A charged silence fell between them.

Sammy was intensely aware of the closeness of her body, the soft floral scent that was always a part of Beth. With just the two of them alone inside the cozy cabin, it seemed they were isolated from the rest of the world.

He stepped backward, breaking the spell. Protecting Beth was his job, and he'd better remember that fact. "I'll get the rest of the stuff in before it gets too dark."

"Right," she quickly agreed, her cheeks flushed pink. "Lots to do before I get settled in."

"Before we get settled in," he corrected.

"I already told you, I'm fine out here. Perfectly safe. No need—"

"I'm staying," he insisted. "At least for tonight."

ICY MOUNTAIN THREAT

USA TODAY Bestselling Author

DEBBIE HERBERT

&

PAULA GRAVES

Previously published as *Appalachian Peril*
and *Smoky Mountain Setup*

ISBN-13: 978-1-335-47369-1

Recycling programs
for this product may
not exist in your area.

Icy Mountain Threat

Copyright © 2022 by Harlequin Enterprises ULC

Appalachian Peril
First published in 2020. This edition published in 2022.
Copyright © 2020 by Debbie Herbert

Smoky Mountain Setup
First published in 2015. This edition published in 2022.
Copyright © 2015 by Paula Graves

For questions and comments about the quality of this book,
please contact us at CustomerService@Harlequin.com.

Harlequin Enterprises ULC
22 Adelaide St. West, 41st Floor
Toronto, Ontario M5H 4E3, Canada
www.Harlequin.com

Printed in U.S.A.

CONTENTS

USA TODAY bestselling author **Debbie Herbert** writes paranormal romance novels reflecting her belief that love, like magic, casts its own spell of enchantment. She's always been fascinated by magic, romance and gothic stories. Married and living in Alabama, she roots for the Crimson Tide football team. Her eldest son, like many of her characters, has autism. Her youngest son is in the US Army. A past Maggie Award finalist in both young adult and paranormal romance, she's a member of the Georgia Romance Writers of America.

Books by Debbie Herbert

Harlequin Intrigue

Appalachian Prey
Appalachian Abduction
Unmasking the Shadow Man
Murder in the Shallows
Appalachian Peril

Harlequin Nocturne

Bayou Magic

Bayou Shadow Hunter
Bayou Shadow Protector
Bayou Wolf

Dark Seas

Siren's Secret
Siren's Treasure
Siren's Call

Visit the Author Profile page
at Harlequin.com for more titles.

APPALACHIAN PERIL

Debbie Herbert

As always, to my husband, Tim;
sons Byron and Jacob; and my father, J.W. Gainey.
Much love to you all!

Chapter 1

He'd found her. Again.

The chill churning Beth's insides had nothing to do with the biting Appalachian wind and everything to do with the letter in her hand. She wanted to fling it into the snow, let the white paper blend and melt into the icy flakes coating the mansion's lawn. But curiosity and a sense of self-preservation would not allow her to act so foolish. She looked up from the stack of mail in her hand and scanned the area.

Nothing marred the pristine white landscape of the exclusive Falling Rock community. Stately homes banked the lanes of the gated subdivision, and smoke curled from the chimneys of several houses. On the surface, all was cozy, civilized and well contained.

Was he watching her now? Delighting in her fear? Beth inhaled the frigid air and braced her shoulders. She wouldn't give him the satisfaction. This was a danger-ous game the recently released convict played. If he'd meant physical harm, he'd already had the opportunity to do so in Boston when he broke into her condo.

She closed the mailbox lid and strolled up the drive-way, even curled her lips in the semblance of a smile—just in case he was watching from the safety of the woods that lined the mountain's ridge. *Take that, Lam-bert.* At last she reached the front door, and her numb fingers fumbled at the doorknob for a moment before she pushed her way inside.

The warmth enveloped Beth as she locked the door behind her and leaned against it, her knees suddenly no more substantial than pudding. The pile of letters slipped from her fingers and dropped to the marble floor.

Movement flickered at the end of the long hallway. Cynthia passed by, wearing black pants and an egg-plant-colored cashmere sweater that was a perfect foil for her brown hair highlighted with caramel streaks. How could anyone look so good so soon after waking? Beth sighed as she removed a striped knitted hat, her hair still wet from an early-morning shower. She hung up her coat on the antique hall tree, kicked off her shoes and picked up the fallen mail, placing her letter at the back. No need to worry Cynthia about that. This was her problem.

"Morning," Beth called as she entered the den and sank onto the leather sofa across from the fireplace. Abbie had already lit a fire, and the oak logs crackled and hissed, releasing a smoky, woodsy aroma.

"Morning. Would you like Abbie to bring you a cup

of coffee?" Cynthia asked. "She's in the kitchen making it now."

Beth resisted a rueful smile. Cynthia fell naturally into the hostess role, but in fact, this house belonged to *Beth* now, not her stepmother. What was Cynthia even doing there? Usually she preferred to stay in Atlanta, close to her son. Beth picked up the mug on the end table beside her. "No coffee. I already have green tea."

"So healthy you are." Cynthia shot her an indulgent smile. "You and your herbal teas. Is that what's popular in Boston with the young crowd? As for me, I need a strong dose of caffeine."

Beth tucked her stockinged feet beneath her and sipped the tea, wishing it were a Bloody Mary. Anything to take the edge off the unease rippling down her spine. Was Lambert out there now? How much longer would he hound her? Hadn't she suffered enough for, according to the convict, the so-called sins of her father?

"Beth? Beth!" Cynthia leaned in front of her, waving a hand in front of her face. "What's wrong with you?"

"N-nothing," she lied.

Cynthia's smooth forehead creased, and she straightened. "I was talking to you, and you stared out the window looking, well, frightened."

Cynthia might be on the self-absorbed side, but she was observant. Too observant. Beth wiggled her toes, considering how much to divulge.

Cynthia eased into a nearby chair. "Go on. Tell me. I'll help if I can."

She'd always been that way. A buffer between Beth and her stern father. Judge Wynngate had remained aloof and unapproachable to his only child right up until his death seven months ago. The chance for a proper father-daughter reconciliation was over.

"I had a bit of trouble in Boston," she admitted. "Somebody had been following me, even broke into my condo once."

"That's terrible." Cynthia drew back, placing a be-jeweled hand with well-manicured nails against her chest. "Did the police catch the intruder?"

Beth shook her head, inwardly wincing as she re-called the cop's skepticism when she'd told him about the strange intrusion. "I'm not even sure they believed me when I reported the break-in."

"That doesn't make sense. Why wouldn't they?"

"Because nothing was stolen. My stuff had been re-arranged, though. My journal and papers were taken from my bedroom and laid open on the kitchen table."

Cynthia gasped. "Why, that's—"

"Here's your coffee. One cream, no sugar."

Abbie placed the steaming mug on the table and gazed at Beth, her freckled face paler than normal and her brown eyes wide with concern. So she'd overheard.

"Thank you, Abigail."

At Cynthia's dismissive tone, Abbie hurried from the room, avoiding meeting Beth's eyes, which were filled with a silent apology for her stepmother's terse man-ner. Cynthia affixed her sharp gaze on Beth. "Go on."

Beth realized she wanted—no, *needed*—to talk to someone about her fear. Someone who'd take her seri-ously. And didn't her stepmother deserve to know about the continued slander Lambert had flung against her dad, Cynthia's late husband? She drew a deep breath and plunged ahead.

"The thing is, just a couple days before that happened, I'd received a threatening letter that said I have to pay for my father's corruption."

"Corruption?" Cynthia's lipsticked mouth fell open. "What's that supposed to mean? Edward was aboveboard in every way."

"I don't know. That's all the note said. I immediately suspected it was written by Dorsey Lambert."

Cynthia's face scrunched in displeasure. "I'd hoped to never hear that name again."

They fell silent, remembering the troublesome case of the drug dealer who'd been led from Judge Wynngate's courtroom, defiant and screaming about corruption in the justice system. Specifically, against the honored judge himself. Lambert had vowed revenge and her father had taken the matter so seriously that he'd installed an elaborate security system for their Atlanta estate. Too bad he hadn't done the same for this house in the North Georgia mountains.

"At least the Boston police checked out that lead for me," she said at last. "Turns out Dorsey Lambert was released from prison only two weeks ago."

"Did they question him?"

"Not personally. They contacted Atlanta PD, who went to the address Lambert provided the Georgia Department of Corrections. His mother vouched for him. Said he was living with her, working a steady job and completely off drugs."

"Of course she did," Cynthia said with an elegant lift of her chin. "What mother wouldn't provide an alibi for her child?"

"Exactly." Beth stared at her stepmother, wondering if Cynthia remembered doing much the same for her son, Aiden. Cynthia's protection of Aiden had come at

Beth's expense, and her father had sided with his wife. The entire incident had created a distance from her dad that was never bridged before his death.

Old news. Let it go. Beth drew a deep breath. "Anyway, after getting that note I returned to the Boston PD to report the latest incident, and they kind of gave me the brush-off. Had me fill out a report and said they'd look into the matter." Beth stopped, flushing as she remembered how the cop on duty had lifted his eyebrows as she'd relayed what happened. He clearly thought she'd been spooked by an admittedly creepy letter and was making mountains of molehills.

"You should have told me earlier. I can make a few phone calls and have the Boston police prodded to do a thorough investigation."

Beth had considered it, of course. But winter break from her art teaching job had been around the corner, and she'd hoped it would all blow over by the time she returned. Her fingers tapped the pile of mail. Clearly, matters had not blown over with Lambert.

Cynthia's gaze dropped to the mail. "What's the matter? Did you get another letter?"

Sighing, Beth picked it up and stared at the envelope, which was postmarked Atlanta and had no return mailing information. Her name and address were printed in a standard computer font. She turned it over and picked at the edge.

"Shouldn't you be wearing gloves?"

"Too late now." Beth ripped it open, then frowned at the tiny scraps of paper littering the bottom.

"What is it?" Cynthia asked, leaning forward.

"I'm not sure." She emptied the bits of paper on the coffee table and spread them out. The small pieces had crisp edges, as though they'd been precisely cut with scissors or some other sharp tool. They were black and white and gray with printed text on the back, obviously clipped from a newspaper. She tried to arrange the text in some logical order but failed. Next, she arranged the scraps on the reverse side and gazed down at the jagged newspaper photo that emerged. Fear fizzed the nape of her neck.

She recognized the photograph. It had been shot at one of the few charitable events she'd attended with her father three years earlier. The judge was seated at a head table, Cynthia and her son, Aiden, on his right, and Beth at his immediate left. Her father held a wineglass in the air, proposing a toast to the guests and thanking them for their attendance.

In the midst of the varying shades of pixilated gray, a red marker circled Beth's body, and in the center of her chest was a red dot.

A lethal target mark.

"Oh my God," Cynthia said. With a loud thud, she set her coffee mug on the table. "I'll call Sheriff Sampson to come here at once. I really wished you had put on gloves like I asked."

"Me, too," she murmured, eyes fixed on the angry red dot.

An unexpected, warm pressure landed on her right shoulder, and Beth jumped to her feet. Twisting around, she half expected to find Lambert had sneaked in and was upon them. Instead, she faced Abbie's troubled eyes.

"Who would do something like this?" Abbie breathed, pressing her hands to her cheeks.

"I can only think of one person."

"Call the sheriff's office," Cynthia said crisply into her cell phone. It instantly obeyed her voice command, and the digital ring buzzed through the den.

"We could just go down to the station," Beth pointed out. If the local officers were anything like the Boston PD, they wouldn't find this latest letter an emergency worthy of their immediate attention.

Cynthia waved an impatient hand, phone pressed to an ear. "I'd like to speak to Harlan Sampson," she demanded.

She and Abbie exchanged a look. How like her stepmother to go straight to the top of the chain. "This is Mrs. Cynthia Wynngate of Falling Rock. It's a matter of the utmost importance."

It was a familiar tone that both embarrassed and irritated Beth. Still, she had to admit that Cynthia's air of confident privilege was one that certainly got results.

"What do you mean he's not in? I need to speak with him at once." Her lips pursed. "A conference, you say? When will he be back?" Pause. "Then send out your next highest-ranking officer. I'll explain when he gets here. The address is 2331 Apple Orchard Lane."

Cynthia tapped a button, then dropped the phone on the sofa. "We should expect them in the next fifteen minutes or so. Abbie, make more coffee and heat up those cheese Danish rolls in the refrigerator."

Abbie slowly returned to the kitchen, casting troubled glances over her shoulder.

Cynthia retrieved her phone, aimed it at the macabre cut-up puzzle and snapped a photo. "The officer will collect this for evidence. Figured it wouldn't hurt for us to keep a backup photo. You can't be too careful. Do you have a copy of the first letter?"

"The Boston PD kept it."

She gave a quick nod, already in her familiar take-charge mode. "We'll have Harlan contact them and co-ordinate an investigation."

"You really think they'll do anything?" Beth asked doubtfully.

"Of course. I contributed to Harlan's reelection campaign. If nothing else, he'll investigate as a favor to me."

A new worry nagged at Beth. What if they sent Officer Armstrong over to the house? No, no. Surely not. Cynthia had asked for the next in line to the sheriff. Hopefully, that person wasn't Armstrong. Could she really be that unlucky? Hadn't her morning been bad enough?

She stared out the patio door with its panoramic view of the Appalachian Mountains. Snow brushed the tips and limbs of the trees and cleanly blanketed the ground.

Except for the large footprints originating at the edge of the woods and ending at their back porch.

Chapter 2

Sammy sighed as he finished his grits, slapped the cash on the counter and took a final gulp of iced tea. Yeah, he was a cop, so he should have been drinking the proverbial coffee and eating doughnuts. Call him a rebel.

"Trouble?" Jack asked, collecting the money and stuffing it in the till.

"Nah. Just duty calling. Catch you later."

He strolled to the cruiser, refusing to acknowledge the slight ping he'd experienced when the dispatcher had given him the name and address. No big deal, he told himself as he drove the short distance from Lavender to Blood Mountain. No need to think Mrs. Wynngate's stepdaughter would be visiting. No reason to believe there was danger brewing.

He waved to the security guard at the gate and breezed into the Falling Rock community with its rows of manicured homes. Blood Mountain was only half the size of its neighbor and sparsely inhabited except for this one exclusive subdivision. When people like Cynthia Wynngate called, they expected immediate attention, no matter the problem. He'd heard that Mrs. Wynngate's husband had died many) months ago. At least he wouldn't be stepping into a domestic disturbance situation. Those were the worst.

He knew exactly which showcase house belonged to the Wynngates, even if he hadn't been there in years. Sammy parked in the semicircular brick driveway and strode to the door, automatically surveying the area and cataloging details.

The Massachusetts license plate on the sleek BMW was the first sign of trouble.

Cynthia Wynngate's cold welcome at the door— "What took you so long to get here?"—was the second sign.

The final confirmation of trouble was the woman pacing the den. Pewter eyes, cool as gunmetal, slammed into him—she was clearly as unhappy to see him as he was to cross paths with her again. A younger girl he didn't recognize stood in the corner of the room, polishing a cherry hutch, trying to act inconspicuous but watching everything from the corner of her eyes.

Mrs. Wynngate didn't bother with introductions. He'd met her a few times over the years at local charity events and political fund-raisers. Not that she'd remember him. He was a law enforcement officer, a guy with a badge who served a function if she ever needed his service. Nothing more. She waved a hand at the coffee table as she sank onto a sofa. "Beth, tell him what's going on."

Beth uncrossed her arms and reluctantly made her

way over, pointing at scraps of paper littering the table. "This came in the mail today."

He took a seat and peered down. "What is this? A cut-up old newspaper photo?"

Beth leaned over him, and he inhaled the clean scent of shampoo and talcum powder. A sudden, inexplicable urge to pull her into his lap and inhale her sweet freshness nearly overwhelmed him. *Stop it. Concentrate on the job.*

"Yes," she answered. "The photo's from many years ago. And that red dot is where he marked my chest."

The crimson ink made the hairs on his forearms rise. Why would anyone want to harm Beth? Perhaps it had been a particularly bad breakup with a boyfriend. Or an encounter with a guy who'd harbored hidden stalker behavior. "Any idea who might have sent this?"

"Dorsey Lambert," Beth answered at once. "He threatened retaliation against Dad when he was sentenced twelve years back."

His forehead creased. The name didn't ring a bell. "But that was a long time ago. How can you be so sure—"

"They released him two weeks ago. Within days, I got a letter in Boston saying I'd have to pay for my father's corruption."

Mrs. Wynngate made a ticking noise of disgust as she rose from her seat and signaled to the young girl by the hutch. "Such a ridiculous accusation. Abbie, see if the officer would like coffee or refreshments."

Sammy flashed a quick smile in the girl's direction and held up a hand. "No, thanks," he told her, returning his attention to the photograph.

A disgruntled ex-con. Should be easy enough to track

down the guy and have him questioned. He was obviously trying to scare Beth, but odds were he'd never take action. Often, these kinds of cowardly threats amounted to nothing more than bluster. But he'd definitely investigate. If this Lambert guy was released on parole rather than end-of-sentence, then he'd report the threats to Lambert's parole officer and have his parole revoked.

"I'll check this out," he promised Beth.

"Hope that means more than a phone call to the Georgia Department of Corrections," she said stiffly. "Because that's all the Boston PD did for me."

"I told you I'd follow up. As soon as I have information, I'll call you."

The skeptical look on her face made him want to groan. Of course she had no reason to trust him, of all people. She opened her mouth, no doubt to utter some sharp retort, but her stepmother interrupted.

"Tell him about the footprints," Cynthia said.

Footprints? That was definitely more foreboding than anonymous mail. It meant danger was close by. It meant someone intended harm.

With a sigh, Beth strolled to the French doors overlooking the backyard. "Right there," she said. "They start at the tree line by the back of the property and come all the way to the patio."

A Peeping Tom, perhaps? Yet he couldn't disregard the coincidence of them appearing on the same day as the letter. He eyed the prints. Large and wide, probably from a male.

"Tell you what. I'll snap some close-up photos of these prints and follow them out to the woods. Take a look around. I'll be back shortly to collect that mail as evidence. In the meantime, don't touch it anymore, okay? The fewer fingerprints on it, the better."

"Of course," she muttered, and he had the feeling she was barely able to refrain from rolling her eyes.

Sammy stepped outside and withdrew his cell phone, then bent on one knee and observed the footprint. About a man's size thirteen, he guessed. It wasn't much to go on. The snow was so light that no identifying shoe treads remained, only the outline of the shoe and the dark earth beneath the dusting of snow. He snapped several photos, then followed the tracks to the woods.

At the woods' edge, a *whish* sounded from behind, and he spun around.

"I wanted to see if you found anything." Beth stood before him, a stubborn set to her heart-shaped face.

It was an expression he'd witnessed several times before.

"Not a good idea. Better get back to the house, just in case. Those tracks were fresh."

"I'd rather not. And this is our property, after all. I have a right to know if anyone's trespassing."

"You also have the right to get hurt if someone's still out here," he retorted.

She said nothing, merely crossed her arms over her chest and lifted her chin a fraction. Clearly, she didn't intend to listen to reason. Especially not coming from him. He shrugged. Whoever had been here had surely seen him pull up in the sheriff's department cruiser and had hightailed it out. "Suit yourself. But stay behind me and keep quiet."

Surprisingly, she complied. He carefully picked his way through dead vines, leafless shrubs and evergreen trees, eyes peeled for any sign of broken twigs or an object left behind. But the snow hadn't drifted down past the heavy canopy of the treetops, and there were no tracks evident, only mounds of seemingly undisturbed pine needles and twigs. Only ten feet into the woods, the ground dropped off sharply along the ridge forming Blood Mountain.

Sammy scanned the area. From here, he could view the dirt road below and the much larger Lavender Mountain, which loomed across from them. There was no evidence that anyone had recently tromped through these woods, and the unpaved road below sported an untouched sprinkling of snow. Whoever had been at the Wynngate estate was either still hiding somewhere in the thick woods, or he'd parked an ATV farther down the dirt road, well out of their sight. He stood silent for several minutes, trying to make out any unnatural rustling or spot anything out of the ordinary in the green, brown, gray and white landscape.

Nothing.

"He's gone," Beth whispered, stepping beside him.

"Appears that way. Soon as I leave here, I'll get the department's ATV and drive down the dirt road. See if there're any recent road tracks."

"You will?"

Again with the skeptical tone in her voice. "If I say I'm going to do something, I do it."

She nodded, started to turn away and then faced him again. "Thank you."

Must have killed her to say that. She clearly still held a grudge. He followed her back to the house, and just as Beth was about to reach for the patio door to reenter the den, he decided to try, one last time, to explain about that night so many years ago. He tapped her shoulder for attention and let his hand drop when she faced him.

"Look, Beth. Hear me out. I'm sorry for what happened back then. It wasn't fair that you were left taking all the blame that night for a situation that had clearly grown out of your control."

Her mouth pursed in a tight line. "Damn right it wasn't fair. The house was packed with people, and I was probably the only person in it not drinking or smoking pot."

"It was filled with *underage* people at *your* house," he reminded her. "And we found traces of heavier drugs. Not just marijuana."

"But I knew nothing about that. I didn't even know most of those people or where they came from. I was only seventeen, and somehow, a small party while my parents were away turned into something I couldn't control."

"I understood that, even as a rookie cop. But I had no—"

"I needed your help. If you understood the situation, then why the hell did you have to arrest me?"

The question hung between them.

Again he tried to explain. "Like I said, I was a rookie. My partner was an experienced patrol officer, and I was only a few weeks into my probationary period. He took the hard-nosed approach, and I had no choice in the matter."

He remembered Beth's panicked eyes that night, her tear-streaked face as she'd opened the door and let them into the house where the party raged uncontrollably. "Thank God you're here," she'd said. "I can't find Aiden anywhere."

She'd recognized him that night. He and her brother had played baseball together in the Lavender Mountain Youth League every summer for years. They'd been close friends up until high school, when Aiden had run with a different set of friends that were more into parties than sports, and they'd drifted away from each other.

"You have no idea how that arrest affected me." Beth crossed her arms and bit her lip, as though regretting that admission.

"It wasn't fair that everything came down on you," he admitted.

Sammy had no doubt Aiden was responsible for the wild crowd that evening. Yet the Golden Boy had managed to escape the debacle with no arrest record to mar his future career as a criminal attorney. Actually, everyone had gone free, save Beth. The herd of partygoers had stampeded out the back door, leaving behind all the drugs and alcohol. The quiet mountain subdivision had roared with the sound of their vehicles hastily exiting the premises.

"Forget it," she said at last, her back stiffening.

"I would, but apparently you can't," he said. "I was only doing my job that night. I hope you understand."

She gave a grudging nod. "I can appreciate that. I just wish…that you'd been able to intervene on my behalf. I was scared and unsure what to do."

That had been obvious. But Sergeant Thomas had been unmoved, ordering Sammy to handcuff Beth and place her in the cruiser.

"Did you really try to soften the older cop, or did you blindly follow orders?" Beth asked.

And there was the crux of the matter. He'd voiced his opinion, but once the sergeant shot down his objection, he'd kept his mouth shut. If he'd had it to do all over again, Sammy liked to think he'd have acted differently, have insisted that Aiden be held responsible for what had happened in that house.

He cleared his throat, about to defend himself once more, when he spotted movement within the house. Cynthia Wynngate emerged from the hallway into the den, rolling a large piece of luggage across the gleaming walnut floor.

"Does your stepmother have plans to go somewhere?" he asked.

Beth frowned and pushed open the door. "Not that I'm aware of."

They reentered the warmth of the spacious living room, where Abbie collected used coffee cups.

"Where are you going?" Beth asked Cynthia.

"Back to Atlanta. I couldn't possibly stay here after all this."

Actually, that wouldn't be a bad idea, Sammy mulled. If they left for the city, they might be safer in a new location that wasn't so isolated.

Mrs. Wynngate turned to Abbie. "I left your paycheck on the mantel. I won't be needing your services again until all this is cleared up." Her gaze flickered to where they stood by the door. "Beth, be careful about keeping the house locked tight. Officer—" her eyes scrunched as she peered at his ID badge "—Officer Armstrong. Can your department be sure to patrol by the house and keep surveillance on it? So many neighbors have already vacated their homes during the off season, and I don't want any trouble."

He blinked at the elegant woman before him. Was she really going to leave Beth behind and not even offer her the option of returning to Atlanta with her? Apparently, her only concern seemed to be for the house itself. What kind of person left another to face danger alone? Especially a family member?

Abbie spoke up. "I'll stay with you if you'd like, Beth."

"That would be great, Abbie," she said softly. "Thank you."

Mrs. Wynngate frowned. "But she's no longer in my employ."

"Abbie and I will work something out," Beth said.

He marveled at Beth's composure. Did she not even see how she'd been so coldly dismissed by her stepmother? That Cynthia had even made it clear she wasn't footing the bill for Abbie's sleepover? Or maybe this was all par for the course, and Beth expected nothing from the woman.

Strange family.

Chapter 3

Something was…not quite right.

Beth snapped from the void of sleep to alertness. Slivers of moonbeams jabbed through the blind's slats, etching vertical patterns against an onyx darkness. Although the house was silent, she was sure there had been a noise. A click of a latch, perhaps…a brief metallic ping that had no place in the dead of night.

She hardly dared move, her right hand tightly bunching a mound of down comforter as she eased into a sitting position. Seconds passed, then several minutes, the only noise a loud whooshing of her unsteady breath.

Her mind scrambled for an explanation. Maybe Abbie had awakened and gone to the bathroom down the hall, locking the door behind her. Yes, that made sense. All this business with Dorsey Lambert had troubled her so deeply that it had invaded her dreams. Yet

Beth remained upright in bed, waiting for the bathroom door to creak open.

It didn't.

Cautiously, she swung her legs over the side of the bed and gently lowered her feet to the floor. Without flipping on a light, she unplugged her cell phone from the charger at her nightstand and walked to the door, her bare toes plunging into the plush carpet. Her hand grasped the doorknob, turned it ever so slowly, and then pushed the door open an inch. Just as deliberately as she'd turned the knob clockwise to open it, she released it counterclockwise and peered down the hallway.

No splinter of light shone beneath the bathroom door.

The large windows of the den's cathedral ceiling provided enough illumination to inch forward. She continued down the hallway toward the guest room at the end of the hall where Abbie was staying. At the girl's door, Beth raised a hand to knock, then hesitated. How foolish she'd look if she awakened Abbie for no reason.

Kerthunk.

Beth jumped at the sound that had emanated one story below. Her father's old study. It sounded as though one of the books had tumbled from the shelf onto the hardwood flooring. The first logical explanation that came to mind was that some nimble feline had accidently knocked over a heavy object.

Too bad Cynthia didn't have a cat.

She swallowed hard past the lump in her throat, not wanting to acknowledge the other logical conclusion: someone was in the house. Indecision tore at her. Should she call the cops and barricade herself and Abbie in the guest room, or try to figure out what the hell was going on?

The unmistakable rustling of papers from below prompted her to immediate action. She opened the bedroom door and hurried to the bed.

Abbie wasn't there.

Confusion spiked her mind. Had she entered the wrong guest room? No, the girl's overnight bag was on the dresser. So where was Abbie? Beth put a hand on her chest and willed her racing heart to slow. Now was the time for level thinking.

Perhaps Abbie was the one in the study. She'd gotten up in the middle of the night and, unable to sleep, had gone downstairs to read or watch television. She could have gone in Dad's study to get a book, accidentally bumped against the desk and knocked something over.

Beth almost smiled with relief. Still, she kept her phone on with speed dial at the ready in case there was a more sinister explanation. She almost hadn't let Sammy put his number in her phone, but he'd appeared unwilling to leave until she allowed him to do so. And she'd wanted him to go. His presence unnerved her.

Careful to make no noise, she returned to the hallway and made her way to the winding staircase leading to the den. At the bottom of the stairs, she picked her way through the den and the kitchen. Sure enough, the study door was cracked open several inches, and dim light spilled from the lamp on Dad's desk.

She'd been right. Pleased with her logic, Beth opened her mouth to call out a greeting to Abbie, but the words died in her throat.

A man wearing jeans and a black hoodie was rifling through the file cabinet.

Not. Abbie.

He jerked a handful of papers out of a file and thrust

them under the lamp, studying their contents. The intruder wore black gloves—and that detail terrified her more than the hoodie drawn tightly about his face.

She tried not to make a sound as she again picked her way back through the kitchen and then the den. Where the hell was Abbie? Beth ran up the stairs, hoping the carpet muffled her footsteps. At the top of the stairs, she paused. She didn't dare dial Sammy, afraid the intruder would hear her speak. Instead, she shot Sammy a text: There's someone in my house.

She hit Send, and then immediately typed a second one: Hurry.

She watched until the gray bar on the text screen read Sent and then Delivered. Good. She'd follow up with a phone call once she'd locked herself in her room. But before she even reached the bedroom door, the phone vibrated in her palm. Beth waited until she was safely tucked into her room before reading the message.

On my way. Lock yourself in your room. Don't open it for anyone but me.

Thank heavens he'd responded so quickly so late at night. Yeah, she could lock herself up. But what about Abbie? She couldn't leave her to fend for herself. Beth wished she had Abbie's phone number to warn her of the danger. A sudden thought clutched at her heart: Had the intruder tied and gagged Abbie? The longer the silence, the more convinced Beth grew that it must be the case.

She padded to the window and peered through the slats. Abbie's car was still in the driveway. The girl was in as much or more danger as she was. No way Beth would cower in her room and let Abbie come to any harm. What if the intruder decided to kill her when he'd finished his business?

Before losing her courage, Beth again tiptoed out of her room. She'd grab the poker by the fireplace as a makeshift weapon. Dad used to keep a firearm in his bedroom, but she doubted Cynthia still had it. She'd always claimed that having the gun made her nervous.

Slowly, slowly, *slowly* Beth descended the stairs, vigilant for any noise or shifting patterns in the darkness. Another faint rustling of papers came from the study. At least she knew where the man was. Hastily, she scurried to the fireplace and clasped the poker. The cold, hard metal in her palms allayed her fear only an iota. If the man had a gun, the poker was useless. Still, it was better than nothing if he tried to rush at her.

She surveyed the den, seeking a bound and gagged Abbie, but the sofa and chairs were empty, and there were no signs of a struggle. Beth walked softly out of the room and went on to check the downstairs bedrooms, bathrooms and dining room. Nothing, nothing and nothing.

How much longer until Sammy arrived?

Could she have missed seeing Abbie somewhere in the kitchen? If Abbie were lucky, she'd have seen or heard the intruder and slipped outside to the patio, probably caught unawares without a phone or car keys. Even now, she might be out in the cold, shivering and frightened. First, Beth would check the kitchen, and then proceed outside.

A murmur emanated from the study, and her heart slammed in her ribs. Was the man talking to himself? More murmurs, an exchange of different pitches in the low warble of the voices.

There were *two* of them.

Her hands convulsed against the poker, and her eyes flicked around the den. A swish of fabric sounded as someone moved toward the kitchen. Whoever he was, his steps were deliberate and unhurried. She glanced over her shoulder, eyeing the distance between where she stood and the comparative safety of the hallway. It seemed to stretch as long as a football field.

No time to retreat. Beth ducked behind the sofa and prayed they were heading for the back door and leaving as quietly as they had entered.

Her nose prickled—the involuntary tingling of an oncoming sneeze. No! Not now. Fear danced in her gut. She splayed a hand across her nose and mouth, trying to suppress the telltale reflex. A muffled explosion escaped her mouth.

The fabric swishing stopped.

"What's that?" one of the men asked, his voice so near that horror chilled every inch of her flesh.

"Someone there?" another man called out.

Elliptical beams of headlights and a dizzying blue strobe pierced the glass panels lining the front door. Judging by the profusion of colors, more than one cop car had arrived at the scene.

"Damn it!"

"Let's get outta here!"

The two men raced toward the back patio and jerked open the French doors, flinging them aside. Glass exploded with a crash. Shards rained down with a loud, scattered tinkling, and a cool burst of air swept through the room, chilling her arms.

She was going to live through this nightmare. Now to

find Abbie. Beth rose, still clutching the poker. "Abbie?" she called. "It's safe now. Where are you?"

A high-pitched cry exploded through the open patio door. Abbie was alive.

Beth ran forward. "Abbie? You all right?"

Abbie ran in the door, her red hair sprinkled with snow and her arms clasped around her waist. Blood dribbled from a cut in her forehead, and she shivered violently.

"They hurt you!" Beth cried. She grabbed a woolen afghan from the sofa and draped it over Abbie's shoulders. "You must be freezing. You're safe now. Let the cops in the front door while I lock the patio doors."

Outside, the stygian atmosphere wholly absorbed any sight of the trespassers. The intruders' dark clothing had allowed them to slip into the black velvet of the night. Hastily, she pulled the door shut and fastened the lock. More glass splintered and crashed to the floor. One good kick and the whole glass door would completely shatter. Hardly did any good to secure it shut, but maybe it would buy a few seconds' time if the intruders returned and had to kick the remaining glass.

"Beth! Are you okay?"

She swiveled at Sammy's shout, surprised at its underlying sound of concern.

"We're good," she called.

He entered the den, his eyes immediately fixating on her face. She pointed at the door. "They ran outside."

Footsteps trampled in the hallway as more officers entered. Sirens blared, signaling that more were on the way. Beth rubbed her arms, suddenly conscious she was clad in an old T-shirt and pajama bottoms.

Sammy stood beside her, draped a blanket over her

shoulders and wordlessly guided her to the sofa. Abbie was already seated nearby, speaking with an officer.

His kind brown eyes calmed her as he waited, letting her catch her breath. Old memories suddenly resurfaced. Instead of seeing Sammy as an emblem of the great divide in her life that had spiraled her fortune downward, Beth remembered her teenage crush on him. He was Aiden's close friend, several years older and totally out of reach. During their summers at Blood Mountain, she'd attended every baseball game he and Aiden played, secretly thrilling at his muscular physique in uniform, the speed with which he ran bases, the skill and power with which he batted.

The house suddenly blazed with swirling blue lights from every window. Out back, a floodlight flicked on and illuminated the yard all the way to the mountain ridge. The rooms buzzed with the cackle of two-way radios and men shouting orders as they spread through the house, guns drawn. Beth dropped her gaze from Sammy, pushing the memories away. "Thanks for getting here so quickly."

"I told you to call whenever you needed me. I'm glad you did."

She looked back up, studying the gentle and determined set of his face. The chaos surrounding them melted away, and only his dark eyes remained. For the first time all day, she felt warm and safe.

Until he opened his mouth.

"How well do you know this Abbie girl?"

She shrugged, surprised at the question. "Well enough, I guess. She's worked two or three years for Cynthia, and we've talked a bit during my brief visits.

She works part-time here and goes to community college. Why? What about her?"

"Do you even know her last name?"

Sheepish, Beth glanced down at her bare feet. "Honestly, no. But what does that matter? She's always—"

"It matters plenty," he cut in, his tone rough with suspicion.

Beth gave Abbie a quick glance. The girl's forehead was already beginning to swell and bruise. Someone had handed her a tissue, and she blotted at the trickle of blood still seeping from her wound. Beth already sensed Sammy's answer, but she had to ask anyway. "What's Abbie's last name?" she whispered.

"It's Lambert."

Chapter 4

"Lambert?" Beth's body recoiled in surprise.

Pretty much his reaction when he'd checked up on the girl this afternoon. "Actually, it's her maiden name. But yeah."

"She doesn't look old enough to be married." Beth studied Abbie from across the room.

"Married at seventeen, divorced at twenty-one. Legal name is Abigail Lambert Fenton."

"I had no idea. Cynthia couldn't have known that either when she hired her."

"To be fair, Lambert's a common name in these hills. Dorsey was originally from Ellijay, only thirty miles from here. Man's got plenty of extended family in the area."

"Seems I ran straight into the lion's den," Beth said with a snort. "Should have stayed in Boston."

"Could be her relationship to Dorsey is distant, and this is all a coincidence." Not that Sammy believed that for a minute. Abbie Fenton was probably involved up to her freckled little neck in this mischief. With any luck, he'd put a stop to it all this evening. No more threats and break-ins.

"She seemed so nice." Hurt chased across Beth's eyes.

"You know what they say. Got to watch those quiet ones," he said, attempting a smile to alleviate her worry. "Woman even volunteered to stay the night with you. Call me jaded, but that rang an alarm in my mind. I'd intended to come back this morning and have a chat with her. Imagine my surprise when I got your text."

Beth's gray eyes widened. "You don't think she had anything to do with those intruders, do you? I mean, she's hurt."

"A superficial cut on the forehead. Could be self-induced. And at first glance, I see no signs of forced entry. Officers are checking all the windows and doors as we speak."

"Surely you don't think… Are you saying Abbie *let* them in?"

"We're not ruling anything out at this point. Now tell me everything that happened tonight. What first alerted you—"

Beth shoved the chair from beneath her and strode to where Abbie sat with an officer. The woman's mouth opened in surprise when she spotted Beth headed her way. Abbie's eyes hardened, and she stiffly drew up her slight frame, clearly signaling she expected a confrontation and was prepared to dig in her heels.

"Did you let those men in my house?" Beth asked, voice tight with anger.

A sullen Abigail lifted her chin and refused to respond. She looked older now, a certain sternness in her features that hadn't been there earlier. Officer Graham raised a quizzical brow at Sammy.

Quickly, Sammy rushed to Beth's side. "Let us ask the questions," he admonished.

Beth ignored him. "Well, did you?" she persisted. "Why? What do they want?"

Abbie kept her face averted, eyes focused on the patio door, her mouth set in a grim twist.

Sammy took Beth's elbow and steered her to the kitchen. Beth still wasn't through. "How could you do such a thing?" she called over her shoulder. "We trusted you!"

"Let Officer Graham ask the questions and do his job. In the meantime, I want a statement from you."

"Can I at least put on a sweater and start coffee?" she grumbled.

"Be my guest." There was no hurry. He'd stay here all night if necessary. He wouldn't rest until the intruders had been found and Abbie had confessed to her role in tonight's invasion. More important, he wouldn't leave Beth alone in this house until he knew she was safe.

She hurried from the kitchen, nearly colliding with Officer Markwell. Both officers watched as she slipped from the room.

"No signs of forced entry anywhere," Markwell reported without preamble. "No open or broken windows, no damaged doors and no footprints around the sides of the house. Point of entry appears to be the patio door, where we found several sets of footprints leading to the woods at the back of the property."

"No damage to the patio door locks?" he asked.

"None."

The two-way radio at his belt crackled, and the voice of Officer Lipscomb cut in. "No sign yet of anyone on the property. Heading to the road below to see if there are any tracks."

"Ten-four," he answered before turning to Markwell. "Sweep through every room. Make sure they're empty and mark any signs of disturbance."

Markwell left, and Sammy stared at Abbie. Her lips were pinched together, and her chin lifted in stubborn defiance. She was going to be a tough nut to crack.

Beth reentered the kitchen wearing a long, loose cardigan sweater. She'd also donned a pair of thick woolen socks. Without sparing him a glance, she poured water into the coffee maker. "Want a cup?" she asked, her back to him.

"No, but I'll take a soda if you've got one."

"In the fridge. Help yourself."

He got out a can and opened it, taking a long swallow as he watched Beth. Her hands trembled as she pressed the machine's buttons. Now that the shock had worn off, the reality of what had happened was settling in. He'd seen it many times before.

"We won't leave until we're sure your place is locked up tight," he assured her. "And we'll keep a patrol outside, too."

She looked up, and her lips trembled before she offered a tight smile. "Thank you. Really. I don't know what might have happened if you hadn't arrived so quickly."

For the first time in ages, Beth gazed at him without a trace of acrimony. The air between them crackled with an electrical charge, one not caused by animosity. That was certainly new.

The aroma of coffee filled the air, and she jerked her gaze away, busying herself with retrieving a cup from the cabinet. After she'd fortified her nerves with the brew, he'd walk with Beth to the downstairs study and ask her to check for any missing items.

What had those men been after? This went way beyond the scare tactics of menacing mail. And if it had been a robbery, they would have gone after electronics or searched for jewelry and money. Beth's purse hung on the back of one of the kitchen chairs, apparently undisturbed.

"Check your bag," he said. "See if anything's missing."

Beth gasped and went to her purse. "Didn't even think of that." After riffling through it and opening her wallet, she shook her head. "Everything's here— my credit cards, cash and driver's license."

No simple burglary, then. Of course, he'd known that anyway because of Abbie's obvious connection with the Lambert clan. But what had they been after? Again, his gaze drifted to the recalcitrant, unremorseful Abigail. Doubtful she was going to volunteer any information.

Did she and other members of Dorsey's disreputable family really believe that Judge Wynngate had been corrupt? Had they planned tonight's invasion to search for evidence to back their wild claims?

It was the only explanation that made sense. As Beth sipped coffee, he strolled to the kitchen window, watching snowflakes sift quietly to the ground. Had the men found what they'd come to collect? Would they return? If they did, it would be incredibly stupid, but no one said criminals possessed the brightest brains.

Returning would be a grave mistake on their part. There'd be no more Abbie to silently open the door and allow them easy access. Still, he should probably convince Beth that she wasn't safe here, that the best thing she could do was return to Boston as soon as possible. At the very least, she needed to spend the rest of her visit with her stepmother in Atlanta—whether Cynthia Wynngate wanted her there or not.

Sammy quashed the small dash of disappointment that arose at the prospect of Beth leaving. She intrigued him, even all those years ago when she'd sat in the stands watching him and Aiden playing baseball. But their age difference had seemed too great then, and she was his friend's sister, after all. Back then, Aiden's friendship had been important to him. Aiden…a solution popped into his mind.

"Maybe it's time you paid a visit to Aiden," he suggested. "At least until we've made an arrest and it's safe to return. How long were you planning to stay on vacation, anyway?"

She lifted a shoulder and let it drop. "No idea. I like to play things by ear. Keep it fluid. I'm free until after the New Year, when classes start up again. I teach art to middle schoolers."

Aiden had mentioned that Beth had an "artsy" job teaching children. He'd said it with a smile that Sammy couldn't decipher, either proud of his sister's occupation or indulgent in a patronizing way.

"So what about visiting your brother?" he asked again, aware she'd sidestepped the question.

She lifted the cup to her lips and took a small sip before answering. "Maybe."

He didn't push. His peripheral vision picked up Officer Graham motioning to him. Sammy started in his direction, and Graham met him halfway.

"The suspect's refusing to answer questions. How about I take her to the station?"

A change of environment might loosen her tongue, especially when faced with the chill starkness of an interrogation room. Members of the Lambert family were no strangers to a jail's ambience, but perhaps Abbie was young enough never to have witnessed it outside of family visitation days. Being questioned and held in a cell didn't compare to the inmate guest experience.

"Yep. Get her out of here," he told Graham. "And don't release her unless you check with me first."

Graham returned to the den, took Abbie by the arm and guided her toward the foyer. She pointedly kept her face averted to avoid Sammy's gaze. Or Beth's. Either way, Sammy took it as a sign of guilt. If Abbie were innocent, she'd be pleading her case to Beth.

"Glad she's gone," Beth muttered. "I hope to never see her again."

"You won't have to. Next time, Cynthia needs to be more thorough in hiring help."

"Agreed." Beth set down her cup. "Ready to take my statement?"

"First, let's go to your dad's office. Take a good look around and see if anything's missing."

Beth tugged the sweater and gave a brisk nod. Wordlessly, she strode past him, and he followed her through the main floor and then down one level to the study.

The room was brightly lit from an overhead fixture

as well as a lamp atop a huge mahogany desk. Two matching mahogany file cabinets, most of the drawers hanging open, banked a side wall. Behind the desk, legal tomes crammed a floor-to-ceiling bookcase. A steady, studious office with an old-fashioned vibe. All befitting a judge.

Several files were scattered across the desk's gleaming surface, along with an open laptop. Papers littered the floor where the intruders had dropped them in their haste to leave. Without touching the papers, Sammy leaned down to peer at the words. Seemed to be court records of various convicted felons. He put on a pair of plastic gloves, and with the tip of a finger, he turned the computer to face him. The screen was black. He tapped the keyboard, and a desktop wallpaper featuring the Atlanta federal courthouse sprang to life. In the center of the monitor was:

Edward Preston Wynngate III
Invalid Password. Try again.

The intruders hadn't cracked the code, so they weren't dealing with experienced hackers. Sammy wondered if they'd planned on stealing the laptop to investigate further, but the unexpected arrival of the cops had interrupted their plan. "Do you know your father's password?" he asked Beth.

She shook her head. "Sorry. He was a reserved man and preferred we not even enter his office while he was working. Said it disturbed his concentration." Her eyes scanned the room. "Actually, he didn't like people coming in even when he wasn't at work."

"Why?"

"He was very meticulous. Probably afraid we'd mess everything up."

Sammy could think of another reason. One that had to do with keeping secrets. "To your knowledge, does Cynthia ever use this computer?"

"I doubt it. She prefers to do everything either on her phone or tablet."

Then Mrs. Wynngate should have no objections to them temporarily confiscating the laptop and having a computer forensic expert review its contents. The sooner they got to the bottom of what Dorsey Lambert was seeking, the safer the Wynngate family would be. Sammy made a mental note to call her first thing in the morning.

"Take a good look around," he urged Beth. "Anything valuable your father kept down here?"

"Not that I'm aware of. But like I said, it isn't a place I entered very often."

He skirted around to the back of the desk and opened a few drawers. Nothing but standard office supplies, neatly arranged and stacked.

His mind flashed to his infrequent meetings with the judge over the years. The man had been physically fit for his age and pleasant enough. But something about his rigid stance, even in the comfort of his home, and his meticulous formality had been off-putting to Sammy— as though with a glance, the judge had taken stock of Sammy's blue-collar background and had merely tolerated him as Aiden's temporary buddy in the weeks they lived at Falling Rock each summer.

Beth sank onto the desk chair and groaned, placing her head in her hands. "What do these lunatic Lamberts want?"

Proof. The answer sprang into his mind fully formed, pure and simple. They must believe Lambert was unfairly sentenced and were out to avenge the family name. Had there been anything shady behind the conviction on the judge's end? He'd question Beth as tactfully as possible.

"Any possibility your father might be involved in something unethical?"

Her head snapped up, and she glared. "Dad was beyond reproach. The most ethical person you'd ever meet. You could even describe him as unyielding when it came to his principles. Maybe too rigid."

Her eyes grew unfocused as she strummed her fingers on the polished mahogany. Obviously, her thoughts had drifted away from the present situation. Sammy could well imagine the judge as a stern, remote father who imposed a strict code of justice. He'd never particularly cared for the guy, but he pushed aside his personal feelings. Had Judge Wynngate truly been on the take or involved in criminal activity?

Dorsey Lambert sure held a grudge against the man. He'd have a talk with him and ask what he, or his family, believed the judge might have in his office and why they'd sent Beth threatening mail. Bad enough she'd been the one left holding the bag when Aiden and his buddies had disappeared from that ill-fated party years ago. Hadn't she already suffered enough for a family member's transgression?

He wouldn't let it happen again.

"Do you have somewhere to stay tonight?" Sammy asked, breaking her reverie. "A friend you can stay with? At the very least, you could drive to Atlanta and stay with Aiden for the time being. I'm sure he—"

"I'm not calling him at this time of night," she answered stiffly. Clearly, Beth was still rankled over his earlier remark about her father.

"I don't want to leave you alone here with the broken door."

She rose and brushed past him. "Of course I won't stay here tonight. I'll go to a motel until I figure out what to do in the morning."

"Good plan. I'll drive you over."

Her gray eyes bore into him. "You've done enough. I'm perfectly capable of driving myself."

Seems when it came to Beth Wynngate, he just couldn't win.

Chapter 5

Sammy's question about her father's integrity pricked Beth's heart like barbed wire. If he'd known her father, he'd never doubt the man's honesty and rigid moral code. Her spoon clanked so loudly against her cup she was surprised other customers at the coffee shop didn't glance her way.

Bells tinkled, and a gust of cold air whipped through the room as the door opened. Lilah Sampson walked in, golden curls enveloping her in an angelic aura. People craned their necks to catch a glimpse of her, their eyes softening and mouths involuntarily upturning at the fresh cheerfulness she naturally bestowed upon everyone. Lilah scanned the shop and then waved at Beth, hurrying over to her table.

"Hey, Beth! It's good to see you again." Lilah gave her a quick embrace, her pregnant belly bumping into

Beth's abs. Lilah released her and awkwardly dropped onto the opposite chair, hands gripping the table for balance.

"You look so happy. And healthy," Beth said. Pregnancy certainly agreed with her old friend.

"I'm both of the above," Lilah agreed. "Although sometimes I wonder how I'm ever going to take care of a new baby when Ellie is a little hellion."

"How old is she again? Two? Three?"

"Almost four years old." Lilah extracted her cell phone from her purse. "Just one quick picture, I promise."

Dutifully, Beth cooed over the photo of the blue-eyed blonde—which was easy to do, as Ellie was an adorable mini version of her mother. "Here," she said, pushing the plate of doughnuts toward Lilah. "Chocolate frosting with sprinkles."

"My fave. I shouldn't, but I can never say no to them. Especially now." Lilah picked up a doughnut, brought it halfway to her mouth and then stopped. She set it back down, her face tight with concern. "The smell of chocolate in this place must have scrambled my brains. How are you? I mean, I know what happened at your place yesterday."

"Figured Harlan would fill you in." As sheriff, her husband had a pulse on everything that went down in Elmore County.

"I wish he'd told me last night instead of waiting until this morning. Why didn't you call? You know you can stay with me until you need to go back to Boston."

She loved her old friend but staying with her for more than a day or two was out of the question. Lilah kept busy enough with her own family and work without an additional burden. "I stayed at a motel last night. I'll probably go visit Aiden a few days. But first, I want to oversee getting the patio doors fixed this afternoon. Cynthia would have a fit if she knew they were busted."

Lilah's eyes flashed confusion. "You mean she doesn't know about the break-in yet? Thought you would have called her immediately."

"There was no point worrying her so late in the evening. Nothing was stolen. Guess I should run it by her, though, if Sammy hasn't already told her about it. Cynthia needs to be careful not to hire any more Lamberts."

Lilah shrugged, and her mouth ticked upward in a wan smile. "The Lamberts are the only family whose name has a worse reputation around here than the Tedders."

The Tedders were infamous moonshiners and outlaws. Their penchant for crime had even become national news four years earlier. Still, as far as Beth was concerned, Lilah's brush with a serial killer in her family was worse than her own scare the previous night. "But you're not a Tedder anymore," Beth reminded her. "You're a Sampson."

"Ha! As if anyone in Lavender Mountain's going to forget my maiden name." But Lilah smiled and took a bite of her doughnut as though she couldn't care less about other people's opinions. Harlan Sampson might not be Beth's cup of tea, but he made Lilah happy, and that was all that mattered.

"Bet Cynthia hasn't forgotten my background," Lilah said with a roll of her eyes.

Beth's stepmother had never approved of her friendship with, as she put it, "that Tedder girl." But surprisingly, her father had overruled his wife, saying that Beth needed a friend during the summers spent at Blood Mountain. And Lilah had been a true friend. Their friendship had remained strong even after Beth had been exiled to a private school for troubled rich kids. Beth would never forget Lilah's kindness, especially since her former friends at the elite Atlanta academy where she'd attended high school regarded her as a social pariah. She'd never heard from any of them again.

"The important people in our lives don't care about our past," Beth reminded Lilah. A current of understanding bolted through the short distance between them. If they lived to be a hundred, they'd always have this bond.

Lilah bit into the doughnut again and momentarily closed her eyes, apparently blissed out on sugar. Guilt nibbled in Beth's stomach. She hadn't invited Lilah over for a casual chat. Best to just ask the favor and get it over with. "How much did Harlan tell you about last night?" she asked.

Lilah's eyes flew open. "Everything," she admitted. "Hope you don't mind. He knows we're close, and I'd want to hear it from him before anyone else."

"Even about…the possible motive behind the break-in?" Sammy's question about her father still stung.

"Yeah," Lilah nodded. "They have to explore every angle and ask the tough questions. Part of the job."

Beth tamped down her reluctance to ask for the favor. Was she as bad as Cynthia, expecting to get preferential treatment because of her social status? No, she decided. This was merely a request from one friend to another. Cynthia wouldn't ask—she'd demand. She wasn't anything like her stepmother. Beth went out of her way not to flaunt her name or her money. Her only motive in asking the favor was to keep Sammy at arm's length. Besides questioning her father's character, he brought up too many memories and made her uncomfortable. She drew a deep breath and then blurted, "Is there any way Harlan can oversee the investigation?"

"You mean, instead of Sammy?"

"Exactly."

Lilah cocked her head to the side. "Harlan's involved in a big case right now with the Georgia Bureau of Investigation. It eats up all his time."

Disappointment seeped into her. At least she'd tried.

"What's the problem?" Lilah asked. "Sammy's his right-hand man. Besides, have you met Sammy's partner, Charlotte?"

"No. She wasn't there last night."

"Well, Charlotte's great. She used to work for the Atlanta PD and has lots of experience. They'll get to the bottom of the case."

A wry voice beside them cut through their conversation. "Thanks for the vote of confidence."

Beth almost jumped at the sight of the officer who glared down at her, clutching a white bag of pastries. The buttons of her brown uniform blouse stretched tightly across her heavily pregnant belly, threatening to pop open at any moment. Her red hair was pulled back in a ponytail, and her eyes stared accusingly at Beth.

"You don't get to decide which officer investigates which case," the fierce redhead said stiffly.

Lilah quickly tried to defuse the situation. "Beth, this is my sister-in-law, Charlotte. Sammy's partner." She flashed a placating smile at Charlotte. "We were just talking about the break-in."

But Charlotte ignored Lilah and kept her gaze directed at Beth. She read the woman's name badge: C. Tedder. What rotten luck that she happened to be walking by at the exact moment she'd asked Lilah for a favor. Beth had forgotten how frequently this kind of chance encounter could occur in a small town.

"I assure you that your case will receive due diligence on our part," Officer Tedder said in a clipped voice.

"Good to know," Beth muttered.

"You have any complaint with the way we're conducting our investigation?"

The woman was relentless. Determined to put her in her place. "Not yet," she mumbled.

"Charlotte and Sammy are the best," Lilah said easily. "What flavor doughnuts did you get?" she asked her sister-in-law in an obvious attempt to change the subject.

Charlotte answered, keeping her gaze affixed on Beth, "Lemon custard."

A sour treat for a sour cop. But Beth didn't dare say it aloud. At last Charlotte broke eye contact and regarded Lilah. The stern set of her jaw softened as she gave her a small nod. With a start, Beth realized the woman was actually pretty when she wasn't being such a hard-ass.

"See you at dinner this evening?" the woman asked. "James plans to grill steaks."

"Wouldn't miss it."

With one final glare in Beth's direction, Charlotte eased away from their table.

"Whew." Beth let out a sigh as she watched Charlotte exit the building. "I'm not winning friends and influencing people today, am I?" she joked.

Lilah merely laughed. "She'll get over it. Maybe we can all have lunch together one day."

She'd as soon have dental surgery than endure a meal with Officer Tedder. But it was too late to do any good, so Beth kept her mouth shut. No need to alienate anyone else affiliated with the sheriff's office. Poor James. What must it be like for Lilah's brother, married to a woman like that? Beth sighed, resigned now to having Sammy and Charlotte as the investigators of record. She wouldn't be around much longer, anyway, so no big deal. Might as well enjoy time with her friend while she had the opportunity. The rest of her get-together with Lilah was pleasant, as Beth put the encounter with Charlotte behind her.

Thirty minutes later, bundled against the winter chill, Beth returned to her car. She kept her head bent low, away from the full force of the biting wind. A pair of large men's boots beneath two tall columns of denim suddenly appeared in her view, and she moved to the right to get out of the way.

A large hand clamped on her right forearm. Startled, she stared up at a giant of a man. He glared, blue eyes lasering through the frosty air. Thick red hair curled out beneath his knitted hat, and a scarf covered his chin and mouth. A muffled, guttural sound tried to escape the woolen scarf.

"What are you doing? Let go of me," she snapped, trying to snatch her arm from his grasp. He tightened it several degrees. Even through the thick coat, his fingers dug painfully into her flesh. Where was grumpy Officer Charlotte Tedder when she actually needed her? Beth scanned the practically vacant street. Nowhere, evidently. *Figures*.

The stranger lowered his scarf and growled. "You owe us."

What the hell did that mean? Was he a bill collector? All her bills were paid. Maybe he had her confused with someone else. "Are you a car repossesser or something? You must be mistaken. Now let go of me before I start screaming."

"Ain't no mistake, Elizabeth Jane Wynngate. Pay us back the fifty grand, and we'll go away."

"Fifty grand?" She practically snorted in derision. "Let me just get my checkbook out of my purse." His demand ricocheted in her brain. "Wait a minute. *Us?* Who is *us?*" And then she understood.

"That's right," he nodded, evidently seeing the light dawn in her eyes.

"Are you Dorsey in the flesh or another family member ordered to harass me?" She'd guess family member. From what she'd seen in the news media years ago, Dorsey had been a short, thin man with skinny wrists and ankles. His prison uniform practically fell off his small frame as he'd been led from a Department of Corrections van into a federal court building.

Her father's courtroom.

"We only want what's due us," he said gruffly. "Play fair."

"Your due for what? You think it's fair to intimidate me into giving you my money? Extortion's a serious crime. I'm not paying a dime just to get you off my back. Leave me alone before I call the cops on you."

The fingers on her arm loosened. With his free hand, the man dug into his coat pocket and pulled out a slip of paper. "Get the cash. By tomorrow evening. Then call this number, and we'll come collect." With a gloved hand, he thrust the paper into her palm. "Don't be stupid. The number goes to a burner phone. And no matter where you go, remember, we're watching you."

He pivoted and, with surprising speed for a man his size, hurried down the alley adjoining the coffee shop and an antique store. Beth glanced down at his large footprints in the snow. Was he one of the same men who'd been sneaking around their property? Maybe he was even one of the masked intruders who'd eluded the law last evening.

Anger overcame her fear. Perhaps if she followed him, she could get his car tag or another clue for the police to find him and bring him in for questioning. Quickly, she raced to her car and started the engine. If she hurried, there was a chance she could make it around the block and onto the street running parallel before he got away. Beth accelerated from the curb, thankful that the streets were practically empty. At the stop sign twenty yards ahead, she barely slowed as she turned right and then took an immediate left.

Ahead, she spotted the Lambert family member hopping into a rusty pickup truck and speeding off as fast as the old engine allowed. Without stopping to examine the risk, Beth hit the accelerator on her sleek sports car. If it came to a speed race, she'd be the clear winner. If nothing else, she had the make and model of his vehicle now. But if she could draw a little closer, she'd get the real prize—a tag number.

Beth pulled up Sammy's number on her Bluetooth dashboard and punched the button. It rang over and over. His deep, disembodied voice sounded. "Sorry, I'm unable to come to the phone right now. At the tone, please leave a message, or if this is an emergency, please call 911."

She smashed a palm on the dashboard. Where the hell was he? She didn't let up on the gas as the truck she followed left town and turned onto a county road, its wheels screeching in the haste to put distance between them. They both began their ascent up Lavender Mountain. The road narrowed and twisted up the steep incline.

Finally, *finally* the voice recording ended with a loud, drawn-out beep.

"Sammy? It's me. Beth. I was harassed in town today by someone sent by Dorsey. I'm following his truck now. It's a rusted-out blue Ford. And the tag number is..." She squinted her eyes. The sun reflecting off the white snow was almost blinding. "It's GA 9—"

A cannonade sound erupted, followed by a steep drop on the right side of her car. Her vehicle swerved, and she gripped the steering wheel, praying she didn't spin out of control down the side of the mountain. The entire right side of her car swiped the flimsy guardrail, the metal screech ringing in her ears. At the last possible second, Beth righted the vehicle's course. A sharp pain bulldozed down her back at the whiplash movement. What had she run over that had flattened her tire and caused so much damage? The truck driver leaned out of the open window on the driver's side and leveled a shotgun.

Oh, hell. That explained everything. The first shot had blown out a tire. Was she the next target?

Beth slumped beneath the dashboard and hit the brakes. Her car skidded on the icy road.

Boom.

The BMW dropped a foot on the left side. The man had shot out her other front tire. She couldn't stay behind the dashboard any longer with her car spinning out of control. Death could as easily come from a crash

off the mountain as a bullet. Beth rose up and managed
to bring her car to a complete stop. The muscle pull in
her back spasmed, and she caught her breath, forcing
her lungs to take in oxygen more slowly and shallowly.

The blue truck rounded a bend in the road and passed
out of sight. She supposed she should be thankful he
didn't hop out of the truck with his shotgun and approach. But he wasn't trying to kill her. Not yet, anyway.
He—they—wanted her money, and that meant keeping
her alive.

But what if he came back anyway? This could be a
chance to kidnap her and force her to withdraw money
from an ATM or write a check. She needed the cops.
Beth inserted the car key into the lock, but it wouldn't
turn. Something had jammed the ignition. Okay, then.
Her car was dead, but she still had her cell phone to call
for help.

Only…where had it gone? Frantically, her gaze
roamed the floorboards, but it wasn't there. She reached
behind her to pat her seat, but the movement shot another burst of pain through her spine. She groaned,
more in frustration than from the hurt. The phone had
to be there somewhere. Steeling herself, she gingerly
scooted forward, then extended her arm backward, but
her hand only brushed against the smooth leather seats.
She really didn't want to do this, but the alternative was
to remain where she was—a sitting duck if the man returned. For all she knew, he might have collected one
or two more of his family to come kidnap her and do
Lord knows what.

Cautiously she reached a hand under the driver's
seat. She gasped; a sharp knife of pain shot through her
as her back protested the movement. Her vision went

dark, and she collapsed forward. Deep, deep breaths. Her sight might have forsaken her, but she could hear the wind in the trees, the far-off sound of cars in town. She'd read once that your hearing was the last thing to go before unconsciousness. Unfortunately, she now knew it to be true.

Everything's going to be all right, she repeated to herself like a mantra. Someone was bound to be along this road shortly. They'd call the police. Sammy would find her. And probably be furious that she'd been so foolish as to chase after a man who'd threatened her. She deserved a scolding, too, not that she'd admit such a thing.

And then she heard it. The roar of a vehicle approaching. The direction the noise came from was in front of her, which meant the person was descending the mountain. It wasn't someone from town climbing back up. The abrupt squeal of brakes rang out, and then a door opened and slammed shut.

Blood pounded in her ears, and she hardly dared try to lift her head and open her eyes. Good chance that whoever approached might be her tormentor and not her savior. Heavy footsteps crunched through snow and came to an abrupt halt by her car. She feared that if she opened her eyes, she'd find an enemy within a couple of feet of where she slumped, easy prey for the taking.

Chapter 6

From the corner of his eyes, Sammy caught Charlotte waving at him. He pushed away from his desk and crossed the aisle where she sat, phone glued to an ear. *Lambert*, she mouthed.

He plopped into the metal chair beside his partner, eavesdropping. He'd tried several times that morning to make contact with the forwarding phone number on file for Dorsey Lambert. No one had answered his call, and despite his repeated message that it was urgent they speak, they hadn't bothered to call back, either.

"Yes, Mrs. Lambert. Good to hear your son's found a job and is staying out of trouble," Charlotte said in her most soothing tone. She flashed him a wink. "There's no problem that a simple conversation with Dorsey wouldn't clear up. When do you expect him home this evening?"

A long pause.

"I promise we're not out to fling him back in jail if he's staying clean. We've got a little matter in Elmore County that we believe he can help us with, that's all."

Charlotte held up crossed fingers at him, and he returned the gesture. With any luck, they'd get answers from the ex-convict tonight.

"Seven o'clock tonight is perfect. Yes, ma'am. And thank you."

She hung up the phone and gave a satisfied smirk. "Mama Lambert is convinced her son is a new man. Prison reformed his sorry ass."

Sadly, he shared her cynical outlook. He'd seen the recidivism rates on felons, and recent circumstances had done nothing to make him believe Dorsey Lambert was going to prove an exception to those abysmal statistics.

Charlotte's two-way radio emitted a loud crackle, and she unclipped it from her belt. Sammy glanced down at the desk blotter and read the scribbled address for Rayna Clementine Lambert. Ellijay would be a short trip. He'd contact Sheriff Roby in Gilmer County beforehand as a professional courtesy.

"Ten-ten at the Flight Club," Charlotte announced abruptly, standing and then quickly heading to the station exit.

"This early in the day?" He shook his head as he leaped to his feet and followed on her heels. "Where's Graham and Markwell? They can take this call."

He didn't say what he was really thinking. If he did, Charlotte would give him a good blistering for trying to protect her. Despite starting maternity leave in a couple of weeks, she refused to ask for special accommodations and insisted on carrying out business as usual.

Her husband, James, had given up trying to convince her to take the temporary desk job Sammy had offered.

Despite her stubbornness, Sammy had to admit she was the best partner he'd ever had. He worried she wouldn't want to return to the job after her maternity leave was over, but she'd assured him otherwise.

With an efficiency born of a long working relationship, Charlotte proceeded to the driver's side of the cruiser—it was her turn to drive—while he slipped into the passenger seat. She flicked on the blue lights, and they pulled out of the station.

"Who you reckon it's going to be this time?" he asked. "The Halbert brothers?"

"My money's on Ike Johnson starting up trouble again."

"Usual bet?" he asked.

"You're on."

She sped through the main street intersection and onto the county road heading south. The Flight Club was less than two miles down the road, an ugly concrete square of a building with a dirt parking lot always filled with worse-for-the-wear vehicles, no matter the time of day or night.

A roll of unease rumbled through his gut as they pulled up to the building, the way it always did whenever he caught sight of the run-down bar. As a teenager, he'd spent way too many evenings here coaxing his inebriated father to get in his car so he could drive him home.

Before they exited the cruiser, two men tumbled out the front door, each grabbing a shirtful of the other as they dragged their fight outside. Bert Fierra, the club's owner and bartender, stood in the doorway, scowling at the men.

"The Halbert brothers," Sammy said to Charlotte as they approached the fighters. "You owe me. I'll take Hank while you take Charlie."

She shot him a suspicious look. Charlie was the smaller of the two brothers. Lucky for him, there was no time for her to argue that she was capable of taking on the bigger guy.

Within minutes, they had the two separated, hands cuffed behind their backs and inside the cruiser. Both were too drunk to offer much resistance. As was their habit, the two brothers quickly made up and were contrite by the time they'd reached the station and been placed in lockup.

"Not only do you owe me a six-pack of soda, you get to handle the paperwork," he told Charlotte smugly once they returned to their desks.

"I can finish it in half the time it takes you," she bragged.

"Then you should file the incident reports every time."

"You wish."

"A guy can try." Sammy chuckled as he slid into his seat. "We make a good team."

She slid him a sly glance. "Too bad Beth Wynngate doesn't appreciate our awesomeness."

His amusement melted. "What do you mean?"

"Overheard her talking to Lilah this morning at the doughnut shop. Seems she wants to pull the friendship card and get Harlan to take over the case."

Surprise, then resentment, flushed over him. "Did she say why?"

"Isn't it obvious? She must hold our investigative skills in low regard."

Either that, or Beth was still put out that he'd questioned the judge's possible involvement in something unethical or illegal. "What did Lilah say?"

"Basically, that Harlan was too busy at the moment and that she should trust us."

"Bet that thrilled her." If Beth was anything like Cynthia, she'd keep demanding until she had her way. Sammy tried to let the insult roll off his shoulders, but found it surprisingly difficult.

He dug his cell phone from his jacket pocket and laid it on the desk. Missed call. Voice mail message lit up the screen. In the bustle of taking in the Halberts, he hadn't noticed the phone ringing. He tapped Play on the voice mail app, and Beth's voice, tinny with excitement and fear, spilled into his ears. His chest tightened as he listened and then nearly burst at the unmistakable crack of a bullet erupting. Had Lambert found her? Or had he sent a hit man? Tires squealed on the road. The message played on in eerie silence for thirty seconds before the recording ended.

"Damn it!" He slammed his hand on the desk. What had happened? Where was she now? He checked the time of the recording: 10:18 a.m., almost ten minutes since she'd dialed.

Charlotte quirked a brow. "What's up?"

"Check with the dispatcher. See what calls have come through in the last fifteen minutes."

Charlotte grabbed her phone while he dialed her number. Beth's cell phone rang three times before switching to voice mail. He dialed again. And again. He dug the cruiser keys from his pocket. If nothing else, he'd drive out toward Falling Rock to see if there'd been any accidents. If she were alone and injured, or in grave peril, he had to find her. At once.

"A ten-fifty-two call came in less than a minute ago," Charlotte announced. "Fuller's en route."

An ambulance request? Sammy raced to the front door as Charlotte followed at his heels, passing along more information.

"Address given was County Road 190, about a third the way up Lavender Mountain. A citizen reported a green BMW Z3 blocking the road. A woman was slumped over the dashboard and unresponsive."

Beth's car. The tightness in his chest twisted deeper, squeezing his lungs. Had she been shot? Sammy's mind whirled as he got in their cruiser, Charlotte beside him, and peeled out of the station and toward the accident scene.

"What's going on?" Charlotte asked.

He nodded at his cell phone on the console. "Play the last voice mail."

Charlotte did. Again the crack of a bullet and squealing tires ripped into him, doubling his tension.

At last they turned onto the county road. A police sedan was ahead of them, lights flashing and siren blaring. Sammy hit the gas until he nearly overtook Officer Fuller responding to the call. From behind, the wail of an ambulance sounded.

"Don't get us wrecked trying to assist Fuller," Charlotte warned. "You're no good to Beth hurt."

But he could think of nothing except Beth needing him at once. If Lambert had managed to get to her, this was his fault. He should have protected her. Insisted that she get away from the area and go into hiding.

Fuller came to an abrupt stop, and Sammy slammed on his brakes, jumping out of the vehicle the moment he slipped the gear into Park. He ran past Officer Fuller, nearly falling on the slick, snowy road in his haste. The nose of Beth's BMW sloped downward, the front two tires completely depleted of air.

Her head and shoulders were slumped over the steering wheel, and her long brown hair hung down, veiling her face. In spite of all the chaotic sirens and lights, Beth wasn't moving. Sammy rapped his knuckles at the driver's-side windows before flinging open the door.

"Beth! What happened?"

No blood was visible on her body or in the car's interior, from where he stood. No apparent bullet wound. This was a good sign. His chest and lungs loosened a notch. Careful not to move her body in case of a neck or back injury, Sammy smoothed back her hair. Beth groaned and leaned back into the seat. Blood poured from a gash on her forehead. Her eyes flickered open, confusion clouding the gray irises. "Sammy?" she whispered, so softly he barely heard her.

"An ambulance is on the way. How badly are you hurt?"

She lifted an unsteady hand to her injured temple and frowned. "I… I'm not sure. Not too bad?"

The EMTs would be there in a moment. "Can you tell me what happened?"

"He shot at me."

"Who?"

"Don't know his name." She straightened and licked her lips. Color returned to her face as she apparently rose from the fog of unconsciousness. "I tried to call you."

"Right. I got your voice mail. Describe the man who harassed you. What exactly did he say?"

"Big giant of a guy with red hair who demanded I pay him fifty grand. He gave me a piece of paper with a phone number to call when I got the money together. When he left, I tried to follow him—"

"Damn it, Beth," he muttered.

"Coming through!" an EMT shouted by his elbow.

Their time was up. "Anything else you remember about the guy or the truck he drove?" he asked quickly.

"No."

Sammy nodded. "We're on it. If you think of something later, call me." He started to turn away, but Beth caught his arm. "Did you remember something?"

"I just wanted to say…" She offered a wan smile. "We should stop meeting like this."

Sammy stared at her dumbly before he realized Beth was making a joke.

Brad Pelling, an EMT he'd met many times, squeezed between him and Beth. "Got to do our job," he explained apologetically, feeling the pulse at Beth's neck.

"Of course." Sammy watched as Brad questioned Beth and continued taking her vital signs.

"She's fine." Charlotte moved to his side and searched his face, her eyes much too sharp and knowing. "Seems you are unusually focused on this particular victim."

"We've known each other for years. Her brother used to be a good friend." He gave a casual shrug but knew his partner wasn't fooled. What was his deal when it came to Beth Wynngate? As he'd explained to Charlotte, she was merely an old friend's little sister. Nothing more or less.

But as Brad and another EMT pulled out a stretcher and laid Beth on it, he swallowed hard past a thick lump in his throat.

"Go with them and stay with Beth," Charlotte quietly urged. "I'll run what I can on the information she provided and ask around to see if there were any witnesses. If I come up with anything, I'll ring you."

He was torn between wanting to leap into the case and find who'd hurt Beth, and a desire to stay with her until she was released from the hospital.

"You know the hospital is unlikely to keep her overnight, even for a concussion," Charlotte said. "We need to consider how to protect her from another attack when they let her go."

That settled the matter. He forked over the cruiser keys. "Call me if you get any leads. After Beth is somewhere safe, I'll head to Atlanta and pay Lambert a surprise visit."

"Sounds like a plan. This situation with the Lambert family needs to be handled quickly before someone is seriously hurt or killed. Be careful."

"You, too." Bad enough he hadn't protected Beth—he didn't need an injured partner on his conscience, as well. James Tedder, Charlotte's husband, was his best friend, and he'd be damned if James's wife and their future baby suffered because he'd overlooked a hidden danger.

Chapter 7

Beth fought the effects of the prescription painkiller and anti-inflammatory pills the hospital had administered. At least she'd talked them into giving her only a mild dosage. She'd need all her wits for the coming interview. Sammy didn't know it yet, but she was going to confront Dorsey Lambert. No way she'd miss the opportunity to get answers.

The rolling hills of North Georgia gave way to the crowded metro Atlanta area with its skyscrapers and traffic. Lots of traffic. Gingerly, she touched the bandage by her temple.

"Your head starting to hurt?" Sammy asked.

"No." She shrugged and relented at his raised brows. "Well, maybe a little. I consider myself lucky not to have a concussion." She quickly rushed to change the subject. If she wanted to see Dorsey, she couldn't let

Sammy harp on her injuries. He'd use it as an excuse to exclude her access. It'd been hard enough convincing him to let her go with him to Atlanta. "Does the traffic bother you?"

"It doesn't thrill me."

Sammy wasn't in the best of moods. En route, he'd contacted the Atlanta PD to provide backup while he questioned the suspect. They'd responded that there were no available officers and wouldn't be for several hours—if then. Sammy had told her that he'd almost turned around but decided the risk of her getting hurt again was greater than the danger of facing the man alone.

She covertly studied his profile. Sammy Armstrong was like a bad-luck charm that showed up at some of the worst moments in her life—the teenage arrest, the break-in at her house, and today's mess. But maybe it was good luck instead of bad, even the arrest. If he and his partner hadn't broken up the party when they did, the aftermath might have been even worse for her.

Sammy turned onto I-20, and a couple of miles later, they were driving through East Atlanta Village with its older homes, quirky shops and even an urban llama farm nestled less than a mile from the interstate mayhem. It was unlike the other parts of Atlanta Beth was used to. Their old family home, which Cynthia still occupied, was in Sandy Springs, which sported an old-money vibe with scenic mansions sprawled along single-lane roads. Aiden favored the affluent Buckhead area and lived in a high-rise condo near his law practice. Beth appreciated their different styles, but as for herself, she enjoyed the SoWa section in the South End of Boston, which served as a mecca of the arts.

Sammy pulled into the driveway of a modest ranch-style home with an old Plymouth Duster parked out front. He shut off the engine and then frowned when he caught her undoing her seat belt. "No way. You stay locked in here. It shouldn't take me long. Chances are he's not living here with his mother, anyway. Probably only listed her address to provide an answer on the Corrections release form."

"I'm not seeing her alone. I'm with an armed law enforcement officer. I couldn't possibly be any safer."

Lines creased on his forehead. "But—"

"No *buts*." Before he could answer, she hopped out of the car and shut the door. She offered him a breezy smile and sauntered toward the porch walkway.

Sammy exited the vehicle and let out a sigh that she guessed could be heard all the way down the street. "You let me do all the talking. I'll explain your presence as a recently hired detective. She'll assume you're in training. Agreed?"

"Of course," she assured him. *Unless I have a burning question for Lambert that you don't ask him yourself.* "Want me to stand at the back door in case he's home and tries to make a run for it?"

The look he threw her was so stern she instantly realized her mistake. "Just kidding," she offered. Quickly, she scooted up the porch steps in case he changed his mind. Sammy moved in front of her and rapped at the door.

A game show played on the TV until someone inside suddenly muted it. "Who's there?" called a raspy voice that could have been male or female.

"Elmore County Sheriff's Department."

Silence.

The peephole darkened briefly, and then the door flung open. A woman stood before them in a floral muumuu. Unkempt gray hair floated past her shoulders, and she sported the lip wrinkles associated with a long-term cigarette smoker. "You ain't got no jurisdiction in Fulton County," she pointed out in a gravelly voice. "What do you want?"

"Mrs. Rayna Lambert? We'd like a word with you about your son, Dorsey. You told Detective Tedder this morning that he lives with you at this address?"

"Like I told that woman, he ain't here," she offered unhelpfully. "He's at work down at the Coca Cola plant. Won't be home for hours."

"I'd like his cell phone number. I can meet him at the plant. Won't take but a few minutes of his time."

Rayna spat out a series of numbers that Sammy punched in his own phone. Beth peered past the woman's bulky frame and into the den, which was surprisingly well furnished and neat. Mrs. Lambert took more care with her housekeeping than she did her personal appearance. From the den, she had a view of the kitchen and a hallway that led to more rooms and a back door. A flash of red hair poked from one of the hallway rooms. The man had a gaunt, pale face with eyes focused on where they stood on the porch. He had the intent furtiveness of a hunted animal assessing danger. He caught her stare, and his eyes widened. Before she could alert Sammy, the man bolted from the room and sprinted to the back door.

"Hey, he's here!" she said, tugging on Sammy's jacket. "He's making a run for the back!"

"Halt," he called out, trying to push past Rayna Lambert's hulking frame. "We just have a few questions."

"Guess he don't want to talk to you," she said without a trace of humor in her flat voice.

Sammy flew down the steps. "Get in the car," he ordered.

Like hell. Beth waited until he'd sped past the corner of the house before she ran after him.

Magnolia trees haphazardly dotted the large backyard, but enough snow lay on the ground to show Lambert's footprints leading straight to the neighbor's abutting property. Lambert was thin and lithe and had the adrenaline rush of the hunted as he scaled the privacy fence and disappeared from her sight. Sammy was close behind, and he also quickly climbed over.

Unlike Aiden, she'd never been the athletic type, preferring the solitary pursuit of painting while he went to ball practice. Scaling a six-foot fence was not in her wheelhouse, especially after being banged up in the car. Instead, she sped to the side of the property, arriving in time to watch as Sammy pursued Lambert down the tree-lined street and then around the bend in the road.

Should she call 911? She tapped the cell phone in her back pocket but decided Sammy might not appreciate her interference. It might be best to let him either apprehend Dorsey on his own or make arrangements to return later with a police officer. But retreat to the cruiser? Beth slowly turned around, facing Rayna, who stood rooted on the back porch, hands crossed over her chest, watching the drama with a stone-faced expression.

Dorsey might have given them the slip, but his mother hadn't. She slowly walked toward her, as though Rayna were a wild animal who'd balk at the slightest provocation and retreat into her lair. But the Lambert matriarch was made of sterner stuff than that. She eyed

Beth dead-on and never flinched a muscle, even though her son was running from the law, even though she was clad only in a thin housedress in the frigid cold—cold for Atlanta, that was—and even though a stranger approached.

Beth stopped at the edge of the back porch, staring into the woman's implacable face. "Why?" she asked simply.

Rayna pulled a pack of cigarettes and a lighter from the pocket of her dress, expertly cupped her hands over her mouth to shield the flame from the wind, and lit up. She drew heavily and then exhaled a noxious cloud of gray smoke. "Why what?" she asked abruptly.

"Why is your son out to get me?"

"First of all, I don't even know who the hell you are."

"Beth Wynngate."

"Ah." The pale eyes flickered. "You must be related to Judge Edward Wynngate." She spat out the name as though she'd accidentally swallowed a morsel of something putrid.

Beth squared her shoulders, unashamed to claim the familial connection. "His daughter."

Rayna cast disapproving eyes over her from head to toe, and Beth was conscious of how she must appear to the older woman—a tasteful Berber knitted cap with matching scarf, diamond studs discreetly gleaming on her earlobes, a wool coat of the finest quality, tailored trousers and designer boots. And there was also the little matter of the bandage over her right temple.

"Go on," Rayna urged. "What's Dorsey done got himself into?"

"I've been threatened. Several times." She touched the bandage. "Most recently this morning. Your son

seems to hold some kind of grudge against my father—
who died seven months ago, by the way."

If she'd expected sympathy, she'd have been disappointed. Rayna's features didn't soften for an instant.

"Anyway, a man confronted me this morning, saying I needed to fork over fifty thousand dollars to make all this go away."

"But it weren't Dorsey."

"No. But it has to be someone he sent, probably a member of the family, judging by the red hair."

"Sounds like a pretty flimsy connection to me."

She didn't want to give away any specific information to this woman, so she merely stated the obvious. "Oh yeah? Then why'd your son run from us?"

"He's an ex-convict. Why wouldn't his first instinct be to run from the cops? He never wants to be behind bars again." She drew on the cigarette. "I don't want that for him, either."

"Then work with us. If Dorsey isn't behind this, he can clear his name."

"Like you'd believe anything he'd say."

"Can you just get him to leave me alone?" she asked, burying her pride. "I haven't done anything to him. Whatever grudge he had with my father, that's in the past. The man's dead, and his sentencing was always fair and within the bounds of the law. This vendetta is ridiculous."

"Poor little rich girl. Daddy's dead, and here you stand, looking like a million bucks. Must have inherited a nice bundle."

Beth said nothing. What was the point in denial?

Rayna tilted her head back and blew out a series of spiral smoke rings. "I'll tell you this much," she said at last. "Dorsey may be a lot of things. Bad things. But he ain't gonna rough up no woman. And he certainly ain't a killer."

Delusional mother. "Maybe you don't know him as well as you think you do. And what about the rest of the family?"

Rayna tossed the cigarette in the snow, snuffing it out. "I'll speak to him."

"Thank you." A modicum of relief swept through her. Even if Sammy couldn't catch up to Dorsey, perhaps some good had come out of this trip.

"I ain't doin' it for you, missy." Rayna started to turn away. "Now get the hell off my property."

What are you going to do if I refuse, call the cops? But of course, Beth didn't say it aloud. No point in antagonizing the woman and calling her out over an idle threat. Rayna retreated inside, and the door slammed shut.

Beth hunched forward, bracing against a chilly gust of wind. Where was Sammy? Was he okay? Dorsey's small build wouldn't match up well with Sammy's fit, muscular body, but a cornered rat might prove dangerous. If she had the cruiser keys, she could search the neighborhood. She was just lucky he'd left it unlocked for her.

She looked over her shoulder, but there was no sign of either man. Might as well wait in the warm car rather than stand out here in the cold, her very presence ticking off Rayna Lambert, a possible ally. And even if she didn't want to admit it to Sammy, her head and back ached from the wreck. She'd been lucky the guardrails had held and that her car hadn't crashed down the mountain. Just imagining being trapped inside the twisted metal heap as it flipped and landed in the hollow below made her knees weak.

Once in the cruiser, Beth leaned back in the seat and closed her eyes, willing herself to relax and have faith that Sammy knew what he was doing and was in no danger. They'd caught Dorsey unawares, so it was unlikely he had a weapon on him as he'd raced from the house. Actually, he'd been wearing a T-shirt and long johns, and he'd been barefoot. A distinct disadvantage against Sammy. She hoped that helped make up for Sammy's lack of knowledge about the layout of the neighborhood, but she pictured Dorsey slunk below the foundation of someone's house, curled into a tight ball like a stray animal hiding.

The car door suddenly slung open, and she jumped in her seat. Her heart jackhammered against her ribs until she saw it was Sammy.

Alone.

"He got away, huh?" she asked. "Figures. He's like a pesky rodent scurrying out of trouble."

"I'd say more than pesky," he answered, pointing at her injury.

Sammy started the car, and they rolled away. A slight lift of the curtain at the front of the house told Beth that Dorsey's mother had been keeping a close watch. Her son would slither back home soon enough.

"Are you going to contact the Atlanta PD again and update them?"

"Already did." His jaw was tight and his hands white-knuckled as they gripped the steering wheel. "I knew I should have waited until they had an officer available."

"You couldn't have known if Dorsey would even be

home tonight," she pointed out. "Are we going to drive around the neighborhood and see if he's around?"

"We can. The local cops agreed to put out a BOLO. Maybe they'll capture him."

He circled around the block and then widened the search to another neighborhood in the direction Dorsey had run.

"Could be he's got friends or relatives close by that've already taken him in. But the good news is that Rayna Lambert agreed to see if she could talk some sense into her son."

Sammy snorted. "Don't count on that happening. Apple doesn't usually fall far from the tree."

Let him be cynical. Beth believed Rayna would try. After all, she was his mother, and it was obvious that if Dorsey didn't stop pursuing her, this wouldn't end well for him. "Time will tell," she said in a you'll-see tone.

"This is pointless," Sammy said at last, running a hand through his dark hair. "Now to figure out what to do with you."

"What do you mean?"

"You're obviously not safe in Blood Mountain. While we're in Atlanta, maybe you should pay your stepmother a visit. Surely you can stay with her until Lambert is apprehended."

The too-casual way Sammy threw out the suggestion didn't fool her. She had the sneaking suspicion this had been his intent all along in coming to Atlanta—to dump her off on Cynthia. Her stepmother would hate that even more than she would.

"No way. I'll take my chances back home."

"Home? Meaning…you're going back to Boston?"

"Blood Mountain." Strange that she considered it

home rather than her dad's old house in Sandy Springs or her apartment in Boston.

He frowned. "Then stay with Aiden."

"He's still out of town."

Sammy pulled onto the interstate, his fingers tapping out a beat against the dashboard. "There has to be a safe place for you somewhere." He cleared his throat, as if uncomfortable with what he was about to say. "Would you consider staying with me? I have a guest room." His voice was no-nonsense, but she detected a note of tension in it, as if afraid of her answer.

"Nope. That's not happening. I can't imagine your boss would cotton to that idea, either."

"Harlan's a friend. Speaking of which, Charlotte mentioned you could stay with Lilah, if being with me bothers you so much."

"Lilah's busy. I wouldn't feel right imposing. Not when her baby's due any moment."

"Stubborn," he mumbled, shifting in his seat.

"I heard that." She wasn't offended, though, especially considering that it was the truth. She'd lived too long in places where she wasn't truly wanted. Once she'd left high school, she'd sworn she'd never again be a millstone around another person's neck.

"There's always Boston." Her heart wasn't in the suggestion, though, since it had proven unsafe once before. But it would put distance between her and the Lamberts.

"That's no good. You were followed up there."

"True. But I think Rayna can put a stop to Dorsey's stalking."

"Don't kid yourself on that score." He shot her a hooded glance. "Is the thought of staying with me so disagreeable? Are you worried about what people will say?"

"It's not that."

"Then what is it?"

"I won't put anyone else in danger again."

"I can take care of myself while I protect you. For crying out loud, Beth. I'm a cop."

"Out of the question," she insisted.

Sammy shook his head and mouthed the word *stubborn*.

She was refusing for his own good, even if he couldn't see it. His offer was tempting. But no matter how easily Sammy shrugged off the impropriety, it wouldn't look good for him professionally to have her, a targeted victim, living in his home. So the problem remained. Where could she stay, besides possibly a string of impersonal hotels, where no Lambert would find her? Someplace where her presence wouldn't be a danger to her host?

A fully formed image blasted into her mind—a small but comfortable cabin near Lavender Mountain's peak. Her dad's former hunting cabin was so isolated that she doubted anyone else even knew of its existence.

If she couldn't hide out there in the wilds, then no place was safe.

Chapter 8

"I don't like it," Sammy said as he finally spotted the tiny lodge almost hidden from sight. Although the oak trees and shrubs were bare, the wooden structure melded seamlessly behind a copse of evergreen pines, and snow covered its roof.

"You haven't even been inside yet. Give it a chance," Beth said.

His Jeep jostled as he hit a pothole. The dirt road had become so overgrown from a long period of no travelers that tree branches arching from each side of the embankment met in the middle to form a gnarled, brown tunnel. Limbs scratched the sides of his vehicle; the metal frame rubbing dead wood sounded like a knife scraping against a plate. His forearms momentarily goose-bumped at the high-octave screech.

"Jeep's going to need a paint job before this is over," he grumbled.

She grinned back at him. "Jeeps are made for off-road use. The scratches will give it character."

He couldn't help returning the grin. With every mile they'd put between them and Atlanta, Beth had visibly relaxed. He didn't share her confidence that the danger was past, but he took heart that she seemed to have forgiven him for daring to question her father's integrity. Unless absolutely necessary, he wouldn't tread again in that emotional quagmire.

He pulled the vehicle as close as possible to the cabin, but they still had to trudge a good twenty yards with all the supplies they'd picked up in town after he'd swapped out the cruiser for his own vehicle. Quickly, they hauled their stash inside, hoping to get everything unloaded and a fire started before the sun set. Already the shadows lengthened, birds flocked noisily to find their night's resting place, and the air grew chillier. Night fell quickly in the mountains, and with the darkness came an almost unsettling quiet.

Sammy paused in his work, a pile of firewood in his arms, and surveyed the land. How many years had it been since he and Harlan and James had spent a weekend hunting? Too many. His friends were busy with their own families now, and the realization briefly pinched his heart. *It's understandable. They've moved on.* Once their children were older, they'd probably be able to get away for an occasional all-guy trip. As for himself, the whole marriage-and-kiddos thing held no appeal. He'd seen how much a bad marriage could devastate a man. His dad had been proof of that.

A loud clatter erupted from the cabin, and his heart hammered. He dropped the pile of wood and raced inside. Had the cabin been booby-trapped? A string tied to a shotgun trigger or trip wires set to an explosive? The Lambert men were rugged mountain folks with little regard for the law and notorious for holding grudges. If they knew of the cabin and had gotten there first...

Beth stood in the kitchen, arms akimbo, staring at the dozens of food cans rolling around the rough pine floor. She held up a brown sack with a torn bottom by way of explanation.

He huffed out a breath of relief, almost laughing at his imagination.

"Didn't mean to scare you," she said.

"Are you sure no one outside of your family knows about this place?"

"How many times do I have to assure you? I'm positive no one else has seen this place, not even hikers or hunters. It's isolated, yes, but that's an advantage. No one knows about it. It's private property. I doubt Cynthia and Aiden even come here. Aiden only bothered with it when he wanted to throw parties far away from parental eyes."

Sammy bent down and helped her pick up the strewn cans. "Still can't believe Judge Wynngate liked to hunt. Didn't picture him as an outdoors kind of guy."

"Dad grew up in the North Carolina mountains. That's why he bought the house at Falling Rock and then built this cabin as his own private retreat. His job dictated he live in a big city, but he enjoyed time in nature."

He caught the wistful note in her voice. "I also had the impression that you and your father weren't all that close."

"Not since I was a little girl," she admitted. "When Mom died of cancer, a part of my dad seemed to wither away, even after he married Cynthia a few years later. And once I became a teenager…well, things changed between us."

Sammy was well aware of the wedge her arrest had driven between Beth and her family—an arrest he was partially responsible for making. "I remember your mom. Nice lady."

Beth's gray eyes brightened. "You do?"

"Yep. I do."

A charged silence fell between them, and he was intensely aware of the closeness of her body, the soft floral scent that was always a part of Beth. With just the two of them alone inside the cozy cabin, it seemed they were isolated from the rest of the world.

He stepped backward, breaking the spell. Protecting Beth was his job, and he'd better remember that fact. "I'll get the rest of the stuff in before it gets too dark."

"Right," she quickly agreed, her cheeks flushed pink. "Lots to do before I get settled in."

"Before *we* get settled in," he corrected.

"I already told you, I'm fine out here. Perfectly safe. No need—"

"I'm staying," he insisted. "At least for tonight."

Actually, he planned to stay with her until he got word that the Atlanta PD had Lambert in custody. But he'd fight that battle with Beth later. One day at a time. And who knew? By tomorrow, Dorsey Lambert indeed might be locked away.

Outside, Sammy inhaled the bracing winter air. *This is business only*, he reminded himself. *Get a grip*. He brought in the rest of the boxes from the Jeep. Amazing how much stuff you needed to bring along, even for a short visit. Once all was unloaded, he set to work building a fire. It didn't take long for the small interior to be filled with its warmth and the pleasant scent of burning oak.

"Your gourmet meal awaits," Beth said, carrying their take-out food on a tray into the living area. She'd placed the Mexican fast-food dishes on plates and filled two glasses with soda. They sat across from one another as they ate, Beth on a chair she'd pulled over to the coffee table, while he sprawled on the leather sofa. He dipped a tortilla chip into the salsa bowl and pointed at the canvas frame she'd set in the corner of the room. A sheet draped the front. "What are you working on?"

"A snowscape of Blood Mountain."

"May I see?"

Color rose on her cheeks. "It's not finished yet. Since there's no television up here, I figured I'd pass the time painting. Maybe start a few new ones."

She didn't feel comfortable sharing her work with him. "I suppose most artists don't like showing their works in progress. I can respect that. As someone who has zippo artistic talent, I have to say that I admire seeing it in others," he said.

The blue specks in her dove-gray eyes shimmered as she silently regarded him. "You have an interest in the arts?"

"Who doesn't?" he countered with a shrug. "I may not have access to local museums like you do in Boston, but I can still appreciate beauty. I just get mine from a different source. Like walking through the woods or driving around mountain roads with panoramic views of Appalachia."

"Touché," she said, lifting her glass of soda in a mock toast and taking a swallow. "I wish my family had half as much appreciation for art as you do. They see my painting as dabbling. A hobby. And the art classes I teach middle graders? It's not a distinguished enough career for their respect. They act embarrassed when their friends ask what I do in Boston."

Sammy wasn't surprised. Cynthia Wynngate appeared the sort to only care about social prestige, and Aiden had adopted his mother's attitude over the years. He and Aiden had drifted apart soon after Aiden started college. Sammy heard his former friend spent summers hanging out in the city with new buddies, tossing around money without limits. On the few occasions Sammy had run into Aiden, there had been a subtle change in the way Aiden treated him. Without sports, they'd discovered they had no common interests, and even short conversations became awkward.

"I'm sorry," he said. "I hope their attitude doesn't upset you. It's their problem, not yours."

A genuine smile lit her face. "It doesn't bother me. Not much, anyway. Besides, I only see them once or twice a year. No big deal."

He hoped that was true.

She gestured at the canvas frame. "You can look, if you'd like."

"You're sure?"

"Yes. Just don't expect Van Gogh or something."

He stood and crossed the room, but she remained seated. Carefully, he lifted the sheet and stared at the painting. A plumage of white, yellow, pink and coral clouds drifted over the mountains dotted green with pine and espresso-colored oak trees, their branches glinting with ice. Old Man Brooks's abandoned red barn adorned the right corner of the canvas. The wide swath of snow blanketing the ground reflected the sky's multicolored palette.

Sammy stared at it for long moments before speaking. He felt like he could step into that scene of crisp pastoral elegance. "It's beautiful," he said simply, then turned to look her in the eyes.

"You mean it?" She rose and sauntered toward him. "It still needs a few finishing touches."

"I mean it."

"Thanks, Sammy." Her breathy voice was close by his side, and he swallowed hard. He scanned a couple more paintings, all in various stages of completion, all alive with pastel washes of color. He knew little of art, but he recognized talent when he saw it. Beth had it. Looking at her work was unexpectedly intimate, as though by viewing her art, he glimpsed something of her soul and how she perceived the beauty in the world. Slowly, he faced her.

Firelight flickered golden on her face, neck and arms. Thin strands of cinnamon highlights streaked her sleek sable hair, and Beth's understated beauty made his breath hitch. As it had been earlier in the kitchen, everything seemed to still. There was only the two of them, alone, with the fireplace crackling in the background. His gaze drifted to her lips. Just one taste. What was the harm? Her mouth parted, and she almost imperceptibly leaned into him. This was it. This was the moment. Sammy bowed his head and pressed his lips to hers. They were as warm and intoxicating as he'd imagined.

He lost himself in the softness of her lips. This was where he was always meant to be. As though the kiss had been inevitable from the moment he saw her again, looking shaken by the threatening letter but determined to get to the bottom of the matter.

Aiden's little sister all grown up.

A barred owl screeched nearby, invading his senses, which had grown thick and heavy with passion. He clasped his hands under her forearms and pulled away. He was supposed to be there to protect Beth, not make love to her. "This isn't a good idea."

Beth stared at him wide-eyed, one hand drifting up to touch her lips. Confusion, then hurt, and at last, resignation flashed across her face. "You're probably right."

Part of him wished she'd protested, but a saner inner voice assured him he'd done the right thing. They returned to dinner and went to bed early, Beth retiring to the one bedroom on the other side of the kitchen while he lay on the sofa under a woolen blanket. For hours he stared into the fireplace as the flames crackled, and then the logs dwindled to blazing orange embers. Had pulling away from Beth been a mistake? The longer he lay awake, the less confident he became of his decision. There were so many reasons not to get involved with her—it would be unprofessional; she lived hundreds of miles away; she resented him for arresting her years ago; and the Wynngates were in a different social league. The distance between them and the reasons to keep it that way seemed impenetrable.

Yet he couldn't deny that their kiss had shaken him to his core.

Dawn filtered through the small window of the cabin. Beth huddled deeper beneath the quilt, reluctant to leave the lazy warmth of the featherbed. And getting up meant facing Sammy, who'd delivered a mind-blowing kiss only to reject her moments later.

But what a kiss.

Somehow she'd have to pretend it had never happened and just get on with the day. Surely he didn't plan to hang around too long? She'd have to convince him there was no danger so far into the woods. She'd be careful to keep the doors locked, her shotgun loaded and at the ready. After all, this was her cabin, and she got to decide who had permission to come and go. Being alone was what she needed. Without the distraction of television and the internet, she'd absorb herself with painting, and when she tired of that, she'd curl up in bed with a good book. Plan made, she pulled on jeans and a sweatshirt and headed to the kitchen.

Sammy was already up. He sat on the edge of the sofa, drinking his usual morning drink of soda, and raised his head at her approach. His jaw had an unshaven shadow that looked sexy as hell.

"Good morning," she called out airily. "I'm up. You should head on back to work now."

"I'm not leaving."

"Doesn't your partner need you?"

"Not as much as you do."

"Don't be ridiculous. I'll lock the door behind you. Any sign of trouble, I'll call 911." She nodded at the shotgun above the fireplace. "And don't forget I have a weapon." Beth turned her back on him and rummaged through the cooler for an orange juice pack. "Did you ever call Cynthia about the break-in?"

"Yep. And got her permission to have a tech guy search your dad's computer." He took a seat at the kitchen table and eyed her curiously. "Your stepmother didn't tell you?"

"She called early yesterday morning, but I was talking to Lilah at the time. The right moment to call her back just didn't happen. Too much going on."

Understatement of the year. Luckily, Sammy didn't bother pointing out that now was as good a time as any. She'd call Cynthia back later today, once she was alone and not so frazzled. Beth sat across from Sammy at the table, then picked up a small metal cylinder that hadn't been there last night. "What's this?"

"Pepper spray. Keep it clipped on a belt or a loop on your jeans. It's police-strength and has a range of ten feet."

She eyed it warily. "I'm afraid I'll hurt myself more than the criminal I'm aiming at. How's it work?"

"It's easy. I'll show you."

Sammy demonstrated how to rotate the trigger to the fire position.

"What if I accidently spray myself?"

"You won't."

"Okay. If it makes you feel better." She looped the canister onto her jeans, privately resolving to take it off the moment he finally left.

"Have you ever shot a pistol?"

"No, but Dad taught me to use the shotgun."

"I can teach you—"

"No, thanks. I'm good."

"Then I insist you at least let me teach you a few self-defense moves."

She started to object, then closed her mouth, remembering the tall stranger from yesterday looming over her. "Not a bad idea."

"How sore is your back?"

"Surprisingly good. No headache, either."

"Great." He slammed both hands on the table. "Grab your jacket, and let's get to work."

"Can't we do it in the den?"

"Not enough space."

"Fine," she muttered, grabbing her designer jacket.

Sammy paused in the doorway and cocked his head toward the fireplace mantel, where the shotgun hung. "That thing loaded?"

"Yes."

"I'll test it and make sure it's in running order. Bring it along with that box of extra shells on the sofa."

Beth picked up the items and followed him out the door. How long could it take? Fifteen, maybe twenty minutes tops, and then she'd have the cabin to herself.

They trudged through the snow a good distance to get to a clearing wide enough to test the shotgun. "This'll do," he said at last.

She handed him the gun, and he checked the barrel. Satisfied, he lifted it to his shoulder and shot off a round. Even though she expected it, the blast in the forest silence made her jump. It'd been over a decade since she'd come out here with Dad and shot cans off a fallen tree log for target practice. Back before their falling-out over the party.

"Your turn."

She took the shotgun, steeled her legs in anticipation of the kickback and fired off a round. It felt good. No one would find her out here in the boonies, but if worse came to worst, she wouldn't hesitate to protect herself. She raised the gun in one hand. "Who needs self-defense moves when you've got this?"

"Can't carry it with you everywhere, every moment."

Beth carefully set the shotgun against a tree, resigned to another lesson. "Show me what I need to learn."

Sammy shrugged out of his jacket and tossed it on the ground. "First demonstration. Say your attacker approaches you from the front and grabs your arm." He clamped his hand down on her right forearm and regarded her sternly. "How would you try to escape this hold?"

"Kick you in the nuts?" she guessed.

"Wrong. He'd see it coming and block it." Sammy placed her left fist on his hand that was clutching her arm. "Now point your left elbow up, and then slice down with every muscle in your core."

She tried, but Sammy held fast.

"Give it all you've got," he urged. "Muscle and weight."

It took several attempts, but to her surprise, the move worked to free her from Sammy's grip.

"Good job. Now let's try a different scenario. Let's say someone grabs you from behind and places his arms around your waist."

Sammy moved behind her and held her tight in his arms. His hard body pressed against her back, and heat flared through her. The memory of last night's kiss fueled her awareness of him. If she turned her head an inch to one side, her lips would land on his chin, and then his mouth would seek hers, and—

His arms clenched tighter around her abs and squeezed. "Pay attention," he said, his voice harsh and deep in her ears.

The warm rush of his breath sent shivers down to her core. How could she possibly concentrate when her mind was thick with the possibilities of the two of them kissing? With great effort, she shook off the images playing in her head. "I'm listening," she said. "What do I do next?"

"Grab my arms and then pull yourself in."

"Like this?" she asked, holding tight to his arms.

"That's it. Now swing your hips to one side and make a fist."

Surprisingly, she felt his hold give way, and she held up her fist. "Now what?"

"If this was an attacker, you'd strike his groin with that fist. Hard as you can."

"That should buy me a few seconds," she remarked dryly.

"Use that time to run. If you're out in public, scream as loudly as you can." He frowned. "Next time I'm at the office, I'll get you a whistle."

Beth stepped away from him, glad to put a little distance between them. "Thanks. I'll keep these moves in mind."

He looked at her in surprise. "We're not nearly through yet."

"We aren't?"

"I've got a couple more moves to show you, and then you're going to practice until your reactions become automatic. Otherwise, you won't remember any of this if an attacker comes at you with no warning."

Sweat trickled down her neck and chest, despite the cold air and snow. Beth shrugged out of her coat as Sammy had done earlier. Over and over, they rehearsed her reactions for every eventuality, whether she was attacked from the front or behind.

"Remember the key vulnerable areas—eyes, nose,

throat and groin," he kept reminding her. "Use your head and stay aware of your surroundings. If an attacker aims a gun at you, then run away in a zigzag pattern while seeking shelter."

Forty-five minutes later, Beth's body dripped head to toe with sweat, and she was panting. But she was prepared. "I'm feeling pretty badass," she said with a cocky grin.

Sammy didn't return the smile, still intent on drilling home his message. He made a sudden lunge for her, and she raised her fists by her face, ready to fight. Again and again Sammy came at her, and she fended him off. At last he broke away and gave an approving nod. "I think you've got it. One last thing. If you have no choice but to fight back, commit to it and never hesitate to hit as hard as you can." His eyes darkened. "If you do get over-powered, fake compliance, and then strike again or run at the first opportunity."

"Got it," she said. Beth had never felt more compe-tent. If someone did try to take her by force, she'd at least put up a good fight.

Chapter 9

"So how come you never got married?"

Sammy nearly choked on the vegetable soup they ate for dinner in front of the fireplace.

A flash of worry flickered in Beth's eyes. "Or are you?"

"Wh-what?" he stammered, clearing his throat. His eyes watered, and he hastily swallowed iced tea.

"You okay there?" Beth placed her hand between his shoulder blades and patted.

"What in the world brought on that question?"

She shrugged. "Why not? I mean, we're stuck out here together. Nothing else to do but talk."

He quirked a brow at her. He could think of plenty of things to do besides talking. If she noticed his amusement, she pretended otherwise.

"Well, are you?" she prodded.

"I'm not married, although I was engaged once." He hadn't thought of Emily in years.

"How long ago? What happened?"

"Years ago."

Beth's gray eyes remained pinned on him.

"She dumped me for another guy."

Her mouth rounded in an O of surprise and sympathy flooded her face. "That's horrible. I'm so sorry that—"

Sammy held up a hand. "It was my fault. She kept pressuring me to set a date and I wasn't ready. Frankly, getting engaged had been a mistake from the beginning. It was a decision I later regretted."

"Why? Did you fall out of love? Realize she wasn't the right woman for you?"

More like cold feet. Actually, that had been more than half of the problem. Sammy moved his bowl to the side and faced Beth where she sat opposite him. They were both cross-legged on the floor, casually dining in front of the fireplace—the only warm spot in the cabin. He could give a short nod to her questions, because Beth was partly right, but he wanted honesty between them.

"The idea of tying myself down forever to one woman and raising kids scared the hell out of me," he admitted. "Judging by my parents' marriage, it's a miserable way to live. Guess you've heard stories about my dad. It's a small town."

Her forehead creased, and she bit her lip. "You're almost a decade older than me so it's not like we ran in the same circles. But it seems like I did overhear that he had a drinking problem."

"Stone-cold alcoholic." Sammy drew a deep breath and decided to rip the bandage off as it were. "Mom ran off with my high school math teacher when I was a junior. Even though the marriage had never been great, it broke Dad. He started drinking heavily."

Sammy kept his face averted, not wanting to see the sympathy in Beth's eyes. He believed in letting the past stay buried and rarely mentioned either of his parents.

"That must have been horrible for you as a teenager. I had no idea. You always seemed so happy and cheerful when I saw you with Aiden."

All an act. Sports had been a lifesaver in his teenage years. While Dad spent most of his free time at local bars, playing ball had given him an activity to focus on instead of sitting alone in a dark and cold house waiting for parents who'd both deserted him—in mind if not in body.

"It wasn't that big of a deal," he lied.

Beth's hands closed over his fists. He hadn't even realized he'd clenched his hands into hard knots, or that his body was wound up tight as a swollen tick. Not until the warm softness of Beth's fingers caressed his knuckles, bathing him with light.

"Of course it was a big deal," she murmured. She squeezed his hands and let go. "Do you regret letting her get away?"

"Who?" he asked, confused at the question.

"Your ex-fiancée."

"Emily?" He chuckled. "Not at all. I run into her from time to time. She's happily married with two boys. I'm glad for her. It's what she always wanted. What about you?" Turnabout was fair play.

"Me?"

"Why aren't you married?" That was the real mystery. A woman with her looks, brains and talent must have been hotly pursued.

"Guess the right guy hasn't come along yet. I've had a few close relationships but…" Her voice trailed off.

"I call bullshit."

Instead of taking offense, Beth laughed. "You might say I fundamentally distrust most people. That doesn't make for strong, lasting relationships."

"You trusted Rayna Lambert yesterday."

"Maybe I just wanted to believe there was an easy way out of this mess. That a mom can appeal to her son's basic decency and set everything right."

"That outcome's highly doubtful."

"True."

She turned her head toward the hearth and he watched the play of fire glow on her elegant features. "You seem to trust me," he ventured.

"Also true."

Perhaps she'd had no choice but to do so. "You can, you know," he said gently. "Trust me, that is. I won't let anyone hurt you."

"You can't make a promise like that."

"I just did."

She fixed her attention on him again. "This—" she swept the room with her hand "—is only a brief respite, not a fun getaway in the woods, much as I try to pretend that it is."

"There's plenty going on behind the scenes while we hide out. Charlotte's working on the case, and the Atlanta PD will eventually pick Lambert up now that he's on their radar. Until Lambert's accounted for, this is our best option." He cocked his head to the side and studied Beth. "Is it so bad being stuck with me?"

"Of course not. Only it feels like my entire life's on hold. It's frustrating. I came down to visit friends and family and instead I'm burrowed underground like a mole."

"Not for long." At least, he hoped that was the case. This morning, Charlotte had informed him that Judge Wynngate's computer hard drive was sent to a tech specialist in Atlanta, but that she'd been unable to place a priority on the task. A stalking case in Appalachia didn't rank high in their opinion. To be fair, they had murders and kidnapping cases that rightly took precedent. There was never enough manpower to investigate every potential crime risk.

"Some visit," she mumbled.

Visit. Meaning she'd be leaving soon. He'd managed to keep pushing that bit of reality from his mind. Getting too close to Beth would be a mistake.

So why did his arms reach for her, draw her close into an embrace? He rested his head on the top of her scalp, inhaling the clean scent of shampoo. Her hair was silky and warm against his cheek. She wiggled closer into him. Side by side they watched the flames in the fireplace leap and play in the darkness. Night came early in the mountain woods and it lay thick around them. With no neighbors and no electricity, the only light outside came from moonbeams reflecting on the pristine snowy ground.

He rained down kisses, starting at the top of her scalp, and then trailing the side of her face. Beth turned into him, her lips seeking his own. His tongue sought hers and she moaned softly as her arms wrapped behind his neck, urging him closer—deeper.

She could be gone tomorrow. Sammy tamped down the thought as her fingers traced the nape of his neck and then stroked his hair. *This can never last.* Damn that incessant, rational voice in his brain that fired off warning missiles.

Beth climbed into his lap and straddled him, never breaking their kiss. His pulse skyrocketed, and a fever of need coursed through his body. *She'll only leave you.*

That got his attention. The thought triggered his dad's often-repeated words about how women always left you high and dry and to never trust them.

Sammy broke off the kiss, cupping Beth's chin in his hands. Her eyes were graphite-dark and clouded with passion and her lips were swollen and moist. How could he possibly say *no* to this magic between them?

He couldn't.

And he was experienced enough to know this was more than a physical reaction. Blended with the raw passion was tenderness and awe. His heart was in so much trouble.

Abruptly, Beth stood and then pulled her sweater and T-shirt over her head. Her long, dark hair wildly tumbled around her pale shoulders. His throat went dry as she locked her gaze with his and unhooked her bra. The sight of her semi-naked body took his breath away. Sammy couldn't even speak. Instead, he held out his hand. Beth took it and she kneeled in front of him. Impatiently he pulled loose and stripped out of his T-shirt and then his jeans. Her eyes devoured him as he shed everything and stood before her, his need evident.

And then he was beside her, lying on the soft rug, their bodies pressed against each other. Who cared about tomorrow when tonight was so entrancing? For now there was only the heat of the fire on their nude bodies, the heat of bare skin brushing against bare skin, and the heat of need bubbling inside him like a fiery cauldron.

Much, much later, Sammy drifted in the twilight between sleep and wakefulness as Beth lay sound asleep beside him. He tucked the quilt she'd brought from the bedroom around her shoulders and smiled as she sighed and snuggled closer into the warmth of his body. A peaceful, contented drowsiness lazed through him.

Right now, holding Beth after a night of lovemaking had to be a top ten moment in his life. Scratch that, top five at least. Maybe even the best moment he'd ever experienced… Quickly, Sammy eradicated the thought. The sexual afterglow had clouded his perspective. There was no need to rank or analyze what he was feeling. *Just enjoy this time while it lasts.* Determined to follow his own advice, Sammy yawned and succumbed to the lethargy.

Through the fog of sleep, a slight noise pricked his awareness. Sammy mentally swatted at it, annoyed at the disruption, and drifted back into a doze. A slight flicker of light disturbed the inky darkness behind his eyelids. A slight crackling erupted from the silence, probably the dying flames consuming the last of the oak. Come morning, he'd add more wood to the fire.

Crunch.

Sammy's eyes popped open, alertness splashing over him like icy water. His body tensed, ready to spring into action. A quick glance assured him Beth still slept undisturbed by his side. He waited, as still as a cat ready to pounce.

Crunch, crunch and then *crunch, crunch.* The sound of advancing footsteps muffled in the snow.

Someone had found them.

This was bad. There'd been no noise or oncoming headlights from a car. No phone communication from the outside world warning of an emergency visit. It had to be Lambert or one of his men. Sammy eased the blanket off while his eyes searched the dark room. The fireplace embers provided just enough light to locate his pistol set on the mantel. Slowly, he rose and grabbed it, the cold metal gripped in his palm reassuring. Beth turned restlessly, pulling the quilt up until it almost covered her face.

He pondered the wisdom of waking her. The advantage would be that she'd be his backup, armed with a shotgun. The disadvantage would be that in waking Beth, he'd startle her, and she'd make a noise, alerting whoever was out there that they were awake and onto them. Swiftly, he decided to rouse her. He couldn't very well leave her alone and vulnerable while he searched out the danger.

Noiselessly, he kneeled and placed a hand on her shoulder. No response. He gave her shoulder a little shake. Her eyes flew open in alarm, then softened when she focused on him. Keeping his gun in his right hand, Sammy lifted the index finger of his opposite hand and pressed it against his puckered lips.

Hush.

Her eyes widened with fear, but she nodded understanding. He pointed at his gun and then to the fireplace. *Get your shotgun.* Nimbly, she tossed aside the quilt and rose. They both had on sweats they'd donned before falling asleep in the chilly cabin. He saw her scoop up her cell phone and shove it into a pocket as she went to the mantel. When she held the shotgun, he raised a palm toward her. *Stay here.*

Beth violently shook her head *no.* He glared at her and she returned his gaze with equal determination. Seemed he had a backup after all.

Sammy leaned into her and whispered in her ear. "Someone's out there. I'm going outside."

Beth nodded and whispered, "Let's go."

"Stay behind me."

He walked to the door and disengaged the lock. A barely audible click sounded before he slid the metal bolts to the side. Fighting an instinct to fling open the door and run wildly into the dark, Sammy turned the knob, conscious of Beth's soft breathing behind him and the warmth of her body pressed against his back. He released the pistol's safety mechanism.

Frosty air bombarded him, and his bare feet sank into snow. Thank heavens it'd been so cold that he and Beth had put on clothes before falling asleep in front of the fire. They'd saved precious time.

Impossible to see more than a few feet ahead, but there was no sign of anyone and no car in sight. Had he imagined the noise? Could it have been an animal rather than a human? Slowly, he advanced to the side of the cabin, Beth at his back with her shotgun at the ready.

An explosion of shattered glass broke the night's eerie silence. Sammy ran toward the back of the cabin, gun raised. The shadows shifted, and he made out a large figure running toward the tree line that bordered the county road. The bedroom window was broken.

"Halt!" he shouted. The figure kept running. No way he could see well enough to land a shot, but Sammy fired his pistol in the air, hoping it would scare the man into surrender.

It did not.

Sammy gave chase, his mind racing as fast as his feet running in the freezing snow. Had the attacker heard them approach? Why hadn't he entered the cabin through the broken window. Unless...

He reached out an arm for Beth, relieved when he made contact with the solid strength of her body. "Get down!"

An explosion shook the ground at his feet as he dropped to his knees and then laid his body above Beth's. His ears rang with the sound of an incendiary pipe bomb exploding. Fire billowed from the cabin, illuminating the sky like lightning. Debris flew through the wind—wood, glass and ash. The snow reflected the giant leaping flames, giving the impression of molten lava spilling on the ground.

Sammy tore his eyes from the horrific damage and scanned the area, eyes peeled for any sight of the attacker returning or any accomplices lurking nearby.

From up the road, the beam of car headlights cut through the darkness.

"They're getting away!" Beth said, pushing him off and scrambling to her feet. "We've got to stop them."

She ran toward the cabin, and he caught up to her, tugging at her arm. "Hurry," she urged. "Get the car keys. We can't let them escape."

"I'll get them. You wait here."

"I can help you search."

"Too dangerous."

Without waiting for an argument, he ran past her. Sammy pulled off his T-shirt and covered his mouth and nose. At the gaping door, precariously tilted to the right, he blinked against the plumes of ash and smoke. His keys, cell phone and two-way radio were located on the far left end of the den on the coffee table they'd pushed against the wall last night so they could sleep in front of the fire. Among other things they'd done there. If they hadn't made love and slept together, if Beth had slept in the bedroom as she had the previous night, she'd be dead.

A chill racked his body—one that had nothing to do with winter. His professional training kicked in. *Deal with that later; there's work to be done.* He sucked in a chest full of air and entered the smoky cabin. Acrid fumes assaulted his nose and eyes. Blinking wildly, he put one hand along the wall to move forward without becoming disoriented by the thick curtain of smoke. Sammy crouched low and tried to ignore the heat emanating from the blistered wood that burned his hand and feet.

Even though he tried not to take deep breaths, smoke filled his lungs and he coughed, struggling for oxygen. The hair on his arms bristled painfully from the heat. Fire roared and crackled and pieces of wood haphazardly fell from the ceiling.

Just a few more steps.

Pain shot through the arch of his right foot as a large glass shard cut through flesh. Sammy kept going. He had no choice; they had to pursue whoever had tried to kill them. This might be their only chance to capture the bastard.

He felt the edge of the coffee table before he saw it. Would the radio and phones already be destroyed by heat and smoke? They were fiery in his palms, but he pocketed the items. Where were those damn keys? He brushed the surface of the table, scorching the bare skin of his right forearm. Nothing. They must have fallen on the floor. Still keeping one hand in contact with the wall, he got on all fours and swept his free hand along the floor until they brushed against jagged metal.

Feeling victorious, he stuffed them in his pocket and started to rise back up on his feet. His head bumped against something solid. The easel clattered to the ground.

Beth's paintings! Her stunning, elegant snowscapes.

Violent coughing seized his lungs. *Get out*, brain and body urged. But he couldn't let Beth's art burn to smithereens. All that work, all that beauty. He slid his left foot over until it thumped against the wall, his anchor in the sea of flames and smoke, and then he gathered the canvases that had fallen to the ground, praying that the thick cloth she'd thrown over the paintings had kept her work from being destroyed.

A large beam fell from the ceiling, landing only a foot from where he stood. It was past time to get the hell out of the cabin. Sammy sprinted toward the door, enduring the gauntlet of the hot floor littered with broken glass. At last he hobbled outside and gulped crisp mountain air down his parched lungs. Snow numbed the bottoms of his burning feet that were laced with gashes.

He thrust the paintings into Beth's arms and turned back to make a mad dash for their jackets and shoes, but the singed door frame buckled, and the overhead wooden strip of the frame dangled precariously in the opening.

Barefoot it was.

And there was no time to waste if they wanted to catch a killer.

Chapter 10

Beth gaped as Sammy shoved her oil paintings into her arms. She hadn't given them a moment's thought. After all, how many had she painted over the years? Dozens and dozens. And although painting was her profession—one of the ways she made a living, along with teaching art—no one would ever believe her work so valuable that they would risk death by fire to save them.

Not her father, who, though proud, had viewed her "hobby" with an indulgence she'd found more condescending than appreciative,

Not Cynthia, who filtered everything and everybody through the lens of their monetary value.

Not Aiden, who mostly regarded the world from the same perspective as his mother, mixed with an intellectual vigor that her father had favored and encouraged.

If Mom had lived, Beth felt certain she would have

understood and appreciated her daughter's artistic success, modest though it was. Mom had always insisted
on Beth receiving art lessons and had proudly displayed
her childhood drawings. But Mom had died a long, long
time ago and Beth still missed her love and encourage-
ment. Since a young teen, she'd felt like a misunderstood, undervalued changeling in the Wynngate family.

And then there was Sammy. The man who had arrested her as a teenager. The man she'd blamed for over
a decade for exiling her from her family. She'd mis-
judged him as uncaring, arrogant.

Beth forgot the horrific explosion, the burning cabin
her father had loved, the chill seeping in her bones and
bare feet, and the knowledge that someone was trying
to kill her. There was only Sammy, covered with ash
and grime, rescuing her canvases as though Dad's cabin
was a museum on fire and her work was Van Gogh's.

She couldn't move. Couldn't speak past the pinch
in her heart.

"Let's go!" Sammy ran past her, limping and still
coughing violently.

Beth blinked away the hot tears that had unexpectedly arisen. "You're hurt. I'll drive."

Without argument, Sammy dug in his jeans pocket
and tossed her the keys. Beth tossed her paintings in the
back seat, got in and started the motor. It took a couple
of seconds to find the light switch on the dashboard
panel and get her bearings with a strange vehicle, then
the Jeep lurched forward as she hit the accelerator. She
bounced in her seat as they crossed over the uneven land
of the small clearing and then onto a dirt road. Only one
way out of here and then onto the main road.

She had to catch up to the bomber. If they didn't,

she could never feel safe again. Each attack grew more aggressive. Next time, she might not escape with her life. How the hell had he found them out here? Was it Dorsey? Sammy had been right. Rayna had no influence on her son—either that, or she hadn't even tried to get through to him.

"Maybe I should have wired that fifty thousand dollars," she said, finding and switching to bright lights. "Or tried to promise them I would get them the money somehow. If I had, they might not have come after me tonight."

"Hell, no! You can't deal with criminals that way." Sammy fiddled with a dial and a blast of welcome heat fanned her chilled body. "It's a game you'd never win."

Snow silently whirled through the wind. Pine trees crowded the road alongside of the Jeep. They made it to the paved county road. In the distance, she caught the elliptical beam of headlights rounding a curve. The attacker was heading north.

Beth stayed focused on the twin rays of headlights ahead, steadily gaining on the bomber. Did he know they were in pursuit? She barely registered Sammy's ongoing radio conversation as he called in their location and requested backup. The static stop-and-go talking provided a comforting backdrop of noise as she sped down the lonely stretch of pavement in the moonlight.

Miles flew past, and although she seemed to be gaining on the vehicle ahead, it stayed frustratingly out of eyesight. She wanted that tag number. She wanted an arrest. She wanted this ordeal to be over. Tonight. Not only for herself, but for her family and for Sammy. No one in her circle was safe.

The county road began to twist as they headed back

up the mountain and the elevation rose. With every turn and climb, the wind howled stronger. The snow seemed to swirl faster, and the trees flashed by at an alarming rate. But Beth drove on, jaw clenched with determination even as her fingers painfully clenched the steering wheel. Her bare feet vibrated with the rumble of the Jeep's engine as it strained under the demanding conditions.

Ahead, she caught a glimpse of a yellow Dodge truck. A little closer and they'd have the tag number. But her jubilation was short-lived as the truck turned sharply onto GA 180—Georgia's own deadly version of the Tail of the Dragon roadway. Bad enough during the day when motorcyclists and other thrill seekers often raced down it. But on a snowy winter night? Despite the continued blast of the heater, her whole body began to tremble.

"We don't have to chase him down the mountain," Sammy said. "If we're lucky, one of our cops might get here in time to put up a roadblock."

If they were lucky. Right now, she didn't feel like Lady Luck was on her side. "I'm not quitting," she told Sammy.

"Want me to drive?"

"There's no time to switch places. We could lose him." Before she could change her mind, Beth turned the Jeep onto GA 180. At least she knew what to expect—a road as narrow as the width of a driveway with miles of blind turns and steep elevation changes. As a teenager, she'd driven down it a time or two, only to prove to Aiden that she wasn't a chicken. Whoever they were pursuing must also be a local to even attempt the ride.

She began the descent down the Tail of the Dragon. At the first blind turn, the Jeep's tires skidded on a sudden icy patch and the vehicle slid several feet to the very edge of the bank. Beth's heart beat painfully against her ribs, even after she righted course and prepared for the next turn.

"Careful there," Sammy said tightly. "Didn't know your real name was Mrs. Mario Andretti."

"Who?"

"Andretti. A legendary race car driver."

Beth slowed a fraction. The only worse outcome than the bomber escaping them would be if she crashed the Jeep. Multiple wooden cross memorials alongside the road were a silent testament to the danger.

The yellow truck ahead didn't slow. Seemed the bomber was more desperate to escape them than they were to capture him and demand answers. At the next sharp curve, the truck veered so close to the edge of the cliff that it clipped the guardrail. The sound of tire squeals and grinding metal screamed through the snowy gales.

Down, down she drove, frustrated at the growing distance between the Jeep and the truck but too cautious to try and gain on it again.

"You're doing a great job," Sammy said softly. "We're over the halfway point down now. It's almost over."

"It won't be over until we get—"

Another squeal of tires filled the air—long and shrill. The truck's driver must have lost control of his vehicle. Beth tapped on the brakes, not knowing what to expect when she emerged from the blind curve. If the driver had crashed into the mountain wall on the right, his truck might be flung back onto the middle of the road, a deadly obstruction for their oncoming Jeep.

She rounded the bend—to see her worst fear come true. The truck slammed into the mountain with a deafening crash. Sparks mingled with snow and metal debris flew through the air like firecracker missiles.

"Look out!" Sammy shouted.

This was no time for mere brake-tapping. "Hold tight," she warned, slamming her foot on the brake, arms clenched to the steering wheel in a death grip as she braced for possible impact.

The truck spun out of control and back toward the guardrail. More grinding of metal on metal ensued and an unmistakable human wail of terror rent the air.

The Jeep grounded to a sudden halt, in time for front-row viewing to a nightmare. The truck toppled over the rail, flipping once before disappearing into darkness. But she heard the crash from the bottom of the mountain as it landed once, then twice, and finally a third time. With each thunderous clap of the tumbling truck, Beth winced. Sammy was back on the two-way radio, barking out their location and requesting an ambulance. Again her body shook so hard that her teeth began to chatter. Sammy flung an arm over her shoulders and squeezed her tight. The solid strength of his arms comforted her and warmed the chilly despair that had momentarily overtaken her body.

"You did great, Beth. I couldn't have asked for a better partner tonight. Help's on the way."

Before she could do more than nod in reply, an explosion blasted from below. Tall flames burst high in a column of orange flares. Sirens wailed in the distance. Sammy flung open the passenger door.

"What are you doing?" she cried in surprise. "You can't go out there. You're not even wearing shoes!"

Sammy's gaze flicked to the back seat and he leaned over, plucking a towel and a jacket from a gym bag. He hastily pulled out the larger shards in his feet, then wrapped each item on a foot for makeshift shoes. "Keep the headlights pointed straight ahead," he instructed. "They know we're here by mile marker eight. I'm just going to stand by the edge of the road and take a quick look."

The door shut behind him and she watched as he picked his way through the haphazardly strewn metal wreckage. A compulsion to see the burning truck overcame her common sense. She opened the Jeep door and Sammy spun around.

"Don't come out here. There's glass everywhere."

"I want to see."

He shook his head and then crossed over to her. "Okay. Just for a minute," he said, putting an arm under her thighs and then lifting her out of the vehicle. She leaned into his solid warmth as the mountain wind whipped around them. He only took a few steps before stopping, mere inches from the smashed-in guardrail.

The twisted metal hull of the truck was engulfed by flames. Black plumes of smoke spiraled among the fire. For the second time tonight, the smell of gasoline permeated the air. But now the acrid scent of scorched rubber mixed with the fuel. The Tail of the Dragon was breathing fire tonight as it claimed yet another victim.

"He couldn't have survived," she whispered.

"No," he grimly agreed. "So much for that lead."

His harsh words weighed on her. "But won't you

be able to discover who that man was? Or at least who owned the truck?"

"We will."

"Then we'll be closer to an answer."

Blue lights and sirens snaked up the mountain. Sammy carried her back to the Jeep, and she waited inside as he met with law enforcement officers. EMTs scrambled from an ambulance with stretchers and headed down the mountain. Firefighters joined them and somehow the dark corner of the mountain was flooded with light in all directions as emergency responders set to work. Sammy emerged from the crowd of people and returned to the Jeep, an EMT by his side.

"You need to go with Adam," Sammy told her gently. "He'll take you to the Elmore Community Hospital. You need to be checked for shock and to make sure you don't have any serious wounds."

"Wounds?" she asked blankly.

"You're covered with cuts," he explained.

She glanced down, surprised at the number of bloody scratches crisscrossing her arms and legs. "How…"

"When the bomb went off, debris flew everywhere. You've been too pumped with adrenaline to notice."

"What about you? You've been limping. Did you burn your feet in the fire?"

"I'll be fine—"

"What's this?" A deep voice interrupted. "Are you injured, Sammy?" Sheriff Harlan Sampson suddenly stood beside them, frowning and surveying them with his hands on his hips.

"It's not bad, mostly a gash on one foot," Sammy said, obviously trying to minimize the injury.

Harlan cocked his head toward the ambulance. "Go get it looked at."

"But you need my report and—"

"That can wait. We have enough information for tonight. We'll get your car down the mountain for you." Harlan glanced at her thoughtfully. "Besides, someone needs to watch out for Ms. Wynngate at the hospital. My wife would never forgive me if something happened to her friend."

His manner was not unkind, but Beth suddenly felt a crushing weight on her chest. She'd placed his officer in danger. Harlan most likely would love to see her hightail it back to Boston, far away from his department's responsibility. Far away from Lilah. Not that she couldn't understand his feelings. Danger followed wherever she roamed, no matter how far or remote the location.

She followed Sammy into the back of another officer's cruiser, which rushed them to the hospital. Sammy's foot required stitches and by the time they were fully examined and cleaned up, dawn streaked the sky. Even though the adrenaline had left her body, she felt oddly restless and not in the least tired.

Lilah burst through the examination room, carrying several large plastic bags. She dropped them to the floor and enveloped Beth in a bear hug. "Are you okay? Harlan told me what happened." Lilah stepped back and appraised her. "You look horrible."

"Why, thank you," Beth said, attempting a smile.

"You know what I mean." Lilah retrieved one of the fallen bags and handed it to her. "I brought clean clothes for you." She shoved the other bag at Sammy. "And for you. I believe you and Harlan are about the same size, so these should fit."

"I can't wait to change out of these stinky clothes," Beth said, wondering if the stench of smoke would ever leave her nostrils.

"Ditto," Sammy echoed, hobbling over to the men's room to change.

Lilah followed her into the ladies' bathroom. "So what's the game plan now? You and Sammy should come stay with us until all this mess blows over."

Beth's gaze involuntarily slid to Lilah's pregnant belly. Much as she would enjoy staying at Lilah's, she couldn't put her friend in danger. "I've worked it out already. Aiden returned early from his trip and insisted I come stay with him a few days until Lambert's locked up."

After the abysmal failure of the remote cabin to keep her safe, the busy high-rise condo bustling with people felt infinitely more secure. At least someone would hear her scream if Lambert attacked.

Lilah stuffed the smoke-ruined clothes in an empty plastic bag as Beth changed into jeans and a sweater. "I'll wash these for you," Lilah offered.

"Those old things? Don't bother. Just dump them in the trash can."

Lilah pulled a pair of sneakers and slippers from the bag. "My shoes might be a size too small for you, if I remember right. If nothing else, you can wear these bedroom slippers and stop somewhere on the way to buy a new pair of shoes."

Beth didn't even try the sneakers, opting for the warm, furry slippers. "Thanks, Lilah. I'll return everything to you later."

Lilah waved a dismissive hand. "Is Sammy driving you to Aiden's place?"

"Your husband made sure his car was brought to the hospital. And Sammy insisted on taking me."

"Might be a good idea." Lilah shook her head and held open the bathroom door. "Still can't get over that they tried to kill you."

"They?" Beth's brow furrowed. Lilah must be speaking of the Lambert family in general.

"Yeah. Those two whose bodies the cops found last night. They'd been flung a good distance from the truck."

It hadn't even occurred to her there would be more than the lone driver behind the attack. "So one of them threw the pipe bomb while another waited in a getaway truck?"

"That's what Harlan speculates."

It felt as though a cold ice cube suddenly slivered down her spine. The whole thing had been so…premeditated. "Wonder if one of the men was the same guy who threatened me in town yesterday."

"Maybe. I wouldn't put anything past Marty Upshaw."

Beth stepped into the brightly lit hospital hallway. Now that she'd donned fresh clothes, the scent of smoke was replaced by an antiseptic zing in the air. "And who did the other body belong to?"

Lilah's brows rose. "You haven't heard yet?"

A knot of dread formed in her stomach. Judging by Lilah's reaction, this person might have been someone she'd known. "Who?" she whispered.

"Abbie Fenton."

Chapter 11

Sammy stepped off the elevator, Beth's suitcases in each of his hands. It had been quick work gathering her clothes and toiletries from the Wynngate house before the short drive to Atlanta. He followed her down a long hallway in Aiden's condo building, impressed that even this utilitarian part of the building had a luxurious feel, with chandeliers, plush carpeting and a view of downtown from floor-to-ceiling windows that banked both ends of the hall. Beth, of course, paid it no mind as she strode to Aiden's door and rang the bell.

Unease niggled the back of his mind. With all the danger and forced intimacy between them, he'd pushed away the realization of how different their social statuses were. A blue-collar man like himself would be a real step down in the world inhabited by the Wynngates and others with their wealth.

Steps sounded from the opposite side of the door and he wondered how his old friend would greet him. It'd been at least four or five years since they'd last met. The encounter had felt awkward for Sammy and he suspected it had for Aiden, as well. After only a minute of reminiscing on old times, he'd found himself floundering in the conversation. There was no longer a common ground between them.

The door flung open, and Aiden filled the doorway with his tall, charismatic presence, throwing Sammy a grin as he hugged Beth in welcome. "You always bring the excitement when you visit us," he teased.

"Sure you don't mind me crashing a few days?"

"Don't be silly. 'Course not." Aiden thrust out his hand to Sammy. "How you doing, buddy?"

"Fine," he answered, as though he and Beth hadn't been through hell all last night.

Aiden opened the door all the way and gestured them inside. The industrial, minimalistic feel of the place struck Sammy as coldly formal. Everything was gray or dull white. The room would be much improved if Beth's colorful paintings graced the stark walls. Odd that her brother didn't display any of them, but he supposed everyone should be allowed to live with their own tastes in their own home. Beth stood beside him and leaned into him, resting her head against his chest. He slung an arm over her shoulder and gave her a reassuring squeeze. The worst was over. Now they needed to rest and recoup.

If Aiden wondered about the connection between his sister and old friend, he didn't remark on it. "You both must be dead on your feet," he said. "Come on in and sit down."

"That's okay. I should be going—"

"Nonsense."

Beth pleaded with her eyes. "You should rest before driving back to Lavender Mountain. Maybe even take a nap?"

"Good idea," Aiden said approvingly. "I have a couple of empty guest rooms. Stay as long as you want."

"No, I really need to get some paperwork done today," he argued. Not to mention there were so many angles he wanted to follow up on. With any luck, Charlotte might have unearthed something useful in the investigation. He could use a bit of good news right about now.

"At least sit down and drink some coffee," Beth urged.

Aiden clapped his hands together. "Excellent idea. I have an espresso machine that makes a mean cup of joe."

Of course he did. Sammy would have preferred a soda, but he gave Aiden a nod. "Sounds good."

Beth lifted the two suitcases sitting by the doorway. "If you don't mind, I'm going to take a quick shower."

He needed one, as well, but he'd wait until he got home. Sammy followed Aiden into the kitchen with its broad expanse of marble countertops and stainless steel appliances. "Nice place," he commented.

"Isn't it?" Aiden agreed with an appreciative smile. "And you should see the gym and pool downstairs. We even have an indoor racquetball court." He beamed with pride as he ground fresh coffee beans and then emptied them into a complicated-looking machine. "There's even a five-star restaurant on the lobby level that delivers room service on nights I'm too beat to cook or go out. Best of all, my office is less than a quarter mile away. So convenient."

"Must be nice," he offered, watching as Aiden fussed with the espresso maker and retrieved glass cups from a cabinet. From the bank of windows over the sink, he could see a line of cars inching forward on the bypass. Good thing Aiden lived so close to his law firm. Otherwise, the commute would be a bitch.

No thanks. He'd take the slow pace of Lavender Mountain any day. Frowning, Sammy eyed the button-down shirt and tailored gray pants Aiden wore. "Are you going back to work today? I thought you were still on vacation."

"Vacation?" He barked out a laugh. "Is that what Beth told you? I've been on a business trip. No rest when you're the boss. But don't worry, I can work here at home the next few days while y'all get this situation sorted. Any idea when they might arrest Lambert?"

Aiden filled both their cups and pointed at the cream and sugar by the machine.

"Atlanta PD has an APB out on him. Could be any minute now."

Aiden shook his head. "Can't imagine why anyone would want to hurt my sister. Are the Lamberts trying to kidnap Beth and hold her for ransom? Is that the theory?"

"Maybe." If Beth hadn't volunteered more information, he certainly wouldn't. Sammy sipped the coffee. For all the elegant preparation and presentation, it tasted like any old cup of black coffee. Maybe his taste buds, like his life in general, lacked sophistication.

"She'll be safe with me, although we might drive each other up the wall if we're home alone together all day every day." Aiden chuckled. "Between us, Beth can be pretty flaky. If you know what I mean."

He frowned. "No, I don't know what you mean. She seems extremely levelheaded to me. Brave, too."

"Oh, sure, sure," Aiden said placatingly. "But you don't know her as well as I do. She's a typical artist. Kind of moody and always has her head in the clouds. It's cute at first, but it wears thin after a while."

"In what way?" Sammy asked, unable to keep the sharp edge out of his voice.

"Don't get me wrong, she's my sister and I love her of course, but she can be overly dramatic. Not to mention a bit spoiled, too. The judge sent her to the finest schools and left her a substantial inheritance. And what does she have to show for it? A job teaching art to middle schoolers." He gave a smug snicker.

"There's nothing wrong with the teaching profession. And Beth happens to be a highly talented painter."

Aiden sipped his coffee and then set it down. "She's a dilettante. By now, she should be seeing someone in our crowd or going to graduate school and learning a real profession."

Anger burned his cheeks and the nape of his neck. Could Aiden have been more obvious in his disapproval of his and Beth's attraction? With one broad stroke, he'd managed to insult Beth as a flighty no-talent hack and himself as a poor, unacceptable match for a member of the Wynngate family.

"Maybe what Beth wants isn't the same as what you believe she needs," Sammy said, striving to keep his anger in check. "And give her a little credit. Beth is a smart, talented and capable woman who makes her own decisions."

Aiden frowned. "You misunderstand what I'm saying. I'm only—"

A sharp voice sounded from behind. "Your message was unmistakable." Beth glared at her brother, pushing back a lock of wet hair from her face. "Nice to know your real opinion of me—an overly dramatic, spoiled dilettante."

"You're twisting my words," he protested. "And how long have you been eavesdropping?

"I'm repeating exactly what you said. And I couldn't help but overhear as I walked over."

"C'mon, Beth, I'm sorry. Don't be so sensitive. I didn't mean anything by it."

A bitter laugh escaped her mouth. "Of course you meant something by it. And you insulted Sammy, too. Apologize to him."

Although gratified at Beth's quick defense, Sammy didn't want to cause trouble between her and her brother. "It's okay," he said quickly.

Aiden's face flushed crimson and he didn't spare Sammy a glance. "You're making a big deal out of nothing," he insisted.

"You implied he was unsuitable. Not good enough for a Wynngate."

"I didn't say that." Again Aiden refused to look him in the eye.

"Bad enough you put me down, but I'm not going to stand by and let you do the same with my friends. At least Sammy hasn't come to me with his hands out, asking to borrow money."

"I asked if you wanted to invest in my new law firm. Not to borrow." Aiden carefully set his coffee cup on the counter. "There's a big difference. It's not like you don't have the money."

Sammy started to ease out of the kitchen. This was family business and he didn't belong.

"And I gladly lent you thousands of dollars," Beth said, her voice calmer now. "This isn't about the money. It's about respect."

Aiden held up his hands, palms out. "You're right. I don't want to argue. Sammy, don't leave. Seems I owe you an apology. No offense, okay?"

"Sure," Sammy said, not believing for a second that Aiden was sincere, but to ease Beth's feelings. She'd been through enough the last few days without him contributing to this sibling conflict. So what if Aiden looked down his patrician nose at him? He really didn't give a damn. Their friendship had been over for years.

"See? Sammy's fine. And I promise, you'll get your money back within the year. With interest."

Sammy cleared his throat. "Guess I'll be heading down the road. Thanks for letting Beth stay with you a few days, Aiden."

"My pleasure—"

"I'm not staying." Beth strode out of the kitchen and headed for the door.

Aiden trailed after her. "But—I thought you needed a safe place to stay."

Sammy sighed. He couldn't blame Beth for not wanting to hide out here. But where could she go now that was safe? She'd already refused to stay with him, and her stepmother obviously didn't want Beth at her place or Beth would have gone there.

Beth snatched her bags from one of the bedrooms and reemerged with her face still set in stony resolve,

Aiden at her heels and trying to convince her not to leave. Sammy held the door open and Beth faced her brother one last time. "We'll talk later. I'm too upset right now. Bye, Aiden."

Sammy gave a quick nod to the chagrined Aiden and they silently proceeded to the elevator. Once the doors closed behind them, Beth gave him a rueful smile. "Sorry you had to see that. It was ugly, wasn't it?"

"A little. Can't say I blame you for walking out, but now we have to figure out our next move. Have you changed your mind about staying with me in Lavender Mountain? I can provide 24/7 police protection."

"No. I won't put you in that kind of danger. Plus, there's too many eyes in that town. Word would get around where I'm staying."

"Let me decide about the risk. My main concern is your protection. I don't want anything to happen to you."

Chapter 12

Sammy's worry about her safety thawed the chill in her heart left from Aiden's harsh words. But then, how much was merely professional concern on his part? Couldn't look good on a deputy sheriff's record to have someone hurt while under his protection. Beth shook off the depressing thought, her usual optimism starting to surface. A good breakfast and a few hours' sleep in her favorite hotel was in order.

"This is it," she announced. "Pull up to the lobby entrance and let's spring for valet service."

"Fancy," Sammy commented as he whipped the Jeep to the door.

The downtown W Hotel gleamed like a skyscraper diamond in the morning sunshine—all glass and chrome, a tall beacon promising warmth and comfort. It was her favorite place to stay in the city. On annual home visits, she often opted to stay at the W in a private suite instead of with family. That way she, Cynthia and Aiden didn't get into each other's hair too much.

With quick and courteous efficiency, they were ushered into the studio suite she preferred. The corner room featured floor-to-ceiling windows that offered stunning views of Atlanta. The energy of the city was also captured in the vibrant turquoise-and-magenta color scheme that clicked with her artist's eye.

"This is amazing," Sammy said, surveying the room. The dazed, appreciative expression on his face spoke volumes. Luxury suites probably weren't much on his radar, living as he did on a deputy sheriff's salary. She hoped she hadn't made him uncomfortable. Perhaps this wasn't the best choice after Aiden's so-recent snobby remarks. Although she'd inherited a substantial amount of money from her parents, she wasn't one to flaunt her wealth. But after everything they'd been through last night, she wanted to treat them both to the very best.

Beth flopped onto the king-size bed and sought to put him at ease. "I hope you love it here as much as I do. It's 'old-fashioned Southern hospitality meets modern chic meets artistic flair.'"

"I suppose this room will be okay," he remarked dryly. "Although I could do without the hot-pink blanket and pillows."

"Think of it as a rich shade of magenta, not pink."

"Tell it to my hormones. My testosterone level dropped the moment I saw it."

Beth laughed and sprang to her feet. "Let's order room service for breakfast and then catch a nap."

"I really should head back to the station. Harlan will be expecting a report by the end of the day."

"Harlan would expect you to rest and then do whatever you have to do. Besides, you can order a laptop brought here from the hotel's business center and email a report. No need to drive all the way back to Lavender Mountain."

"They would do that?" he asked in surprise.

"Of course. Welcome to the twenty-first century."

"The technology isn't what surprised me. I'm talking about the service. You don't get that at the local motel chains I use."

She searched his face for a hint of rancor but, to her relief, found none. Treating Sammy to the very best was going to be fun. In short order, they were seated at the window table and dining on a brunch of shrimp and grits, fried green tomatoes and bacon biscuits. The coziness felt extra intimate as they watched office workers and shoppers crowding the streets below under a light dusting of snow.

Once their hunger was sated, a different physical appetite was aroused. His eyes blazed across the table at her as he slowly set his fork down. Wordlessly, Sammy took her hand and led her to bed. That large luscious bed with its soft mattress—a stark contrast to the hard floor of the cabin where they'd made love last night. Not that she was complaining. She'd always treasure the memory of discovering the feel of his strong, sleek body and the taste of his mouth as the fireplace crackled in the background.

Beth never imagined it possible but making love to Sammy the second time around was even more exciting than the first. He kissed and touched her in just the right places, already an expert on her sensual desires. Need welled in her, frantic and desperate until at last he entered her. She met each thrust with wild abandon. Pleasure at last ripped through her and she held on to him as the tremors subsided. Only then did he allow his own orgasm and she marveled at what a skillful and tender lover Sammy was.

The long, sleepless hours finally caught up to her. Beth closed her eyes and snuggled into Sammy's warm arms, drifting into welcome slumber.

A cell phone rang, jarring her out of sleep. The illusion of safety and isolation from the rest of the world lifted in an instant. Sammy rolled away from her and picked the phone up off the nightstand.

"Armstrong, here." A pause and then he sat up, all business. "You've got him? I'll be right down."

"What is it?" she asked breathlessly. "Has Lambert been found?"

"Found and arrested. Atlanta PD are holding him at their midtown station." Sammy slid out of bed and picked up his clothes lying on the floor. "Can't wait to interrogate the little bastard."

Beth got out of bed and snatched up her clothes, as well. "I'll go with you."

"No need. Go back to sleep. I could be gone for hours." He quickly began dressing.

She paused, about to pull her T-shirt over her head. "Are you sure?"

"Positive." He grinned and drew her in for a brief, fierce kiss. "You're safe now," he proclaimed. "We're shutting Lambert and the rest of his family down. It's finally over, Beth."

Just that quickly. It was almost hard to take in. "Safe," she echoed. "I like the sound of that."

Sammy grabbed his jacket. "Let's celebrate when I

get back. Anywhere you want to go." He gestured at the windows. Already, lights twinkled in the gathering dusk. "The city's finest dining and entertainment. You decide."

"Perfect."

With a quick wave, he left, and the door shut behind him, only to open a second later. "Dead bolt the lock behind me."

"Thought I was safe," she said with a laugh.

"Can't be too careful."

Once a cop, always a cop. Although Beth couldn't say she minded his attention and concern. She'd lived alone too long not to appreciate the caring behind the admonitions. Dutifully, she crossed to the door and secured the lock. Turning around, she faced the rumpled bed where they'd just made love. Should she crawl back in and catch more sleep?

The idea had no appeal. She was too excited to go back to sleep. At the windows, she glimpsed the valet bringing around the Jeep and the slight limp in Sammy's step where he'd had stitches. He drove off and she sighed, wishing she'd insisted on going with him. Although, what good would that do? She wasn't a cop and they wouldn't let her listen in on the interrogation. She'd be stuck sitting in the dismal precinct atmosphere for at least a couple of hours sipping bad coffee and munching vending machine potato chips.

Beth sat in a turquoise-and-pink chair by the window and gazed at the view. The blue-top dome of the Polaris lounge caught her eye. Instantly, her mouth watered with the remembered taste of the peach frozen daiquiri they were famous for making. The place had its own bee garden to harvest honey for their handcrafted libations. Plus, the domed restaurant atop the Hyatt Regency rotated, offering spectacular views of Atlanta at night. Sammy might get a kick out of the fresh vegetables grown on their rooftop garden.

Decision made, Beth called and made a reservation. If Sammy had time tomorrow, they could extend their celebration and spend the day at the Georgia Aquarium. She glanced at the time on her cell phone, noting that only twenty minutes had passed since Sammy left. She paced the room, wondering what Dorsey Lambert was telling the police. Would he rat out members of his family he'd recruited to help him? She thought of Abbie. So young to have died. The violence of the truck crash played out in her mind—the sound of it as it flipped and rolled down rocky mountain terrain and then burst into flames. In a way, the sights and sounds of the crash made her cringe as much as the exploding pipe bomb in the cabin. At least that disaster had been unexpected. They'd never seen it coming. But that icy race down the Tail of the Dragon had seemed to go on for hours and hours.

At last she managed to rest for a while in the comfortable chair, even dozing a little as she waited for Sammy's return. She didn't know how long she conked out but eventually she roused, blinking her eyes fast to reorient herself.

From the hallway, an elevator door pinged open and shut. It was a busy time of day for guests to head out for cocktails and dinner. More footsteps shuffled outside and then came to an abrupt halt by her room. Beneath the door slat, a pair of dark men's shoes blocked the hall light. The lock jiggled. Her heart hammered, and her throat went dry.

A drunken businessman mistaking her room for his?

A sharp rap hammered the door. Beth didn't move.

Didn't speak. Maybe whoever was out there would realize his mistake and just go away.

Another loud knock. *You're safe now*, Sammy had
said. She'd known it was too good to be true.

Beth grabbed her cell phone and punched in 9-1-1
with trembling fingers. If whoever was out there tried
to break down the door, she'd hit the call button.

"Beth?" a deep voice called out. "Beth, are you in
there?"

"Wh-who is it?" she asked, a hand at her throat.

"It's me, Aiden. Come to apologize. Let me in."

Aiden. A tsunami of relief swooshed through her
body and her knees threatened to buckle. She grabbed
onto a chair to keep from falling to the floor. Drawing
a deep breath, she hurried to the door and flung it open.
Aiden grinned down, holding up a bottle of merlot. "I
knew you'd be at this place. Figured I'd bribe you to let
me in with your favorite wine."

She gave a weak laugh. "You scared the hell out of
me. Come on in."

Aiden sauntered inside and surveyed the room. "Nice
digs. You always liked this place. Where's Sammy?"

"At the police station." She shut the door and reset
the dead bolt. "They called not thirty minutes ago saying they had Dorsey Lambert in custody. Sammy will
be back before too long."

"They've got Lambert? That's fantastic news! Let's
have a drink and toast an excellent bit of police work."

"You didn't have to come bearing gifts," she admonished, though secretly glad for the company.

Aiden set to work, gathering two crystal glasses from
the kitchenette and setting them on the table. He popped
the cork and began to pour.

"I'll join you in a second," she said.

Beth scurried into the bathroom and winced at her reflection. As she suspected, the mussed hair and streaked mascara made it appear as though she'd just rolled out of bed—after being thoroughly pleasured by a lover. Which she was. But she didn't need to parade that fact in front of her brother, because…just *eww*, he was her brother. Hastily, she brushed her hair and swiped at the makeup under her eyes. Much better.

When she returned to the table, Aiden was already seated, drinking wine. He gestured to the other poured glass and she gratefully sipped. The merlot was smooth and flavorful but a bit on the dry side, with the faintest afternote of bitter. Still, it was delicious and just what she needed after the last few harrowing days. If only Sammy was here to join them, the evening would be perfect.

"You've been through a hell of an ordeal, haven't you?" Aiden's dark brown eyes were warm with concern. "And then I heaped more trouble on you when you came to me for help. I was way out of line. I'm really sorry. Forgive me?"

"Of course." And she meant it. The Aiden seated across from her was her brother of old, his refreshing tenderness a quality that always helped brush over Cynthia's sometimes cutting indifference.

Aiden glanced at his expensive watch. "How long before Sammy returns? An hour? Two hours?"

"Two at the most. I'm hoping he'll be back within the hour."

"Heading home when he returns?"

"Nope. Going out to celebrate. Come with us for cocktails and dinner at the Polaris."

"Maybe."

"Anything wrong?" she asked. "You seem on edge this evening."

"No, no. Everything's fine. Matter of fact, I've got some good news, too."

More good news. Tonight was certainly her lucky night. Everything was nicely turning around. "Tell me."

Aiden raised his glass. "Drink up first."

Beth took another long sip. "Now what's up?"

"My firm's finally in the black. We got a large civil suit settlement and several more excellent prospects lined up. Wynngate LLC is starting to attract prominent customers."

Beth flushed with pride that her family's name was being honored by her stepbrother's firm. Dad had adopted Aiden when he married Cynthia and Aiden had always aspired to follow in his footsteps. "That's great. I'm so proud of you, Aiden. I knew you'd make a success of it."

When he'd first approached her six months ago to invest in his new criminal defense law firm, she'd had a few misgivings. Particularly when she heard the office would be in a new, swanky building situated in the trendy Buckhead area of the city. "Takes money to make money," Aiden had assured her. And spent money he had. Her brother was always wining and dining potential clients, but it looked as though the hard work was finally paying off.

Aiden raised his glass and pointedly looked at hers. Beth obligingly took another swallow.

"Best of all," he continued, "I should be able to repay you—with interest—by the first of the year."

Beth tried not to show her relief, afraid Aiden would

take it as a lack of faith in his abilities. But more than the money, she wanted their sibling relationship unencumbered by awkwardness over the loan.

He clinked his glass with hers and they toasted his good fortune. Aiden picked up the merlot bottle and refilled her glass.

"I'm not sure I should have another," she protested. "My heart's set on a peach daiquiri later."

"Lighten up," he said with a laugh. "You deserve this. And I certainly don't want to drink alone."

A second glass of wine never hurt anybody. Beth shrugged and took another sip from the full glass. Already, her body seemed to be floating and her head swam. With shaking hands, she carefully set the goblet on the table, oddly mesmerized by the shimmer of the crimson liquid under the lamp.

"No more for me," she stated with an uneasy laugh.

"Well, you're no fun. I bought this merlot just for you."

"Doesn't mean I can drink it all in one sitting."

"That's my Beth. Always were a bit of a spoilsport. Never one to party hard like me and my friends."

And yet, she was the one who had paid the price years ago when his friends had left her high and dry at the party when the cops arrived.

"I thought you artsy types were supposed to have a more live-and-let-live lifestyle."

Was his tone faintly mocking or was the alcohol screwing with her judgment? "Those stories of wild artists are mainly a myth."

"So you consider yourself an artist and not a middle school teacher?"

Again his words seemed laced with a trace of superiority. "We can't all be hotshot lawyers and judges," she countered.

"You're right. It takes a particular intellect to succeed in those fields."

Beth swallowed an angry retort. Aiden couldn't help being a bit of a snob, considering he was raised by Cynthia. She rose to her feet and then quickly grabbed the table to keep from losing balance. Wine had never affected her so quickly before. Drinking on an empty stomach didn't agree with her. "Thanks for bringing the wine, Aiden, but I think I need to take a little nap before Sammy comes back."

Aiden chuckled. "It's catching up to you, huh?"

No point denying it. "Yes." She gestured to the door. "We'll talk later. Congratulations again on your firm's success."

"This wasn't much of a celebration. Tell you what, let's you and me go on over to the Polaris. Sammy can join us when he finishes business."

"I don't feel like going out."

"You need food," he said firmly. "How long since you've eaten?"

She thought through the fog clouding her mind. "Not since a late breakfast."

"There you go then. The Polaris is only a few blocks away. You can walk off the effect of the drink and eat dinner. You don't want Sammy to see you sloppy drunk, do you? What would he think?"

"I suppose you have a point," she said with a longing glance at the bed.

Aiden took her arm, leading her to the door. "I'll get a taxi. Trust me, going out to eat is just what you need."

With a sigh, she looked around for her purse, then spotted it on the nightstand. "Let me get my purse."

"No need. This is my treat."

"If you're sure—"

"Least I can do after all you've done for me. I couldn't ask for a better sister. It was my lucky day when Mom married your dad."

Aiden unlocked the door and she stumbled into the hallway. The floor felt uneven and her stomach rumbled. "I feel sick. Maybe I better—"

"No." His grip on her arm seemed to tighten.

"But—"

Instead of slowing down to accommodate her wobbly feet, Aiden quickened his pace and they walked past the elevators.

Beth frowned and tried to sort what was happening. "Why aren't we getting on the elevator?"

"We'll take the stairs."

"But why?"

"You need to walk, sis. You're right—that wine went straight to your head. Besides, I can't be seen with you stumbling around in public. What if I ran into an important client or a colleague?"

Heat rose in her cheeks. "Going out was your idea." She tried to jerk her arm free, but Aiden tightened his grip even more.

"Don't be so sensitive," he chided. "I'm doing this for you, not me."

They reached the end of the hallway. Beth dug in her feet at the exit stairwell door. "I've changed my mind."

He tugged at her elbow, his jaw set stubbornly. "Too late for that."

Chapter 13

Sammy entered the interrogation room, noting that it looked almost identical to the one in Elmore County. He suspected every such room at any police station looked much the same—windowless, dreary colors, cheap linoleum floors and no furniture except for a table and couple of metal chairs.

Dorsey Lambert sat slumped in a chair, scowling at the gouged surface of the table. He didn't raise his head when Sammy entered. A uniformed cop rose and nodded as he exited the room. "He's all yours."

Sammy took a seat across from Lambert, who stubbornly refused to face him. He waited, sweating him out. A full minute rolled by before the suspect met his gaze. "Who are you supposed to be?" he demanded, evidently expecting to see someone in a cop uniform or a detective with a suit sporting a badge.

"You don't remember me? I chased you a good three or four blocks when you bolted from your mom's home."

Recognition sparked in Lambert's unnaturally intense blue eyes. He scrubbed at his jaw, speckled with auburn stubble. The man was skinny and, as Sammy recalled, rather on the short side. But he carried himself like a mean yard dog itching for a fight and no doubt he could probably hold his own with most men twice his size. Sammy tried to think back on the height of the pipe bomb suspect who'd run away. Could there have been a third person there that night that they didn't know about? But Sammy couldn't recall anything concrete about the suspect that had tossed the bomb; it had been too dark and too brief an encounter to hazard a guess on the man's size.

"Are you the reason I'm here?" Lambert groused, lazing back in his chair. "Whatcha want with me?"

"You know why."

"No, I don't."

"Haven't you spoken with your mother?"

Lambert suddenly leaned forward and practically growled. "Leave Momma and my kin outta this."

Interesting to note the suspect felt such loyalty. "So it's okay for you and your family to terrorize a woman but then not man up when the law finally catches up to you?"

"Man up? That what you call snitching on your own family? 'Cause that ain't happening."

"I'm not here to debate semantics with you." At Lambert's blank look, he leveled him with a grim smile. "Let me put it another way. Either you cooperate, or I'll be questioning your mother every day until you confess."

Lambert sprang to his feet, chest puffed out. Sammy also rose and stared him down, daring the man to strike.

The door opened. "Need any backup?" a uniformed cop asked.

Dorsey's eyes darted nervously; he knew he was trapped.

"That's okay. I think we're ready to have a civilized conversation now, aren't we, Lambert?"

Dorsey didn't respond but slumped back down in his chair. Sammy also took a seat and tried a new tactic. "Two cousins of yours—Abbie Fenton and Marty Upshaw—are already dead. Do you really want more lives wasted? Let's end this. Right here, right now."

Dorsey's mouth twisted. "End it? You mean arrest me for only trying to get what's due me." His voice oozed with bitterness. "Ain't that always the way, though? Rich man gets away with everything while people like me and my family are the ones who suffer."

Sammy picked up on his earlier statement. "What do you mean by trying to get what you're due?"

"Judge Wynngate was dirty. Everyone knew it. With the right amount of money, you could buy an innocent verdict or get your jail time cut in half."

"Why should I believe you?"

"Why would I lie about it? I paid fifty thousand bucks and what did that bastard do for me?"

Sammy stared back at him impassively, waiting for Lambert to continue. Dorsey slammed his hand on the table. "Nothing! He did nothing. Wynngate took my money and then gave me the maximum sentence possible. All I wanted was to get my money back. That kind of money don't mean nothing to some rich bitch like his daughter. She should give it back to me."

Sammy grabbed a fistful of Lambert's flannel shirt. "Don't you dare call her that." Conscious he was being watched, Sammy reluctantly let go. "Beth Wynngate has nothing to do with her father's so-called crimes."

"Yeah, but she inherited his dirty money, now, didn't she? I seen it in the papers after he died. She got nearly all of it. All I ask is that she give back what's rightfully due me and my family. Scraping together that money was a real hardship on us. And while I was in prison, I couldn't hold down a job and help out my momma. Without my paycheck, she lives off a measly government check that don't cover all she needs."

Regular paycheck? Dorsey Lambert was a known drug dealer, not a stalwart employee earning an honest income, but Sammy let that go for now.

"I fail to see how killing Beth Wynngate is going to get your money returned to you."

Dorsey's eyes widened, and his jaw slackened. "Kill her? Ain't nobody trying to kill her."

"Don't lie to me! Why else were Marty and Abbie out there when the cabin exploded?"

Confusion clouded his eyes. "What cabin explosion?"

Sammy narrowed his eyes at him. Dorsey appeared surprised, but ex-cons were often good actors. His department hadn't reported the arson crime to the newspapers so the few Lavender Mountain locals who knew the fire department had been called out didn't know what had caused the fire.

"I know about the high-speed chase. Weren't no mention in the papers about a cabin exploding. We ain't got nothing to do with that."

"You saying your cousin Marty didn't have anything to do with it?"

"No, sir." Some of Dorsey's defiant bravado faded. "I admit they were out there keeping watch on Wynngate. I told them to wait for an opportunity when she was alone and then lean on her again about the money. Last time I talked to them, they'd followed y'all out to the cabin. Figured you'd return to work the next day and Wynngate would be alone at the cabin. The perfect opportunity to squeeze her for the money."

Sammy's blood chilled at the thought of Beth being alone in the woods and "squeezed" for money. "Let's back everything up a minute. Tell me more about your claim of paying off Judge Wynngate."

Dorsey shrugged. "Everybody knew he could be bought."

"You got any proof you paid him this money?"

"No," he admitted, his voice souring again. "I didn't pay him directly. I paid one of his collectors. Cash. Just as I was told to do."

"Who took your money?"

A cagey look came over his face. "Don't know his name."

"You're lying. You expect me to believe you paid a stranger fifty thousand in cash?" Dorsey wasn't the sharpest tool in the shed, but he did appear to have some street smarts.

"I did. I swear it's true. Some buddies of mine got time shaved off their sentences doin' the same thing."

"And how do you know this collector didn't just pocket the money and never forwarded it to the judge?"

"He paid him," Dorsey insisted. "Just my bad luck that federal heat was coming down on the judge not long after he took my money. The middleman told me I'd have to wait it out a few months. If Wynngate gave me a light sentence, it could be viewed in a negative light for the judge. The feds were looking for a pattern. Guy told me that when the heat died down, the judge would lighten my sentence on appeal."

First thing he needed to check was Lambert's claim of a federal investigation on the judge. He'd see if Harlan could use his contacts to find out unofficially. That should prove much faster than a formal inquiry.

Dorsey kicked at the empty chair beside him in disgust. "Then the bastard up and dies on me. Can you believe that crap? All that money wasted."

"Forget about the money. It's gone and you'll never get it back. You've already done your time. It's over. Think of the future. Now you're looking at a bigger mess. Attempted murder."

Dorsey threw up his hands, eyes wide with panic. "I wasn't anywhere near that cabin. I've been here in Atlanta at my mom's house. Didn't even know about the explosion until you told me five minutes ago."

"Yet you readily admit you had family members there that night, working for you."

"They didn't do it! I know them. They wouldn't kill nobody."

"Why should I believe a word you're telling me?"

"Ask around. Check with the feds about my story. Look, man, all I wanted was my money back. I ain't never killed anybody and don't plan on starting now."

Sammy steepled his fingers and regarded Dorsey's pleading eyes. "So you say. But greed and revenge are powerful motives for murder. I'd say both of those factors are at play in your head."

"I didn't do it!" He kicked at the chair again.

"If you're not guilty we'll find out soon enough. But your admission about involving your cousins in a scheme to extort money from Beth Wynngate is pretty damning. It places them right at the scene of the crime."

"That don't prove nothing. You can't keep me here."

"Of course we can. You've technically broken parole."

Dorsey squeezed his eyes shut and crinkled his nose, evidently regretting his words. He crossed his arms over his chest. "I want a lawyer."

Of course he did. Sammy nodded and rose. "Don't even think about asking anyone else in your family to come after Beth Wynngate. If you do, I'll make sure you're so old by the next time you get out of prison that you'll go directly into a nursing home to live out whatever's left of your sorry life."

"I ain't messin' with her no more. You have my word," Dorsey said, surprising him. Then again, a man would say anything to avoid returning to prison.

As though reading his mind, Dorsey spoke once more. "Like you said, the past is the past. My money's gone. Best I can hope for now is to live out my days in peace. Try to be an honest man."

Sammy walked to the door, but Dorsey hadn't finished speaking his mind.

"Sounds like someone's trying to kill that girl, but it ain't me."

The Atlanta traffic was heavy. Sammy kept hitting redial on his phone, but Beth didn't answer. With every failed ring, his unease grew. Surely she hadn't already gone out on the town on her own. And not while there were so many unanswered questions. Hell, they still bore the scars from last night's attempt on her life. Impatiently, he began weaving his way through the clogged lanes as fast as possible. At the hotel, he left the Jeep parked at the main entrance. "Back in a moment," he told the startled valet drivers.

Sammy raced through the lobby and entered the elevator, punching the button for the thirty-third floor. When the elevator door opened, he pushed through and scanned the hallway. To his left, he took in the sight of a man and a woman about to enter the exit stairwell. Relief washed over him.

"Where are y'all going?" he called out to Aiden and Beth, rushing over to them. "I've been trying to call."

Something was off. Beth looked disgruntled and wobbly all at once. Aiden's eyes flashed with an annoyance that was replaced so quickly with his usual effervescent charm that Sammy wondered if he'd seen it in the first place. And after the scene at his condo earlier, why the hell had he come around? That must account for the frustration in Beth's eyes. She was still upset over his remarks a few hours ago.

"We were going to go out for a drink at the Polaris, but Beth changed her mind," Aiden said smoothly. "She decided to wait for your return. Tells me you're planning a celebration this evening."

Sammy glanced at Beth. She placed a hand on her forehead and shot him a rueful smile. "I might have to take a rain check on the celebration dinner. Aiden brought over some merlot and it's hit my system like a ton of bricks."

Aiden chuckled. "Seems my sister can't hold her liquor."

That didn't sound like Beth to overdrink. It seemed out of character. "The celebration can wait," he said.

"Sounds good. Guess I'll head on back home." Aiden extended a hand to Sammy. "We'll do it another night?"

"Sure. I'll call you."

"Great. Catch you later." Aiden raised an arm at the stairwell door. "Guess I'll take the stairs and burn some calories."

Beth started back toward their room and stumbled. He grabbed her elbow to keep her from falling. "Easy now."

She drew a deep breath. "Thanks. I can't believe how dizzy I am."

"If you're dizzy, why in hell were y'all going to take the stairs instead of the elevator?"

She grimaced. "Seems that in my present condition, Aiden was afraid I'd embarrass him in the lobby."

"Then he shouldn't have taken you out. Period. Besides, you'd have been in public with him anyway at the Polaris."

Beth shook her head, as if to clear mental cobwebs. "Right. Who knows what he was thinking? I love my brother, but sometimes he befuddles me."

"What was he doing here? Apologizing again?"

"Yep. Showed up with a bottle of merlot and a hangdog expression." She gave a soft chuckle. "I can't stay angry with him when he pulls that."

For the second time that day, unease prickled down his back and he slowed his steps. Beth cocked her head to the side and smiled. "What's the matter? Somebody step on your grave?"

He tamped down the apprehension. Beth was here with him, a little tipsy, but they were both intact. A small miracle considering last night's attack. This was still a cause for celebration. Maybe he should wait until tomorrow to tell her of Dorsey's claims. After all, the ex-con could be lying. And she'd been so angry at him when the intruder had entered her house and he'd asked if the judge might have had some secret. He and Harlan would investigate his allegations about her father. If they were true, then Beth would be the first person he told.

Inside their room, he led her to the bed and propped her up with pillows. "I'll call room service and we'll have dinner by candlelight right here. No need to go out."

"Perfect," she agreed with a grin. "Just don't order celebratory champagne. I'm not up for it."

Neither was he, matter of fact. Thanks to Dorsey Lambert. A small corner of his mind remained disquieted. The case still didn't feel over.

Not yet.

Chapter 14

Beth glowed with contentment as she gazed around her Falling Rock home. In only two days, Cynthia had arrived and taken charge of the holiday decorations. A twelve-foot-high balsam fir in the den was lit with twinkling lights and the fireplace mantel decorated with fresh garland and cinnamon-scented pine cones. In every room, even the bathrooms, Cynthia had set out scented candles and holiday figurines. Beth had to hand it to her stepmother; she was a whiz at creating a warm, cozy atmosphere at Christmas, right down to the aroma of freshly baked gingerbread and cookies. Her nesting instincts at this time of year contrasted with her usual social activities of superficial cocktail parties.

The oven alarm dinged. "Pull out that pan for me, hon," Cynthia called out, elbow-deep in a new batch of cookie dough.

Beth retrieved the lightly browned chocolate chip

cookies and set them on the cooling rack. Much as she was enjoying the domestic bonding with Cynthia, a small part of her remained hurt that she'd cut out on Beth last week after the first sign of trouble. Of course, she hadn't expected Cynthia to stay in the house, but it rankled that her stepmother hadn't even offered to have her as a guest at her Atlanta home until the danger had passed.

At least she was thankful that the threat had been removed. Nothing suspicious had happened since Dorsey Lambert's arrest. Even though he'd been released yesterday, Beth hadn't received even a hang-up call or any hint she was being followed. The only matter casting a tinge of sadness today was the thought of returning to Boston next week. How much did Sammy care that she'd be leaving? They'd been almost inseparable the last few days. When he wasn't at work, he spent all his free time with her. The thought of their returning to their normal lives living hundreds of miles apart made her heart pinch.

As though she'd conjured Sammy from sheer willpower, his Jeep pulled into the circular driveway.

"You should fill a tin with cookies for him," Cynthia suggested. Beth shook her head in bemusement. Since arriving, Cynthia had been friendly with Sammy instead of acting formal and vaguely condescending. Beth wasn't naive enough to think she actually approved of her choice in boyfriends, but her stepmother probably figured there was no harm in their temporary relationship. Beth would be leaving soon enough.

She strode to the front door and flung it open, determined to enjoy whatever time was left with Sammy.

He didn't return her welcoming smile.

Now what? "Is it Lambert? Has he done something?" she asked, holding the door open.

He entered, glancing into the kitchen where Cynthia hummed along with a Christmas carol as she continued baking. "We need to talk. Somewhere private."

Must be serious. "Downstairs, then."

Only when they were seated in the recreation room did he lean forward and speak. "When I interviewed Lambert earlier this week he claimed that he paid a middleman to have your father reduce his drug sentence."

"That's absurd," she scoffed, raising her voice. "What a piece of—"

"Don't shoot the messenger."

Beth gritted her teeth. "Go on. What else did he lie about?"

"As I was saying, Lambert claimed to have paid fifty thousand dollars for your father to lighten his sentence. He started harassing you in the hopes of getting his money back. He had two family members, he wouldn't name names, search your father's study that night, seeking proof of payment."

"What good would that do? Even if there was, it's not like he could enter a store and show a receipt to return merchandise and get his money returned."

"I'm sure he believed you'd do anything to protect your father's reputation, including paying him off."

"Blackmail," she said grimly. "Not that I would ever have agreed to such a thing."

"No doubt Lambert wouldn't be satisfied with merely getting his money back."

"He'd start asking for interest, then payment for the pain and suffering of being incarcerated. It would never end." She observed Sammy's set face more closely. "But Lambert's claim is nothing new. What else did he say?"

"That federal authorities were investigating your dad several months before he died."

Beth couldn't speak right away, and she bit the inside of her mouth to stop the involuntary tremble of her lips. "You wouldn't be telling me this if you didn't think it was true."

He nodded. "I checked it out. Your father was under investigation after numerous allegations that he accepted bribes."

"Go on," she whispered at his pause, expecting the worst.

"There appeared to be some validity to the claims, but they dropped the investigation upon his death."

"I see." She pictured the last time she'd seen her father, in the hospital ICU unit after triple bypass surgery. Had the stress of an investigation contributed to his heart attack? Sammy took her hand and gave it a squeeze.

"But it's possible Dad was innocent," she insisted. "I mean, they didn't actually declare him guilty of any crime."

"Anything's possible."

Beth blinked back tears. Sammy was just being kind. More than likely, her dad had been involved in shady business. He drew a nice salary as a federal judge, but they'd enjoyed a very luxurious lifestyle—expensive schools, oversea travels, gorgeous homes. Perhaps, in hindsight, that had been a bit of a stretch based on his salary. But she'd always attributed the wealth to his smart investments and side businesses.

With a sinking heart, she remembered one odd fact that had struck her after Dad died and the will had been probated. He'd owned several companies, but four months prior to his death, he'd liquidated them all. At the time, she'd wondered if he'd done so because he had a premonition of his deteriorating health and wanted to simplify his financial affairs.

"Does Cynthia know about that investigation?" she asked.

"You know her better than I do. What do you think?"

Beth considered her own question. She hadn't been living nearby to see them regularly while all this had been going on, but she didn't recall anything that would lead her to believe Cynthia was aware of possible impending doom. There had been no whispered conversations, or sudden talks of Dad retiring early. Nothing to indicate they were anything but settled and happy in their comfortable life.

"I don't think Cynthia knows anything," she said slowly.

"I don't know what?"

They both whipped their heads around. Cynthia stood halfway down the carpeted stairs, an oven mitt in one hand and a tray of cookies in the other.

Beth stood and ran a hand through her hair. "I didn't hear you coming."

"Obviously." Her stepmother gazed back and forth between them. "What's going on?"

Sammy shot her a sideways look that said, "This is up to you."

"Maybe I should tell her. I mean, if Lambert came after me for money, she might be in danger, too."

"Danger?" Cynthia slowly made her way down the steps and laid the cookies on a coffee table. "Tell me what's going on. I thought Lambert had been arrested."

"He's already been released. You better sit down for this." Beth gestured toward the couch and they sat, Sammy across from them. "You know Sammy interviewed Dorsey Lambert earlier this week and he claimed to have paid Dad for a lighter sentence."

Cynthia's lips pressed together for an instant. Her face reddened, and she removed the mitt from her hand, smacking it down on the sofa. "He's nothing but a liar. Surely you don't believe him, do you?"

Sammy cleared his throat. "Actually, there was an ongoing federal investigation prior to your husband's death. Were you aware of that?"

Cynthia's mouth parted in astonishment. "Investigation? Are you sure?"

"Yes, ma'am. I personally spoke with the federal officer overseeing it."

"Why, I—I don't know what to say. Edward never said a word to me." Cynthia cast her a bewildered glance. "Beth?"

"He didn't say anything to me, either."

Cynthia leaped to her feet. "I refuse to believe any of this nonsense. Lambert and other convicts are just scumbags. The dregs of society. They'll say anything to cause trouble."

Sammy pulled out his cell phone. "Be that as it may, take a look at this latest mug shot of Dorsey Lambert. Wouldn't hurt for you to be aware of his appearance, so you can be on the lookout."

Cynthia gave it a quick glance, her lips curled in a sneer. "He looks thoroughly disreputable. I can't believe you'd entertain him, or others like him, for one minute. Do you really think my husband could have done such a despicable thing?

Sammy tucked the cell phone back in his pocket. "I

don't know, ma'am. We might never know the full truth given his untimely death."

"I know the truth. You didn't know him like I did. Like *we* knew him. How dare you come in my home and besmirch Edward's name?"

"Sammy's only doing his job," Beth said, gently patting Cynthia's arm. "He's not accusing Dad. He came here to warn us."

"Fine. I've been warned." Cynthia stood and lifted her chin at Sammy. "Now I want you to leave my house. And Christmas Eve dinner tomorrow night? Forget it."

Beth's face flamed with heat. It was one thing for her stepmother to assume that superior air with her, but she wouldn't tolerate it being aimed at someone she cared about. Sammy started to rise, apparently unruffled at Cynthia's outburst, but Beth gestured for him to stay seated.

"Actually, Cynthia, if you want to get technical about it, this is my house. Dad left this place to me and the Atlanta home to you. So Sammy is staying and he's having dinner with us tomorrow, too."

Cynthia's haughty mien crumbled in an instant. She opened her mouth to speak, and then clamped it shut. Tears pooled in her eyes.

Damn. She hadn't meant to hurt her feelings; she'd only wanted to stop her from trying to order Sammy around. Cynthia spun on her heel and headed to the stairs.

"Wait a minute, I'm sorry," Beth began. But Cynthia held up a palm, warding off her apology. She disappeared from sight, and seconds later the door slammed shut behind her.

Sammy gave a low whistle. "Didn't mean to cause

trouble for you. Is it always this tense between the two of you?"

"Without Dad as a buffer—yes. It's not like we have a whole lot in common. Things are better when Aiden's around. He keeps the conversation going and smooths out any friction. Thank heavens he's coming in tomorrow and staying over the weekend."

"You know, you're always welcome to spend the holiday with my family," he offered. "It's a large, boisterous household when we all get together. There's my uncle and his bunch, and several cousins and their kids. Always plenty of commotion and conversation," Sammy said with a grin. "It may make you want to come running back here for a little peace and quiet."

No, what it sounded like was a loving family who enjoyed getting together. Would they really appreciate an outsider horning in on their celebration? "I'm already spending Christmas Day with you at your dad's. Don't want to overstay my welcome."

"You won't be." He hugged her and planted a quick kiss on her forehead. She rested the side of her face against the crisp cotton fabric of his uniform shirt, inhaling the clean linen smell mixed with a hint of a leathery aftershave. Her dismay at Cynthia's outburst seeped out of her body. She'd work things out with her stepmother. They always had before. She could suck it up a few more days until Cynthia returned to Atlanta and she to Boston.

Boston.

She pulled Sammy to her a little tighter, wanting to savor every possible moment they were together.

"You okay?" he asked in a husky voice that sent shivers—the good kind—down her back.

Beth pasted on a bright smile. "Fine. Guess you need to get back to work, huh?"

He held her shoulders, gazing deep into her eyes. "I have a few things to check on, but if you need me, I'm all yours."

"No, you should go. I'll talk to Cynthia now."

It took a few minutes to reassure him all was well, but at last she waved at him from the doorway as he drove off. Cynthia was nowhere in sight. Beth walked through the kitchen, noting that the oven had been turned off and all the baking supplies put away. Cynthia wasn't in the dining room or den, either. Had she been so upset that she'd packed up her things and left?

She opened the door and peeked into the garage. Cynthia's silver Town Car was still there. Perhaps she'd retired to her bedroom, unwilling to face her. She should apologize for sounding so harsh. Beneath her somewhat icy exterior, Cynthia was an emotional woman.

As she passed by the French doors in the den, a movement from outside froze her midstride. A camo-colored ATV motored by the edge of the woods. On her property.

Anger infused her body and without thinking, she hurried to the door and opened it. "Hey," she called out. "What are you doing?"

The driver braked and stared at her for an instant. He was tall and wore a large brown parka. A black ski cap covered his head, but strings of long red hair peeked out.

Not Dorsey, but he could definitely be a member of the Lambert clan. Her breath caught, and she hastily stepped back inside. In a burst of engine pedal-hitting-metal noise, the man drove the ATV into the woods and out of sight.

But not out of mind. Beth slammed the door shut and locked it, remembering how recently two men had broken into her home and destroyed the previous door. She placed a hand on her heart, feeling it pound inside her rib cage. Should she call Sammy? Grab Cynthia and insist they leave at once and spend the holidays in Atlanta?

In the end, she did neither. *Probably only a hunter scouting locations*, she told herself. *Or somebody just bored and out for a ride.* It wouldn't be the first time they'd seen people along the tree line of Blood Mountain. ATV riding was a popular activity in the area.

Beth rubbed her arms, relieved she wasn't alone in the house. There was safety in numbers. Maybe she should give Aiden a call and see if he could come earlier than originally planned. It would soothe Cynthia and lighten the mood. Impulsively, she lifted the receiver of the landline to call him.

"I miss you so much, baby. I hate we're so far apart."

Oops. Cynthia was already on the line. She must have wanted Aiden to come home earlier, as well. Beth started to hang up the phone when an unfamiliar, deep voice spoke.

"Ditch the family. It's been a year. Bad enough we had to sneak around when your husband was alive. But now?"

Surprise rooted Beth to the spot, hand gripped on the phone that she held to an ear. Who the hell was this man? Cynthia was a cheater. Had Dad discovered this before he died?

"Just a little longer, sweetheart," her stepmother murmured. "If we're seen together too soon, people might start to wonder how long we've been a thing."

"I don't give a damn what people think and neither—"

"And from there, some might even speculate how convenient it was for us that Edward died while I was having an affair. After all, I did end up collecting some of his money in the will."

Beth held her breath and an ominous chill ghosted across her flesh. She could hardly reconcile the grief-stricken Cynthia at her father's funeral with this woman speaking so casually to her lover about the will. She hoped Dad had never suspected. That until the very end he'd been happily married and blissfully ignorant of his wife's deceit.

"You should have gotten *all* the money," the mystery man groused.

Cynthia laughed. A high-pitched artificial sound that grated on Beth's ears. "I couldn't agree more. But what's done is done. I had no idea I wouldn't collect everything. If I'd known seven months earlier that Edward would leave Beth most of his estate, then I would have done things differently."

Things? What things? What had her stepmother done?

"Did you hear something on the line?" Cynthia asked sharply.

Beth bit her lip and wildly glanced around the room. If she hung up now, they'd definitely hear a click as the call disconnected. She raised a shaky hand to her mouth to stifle any betraying gasp.

"Nope. You're paranoid," the man said, barking out a small chuckle. "Always worried others will discover your little secrets. Why the hell did you call me on the landline anyway?"

"I forgot to charge my cell phone battery last night.

Anyway, I should get off the phone, just to be safe. I'll call you later tonight."

"Come home soon," he said.

The line went dead. Beth immediately placed the phone back on the receiver. *That's what you get when you eavesdrop on people*, she heard her father's reproving voice scold in her mind. *It will never be anything good.* But it wasn't like she'd meant to listen in on a private conversation. Not really. Not until the conversation had taken such a dark, twisty path. Then she'd been hooked and there was no going back.

The scent of chocolate and caramelized sugar suddenly turned cloyingly sweet. The air felt oppressively hot and humid from all the residual heat still radiating from the oven.

She had to get out of there. She couldn't face Cynthia. Not now. Not until she'd worked out everything she'd overheard. Beth scrambled through a kitchen drawer, searching for pen and paper. She'd leave Cynthia a note that she'd gone out for a bit.

A door screeched open upstairs. Cynthia was coming.

Floorboards creaked, and footsteps started down the hallway, then onto the stairs leading to the den. Strange to think of all the times she'd ever spent with Cynthia and now the idea of being alone with her filled her with disgust and anxiety. Beth desperately snatched her purse from the counter and stole a quick glance up.

Cynthia stood at the top of the stairs, looking cool and composed again, a slight smile curving her lips. As though she hadn't stormed out of the recreation room ten minutes ago. As though she hadn't been on the phone with the lover she'd been cheating with while married. As though she bore no ill feelings for her stepdaughter.

A lie. Everything about her was a lie.

Beth rushed to the foyer and pulled on a coat.

"Where are you going?" Cynthia asked.

"Out." Beth didn't dare glance her way, afraid her emotions would be written all over her face.

"Listen, don't go. I want to apologize for losing my temper. Of course, Sammy was only doing his job. He's always welcome here."

A jolt of irritation pricked through Beth's nervousness. How many times did she have to remind Cynthia this was *her* home, not her stepmother's. And it was *her* decision who came and went.

"Good to know," Beth commented wryly.

"You're still upset."

"Of course I am." Beth unlocked the dead bolt and buttoned her coat. "I need to run to the store. Be back later."

Cynthia reached her and ran a hand through Beth's errant locks. It took all of her willpower not to cringe from the woman's touch.

"Okay. I hope you realize I was only upset because of the slur to your father's name."

As if you care, Beth wanted to scream. Had Cynthia ever really loved her father? Or had it always been about the money from day one? Another one of those mysteries she'd probably never learn the answer to.

Without responding, Beth hurried out the door and into the cool, bracing air. After the stifling hot kitchen, the fresh winter breeze was as refreshing as a gulp of iced tea in the heat of a Georgia summer. She felt Cynthia's assessing eyes upon her as she opened the rental car door and slipped inside. Thank goodness Lilah had been so thoughtful to arrange a rental for her to use temporarily.

Her mind swirled, recalling every word of the overheard conversation.

Always worried others will discover your little secrets...

How convenient it was for us that Edward died while I was having an affair...

If I'd known seven months earlier that he'd leave Beth half of his estate, then I would have done things differently.

The more she ruminated, the more sinister the implications grew. Could Cynthia have played a part in her father's death? Perhaps his heart attack was brought on by the shock of discovering her affair. She had to concede that if that were the case, his heart probably wasn't in good condition to begin with.

How could Cynthia have betrayed him like this? Dad had rescued her from a minimum-wage job as a nurse's aide where she'd struggled to make ends meet for herself and her young son, Aiden. Dad had given her everything—a beautiful home, a first-class education for her son, a lifestyle that included travel and security—and all his love and loyalty.

The security guard at the gate waved at her as she passed through. Not that he'd done much good when her house had been broken into the first time. It was way too easy to access the Falling Rock houses via the woods at the back of the subdivision.

Beth shook her head as she left the gated community. What was she doing driving out of her own neighborhood? Instead of fleeing, she should have booted Cynthia out of the house. It had been such a shock to learn of her deceit that her first instinct had been to get away until she was more in control of her feelings. To hell with that. Next opportunity to turn around, she'd take it.

She started down the narrow mountain road and tapped the brakes as she came to the first bend. Nothing. She pressed her foot down until the pedal jammed against the floorboard. The car only gathered speed as it began its descent.

Panic bore down her, squeezing her chest with dread and fear. The car sped faster with every turn. To keep from going over the edge of the mountain, she had to drive in the middle of the road. If someone else came around a curve, they were both toast.

Be calm. Think.

She was already over halfway down. An S curve loomed about fifty feet ahead—bad news—but the good news was that the side of the road broadened at the curve's end. If she could just manage this last curve, she could pull over onto flat land and hope that the car would eventually stop in the wide plain before she crashed into a tree.

If, if, if.

But there was no time to speculate on her chance of survival. She desperately jerked one way on the steering wheel, then the opposite, trying to keep the vehicle from either veering off the mountain or crashing against its rocky side.

This was it. The last bend in the curve. She only had seconds to exit off the road and into flat terrain. Beth yanked at the steering wheel and the car bounced as it traversed the bumpy field. But at least she was losing speed and not endangering anyone else's life. Too soon, the open field ended, and trees jutted the landscape. She was headed straight on to a collision with a copse of pine trees.

Should she open the door and try to roll away from the car's path? Or would she risk injury by staying in the car and jerking the wheel in time to either avoid the tree or have it only hit the rear?

Beth opted to remain in the car. She gripped the steering wheel and twisted it. Her muscles tensed, anticipating impact.

Bang!

Metal crashed against bark and the car fishtailed. She held on to the steering wheel, praying that the force of the collision didn't send her body flying through the front window. Her torso strained against the seat belt. An explosion of sound and force slammed into her consciousness, so powerful her teeth rattled.

The world went white. It was as though she'd been thrown into a blinding snowstorm, so thick that it smothered, choking out the rest of the universe. Only this snow scalded. She breathed in hot fumes of dust. Beth struggled to understand what was happening.

The ivory veil abruptly dropped. She blinked. Dazedly, she glanced down and noted a deflated bag and broken sunglasses on her lap. How did they get there? Pale yellow smoke curled up from the bag and a film of dust coated the dashboard.

The dashboard…she was seated in an unmoving car. How strange. She looked out the shattered window and took in the snowy field and green pines. Where was she? Beth pulled at the door handle, but it was jammed shut. She was trapped.

Yet the idea didn't fill her with alarm. The observation merely floated through her mind like a cloud on a windy day. Again, she glanced down and saw her purse on the passenger floorboard, its contents spilled. The black screen of the cell phone seemed to blink at her as it caught a gleam of sunlight.

She undid her seat belt and leaned over to collect it, wincing as her banged-up muscles protested the movement. The solid weight of it in her palm brought her slowly back into focus, grounding her to the present reality. She'd driven off the road and hit a tree.

The moment of blankness and scalding heat she'd felt was from where the deployed airbag had punched her upper torso. In the dashboard mirror she saw several abrasions to her face and chest.

But she was alive.

And then she remembered the suddenly defective brakes. The terrifying sensation of being at the mercy of four tons of metal careening down a mountain. Had it been a freak accident or had someone tampered with them? Someone who wanted her dead. Someone named Dorsey Lambert.

Fear sharpened her dull senses and she spun her head left to right, searching for anyone lying in wait. To her immense relief, she appeared to be utterly alone. Beth turned off the sputtering engine and punched in Sammy's number.

He answered almost immediately, and she filled him in on the situation.

"I'll be right there," he assured her. "I'll send an ambulance, too. Just to make sure you're really okay."

Beth huddled deeper into her coat, the outside chill beginning to seep inside the idle, smashed car.

Chapter 15

"Here you go." Charlotte placed a Dixie Diner to-go bag on his desk. Sammy's stomach grumbled at the aroma of fried chicken and cornbread, reminding him that he'd missed lunch. He pushed aside paperwork and pulled out the container.

"Jeb says the brake lines were definitely cut," Charlotte said, plopping down on the chair beside him and idly rubbing her belly. "Is that enough to see if the Atlanta PD can pick up Dorsey Lambert again for questioning?"

"Already called them. Lambert's pulled another disappearing act."

She rolled her eyes. "Of course he did."

Sammy bit into a chicken wing, suddenly ravenous. "I want you to see something," he said as he dug into his meal. He pushed the computer monitor toward Charlotte. "Click on that video."

She watched the three-minute video with a puzzled frown. "So who are these people? What's going down here?"

"It's Aiden Wynngate, Beth's stepbrother. He's talking to Tommy Raden, a well-known Atlanta criminal with suspected ties to the mafia."

Charlotte peered more closely and leaned forward as though trying to pick out the men's conversation from the background noise of automobiles. "No better audio with this, I'm assuming?"

"None. Atlanta PD has been following Raden as part of a sting operation. I asked if I could review any recent video or audio of criminals suspected of bribing judges and politicians."

"To see if you could catch Lambert talking to one and collaborate his story?" she asked.

"Yep. Imagine my surprise to find Aiden on my screen."

"What do you suppose it means?"

He wiped his hands and swilled iced tea before answering. "Good question. I know the guy well, or I used to. We were friends growing up."

"But you aren't now?" Charlotte was always quick on the uptake.

"Not since he left for college and I went to work in this place." He shrugged. "Different worlds. We drifted apart."

She tapped the side of her jaw with her index finger, studying him as he resumed digging into the fried chicken. "Do you think he's in league with Lambert to hurt Beth? And if so, what's in it for him?"

"That's what I'm trying to figure out."

"What can I do to help?" she asked, always ready to get down to business.

"Nothing. I've fished around, trolling for the usual information. I'm waiting on some emails to come in. You go on home. If I need you, I'll call you."

"Promise?"

"Absolutely."

Charlotte slowly rose to her feet, wobbled a moment and then swiped a hand across her brow. He frowned. "You need me to call James to come pick you up? Or I could give you a ride home."

She shook her head. "I can drive myself home. See you in the morning."

He watched as she slowly made her way to the lobby, wondering if the baby had decided to make an early appearance. Wouldn't surprise him if James called in the morning announcing the arrival of a baby. It was times like this that reminded Sammy just how alone in the world he'd become over the years. One by one, all of his closest friends had gotten married and most were now raising children.

Sammy mentally shrugged off the disquieting thought. He had plenty of time to muse on his life choices later. Right now, he needed to solve this puzzle of Aiden and his contact with Raden. Aiden was a criminal attorney now, so it was possible Raden was a client. Could there be more to it than just an attorney-client relationship, though?

Could Aiden be responsible for any of the attempts on Beth's life? The question went round and round in his mind. Sammy stood and paced the office, ruminating over dark, dangerous possibilities.

At least Beth was protected for the moment. It had taken lots of persuading, but she'd agreed to spend the night with Lilah. Harlan's place was as good as a safe house. By morning, Cynthia would be ousted from the Falling Rock home and kicked back to Atlanta.

With something of a shock, he realized night had crept up on him. Most of the downtown shops were closed and under the yellow streetlamp beams. The only people out and about were a few coming and going from the diner.

His computer dinged, signaling an incoming email. He hurried back to his desk and saw he had missed several messages. He opened the first one and scanned the bank records he'd requested. Thankfully, he was able to access them because of the ongoing criminal probe of Raden. The numbers confirmed why Aiden had sought a loan from Beth. Both his personal and business accounts had bounced checks and had huge outstanding credit card balances from extravagant expenditures and high rent.

Next, Sammy turned to the message from his friend at the Elmore County Courthouse. After scrolling through pages of legalese he found the bottom line— Judge Wynngate had left seventy percent of his estate to Beth and thirty percent to his wife. It wasn't unusual to see children inherit the majority of an estate upon a person's second marriage, but Cynthia might not have viewed the terms in such a light. Perhaps she was determined to gain the rest of the inheritance she believed rightly belonged to her and not Beth? And if she was, she might have recruited her son in the effort.

He mopped his face with a hand and sighed. Beth's accidental discovery of Cynthia talking to her lover might have saved her life. His thoughts went deeper, darker. Did Cynthia have anything to do with her husband's unexpected heart attack? He made a note to check the hospital records in the morning before that office closed for the holiday and speak with the attending physician of record. Not much hope that would reveal anything, though. If there'd been any suspicion of foul play there would have been an autopsy and the sheriff's department would have been asked to investigate.

With no more avenues to explore, Sammy gazed out the window, absently tapping his pencil on the desktop. He briefly considered dropping by Harlan's place and asking Beth to spend the night with him instead. *No.* He was being selfish and paranoid. She'd looked so tired and haggard when he'd driven her there from the hospital after the wreck, Lilah's fierce nurturing mode had kicked in. She'd immediately embraced Beth and led her inside, fussing over her. Once Beth was seated, Lilah had immediately placed a pillow behind her back, pulled a blanket over her legs, and demanded Beth rest while she cooked a pot of chicken and dumplings.

For all he knew, Beth might have taken one of the prescribed pain pills and already be peacefully dozing.

No, tomorrow morning would be soon enough to see Beth and explore the possibility that the person, or persons, who wanted her dead might be the very ones closest to home.

Chapter 16

After a nap and a home-cooked family meal, Beth at last felt better. Her automobile accident and the conversation she'd overheard earlier had unsettled her. Instead of being afraid, though, she was angry. Furious, actually. And she didn't want to wait until tomorrow morning to have a much-needed conversation with Cynthia. The sooner she got that woman out of her home, the better.

As she fumed over what to do, she reached out to her stepbrother, her hand clenched around her cell as she spoke.

"Did you know about this?" she asked, her voice filled with rage after she told Aiden of his mother's affair.

"Calm down, sis. I suspected something. I'm headed to the house, and maybe we should talk to her together. Find out what's really going on. We can present a united front," he suggested.

Relieved he was willing to help, Beth quickly agreed. She'd feel more in the holiday spirit if she settled this with her stepmother first.

Despite Lilah objection's, Beth drove her rental car back to Falling Rock and pulled into the drive. A quick glance into the garage window showed it was empty. Had Cynthia left of her own accord, sensing that Beth was angry and onto her? So much the better.

Beth unlocked the door and entered her home, feeling a mixture of both relief and disappointment. She'd been all set to light into her stepmother and demand an explanation for her appalling behavior. But instead, she wandered aimlessly in the quiet house. The kitchen still smelled of fresh baked cookies and the Christmas tree twinkled in the gathering darkness. She marched upstairs and peeked in her stepmother's bedroom.

Cynthia had cleared out. The bed was made and the closets empty.

Beth strolled to the window and looked out over the yard. Snow blanketed the ground. The beauty of the scene made her fingers itch to capture the play of light and shadow in the twilight. Well, why not? It would give her something to do as well as quiet the unease that twisted her gut as she waited for Aiden to arrive. She'd already called him to tell him he needn't come because Cynthia was gone, but he said he was on his way and to just head to bed if she was tired. They still had things to discuss, he'd told her. Quickly, she gathered her painting materials and set to work.

Over two hours later, she'd finished the small painting and regarded it with satisfaction. Beth stood and stretched, contemplating taking another pain pill before bedtime. Ultimately, she decided plain aspirin would suffice. She'd go to bed early, as Aiden had suggested, and call Sammy first thing to tell him she'd had a change of heart and would love to spend Christmas Eve with him and his family. Mind made up, she donned pajamas and slipped into bed. It had probably been for the best she'd not had a confrontation with Cynthia this evening. Tomorrow, she'd be able to talk to her in a more civilized manner. For her father's sake, she'd be polite—but barely. As far as she was concerned, any relationship with her stepmother was officially over. And as for Aiden—the jury was still out. This past week had not brought out the best in her stepbrother. Maybe she'd always been too giving in their relationship, as well. Always the one to forgive and forget. She was glad he'd offered to confront Cynthia together, but she still wondered what his true motives were.

Beth punched at the pillow and rolled over, struggling to find a comfortable position and quiet her mind. Again she recalled the terror of hurtling down the mountain in a car without brakes and the phone conversation she'd overheard—the little innuendos that sent spider-crawls of suspicion skittering down her spine.

Headlight beams pierced the darkness of her bedroom and the sound of a car motor interrupted the night's silence. A spark of involuntary fear paralyzed her for a moment before she pulled back the bedspread and hurried to the window. Keeping cover behind the curtain, she watched from a small slit of windowpane as the familiar dark blue sedan stopped on the driveway. Aiden sprang from the vehicle, a bottle, presumably liquor, tucked between one arm and his waist.

Too bad it hadn't been Sammy. She wasn't sure she had the energy to deal with Aiden so late in the evening.

Had her brother spoken with Cynthia already? Or had her stepmother given him some sob story—that Beth had possibly overheard a conversation and misunderstood everything?

Briefly, she considered ignoring his arrival. No, she couldn't be that rude. With a sigh, Beth turned on the lamp, grabbed her robe from the foot of the bed and donned slippers. Two piercing chimes buzzed through the house as she hurried down to the main level. Already, her back and shoulders ached and protested her sudden movement. The tumble down the mountain earlier had left her body feeling slightly battered.

She flung open the door as Aiden jabbed it yet a third time.

"I'm here," she said irritably. Cold wind slapped against her body and she hugged her waist, belting the robe tighter.

Aiden pretended not to notice her cranky mood. "Where's the party?" he said with a laugh, holding up a bottle of wine. "It's not even eleven yet."

"Guess you didn't hear about my car wreck." Beth stepped aside, allowing him entrance. She'd not told him about it.

Alarm slackened his jaw and his eyes quickly scanned her body. "Oh my God! Are you okay?"

"By some miracle, I'm only sore."

"You've got scratches on your forehead. What happened? How bad was the wreck?" Aiden hung his jacket on the coat rack and followed her into the den. "And where's Mom? She never came back?"

"She never did. I thought you might have tried to reach her to find out what her side of the story was."

"No. Thought we'd talk first. Damn, sounds like

you've had a rough day all around. And I haven't helped things barging in here so late at night. Sorry, hon." Aiden gestured toward the sofa. "Sit down and put your feet up. I want to hear all about it. But first, I'll pour us a glass of bourbon."

She shook her head, then groaned at the jolt of pain in her right temple. "Better not. I took a pain pill earlier today."

"What does it matter? Just a few sips before heading to bed. It won't hurt anything."

"I'd rather not. Didn't work out for me so well last time I drank."

A dark shadow crossed his face. Did Aiden have a drinking problem? Did it make him feel better about his alcohol issue if he wasn't drinking alone? She started to give in, then stopped herself. No, it was high time she put her needs before what her family wanted and right now she didn't want a nightcap.

Aiden sighed. "Okay, okay, spoilsport. How about a cup of tea, then?"

"Great idea," she conceded. "I'll show you—"

"I know where everything is. You just relax. I'll take care of you."

That sounded wonderful. Beth sank against the couch cushions and smiled. "Not going to argue with you. I could use a little pampering after the day I've had."

"Poor kid. Be right back."

Beth glanced out the window as Aiden rumbled around in the kitchen. The night was so peaceful, so beautiful. She actually found herself looking forward to Christmas. Without Cynthia underfoot, it'd be less stressful. It would be fun meeting Sammy's family and then later she and Aiden could chill out here at home watching a couple movies and microwaving popcorn. It'd be like the old days.

Maybe Sammy wouldn't mind if Aiden had dinner with his family, as well. She'd ask him in the morning.

The kettle whistle blew and moments later Aiden appeared with a mug. "Two sugars and a splash of cream, right?"

"You got it."

He placed the mug in her hand and the heat warmed her chilled fingers. Steam spiraled upward, and she inhaled the slightly citrus aroma of the Earl Grey. It made her think of lemon orchards in the middle of winter.

"So where's your boyfriend tonight?" Aiden asked, kicking back in the recliner with a highball glass filled with bourbon and ice.

"Working late." Beth sipped her tea. *Hmm.* The taste was slightly off. Aiden must have accidently only used one packet of sugar instead of two.

"Problem?" he asked.

"Nothing," she hastened to reassure him, taking another swallow. He'd driven all the way from Atlanta and must be tired. She certainly wasn't some diva who insisted on perfection and expected others to wait on her hand and foot. "Want to have dinner tomorrow with Sammy's family? We can come back here afterward for movies and popcorn." Beth frowned. "But I guess Cynthia expects you to be with her tomorrow night?"

He lifted and dropped a shoulder. "We'll play it by ear. Right now, all I can think about is this evening. Tomorrow will take care of itself. We can work things out."

Typical Aiden. Always had been one to live in the

moment. She'd wondered if law school and his new career would make him more cautious, less spontaneous. Apparently, it had not. He took a long swallow of bourbon and she studied his tight face. Despite his casual words and laissez-faire attitude, he didn't seem quite himself. Maybe he was as upset as she was about Cynthia's disloyalty. "Are you really happy in your job?"

"Couldn't be happier. Why?"

"I don't know," she said, cautiously picking her words. "You seem a bit wound up this visit. Under stress."

He snorted. "How would you even know what it feels like to be under stress? Teaching nine-year-olds how to finger-paint is hardly what anyone would call stressful. Besides, you're loaded. Born with a silver spoon, you lucky bitch."

Aiden said the words with a laugh, but they were too harsh for normal sibling teasing. Something more was at play here. She'd had no idea he resented her inheritance so much. After all, Aiden had been left a generous stipend in her father's will and she was Dad's only biological child. Not to mention some of the inherited money had come from her mother.

"Maybe you need to slow down with the drinking," she said. "Your jealousy is showing. Not a good look for you, brother. I think I'll go to bed after all. We'll talk in the morning about Cynthia. My mind's too much in a fog right now."

"No, no, you're right. I was out of line there. It's just that I've been under a lot of pressure at work trying to make a go of my new firm. Go on and finish your tea."

Beth started to rise and then shrugged. It was practically Christmas. She didn't want to argue. It wasn't like she was living with her brother, or even anywhere near him for that matter. Wasn't that what families did when thrown together for the holidays? Try to get along for the brief period of time they had with each other? She swallowed her annoyance and took a large gulp of the cooled tea. The sooner she finished, the sooner she could get to bed and end this conversation. And having Aiden in the house was comforting, what with all the break-ins and threats from Lambert and his family. In the morning, they'd decide what to do about Cynthia.

"More tea?" he asked when she set down her cup and started to rise.

"Any more caffeine and I might not sleep tonight." A rush of dizziness assaulted her as she stood, and Beth grasped the sofa arm and closed her eyes, willing the room to stop spinning.

"Feeling a bit woozy, little sister?" Aiden's voice was singsongy and chirpy. As though he found her unsteadiness amusing.

"A bit."

His hand grasped her forearm. "Good."

Good? What was that supposed to mean? Beth's eyes flew open and she stared at him.

The Aiden who stared back was a stranger. Dead eyes, a lifted chin and a curled upper lip made him appear cold and disdainful. As though…as though he hated her.

"I've got something I want you to sign." He dragged her toward the kitchen, fingers cruelly kneading into her flesh.

Beth fought down the sudden wave of fear. This was Aiden, her brother. He could be a giant jerk, but he meant her no harm. He couldn't realize how his own strength made his grip painful. On the kitchen island, a mound of paperwork lay on the counter, a pen splayed across the top sheet. They hadn't been there before.

"Let go of me. Can't this wait until morning?"

He roughly planted her at the edge of the counter. "Do it now."

She gaped at him, startled at the mean edge in his voice. "What's wrong with you?"

"Just do as you're told. It will go easier for you."

Beth glanced down at the top sheet of the paper. The text seemed to squiggle and squirm. "I—I can't read it. What do you want me to sign?"

"Doesn't matter. Now do it."

Beth picked up the pen with shaking fingers and licked her lips. *Concentrate.* Something was very, very wrong here. She hunched over the counter and squinted her eyes. Several words and phrases leaped into coherent form. It was a legal document of some sorts: *Being of sound mind and body, bequeath to Aiden Lyle Wynngate, my legal heir, seventy-five percent of all my assets, in the event of my death.*

My death.

The full import of the words fell on Beth like a knockout punch to the gut. At least it had the effect of snapping the mental lethargy that had clouded her mind. Aiden applied a deeper, bruising pressure on her forearm. "Sign it."

"Why are you doing this?" she asked, searching his dark eyes for a spark of human warmth. But his eyes were a vacuum, a black abyss of implacable hatred and determination.

He sneered. "Isn't it obvious?"

Her fingers grasped the pen and held on to it as

though it were an anchor. Her mind skittered around the source of its greatest fear and then accepted the monstrosity.

Her brother wanted to murder her for money. He'd not rushed to her side to offer comfort and counsel about Cynthia. She'd be willing to bet that he'd invented some ruse to his mother to ensure that she didn't return here today. He'd been planning on showing up all along. To get rid of her.

She'd deal with the horror of that fact later. For now, she had to keep Aiden talking, to understand every nuance of his plan. "You drugged me," she accused. "What did you put in that tea?"

"A little something to make you drowsy." He grinned, as though mentally congratulating his own cleverness.

"But…why?"

"C'mon, Beth. You aren't the brightest bulb in the pack, but you aren't totally stupid. Do I have to spell it out for you? Fine, then."

He leaned forward, his face inches from her own. The scent of bourbon on his breath made her eyes water. "I want your money. I hate people like you. So entitled. Blissfully ignorant of what it's like in the real world."

"You—you hate me?" Memories rushed past her with cyclone speed—Aiden driving her to get ice cream in the summers before she had a driver's license, Aiden teasing her about past boyfriends, Aiden who always could lighten the tension in the house with his jokes and easy manner.

He released his grip on her arm and gave a slow clap. "Now you're catching on."

"What did I ever do to you?" Beth slowly sidled away from him, hoping his attention was focused on at last spewing all the poison he harbored deep in his soul. "Dad took you and your mom in when you had nothing. He paid for your college, law school and everything in between. Doesn't that mean anything to you?"

"He died and left me nothing."

"That's not true. He left you over ten thousand dollars."

His upper lip curled. "A paltry amount. That pittance ran out four months after he died."

Beth eased another two steps back from his hulking form and eyed the knife block four feet away on the kitchen counter. If she could only divert his attention for a couple seconds, she could make a run for it and grab a knife as she raced out of the room.

"Is Cynthia in on this, too?"

"Are you kidding? She's moving on to the next sugar daddy, as you know." A sly grin flickered across his face. "Actually, she got started on that even before your dad died."

"So I learned today. Cynthia's a lot of things, but at least she isn't a murderer. Like you."

"You're defending her?" Genuine puzzlement creased his forehead.

Beth grasped at the straw that had presented itself. "Yes. No matter what else Cynthia's guilty of, she loves you, Aiden. She's always been the one to rush to your defense in every situation. Even managed to convince my own father to let me be the sacrificial goat when the cops showed up and found pot and alcohol at the party. Remember? The night you cut out and left me to shoulder all the blame."

He smirked. "Couldn't have planned it any better. I called up all my friends and acquaintances and told them to get over here. The more grass, booze and other drugs they could bring, the better. Then, I called the cops myself to tip them off and gave them the address."

"You planned that all along?"

"Of course."

Another step back. She was so close to the knives. But she dared not make a sudden grab while his attention was all on her. "Like I was saying, Cynthia loves you. If you kill me, Sammy will catch you and make sure you're put in prison for the rest of your life. What would that do to your mother to have to come visit you at a penitentiary?"

"I prefer to think of it as eliminating an obstacle, not a murder. Don't worry about her. She won't live long enough to worry about it. I can't have Mom needling me for her cut of your inheritance."

"Wh-what are you saying?"

"Mom's next."

Her gasp filled the kitchen. If Aiden was capable of killing his own mother, he was truly mad. "Think, Aiden. Please. Think this through. You're not as smart as you believe. How's it going to look that I signed a will the day before my death? You'd be the person with the best motive to kill me. Sammy would target you in a heartbeat."

"The will's dated a year earlier, dumb ass."

"And it just happens to come to light now?"

"What better time than after someone dies? That's how wills work. Sign it and I'll safely tuck it away in a file cabinet."

There was no reasoning with a madman.

Aiden turned his back to her and toward the papers on the counter. Now was her chance—maybe her only chance. Beth leaped forward and lunged for the knife. Her right hand closed over the wooden base and she pulled one from the block. A subtle rush of air must have alerted Aiden and he wheeled around.

Beth brandished the large carving knife in front of her as she carefully backed toward the foyer. Aiden advanced, a coaxing smile on his lips.

"We both know you aren't going to use that," he said soothingly.

"Do you really want to try me?"

He frowned and shook his head. "I didn't put enough drugs in that tea."

"Mortal danger is a powerful counteractant to any sedative." Adrenal hormones were probably flooding her body. Beth kept the knife raised as she contemplated her next move. Even if she managed to reach the front door, Aiden would be on her before she could unlock it and run into the yard. Her best bet now would be to pivot, run upstairs, and then try to lock herself in one of the bedrooms. And after that? If only she could grab her cell phone to call the police—it sat, tantalizingly close, charging on the counter. But she'd have to figure out the next step once there was a locked door between her and Aiden.

The shrill ring of the landline phone buzzed through the tension between them.

Beth didn't wait to see if Aiden turned in the phone's direction. Damned if she'd just stand there and let him overtake her. Good chance he'd grab her arm before she could get a lethal cut in.

She ran. As fast and furious as she could pump her legs. She felt his breathing behind her as she climbed the stairs but couldn't risk a look around to gauge how close he was. She made it up the short flight of stairs and began running down the hardwood hallway. Aiden's footsteps pounded close behind. Oh, God, she was never going to make it. The first bedroom was on the right and she headed to it. Only three more steps…two…

Over two hundred pounds of solid flesh knocked into her back, and she hit the floor headfirst. The knife slipped out of her grasp and clattered across the floor. Beth extended an arm, desperately stretching to reach it, but Aiden easily scooped it up first. He rolled her over onto her back and pinned her down with a knee to her stomach. The metal tip of the knife pressed into her throat.

"Let's start over. Shall we? We're going to go downstairs, you're going to sign those papers, and then we're taking a little night ride. Got it?"

Beth blinked up at the brother she'd never truly known. He didn't even appear to be all that angry, merely annoyed that she was causing so much trouble with his plans. But the absence of rage only chillingly brought home how truly crazy he must be.

"Please, Aiden," she whispered, hoping to reach some small sane part of him that might be buried in his soul.

He drew back the knife and pulled Beth to her feet. "No more nonsense now," he chided. "Can't leave a mess behind."

That was the only reason Aiden hadn't killed her yet. He didn't want to leave behind any evidence of foul play, plus he wanted her authentic signature. Once he had that, he'd drive her to a remote area in the hills and…kill her and dispose of her body.

An inexplicable calm settled over Beth as she let him

lead her back into the kitchen. It almost felt as though this whole ordeal was happening to someone else and she was observing from afar. Her survival instinct had kicked in, providing a chance to try and think through her predicament and seek possible opportunities for escape.

Let him believe she'd been frightened into meek compliance. He'd be all the more startled when she seized the perfect moment to try and escape again. Wasn't that what Sammy had taught her that day in the woods? In the kitchen, Aiden sat her roughly down in a chair by the table. Without a word, he shoved the papers in front of her and handed her a pen.

She began writing her name. Should she try to signal something here? If Aiden was successful, if he killed her, shouldn't she leave behind a breadcrumb trail that would lead Sammy to her killer? *Sammy.* The surreal calm crumbled. He would be devastated. He'd find some crazy reason to blame himself for not protecting her. And if he never caught the killer? He'd probably never forgive himself. She didn't want that. Not for anyone and especially not for him.

Slowly, she wrote her first name with, hopefully, enough of an exaggerated script that might raise eyebrows at close inspection—but not so exaggerated that Aiden would notice. Would it be enough? Beth began to write her middle name, deliberating leaving out a letter to further make it look suspicious. She stole a quick peek at Aiden, who was watching her and not the writing. A mad desire arose to scribble the word *help* somewhere on the page, but she didn't dare take the chance.

"Hurry up," he demanded.

She finished her name and set down the pen. He gave

it a quick glance and nodded. "Very good. I'll put these up in a good place later."

Beth swallowed hard. *Keep him talking.* "When you visited me at the W Hotel—you were going to kill me that day, weren't you? I wasn't drunk. You'd spiked my drink then, too."

Aiden scowled. "I had you right where I wanted. Didn't have you sign the will, but I would have forged your signature after. Another ten seconds and you would have plunged headfirst down the hotel stairwell. Damn Sammy for showing up when he did. What a pain in the ass."

Beth shivered, realizing how close she'd come. What did he have in mind for tonight's killing? What would his new method for murder be? Her glance strayed to the knife he'd laid on the table. *Don't dwell on that now.* "Speaking of Sammy, you underestimate him if you think he won't figure out what you've done."

"Sammy Armstrong? The same genius who believes Dorsey Lambert is behind all your accidents?"

Her eyes widened. "You mean— "

"I'm the one who cut the brake line on your car. I'm also the one who threw that pipe bomb in the cabin. Did you really think I wouldn't hunt you down there? I used that old cabin so much for partying as a teenager that it's the first place I thought of for you to run and hide. " He slammed his hand down on the table. The loud *tha-wump* echoed through the kitchen. "I can't believe it didn't kill you both."

The confession confused her. "But Dorsey's cousins were there. They ran from us."

"Oh, the Lamberts have been stalking you all right. At first, I was annoyed. Then I realized I could use that fact to my advantage. Why would anyone suspect me of killing you when Dorsey had motive and opportunity? And *that*, my dear Beth, is what Sammy is going to believe. That Dorsey or one of his kinfolks is responsible for your disappearance.

"Disappearance?" A small hope bloomed inside her chest. Maybe Aiden planned on letting her live, perhaps allowing her to assume a new identity in another country.

"Disappearance or death." He shrugged. "Depends on whether or not they find your body."

With that chilling remark, Aiden stood and grabbed his coat off the back of a kitchen chair. "And now we go for a ride."

"Where are we going?"

"You'll find out soon enough."

No way in hell she'd cooperate without a fight, like a lamb led to the slaughter. Beth jumped to her feet, grabbed a vase on the table and swung it at Aiden. The fragile glass exploded on his right temple. Blood and glass shards splattered through the air. Aiden shook his head, momentarily stunned.

Again she ran. This time she made it to the backdoor and had even managed to release the dead bolt on the lock before a sudden, searing pain exploded on her scalp. Her body was jerked back into Aiden's chest and he twisted her hair locked in his grip.

"Nice try."

She tried to remember the move Sammy had taught her when grabbed from behind, but she couldn't manage anything with the violent pull at her scalp.

He dragged her across the den and then threw her onto the sofa. Beth kicked at him, even landing a few blows to his chest and gut before he wrestled her onto her stomach. His large hands tightly gripped hers, then she felt the rough hemp of rope cut into her wrists. In short order he bound her hands, and then her ankles.

Beth rolled over onto her back and stared up where he lurked above, breathing hard and gushing blood from the head wound. Aiden swiped at the crimson streaks and winced; evidently a few glass shards had embedded into his skin.

At least I made a mess, she thought. Hopefully, enough of one that it would make her disappearance look suspicious. Because right now, it appeared that Aiden had won. She was defenseless and entirely at his mercy.

Aiden tapped a finger against his lips, studying her.

"What?" she asked breathlessly. Maybe he was rethinking his plan. Was he going to kill her right here, right now? *No, no. I'm not ready to die.* Tears poured down her cheeks, hot and salty.

"I'm debating whether or not to duct-tape your mouth shut." He shrugged and dropped his hands to his sides. "Guess there's no need to. No one will hear your screams where we're going."

"Where are you taking me?"

He wagged a finger at her, as though scolding a mischievous child. "You'll see soon enough."

"Please, Aiden…"

But he'd already turned his back, snatching an afghan from the recliner. He threw it over her, smothering her face. Beth rocked her head to and fro, frantic to fight against the sudden darkness and feeling of claustrophobia. Her warm breath was trapped underneath the knitted blanket. Was the end coming now? A death blow to her head? A gunshot wound to the heart? Strong arms gripped underneath her knees and shoulders and he carried her out the front door.

Maybe a neighbor will see him, she thought, grasping at the slight thread of hope. Unlikely given the time of night, but she prayed for it nonetheless. The door of his vehicle opened, and he flung her into the back seat as carelessly as though she were a sack of potatoes. A door slammed shut behind her. Moments later, the front door of the vehicle opened, and Aiden settled behind the wheel. Christmas music blared from the radio and he dialed down the volume, whistling along with the tune. The sedan pulled out of the circular drive.

Beth struggled and slowly managed to sit upright. The car screeched to an abrupt halt. Aiden threw back his head and laughed. "I'm an idiot," he said in apparent amusement. He threw open the driver's-side door and walked past her. The trunk clicked open from behind.

No, no, no.

Aiden flung open her door. In his hands he held a roll of duct tape and a knife. Her gut seized, and she began screaming. "Don't put me back there. Help! Somebody help me!"

Aiden peeled off a strip of tape and then sliced it with the knife. "Knew I should have done this to start with," he grumbled, leaning toward her with the improvised gag.

She rocked her head violently back and forth, but Aiden still managed to slap the tape across her mouth. *I can't breathe.* Her lungs burned. Would she die from asphyxiation before they made it to wherever he was taking her? She inhaled as much oxygen as she could through her nose, but it didn't feel like nearly enough.

"The front gate guard isn't there now, but they might have a camera recording my coming and goings," Aiden mused aloud, as calmly as though deliberating a move in a chess game.

Then he picked her up and carried her once again. She wiggled, trying to leverage her bound body to either butt him in the head or twist from his grasp, but Aiden was too strong, too determined, for her struggles to even slow down his inevitable next move.

Aiden stuffed her in the trunk and slammed the lid shut. Cold darkness enveloped her, and even though no one could possibly hear, Beth whimpered, her screams smothered and trapped under the tape. The closed confines felt like being entombed in a metal casket. *Stop. Get ahold of yourself. There must be something you can do.* She quit screaming but her loud, labored breathing roared between her ears—and still she couldn't seem to suck in enough air. Giving in to hysteria and hyperventilating would not help her live to see the morning.

Beth controlled her breathing to a slow, diaphragmatic pace. Her eyes adjusted to the darkness and in the taillights' pinprick glow she discovered a large metal toolbox in the right corner. She kicked it with her bound feet and it toppled over, its contents spilling out—rough lengths of cord, several knives, black gloves and rolls of duct tape.

Aiden had come prepared.

Beth held her breath, wondering if Aiden had heard the toolbox fall. But he drove on, still humming along with the loud radio music, as though he hadn't a care in the world. And why not? He thought he was smart enough to get away with murder.

But despite all his cool, deadly arrangements, Aiden

hadn't factored in her desperate will to fight for her life, or her ability to devise a plan of her own. As far as he was concerned, she didn't have the brains or the brawn to fend off an attack.

She'd just have to prove him wrong.

With the toolbox knocked on its side, Beth discovered another tiny source of light that shone in the trunk's dark interior—a small handle with a dim glow. She stared at it, wondering what it opened.

Understanding thundered in her brain. A release handle! For at least the past decade, all vehicles made in the United States were required to provide an interior trunk release mechanism. She wanted to cry with relief.

Beth rolled over to it and tried to maneuver her body into a position where her bound hands could pull the handle. Her first priority was escape. She'd work on her bindings next. But no matter how she twisted, her hands couldn't quite grasp it. At last she gave up, panting through her nose, exhausted with the effort. Beads of sweat dribbled down her forehead, stinging her eyes, yet she couldn't swipe them away.

The sedan came to an unexpected halt and Beth stilled, dread churning in her stomach. Seconds later the vehicle rolled onward, and she realized Aiden had stopped at the stop sign at the bottom of Falling Rock. What kind of psychopathic killer obeyed traffic signs in the dead of night when no one was around?

She tried to keep her bearings and figure out where they were going. If—no, *when*—she got out of this damn trunk, she needed to know where she was. How awful it would be to have a chance of escape only to run around in circles and get caught by Aiden again.

If Aiden stayed straight on this road, they'd soon be

in town. If so, it would be her best opportunity to kick the trunk lid and hope that the noise would attract attention. But who would hear her? No one would be on the streets at this hour. There had to be another way. She'd read newspaper stories of people escaping from trunks. What had they done?

An image flashed through her mind, a television reel of a kidnapped child who'd kicked the taillights out of his abductor's vehicle and then stuck his hand through the resulting hole, alerting other motorists that he was trapped inside. She'd do the same, but she'd have to wisely choose her timing. Aiden would surely hear the noise of the taillights shattering. The most opportune moment to make her move would be at the first traffic light in town. With luck, there would be a few late-night travelers for the holidays and someone would see her desperate signal for help.

But instead of going through town, Aiden took a sudden left. Her small ray of hope immediately extinguished. They were on County Road 18, heading away from Lavender Mountain's town area. What ungodly, remote place did Aiden have in mind for her murder?

Okay, scratch the whole kick-out-the-taillights plan. No way would there be a stray vehicle on this lonely mountain road. If she was going to get out of this alive, it was all on her.

Beth searched in the semidarkness until the palm of her right hand came into contact with sharp, cold metal. Now was the time to try to cut her hands free of their bindings. More likely she'd slice her wrists open in the awkward, blind attempt and then proceed to bleed out. But anything was preferable to whatever Aiden had in mind for her.

Cautiously, Beth gripped the knife's handle and began to saw at the rope binding. The top of the blade pricked into her wrist, but she gritted her teeth and readjusted her aim. It was painstaking work and she repeatedly stabbed at her own flesh in the process, but what choice did she have?

To help keep her mind off the pain and the imminent danger of her predicament, she continued to try and map their location. Did he have their burned-down cabin in mind? They were headed in that general direction, but going there didn't make sense. There was no reason to choose it as a murder scene. Perhaps Aiden would arbitrarily stop on this lonesome road whenever he decided the time was right.

The rope bindings began to ease under the wet slickness of her wrists. The sedan suddenly swerved, and she lost her balance. Searing pain sliced through her skin as she fell against the knife blade. Beth moaned and caught her breath, trying again to slip out of the restraints. Her time was short. Aiden had turned onto Witches' Hollow Road and that only led to one place.

She knew exactly where they were going. This was a dead-end lane that ended at an old abandoned gravel pit. Estimated at over sixty feet deep, this time of year the pit would be filled with icy water from melted snow. Her brother's intention couldn't be any clearer. The only question now was whether he intended to kill her before throwing her into the icy pit.

Branches raked against the vehicle in an eerie grinding that set her teeth on edge. The road was narrowing, and the sedan jostled as it ran over potholes.

The binding at last gave loose and Beth freed her hands. Quickly, she ripped the duct tape from her mouth, barely registering the tear of flesh on her face. She gulped in a lungful of fresh air, grateful for the small mercy.

The sedan hit a deep pothole. Her entire body lifted and then dropped. At least this time her arms were free, and she could stabilize herself from rolling all over the trunk. The vehicle slowed as the terrain worsened. Aiden couldn't continue much farther down this path without a four-wheel-drive truck. She was almost out of time. Beth hurriedly cut off the rope binding her ankles. It was now or never.

She located the trunk release lever and popped it. A sweet click, and the top of the trunk flung open, blasting her with the night's frigid air. Beth grabbed one of the knives and lunged forward. The sedan came to an abrupt halt.

"What the hell?" Aiden thundered, opening up the driver's-side door.

Beth scrambled out of the truck and began to run. Her ankles and feet were numb from being bound, but she stumbled forward as fast as she could.

"Stop running," Aiden shouted.

Hell, no. Why should she make her murder more convenient for him?

A shot rang out, exploding into the night. She kept running, waiting for the shock of the bullet as it rammed into her, but nothing happened. She dared not glance behind to see what was happening. Aiden must have fired that warning shot straight up in the air. Beth cut away from the road, slipping into the cluster of trees and dense foliage. Aiden was hot on her tail as she rushed forward, branches and vines cutting into her face, hair and body. This must be what it was like to be a deer or rabbit fleeing from a hunter—only she was the one out of her element here in the bleak, alien woods. Her left foot caught under a root and she fell. Her ankle twisted and burned beneath her. The knife fell from her hands. Beth hunkered down, gathering her body into a tight ball under a knot of woody bramble that cut through her clothes and into her flesh. Her fingers searched for the knife, but all she felt was snow melting into her bare hands.

Dead leaves and twigs crunched all around where she lay on the wet ground. Closer and closer he came. Beth closed her eyes, awaiting the inevitable. All she had left was to try and land a good kick or punch once he discovered her hiding place.

And he would find her.

She knew the moment Aiden spotted her. All sound ceased. A whoosh of air and then a bruising grip ground into her right forearm. Aiden placed a knee against her back. She tasted snow and leaves.

"There you are. Did you really think you could get away from me? Damn, killing you is more trouble than I thought it would be."

"Aiden. Please. You don't want to do this."

"Got no choice now. We've come this far."

The distinctive sound of duct tape unraveling rent the air. Seconds later, her shredded and bleeding wrists were taped. Tears gathered in her eyes. She'd worked so hard to be free and now she was right back where she started.

"I won't tell anyone what happened tonight."

He snorted, not even bothering to point out how ridiculous she must sound. With a grunt, he yanked her to her feet.

"At least you wouldn't get the death penalty if you stop now," she persisted, hoping to reach him by some wild chance. Deep down, she believed some shred of humanity still existed beneath his charming, light-hearted manner. "Quit and maybe you'd end up with only a few years in prison for kidnapping."

Past his shoulder, a cut of light strobed through the trees. It lasted only seconds, then vanished. The dark seemed darker and more absolute from its absence. Had she lost it? Had desperation and fear conjured an illusion? Aiden whipped his head around and surveyed the woods, then shrugged. "Must have been lightning."

Lightning was an unusual phenomenon in winter, though. She didn't have time to dwell on it as Aiden began dragging her back toward the road.

"Don't give me any more trouble," he warned. "Accept your fate and you won't have to suffer. It will all be over quick. But if you do fight me, I'll knock you out cold. Your choice."

Some choice. Stay conscious and face Aiden while he killed her in order to have one last shot at begging for her life and praying for a miracle, or take being knocked out and spared the final horror. Beth decided to fight until the end.

"Someone saw us, Aiden. Those were headlights flashing through the woods. They'll report it. A car with a popped trunk on a dark road? They're probably calling it in right now. Let me go and you can get away."

Aiden ignored her. He crammed her into the front seat and then settled beside her. "I want you where I can see you. How the hell did you manage to get free?"

She didn't answer and rapidly scanned the center console and dashboard for either a cell phone or a make-shift weapon. Only a couple of empty beer cans lay scattered on the floorboard.

"I don't want a blood trail everywhere," Aiden continued. "I'm hoping they never find your body. That way, there's less risk anything will ever be traced back to me."

He cranked the car and the sedan lurched forward. They proceeded slowly, but with the deteriorated condition of the road the sedan scraped ground a couple of times. Beth's gaze switched from Aiden's profile to the wild landscape. In minutes, the car headlights shone on a faded metal sign that read Lavender Mountain Pit & Quarry. Just beyond the sign was a ramshackle wooden building that had once served as the company's modest headquarters. She'd visited the place many times over the years as a teenager. Local legend maintained that the structure was haunted, and it had become a Halloween attraction for older teens looking for spooky thrills. Beth never imagined the creepy place would be the sight of her own violent death.

The car shuddered to a stop and she cast him a quick glance. *Wait until he pulls you from the car, then make your move.* That would be her best shot at making contact.

Unexpectedly, Aiden reached across her and pushed the passenger door open. "Get out," he ordered. She froze, unsure if now was her moment to strike.

"I said get out." Aiden gave her a violent push and she tumbled out. Aiden immediately followed suit. "Turn around," he commanded.

Slowly, she obeyed. He stood before her, illuminated in the car's elliptical beams. He had a gun raised and aimed directly at her. Beth's heart beat painfully in her chest. With his head, Aiden motioned her forward. Behind him, the black abyss of the pit awaited.

But they weren't alone. Someone was watching. She heard a twig break, as if snapped by a foot. She felt them staring, watching in the darkness like a wild beast. Beth crept forward at a snail's pace. Past Aiden's shoulder, a figure emerged out of the woods. Moonlight glowed on his ginger hair. Recognition slammed into her.

What the hell was Dorsey Lambert doing out here? Were he and Aiden working together?

Aiden studied her startled face and then whipped his head around. But Lambert had already disappeared into the shadows.

He chuckled. "You really think that old trick's going to work on me?"

Chapter 17

The phone rang, jostling Sammy from an uneasy sleep. The alarm clock by his bed blinked neon-green numbers—2:46 a.m. Nothing good ever happened at this time of day. Could it be Beth? He picked up his cell phone from the nightstand and frowned at the unfamiliar number. Not Beth then. His racing heart quieted several beats. But an Atlanta area code was on display. Perhaps there was some news about Dorsey Lambert. Quickly, he swiped the screen and spoke. "Officer Armstrong."

"Sammy?" A woman's hesitant voice sounded. "I'm so sorry to bother you at this horrible hour but I'm afraid."

"Who is this?"

"Cynthia Wynngate, Beth's stepmother."

Sammy stood, pulling on his uniform pants he'd

flung at the foot of the bed only a couple of hours ago. "What's wrong? Is Beth hurt?"

"I—I'm not sure."

"Explain yourself."

"We, um, had a bit of a falling-out earlier today. I don't know if she told you?"

"She did," he growled impatiently. "Go on."

"So I asked Aiden to go over and try and help smooth things over between us like he always does."

His heart slammed in his ribs before he remembered Beth was spending the night at Lilah's. Sammy pulled on socks and slipped into his uniform shoes. "Your point?"

"I—I think Aiden might be planning to hurt Beth."

Sammy stilled, hands frozen over the shoelaces he'd been tying. All his niggling doubts and suspicions about his old friend rushed up and merged into a knot of dread. "What makes you say that?" he asked past the lump in his throat.

"It wasn't so much what he said, it's how he said it. His practice hasn't been going so well and when I called him this afternoon, I asked how his firm was doing. He admitted it was in dire straits but that he had a plan to fix everything." Cynthia paused. "He sounded strange… I—I can't explain it exactly. I pressed him what that meant, and Aiden claimed he'd be coming into a large sum of money in the next few weeks. I asked if a big lawsuit settlement was due and he laughed, saying he had a major score to settle with someone."

Sammy cradled the cell phone between his shoulder and right ear as he slipped into his uniform shirt. He wished Cynthia would hurry with her story, but suspected that the more he interrupted and pressed her, the longer it would take.

"Anyway, I asked when he'd leave to see Beth today and he said he had a few supplies to pick up first before leaving the city. Then—and this is what makes me nervous—Aiden said tonight was the night his plan would be set in motion and that people like Beth, born with silver spoons in their mouths, didn't deserve to have such easy lives when people like him had to struggle."

Sammy scowled. What a strange woman Cynthia was to report her son to an officer of the law on the basis of so little. "And from that conversation you suspect your own son...of what, exactly?"

Her voice chilled a notch. "I'm just saying maybe someone should check on Beth. I awoke from a disturbing dream over an hour ago and I've tried to call both of them but get no answer. I even tried the landline at Falling Rock."

Why hadn't Beth answered her phone? Probably only because she saw Cynthia's name on the screen and didn't want to talk to her, he suspected.

"I'll check it out," he told Cynthia, abruptly ending their call. Immediately, he punched Beth's number on speed dial. It rang four times and went to voice mail. "Call me," he said roughly, not expecting to really hear from her. Beth was either asleep or had her phone ringer turned off. To be safe, Sammy called Harlan to make sure all was well.

"Sampson here," Harlan grumbled into the phone. "Sammy?"

"I'm calling to make sure Beth's safe and sound. I got a call from her stepmother warning she might be in danger from her stepbrother."

Harlan muttered an expletive. "She's not here. She left

hours ago, insisting that she wanted to stay in her own home. Sorry, I should have called you. Do we need to—"

Alarm coursed through him. "I'm going over now to check it out. I'll call you later."

Sammy buckled his belt and headed to the den where he grabbed the Jeep keys off the fireplace mantel. Recrimination rose and battered his conscience. He should have asked Beth if he could spend the night with her. He couldn't rest now until he'd either seen Beth or heard her voice.

Chills skittered down the back of his neck as he raced out the door and into his Jeep. Sammy zipped down his neighborhood street and then sped through town. At the entrance of the Falling Rock subdivision, the unattended gate opened automatically, and he shook his head as he drove through. Months ago, their homeowners' association had cut back on manning it with a security guard on duty at nights, citing the difficulty of finding and funding personnel. In his opinion, the gatehouse was now merely a pretentious show of wealth and security that held no real teeth.

Most of the homes were tastefully lit with a Christmas tree placed in an open window and outside strings of white or pale lights draped across porch and roof lines. A few homes had mangers or decorated yard trees that glowed from a single white spotlight. Driving through the elegant neighborhood felt like slipping into a fairyland. Could anything really bad happen here?

Oh, hell yes. Sammy recalled the human trafficking ring they'd uncovered a year ago. A wealthy Atlanta couple had used one of these mansions as a holding pen for kidnapped young women. While there, the victims were physically and emotionally broken down and eventually sold as sex slaves. His partner, Charlotte, had been the one to crack that case.

He turned the corner to Beth's street and gave a brief, involuntary smile at the corner house, which sported over a dozen inflatable holiday cartoon characters, including a twenty-foot-tall Grinch. The home was lit with a mismatch of bright colors on every available surface. Some might unkindly call it "tacky," but he secretly loved it.

Sammy's amusement was short-lived as he pulled into Beth's driveway. His knot of anxiety wouldn't unravel until he saw she was unharmed. Leaving his truck running, he ran to the front porch and stopped, his heart sinking.

The front door wasn't completely shut; it gaped open an ominous inch. Sammy withdrew the revolver on his belt clip and stepped to the side of the door before pushing it open all the way with his foot.

There was no sound or movement from beyond. Slowly, he eased into Beth's home, gun drawn. He stole past the unlit dining room, down a hallway and into the den where a lamp burned near the sofa. At first glance, all appeared in order. Sammy peered closer at the sofa where Beth might have recently sat. Semidry droplets of a dark liquid spotted the floor and couch cushions. Had Beth had an accident of some sort? Or had something worse befallen her? His own blood ran cold at the thought.

Sammy raced upstairs to check out the bedrooms. All were empty and there were no signs of a struggle. Beth's bed was unmade, as though she'd been in it for a time before being awakened. Where had she gone in the middle of the night? He hurried back downstairs and opened the garage door. Her rental car was parked inside. Sammy strode over to it and placed his hand on the hood. It was cold and unused. He opened the door and took a look. Nothing unusual there.

Sammy returned inside, his concern mounting. He called Beth's phone number again and heard it ring nearby. He found it plugged into a charger on the kitchen counter, next to her purse. His shoes squeaked, grinding against some small object. His eyes followed the trail to several large fragments of broken glass. Behind the kitchen island were larger pieces of broken glass, perhaps a vase.

He called her name, then Aiden's. Nothing. Just the sound of his own voice in the empty home.

Beth had not left her home willingly. Not without her purse and phone. He called Charlotte on speed dial. She answered almost at once, although her voice was drowsy with sleep. Sammy found himself suddenly unable to speak past the massive pressure weighing on his chest.

"Sammy? What's up?" Charlotte's voice sharpened. "What's wrong?"

"It's Beth," he said roughly. "She's missing. Foul play suspected."

A muttered curse and then "Where are you? I'm coming over."

He gave her the address. "Call Harlan, too," he added. "We need a manhunt with all available officers."

"Should I put out an APB on Dorsey Lambert?"

"Yes. And also on Aiden Wynngate."

"The man in the videotape. Beth's stepbrother, right?" Charlotte asked.

"Right. I'll explain everything later."

He hung up the phone and swiped a hand through his

hair. Who had taken Beth—Lambert or her stepbrother? Were they working in tandem? It would make sense. Aiden's firm represented persons charged with a crime. As the tape had shown, Aiden had plenty of opportunity to make connections with the criminal underworld.

Think. Where would Aiden or Lambert have taken Beth? Trouble was, there were dozens of remote roads in these mountains. All suitable for murder and burying the victim in a shallow grave that might or might not be discovered by hunters one day. His heart pinched, imagining Beth at this moment, scared out of her mind, believing she was about to die.

Or she might already be dead.

Sammy drew a long breath and shook his head. He couldn't go there, couldn't entertain the thought of Beth not being in this world. They'd find her. There had to be a clue here somewhere. He scanned the kitchen and his eyes rested on a stack of papers on the table. That was as good a place as any to start his search. He glanced at the typewritten words and blinked.

Last will and testament of Elizabeth Jane Wynngate.

Frost flowed through his veins and his heart froze. Abruptly, he rifled through the papers and found what he was looking for. Aiden Wynngate was listed as the primary beneficiary, with his mother, Cynthia, also inheriting a significant percentage. If Aiden had an accomplice, it was Cynthia, not Dorsey Lambert. But why would Cynthia have called him if she was in on it? Maybe she wanted to make sure the finger pointed at her son and not at her?

Unless this was an elaborate red herring planted by Lambert. Sammy immediately struck that idea as not being credible. Everything pointed to Aiden. His strange behavior, association with criminals and one terrific financial need. Greed was always a slam-bang murder motive.

Where would Aiden take her? He knew all these back-roads. Even with a full-blown manhunt it would take hours to check every narrow dirt road that crisscrossed the mountains. His cell phone rang, interrupting his racing thoughts. He glanced down at the screen before answering. It was Charlotte.

"We've got a tip," she said without preamble. "An anonymous caller at the station claimed a woman had been abducted and taken to the old Lavender Mountain quarry."

The old abandoned pit. Of course. He should have thought of that straightaway. "On my way," he said tersely, tucking his phone in his back pocket, then fishing the Jeep keys from his pocket as he ran to the door.

He could be there in ten minutes, twice as fast as any officer in town. But would that be quick enough? It had to be.

Sammy sped out of Falling Rock and raced on the snowy rocks with reckless abandon. *I'm coming, Beth. Hold on, sweetheart.*

He hadn't been to the quarry in years and he almost missed the turnoff. Sammy slammed on his brakes and took the turn like a NASCAR driver on the final lap of a race. The Jeep swerved to the far left, almost plunging into a ditch before he jerked the steering wheel to the right and returned to the road's center. Headlights illuminated recent tire tracks in the snow.

Almost there, Beth.

The truck bounced and rattled on the rough road. All at once, he came upon an unmoving sedan and had to slam his brakes to keep from plowing into its rear fender. Sammy swerved to avoid the collision and the car beams spotlighted two persons standing near the edge of the deep pit—Aiden, eyes wide with shock and bleeding from a cut at his temple, and Beth, looking equally as shocked, her brown hair whipping in the wind.

Sammy retrieved his gun and flung open his truck door, using it as a shield. From the side of the door, he pointed his gun at Aiden. "Hands up, Wynngate."

Aiden pulled a gun from his jacket and fired a round. Pain exploded in Sammy's left shin and his leg gave out beneath him.

"Run, Beth!" he screamed, rolling under the Jeep bed for protection. But he wasn't fast enough. Another bullet slammed into the front of his left shoulder, dangerously close to his heart. He lay on the ground, exposed and vulnerable. The next shot would take him out for good. Had Beth run? Was she safe? A black film seemed to form over his vision, and the world grew fuzzy and unfocused.

A shrill scream pierced through the ringing in his ears. *Beth.* He opened his mouth to urge her again to run, but the words would not come. He struggled to his feet. If it was the last thing he did, he had to shoot his old friend. Had to protect Beth at any cost. Her life was all that mattered. Tamping down the pain, he picked up his gun in his right hand and focused.

Aiden had walked closer to him and only stood a few feet from where he lay, gun raised for the lethal shot. Beth lunged at Aiden's back and he fell. A shot exploded, and Sammy felt a bullet whizzing by his ear, narrowly missing his face. Beth was still in danger. Why wouldn't she run while she had the chance? Aiden's gun lay on the snow-covered ground between them. Sammy began crawling toward it. Aiden also crept forward to retrieve his weapon. Beth lay sprawled on the ground, stunned from the impact of hurling her body at Aiden.

He was going to die. They both were.

From his right, a figure sprang from the dilapidated quarry headquarters. Was he hallucinating? Just as Aiden's fingers grasped the weapon's handle, the man kicked the gun away. Beth scrambled to pick it up.

"Sammy! How bad are you hurt?" she cried.

Dorsey Lambert's eyes locked with his. What the hell was the man doing here? Were the two in league after all? No, that made no sense. Lambert had saved his life.

In the confusion, Aiden jumped to his feet and began running. Dorsey took off his jacket and pressed it against Sammy's wound. The pain was excruciating but necessary. He could feel the warm blood soaking his shirt and jacket.

"Backup on the way?" Dorsey asked. "I called the cops earlier."

"Yes."

Beth dropped to her knees beside him. "Sammy!"

"He's going to be okay," Dorsey said. "That bastard was trying to frame me for murder. I knew I had to keep an eye on him."

Sammy hoped Lambert was right in his pronouncement that this shot wasn't fatal. Even now, sirens wailed in the distance. But his head swam, and strength oozed from his body with every drop of blood lost. And still Beth wasn't out of danger. "Aiden might return," he warned them. "We…" His words began to slur. "Not safe yet. Still in danger."

Chapter 18

Still in danger.

Beth cast a quick glance over her shoulder in time to see Aiden hightailing it to the woods. She knew what she had to do. She'd already witnessed her stepbrother's persistence. He'd come back to finish them off if he had the chance.

"I'll stay with him until the ambulance arrives," Dorsey said with a nod at Sammy. "You go on. Know how to use that gun?"

"Yes." But she hesitated, staring down at Dorsey's hands pressed over Sammy's wound. Blood had soaked through Sammy's jacket and covered Lambert's fingers. Sammy's eyes were closed shut and his face was pale as the snow. Fear clinched her gut. She didn't want to lose him. Not when her heart had begun to love.

"Go!" Lambert shouted, thrusting a flashlight into her free hand. "There's nothing you can do here."

Beth rose to her feet and ran, gripping the gun's handle in her right hand. She knew how to use it but hoped she didn't have to. All she needed was to keep Aiden in sight and make him quit running. The cops could arrest him then and take care of the rest.

She shone the flashlight on Aiden's footprints in the snow. He couldn't escape. Not after all the hell he'd put her and Sammy through. She'd brought this trouble into Sammy's life. Aiden was *her* stepbrother and he'd been after *her* money. Only fair that she be the one to bring him down in the end.

She entered the woods, and the thick tree canopies blocked most of the full moon's light. If Dorsey hadn't had the good sense to bring a flashlight, she wouldn't have had a chance at tracking Aiden. Surprisingly, a narrow trail ran through the terrain. Probably forged by deer hunters, she surmised. Aiden had somehow found the trail. Had he scouted this area ahead of her abduction? Had he devised contingencies in the event he was forced to flee? What if he'd deliberately drawn her into the cover of the woods?

Beth flicked off the flashlight. What she'd imagined an advantage might prove her undoing, since the elliptical beam spotlighted her every move. Her heartbeat went into overdrive and she felt the roaring of blood in her temples. Despite the cold, a sweat broke out all over her body. She strained her ears, listening for the slightest whisper of Aiden's breathing, of an unexplained twig snapping.

But there was only the persistent, haunting howl of the wind rattling through the treetops. An owl hooted, and she bit back a scream. Seemed she'd gone from hunter to hunted. *I'm the one armed with a gun. Aid-*

en's the one who should be frightened, not me. Yet her mind didn't buy the argument. He was close, she could feel it. She had to know where he was. Waiting in the darkness for him to pounce was the worst torture. Beth snapped on the flashlight and circled around.

No Aiden in sight.

Her legs went weak with relief and she leaned against the rough bark of a pine tree. Chasing Aiden was a fool's errand. She'd go back to Sammy and wait for the cops to mount a search. They were the experts. She straightened and turned for retreat.

Straight ahead, the flashlight illuminated a large obstacle that hadn't been there seconds before. *Aiden.* The light trembled in her hands and she almost dropped it. He'd been so quiet in his approach. So lethal.

He grinned. "Hello, Beth."

How could he be so calm—so confident? He'd greeted her as though he'd just stepped into her home for a chat, as though they weren't standing in the woods after he'd attempted to kill both her and Sammy. The grip on the gun at her side tightened. Did he have a weapon, as well? One he'd hidden here earlier?

He stepped forward and she took a step back, raising the gun. "Stay where you are."

A smile ghosted across his lips. "You wouldn't hurt me."

"Don't be so sure."

He didn't take another step, but he didn't retreat, either. "Why, Aiden?" she said gruffly, past the lump in her throat. "Have you hated me all these years?"

"Not always. At first, you were merely an inconvenience. But once your father died, you were in my way."

His words were more chilling than the December

night. *In the way. An inconvenience.* How could she never have seen past his easygoing facade? She wanted to believe there was some good left in him. A modicum of decency.

Aiden stretched out a hand. "Give me back my gun."

She shook her head, trying to wake up from the surrealistic nightmare of the last hour. "Why should I? So you can shoot me?"

"I won't hurt you. I just want to escape. I can't go to prison. It would kill me."

The sirens sounded louder, and he uneasily glanced behind his shoulder. But would they get here in time? She had to keep Aiden focused on her, not the approaching cops.

"Did Cynthia murder my dad?" she asked, hoping the question disarmed him and returned his focus to her.

He faced her again and chuckled. "Good ole Mom. She's inventive, you've got to give her that. Put her LPN training to good use."

"What did she do to Dad?" Beth fought back her tears, her horror. "How did she kill him?"

"*Kill*'s a strong word. Come on. Your dad was old and had a weak heart. He'd have died soon anyway. Mom only helped him along a little."

"How did she do it?" she insisted, her voice tight and hard. "I never heard even a whisper of suspicion on the cause of death."

"After his heart attack, Mom finished him off with an air embolism. Killed by thin air." Again he chuckled. "All it takes is a well-administered syringe of oxygen." He held up a hand and pointed his thumb and index finger like a pistol. "Poke that tiny needle in an inconspicuous place and voilà—an easy solution." He jabbed his index finger above his kneecap and made a tiny, swishing sound. *Whoosh.* "Like I said, she picked up a thing or two at her old job."

The callous description of her father's murder almost shattered the little bit of her composure that remained. Her knees jellied, and the gun wobbled in her hand. Beth struggled to understand why this had happened to her family. "But why? He loved you. Both of you. He took you in and shared everything he had."

Aiden shrugged. "Stop making him out to be a damn saint. He was a dirty judge, remember? You always were in your own little world, painting and drawing. But to answer your question, he got suspicious of Mom having a boyfriend. She denied it, of course, but Mom was afraid that since he was onto her, he'd hire a private detective and find the truth."

Aiden took a step forward, but this time Beth didn't step away. Anger steadied her hand and gave her strength. The sirens kicked up a notch, their ghastly wail drawing closer. The longer honk of a fire engine blasted, as well as the high-low pitch of an ambulance alarm. *Please let them get here in time for Sammy.* He'd have been so much better off if he'd never gotten involved with her. But on the heels of that disturbing realization, Beth realized she could never regret a moment of their time together. The memory of every second—every kiss and every touch—seemed incredibly precious.

"One last question."

He quirked a brow and stilled.

"Does Cynthia know about…about your plans tonight? Are you two working together?"

Aiden flashed a grin, his teeth gleaming as white as the snow in the darkness. "Are you kidding me?

Her methods are more subtle. More untraceable. Mom doesn't have the stomach for the nitty-gritty work."

If she couldn't appeal to Aiden's humanity, perhaps she could reason with his avarice. "You know she gets a large hunk of my money when I die, right? You don't get it all."

"Do you think I'm stupid?" His mouth tightened, and his chin lifted an inch. "I'm an attorney, for Christ's sake. I can read a damn legal document. I know exactly how much she'd receive. But she won't live to enjoy it."

Matricide. Cynthia was a lot of things, but she adored her son. Aiden was her golden child that she protected and defended. Maybe that was the problem. She'd raised him to believe that he deserved anything he wanted and to claim it at any cost.

Aiden was upon her, his breath smelling of bourbon. "Give me the gun. Now. You'll never see me again."

"I don't believe you."

"It's true. I've got a car and a driver waiting for me down the road." He pulled a small leather binder from the inside pocket of his jacket. "Got a passport and a plane ticket, too."

"Where do you think you can run?"

"Like I'd tell you?" He shook his head. "All I'll say is it's warm and their cops turn a blind eye to extradition requests. But I need my gun. I can't outrun the cops without a weapon. There's going to be a standoff."

Alarm chimed through Beth. He'd need more than a weapon. He'd need a human shield. He'd need...*her*.

The woods were suddenly alive with blue and red cop lights strobing through the icy trees and dense underbrush, sirens shrieking in the frigid air—the moment of reckoning was upon them. Aiden's arm began to rise, and she made a move of her own. Her left arm hoisted the heavy steel flashlight in an arc, catching the right side of his face in a crushing thump of bone.

Aiden screamed and staggered backward, holding his head in his hands.

Beth dodged around him, navigating clumsily through the copse of trees. *Head back to the main road.* She didn't need the flashlight now; the glare from first responder vehicles cast a spotlight on the clearing ahead. Aiden clomped behind her, as fast and furious as a bull and gaining on her with every second. Her wet slippers were useless for gaining traction.

She reached the clearing. Several police cars snaked across the narrow road and a couple of them left the road and bumped across the field. Their headlights stung her eyes and she blinked, trying to orient herself in the temporary blindness.

Oomph. A solid mass of weight slammed into her back. An arm encircled her throat, pushing her neck back in a choking hold. She could hardly breathe.

Aiden had gotten just what he wanted. He'd take her down with him if needed. What else did he have to lose?

"Give me the gun," he growled in her ear.

The gun. Thank heavens she hadn't dropped it. He might be faster and stronger, but she wasn't defenseless. Cold metal practically burned into her numbed hand and fingers. Could she do it? Really shoot somebody? Hell, yes. He'd left her no choice. As best she could in the awkward hold, Beth aimed the gun backward and pulled the trigger.

The explosion rang in her ears. The hold loosened, and Aiden screamed in agony. She gulped in a lungful of fresh air. Cops seemed to shout at her from every direction, but she was too wired to make out the words, only the frantic urgency of their voices. *Run.* Aiden wasn't through with her yet. Just as her legs obeyed her brain's command, Aiden lunged at her, knocking her to the ground.

The gun fell out of her hand and she grabbed it. Aiden loomed above her, his dark eyes aglow with desperation and madness and anger mixed with fear. He raised an arm, his hand gripped in a fist. She tried to wiggle out of his grasp but his knee lodged firmly in her gut and his left arm anchored her upper torso. The snow was wet and freezing, seeping through her bathrobe and pajamas. In two seconds Aiden would deliver a knockout punch, take her weapon and make his wild dash to freedom while dragging her along as a hostage. He'd kill her at the first opportunity when she was no longer useful to him.

Beth lifted the gun, not sure if she'd even get off a shot before Aiden's fist shattered her face. With numbed, stiff fingers, she pulled the trigger and fired. The reverberation of the gun tingled in her palm and the blast deafened all sound. All sensation seemed frozen in the frigid night. A chiaroscuro of black, white and grays punctuated with slashes of red.

There was Aiden's widened eyes and slackened jaw;

…the crimson patch blooming on his chest;

…the black nighttide lit by red sirens;

…the white snow falling swiftly and silently—a silent witness to murder.

Oh, God. She'd killed him.

Aiden's body toppled backward several inches and then fell forward. She watched his descent in horror. There wasn't time to move away. Dead weight crushed her chest. Beth screamed until her throat burned raw. Pandemonium erupted as cops and rescue workers arrived, their voices calling out sharp commands and urgent warnings. A volley of camera flashes strobed the area from officers recording the crime scene.

It was all a jumbled mess echoing round and round in her brain. Strong arms rolled Aiden's heavy, slack body away. "Is he...?"

She couldn't form the word, but the man nodded. He had a kind, grandfatherly face that was worn and wrinkled. He awkwardly patted her arm. "Sammy?" she asked.

"They've already taken him to the hospital. Are you hurt?"

Beth eased up to a seated position and blinked at the swarm of people standing above. Two men placed Aiden's lifeless body on a stretcher. She averted her eyes, not wanting to witness the shell of a man she'd believed had cared about her all these years.

"I'm okay but I want to go to the hospital. I need to be with Sammy."

She struggled to her feet, surprised to find her limbs weak and her vision blurry. Two people rushed forward and supported her from either side.

"Need a stretcher?" one of them asked.

She stiffened her spine and cinched the wet, dirty bathrobe closer against her waist. All she needed was Sammy. She had to be with him, to touch him and see his eyes open again.

Not ten yards away, an ambulance awaited, its back door open and the interior lit. She glimpsed two stretchers and lifesaving equipment on shelves. But there was also another vehicle—the side of it emblazoned with the

County Coroner seal. Several workers loaded a stretcher with Aiden's body wrapped in a tarp.

The cops waved an EMT crew over and she was encircled. Safe and protected. But a tight knot of anxiety cramped her stomach.

Please, God, let Sammy live.

Chapter 19

Beth laid her head beside Sammy's chest on the hospital bed where he rested. Despite the uncomfortable chair, she was afraid that if she fell asleep it would be days before she awakened. The weariness went bone-deep. She'd showered in Sammy's private room and Lilah had brought her dry clothes to change into. Her friend, mother hen that she was, had also insisted that she eat a bowl of soup. Now, warmed and sated, her body wanted sleep. She fought the drowsiness, wanting to be the first thing Sammy saw when he awakened.

The doctors had assured her that the surgery to remove the bullet and staunch the internal bleeding had been a success. A couple of nights in the hospital for observation and Sammy could go home.

Home. Beth realized that she thought of Lavender Mountain as her home now. Boston seemed far, far away. Her heart was here in Appalachia—with Sammy. The hospital door opened and Lilah poked her head in, eyebrows raised in question. Beth shook her head no, shuffled to her feet and entered the hallway where Harlan and Lilah stood guard.

"He's still sleeping, which is a good thing. Sammy needs lots of rest." She cut Harlan a stern glance. "He's in no shape to be giving statements or making reports tonight. Probably not tomorrow, either."

Harlan nodded. "Of course. Besides, I spoke with him just before he went under the knife and I know everything I need to for the time being. I also spoke with Charlotte before she was admitted here."

"What happened to her?" Beth hadn't even known Sammy's partner had been on the scene. Dread weighed on her chest. Had something awful happened to the pregnant cop?

"She's fine," Lilah assured her with a quick squeeze of the hand. "Just delivered a nine-and-a-half-pound baby boy. James is beside himself. It's their first baby."

Lilah and Harlan exchanged a tender, knowing smile as Beth sighed with relief. At least something good had come out of this night. "Y'all should go on home," she urged them. "Sammy's out of danger and I'm fine."

Lilah leaned into Harlan's side, patting her round stomach. "I'm not going to argue with you. I'm beat. Come by whenever you're ready. The spare room's yours."

Harlan extended a hand toward her. "You'll always be welcome in our home."

She shook his hand and his unexpected kindness had her blinking back tears. No wonder Lilah was so in love with this man. He often appeared taciturn and aloof on the outside, but underneath, Harlan was a solid, stand-up kind of guy. Lilah had chosen well.

Beth tiptoed back into the room and resumed her seat by Sammy's bed. Some color had returned to his face and the chalk-white paleness was gone. His breathing was smooth, deep and regular.

She huddled under a blanket. After all the hours outside in the winter cold, it seemed her body just couldn't get warm enough. Her lids were heavy, and she gave in to the pleasant lethargy.

Something tugged on her hand and she startled awake. Beth gazed at the unfamiliar, sterile room in confusion for a moment until her eyes focused on Sammy. He smiled at her, his brown eyes warm and gentle. "They told me you were okay," he said. "But nothing beats having you right here in front of me where I can see for myself."

"Ditto," she said past the lump in her throat. "You gave us all a scare."

"Nothing compared to what I saw when I found you with Aiden."

She nodded slowly. "You know he—he's dead now."

"Harlan filled me in on everything. Don't you dare waste a moment of grief for his sorry ass. You did what you had to do."

"I know, but..."

Sammy held out his arms, and she leaned forward, laying her head on his chest and allowing him to comfort her. For the first time since she'd arrived at the hospital, tears slid down her face. But they were good tears this time, healing tears. Sammy's fingers caressed her scalp and then his fingers stroked her hair. Beth sighed and felt peace settle over her at last.

Long, long minutes later, she pulled away. "Forget about me. You're the one who's been shot. How bad does it hurt?"

"I told you I'm fine," he said gruffly.

"If something had happened to you…" Beth squeezed his hand.

He narrowed his eyes. "Sure everything's all right with you? You must be exhausted. And devastated."

"Aiden's not the worst of it. It's what he said about Cynthia that I can't get out of my head."

"Cynthia?"

"Oh, that's right. Harlan didn't get a chance to fill you in on everything. Aiden claimed that she killed my father by injecting him with oxygen. Apparently, an air embolism did him in."

"Damn it. None of us even suspected there was foul play, Beth. Given his age and history of heart trouble—"

"Of course you couldn't have known." Beth stood and began pacing. "I don't know what to believe anymore. If what Aiden said is true, I want Cynthia to pay for what she did to Dad."

Sammy frowned. "Don't expect a confession from her. And I seriously doubt that there's any evidence after all this time."

What about justice for her father? Had her stepmother gotten away with murder? Beth hugged her arms into her chest. "Do you think Cynthia killed him?" she asked Sammy.

"We may never know for sure, but I'm inclined to think the answer is *yes*."

"Me, too." She recalled the grim amusement on Aiden's face as he described how his mother had caused the fatal heart attack. "Harlan told me she called you and rang the alarm about Aiden. Why do you think she warned you I might be in danger?"

"Could have been one of two things. Either she wanted Aiden caught in the act and arrested, leaving her with your inheritance—"

"Or she truly cares about her son and wanted him to get caught before he killed me and possibly ended up on death row," she said slowly. "I'm guessing it's the first option."

"And she might have tipped us off to cover her bases in case an investigation implicated Aiden. That way, she could claim she acted in your best interests over her son's, even throw doubt on any stories he would tell about her possible involvement in your father's demise."

"I bet she hates me now," Beth muttered. "Not that I particularly care about her opinion. Unless she decides to come after me for shooting Aiden."

"You'll never have to see her again, whether or not she's ever convicted of murder. I won't let her hurt you," Sammy promised, his face grim and his eyes flashing in fury. "Soon as I'm able, I intend to have a little chat with her. I guarantee you by the time I'm finished, she'll never want to step within miles of anywhere you might be. If she knows what's good for her, and I suspect a person like her always has their best interests at heart, Cynthia Wynngate will never again step foot in the State of Georgia."

Beth believed him. "There's only one thing left that troubles me."

"What's that?"

"Dorsey Lambert."

"No need to worry on his account. The man saved both our lives tonight."

"That's what I mean. I feel like I owe him."

"You don't owe him a thing. But if it makes you feel better, we can write a letter to the parole board recommending he be released from parole."

"I want to do more than that. After all, my Dad did take his money and placed an undue hardship on his family." She stopped pacing and nodded her head, decision made. "I'm going to provide him a reward. Enough money so that he can start over in a new life."

"That's incredibly generous. Probably more than he deserves. He and his family did stalk you, remember? They also broke into your home and tried to extort money from you."

She cocked her head to the side and regarded him with a smile. "But they weren't killers. And Dorsey saved your life. For that, he deserves a fresh start."

Beth resumed pacing, her heart growing lighter as she thought of the future. There were so many things she wanted to do, so many wrongs to right. As the daughter of a judge, no matter how much her father had erred later in life, her sense of justice ran deep. And she had her dad to thank for it. For many, many years he'd been honest and fair. Whatever had corrupted him later, she'd grown up with his strong role model of integrity.

It was how she'd choose to honor and remember her father.

Her right foot knocked against something on the floor and she glanced down to find what she'd stumbled upon. A black duffel bag was positioned at the end of the hospital bed.

"Harlan brought it over," he explained. "I asked him to bring that and—"

"What's this?" She lifted the square canvas that had

been leaning against the bag. She held it up to the fluo-rescent overhead light and chuckled with surprise. The edges were charred, and soot blackened a good portion of the bottom, but she recognized it as one of the paint-ings she'd been working on at the cabin.

"I can't believe you kept this."

"Are you kidding me? I risked life and limb to get them."

She laughed. "Crazy man. It wasn't worth it."

"Sure it was. It's beautiful. And you painted it."

She couldn't tear her eyes from the ruined painting. She could redo it, or even try and repair the damaged parts. But Beth decided she wanted them to remain. They were a reminder of the day Sammy had run out of the burning cabin with a handful of her artwork.

The day she'd fallen in love.

"Come here," Sammy demanded gruffly, patting the hospital bed.

Beth propped the painting on the metal nightstand and climbed into bed beside him. She ran a hand through his hair, and he planted a kiss on her forehead. "So you think I'm a crazy man?" he teased, his chest rumbling with laughter. "I'll admit, I'm crazy in love with you."

It was hard to believe her heart could go from the depths of despair from only a few hours earlier, to feel-ing as though it would burst with joy. His admission left her speechless. She knew how deeply his parents' divorce had affected his willingness to make commit-ments.

"I'm not asking you to stay here," he said quickly. "I know you have a life in Boston. But we could see each other long-distance. Plenty of couples—"

She kissed him, long and hard. At last she pulled

away. "I don't want a long-distance relationship. I want to stay right here in Lavender Mountain."

"But won't you miss the excitement of Boston?" His brows drew together in consternation. "What about all your artsy friends and visiting museums? We have nothing of the kind to offer here."

Did he want her to stay or not? Was he still afraid of love and commitment? "I see unparalleled beauty in the Appalachian Mountains that no museum painting can ever replicate," she said quietly.

Sammy appeared unconvinced. "What about all your friends? Your art classes?"

"I can teach anywhere, including Lavender Mountain. And as far as friends and family, all I ever want, or need, is one person who loves, supports and believes in me." She jabbed a finger playfully in his chest. "And that person is you. I love you so much."

"I love you more. But are you sure? Really sure?" Hope flickered in his dark brown eyes, but she also read a worrisome, nagging doubt.

"One hundred percent positive," she assured him. Then she pressed her mouth against his, expressing all her love in the kiss. She was where she was supposed to be, now and forever. Sammy held her in his arms, and long after he'd finally fallen asleep, Beth lay beside him in utter peace and joy as she watched the snow fall on Lavender Mountain.

* * * * *

Paula Graves, an Alabama native, wrote her first book at the age of six. A voracious reader, Paula loves books that pair tantalizing mystery with compelling romance. When she's not reading or writing, she works as a creative director for a Birmingham advertising agency and spends time with her family and friends. Paula invites readers to visit her website, paulagraves.com.

Books by Paula Graves

Harlequin Intrigue

Campbell Cove Academy

Kentucky Confidential
The Girl Who Cried Murder
Fugitive Bride
Operation Nanny

The Gates: Most Wanted

Smoky Mountain Setup
Blue Ridge Ricochet
Stranger in Cold Creek

The Gates

Dead Man's Curve
Crybaby Falls
Boneyard Ridge
Deception Lake
Killshadow Road
Two Souls Hollow

Visit the Author Profile page
at Harlequin.com for more titles.

SMOKY MOUNTAIN SETUP

Paula Graves

For my chat pals, Kelly, Jenn and Donna.
Thanks for keeping me laughing.

Chapter 1

The ligature marks on his wrists had long since healed, but the stinging phantom pain of the raw spots the shackles had chafed into his skin sometimes caught him by surprise. Odd, he thought, given the other injuries he'd sustained during his month of captivity, that those superficial wounds were the ones to continue tormenting him.

He'd had cracked ribs, for sure. A dislocated shoulder he'd been forced to reduce himself, since the rough men who'd taken him captive hadn't cared much about his comfort.

Cade Landry had escaped on the thirty-first day of his captivity, and he'd been running ever since.

Given the icy chill in the air and the heavy clouds overhead threatening snow, he should have headed south to Mexico instead of wandering around the Southern Appalachians while he tried to figure out what to do

next. He could be sipping cerveza on a beach somewhere, flirting with pretty cantina waitresses and soaking up the tropical sun.

It wasn't as if he had any kind of life to get back to
now.

And still, somehow, he'd never completely given up
on the idea of clearing his name, though he'd spent the
past several months avoiding the issue altogether.

No more. It was time to see if there was anything
left of his life to reclaim.

Clouds overhead obscured the sun he'd been using as
his compass, but he was pretty sure he was still headed
west, which would take him out of these mountains
sooner or later. Sooner if he was on the Tennessee side,
later if he was in North Carolina.

Either way, he was heading for Purgatory.

Where *she* was.

You don't know if you can trust her anymore.

Maybe not, he conceded to the mean little voice in
the back of his head. But she was the best shot he had.

He squinted up at the gray sky overhead, enough
sunlight still filtering through the clouds to make his
pupils contract. Definitely still headed west, he decided,
but he hoped he'd reach civilization sooner rather than
later. He had to make a stop in Barrowville first. He'd
made a point to shave that morning, to clean up and
look his most presentable. Maybe he'd get lucky and
somebody would give him a ride into town.

The money he'd hidden away before his abduction
had still been there when he'd escaped, thank God, but
months of living under the radar had taken a toll on his
cash reserves. He needed to see if the money they'd put
away a couple of years ago was still in the bank. It was a

risk, but one he had to take if he wanted to get through the long, cold winter.

Technically, the account was in *her* name, but he was on the account, as well, and as far as he knew, she'd never closed it out.

Maybe it had been as hard for her to let go as it had been for him.

Landry could tell from the color of the sky and the chill in the air that snow was coming, and he'd lived in eastern Tennessee long enough to know that snow-storms in the Smokies could rise up fast, like a rattle-snake, and strike with power and fury.

Just like the men he'd escaped.

Olivia Sharp poked at the fire behind the grate and wrapped her sweater more tightly around her shoulders. Winter in the Smoky Mountains had so far proved to be a cold, damp affair, but tonight they were supposed to get the first snow of the season for the lower elevations.

Growing up on Sand Mountain in Alabama, she'd seen snow now and then, but rarely enough to blanket everything and shut a person in for more than a day or two. But the TV weathermen out of Knoxville were call-ing for as much as a foot and a half in the higher eleva-tions, and the lower elevations could expect five or six inches by morning.

She was safe and snug, tucked in with about a week's worth of background checks to read through. In a com-pany like The Gates, which specialized in high-stakes security cases, everything lived or died on the qual-ity of personnel who worked the cases and kept the company running at peak performance, and the CEO,

Alexander Quinn, had put her in charge of profiling prospective hires.

She was lucky to still have a job at all, she knew. Her first big job at The Gates had been a spectacular failure. Tasked with finding a traitor in their midst, she'd failed to smoke him out until it was nearly too late. Quinn would have been well within his rights to terminate her employment on the spot, but he'd given her another chance.

She had no intention of screwing up again.

She had made it through three files and was starting a fourth when her cell phone rang. No information on the display, which usually meant her caller was Quinn or another agent who didn't want his identity revealed. "Sharp," she answered.

"Hey, Olivia, it's me." The distinctive mountain drawl on the other end of the line belonged to Anson Daughtry, the company's IT director and one of the people who'd saved her bacon during the investigation into the mole at The Gates, mostly by putting his own ass on the line.

Of course, he'd had a good incentive—the pretty payroll accountant he'd fallen hard for had been right in the middle of the danger.

"I thought you were on your honeymoon."

"I am." She could almost hear him grinning. "Ginny says hi."

"Hi, Ginny." She couldn't stop her own smile. She might like to play the role of a tough woman of action, but two good people crazy in love still had the capacity to make her go all squishy inside. "Seriously, Daughtry, why are you calling me on your honeymoon?"

"You remember that bank account you asked me to start monitoring for activity a few months ago?"

She sat up straighter, the muscles of her stomach tightening. "Of course."

"I got an alert in my email. Someone accessed the account a little after one. Withdrew five thousand dollars."

Olivia glanced at the clock over the mantel. About an hour ago. "Any idea what branch?"

"That's the interesting thing," Daughtry said. "It was the one in Barrowville."

"Oh." A cool tingle washed over Olivia's body, sprinkling goose bumps along her arms and legs. "Okay. Thanks for letting me know."

"Is there anything else you need me to do?"

"No," she said quickly. "I just needed the information."

She could tell from Daughtry's thick silence that he had questions about her request and what the information he'd just imparted to her meant. But she simply said, "Thanks. Go enjoy your honeymoon," and hung up the phone before he could ask anything else.

She could be in Barrowville in fifteen minutes. Ten if she drove fast, although the first flurries had already begun to fall outside her cabin window.

No. He wouldn't still be there an hour later. And the information she needed from whichever bank teller had handled the transaction, she could get over the phone.

She looked up the phone number for the bank and made the call, finally reaching the teller in question after a long wait. "How can I help you?"

"My name is Olivia Sharp. I have an account at your bank." She rattled off the account number she'd memorized ages ago. "I just received an alert that some of the money has been accessed and you were the teller who handled the transaction."

"Yes, ma'am," the teller answered. She sounded young and worried.

"He gave his name as Cade Landry?"

"Yes, ma'am. He had the right identification and he knew the account number. He's on the account."

"I'm sure you handled things by the numbers. I just need to know if you remember what he looked like."

The teller was silent for a moment, long enough for Olivia to fear the connection had been lost. But as she was opening her mouth to speak, the teller answered her question. "He was tall. Dark hair. Nice eyes. I don't remember what color, just that they were nice. Friendly, you know?"

Olivia knew about Landry's nice eyes. She knew their color, as well, a soft hue somewhere between hazel and green. "What about his build?"

"His build?"

"You know—heavy, slim—"

"Oh, right. It was…nice. You know, he looked good." There was a nervous vibration in the teller's voice. "Built nice."

"Athletic?"

"Yes, definitely. He looked athletic."

Olivia closed her eyes. "What about his voice? Low? Medium? Did he have an accent?"

"It was deep, I'm pretty sure. And he didn't have an accent, exactly. I mean, he was from down here somewhere."

"Down here" meaning the South, Olivia assumed. If it was really Cade Landry, he'd have spoken with a Georgia drawl. "I see."

"Is there a problem? Our files show Mr. Landry is still authorized to withdraw funds from the account."

The teller was starting to sound worried. "Should I put the bank manager on the phone?"

"No," Olivia said quickly. "Mr. Landry is authorized to withdraw funds. I just wasn't aware he was planning to. Thank you for the information." She hung up the phone and tugged her sweater more tightly around her, trying to control a sudden case of the shakes.

So, someone claiming to be Cade Landry, someone who fit his description and spoke with a Southern accent, had withdrawn $5,000 out of a savings account she'd set up almost two years ago, back when the relationship between her and her FBI partner had been going strong.

Before the disaster in Richmond.

But if it really was Landry who'd withdrawn the money from the account, where the hell had he been for the past year?

The chill in the air had grown bitter as the cold front rolled in, sending the temperature plunging. Overhead, clouds hung low and heavy, threatening snow.

The bank in Barrowville hadn't given him any trouble with the withdrawal, so clearly Olivia hadn't removed his name from the account.

Maybe that was a good sign.

He pedaled harder as the newly purchased thrift-store bike started uphill on Deception Lake Road. Getting her new address had been easy enough—he'd asked for and received the latest copy of the bank statement, which included her home address in Purgatory, Tennessee.

It had been a little too easy, really. What if he'd been an ex-boyfriend stalking her?

Isn't that sort of what you are? The mean voice in his head was back.

Fine, he thought. *I'm her ex-boyfriend. And I'm about to drop by her place unannounced. And I'm armed.*

But the last thing he'd ever do was hurt Olivia, no matter how badly she'd hurt him. He just needed to talk to her. He might not be sure he could trust her, but he knew there was nobody else he could trust.

He'd learned that painful truth the hard way.

By the time he reached the turnoff to Perdition Gap, sleet had begun to fall, making crackling noises where the icy pellets hit the fallen leaves blanketing the roadside. He picked up speed as the road dipped downhill toward the narrow gorge cut into the mountains by Ketoowee River, hurried along by the bitter westerly wind that drove sleet like needle pricks into his bare cheeks.

He'd made his choice. Set himself on a course it was too late to alter, at least for today. Snow was coming, and he had to find shelter soon.

And the cabin looming out of the curling fog ahead was his only choice, for good or for bad.

There was a car parked on the gravel driveway, the same sleek black Mazda she'd driven when they had been together. It gave him pause, the sight of something so achingly familiar in a world that had turned alien on him almost two years ago.

He dismounted the bicycle and walked it slowly up the driveway, still staring at the Mazda, noting a tiny ding in the right front panel that hadn't been there the last time he'd seen it. And there was a small parking decal on the front windshield, as well.

The sound of a door opening drew his gaze back to the house.

She stood there in the doorway, dressed in jeans and a snug blue sweater that hugged her curves like a lover. In one hand she held a Mossberg shotgun at her side. He knew from experience that she could whip that thing up and fire before he could reach for the pistol tucked in his ankle holster, so he froze in place.

He realized he could see her better than she could see him. He was bundled up against the cold and damp, a scarf wrapped around the lower part of his face and a bike helmet perched atop his head.

"Hey there, Sharp."

She stopped short.

"Sorry to drop by without calling," he added, moving slowly toward her again, pushing his bike closer to the cabin.

She took a few steps closer to the porch steps, a tall, fierce warrior of a woman blocking the entry. "So it *was* you at the bank."

He stopped at the bottom of the steps and looked up at her. God, she was beautiful, he thought, taking in the perfect cheekbones, the snapping blue eyes and the windblown blond waves framing her face. She'd cut her hair since they'd worked together. The short style suited her.

"It was," he admitted. "I was afraid you'd closed the account, but I thought I'd take a chance."

"Is that how you found me? Through the bank?"

"Your address was on the account."

"And you found a way to get the teller to show it to you." The faintest hint of a smile made the corners of her mouth twitch.

"I did."

She took a deep breath and released it. "But now

you've left a paper trail. You have to know it won't take long for people to connect you to me and come looking for you."

"It was a calculated risk." He was beginning to feel a potent sense of unreality, standing here in the cold, gazing at a woman he'd once loved more than anyone or anything in his life.

Sometimes, he thought he still did.

"You should turn yourself in."

"Already tried that," he said bluntly, the heat of old anger driving away some of the cold. "Ended up chained in a backwoods cabin for a month. You'll forgive me if I'm not eager to try it again."

Her eyes narrowed. "Is that supposed to be a joke?"

"No. Believe me, there was nothing funny about it." The phantom sting in his wrists returned. He tried to ignore the sensation, hating the frisson of dread that jolted through him each time he experienced the burning pain.

"You look cold."

He couldn't stop a wry laugh, looking around him at the light snowfall. "You think?"

She made a huffing noise but stepped back, opening a path to her door. "Get inside before you freeze."

He grabbed the used duffel full of thrift-store clothes and climbed the stairs slowly, keeping an eye on her and her Mossberg. She didn't look as if she was inclined to shoot him where he stood, but a lot had changed between them since Richmond.

She entered the cabin, leaving the door open for him. A wave of delicious warmth washed over him when he entered, and he quickly closed the door to shut out the cold.

As he started to turn around, he felt cold steel against his neck.

"Put your hands on the door where I can see them." Olivia's voice was calm and cool. "And spread your legs."

"I'm armed," he warned her as he dropped the duffel bag and complied.

"I figured as much." She started to pat him down, her hands moving quickly over his arms, then slowing as she reached his waist. He couldn't quell a shiver of pure sensual awareness as she slid her hands over his hips. "You've lost weight."

"Meals have been hard to come by recently."

She discovered the pistol stashed in his ankle holster and relieved him of it. "Where have you been?"

"Here and there." He felt her retreat, cool air replacing the warmth of her body. "Can I turn around now?"

"Knock yourself out."

He turned to find her emptying the magazine of his Kel-Tec P-11 onto a rolltop desk by the wall. His duffel bag was on the floor by her feet. "Is that really necessary?" he asked with a nod toward the pile of ammunition.

"For now." She removed the round in the chamber and added it to the pile of ammo on the desk before she set the pistol down and turned her cool blue gaze on Landry. "Why did you come here?"

"Nice seeing you again, too, Sharp. It's been such a long time."

She shook her head, her eyes narrowing. "You disappeared nearly a year ago after McKenna Rigsby's undercover mission went very wrong. At least one corrupt FBI agent has gone missing, and the Bureau is scrambling like crazy to find out what other agents might be compromised. You are on the top of their list."

"I know."

"And yet, here you are. Did you think I would just turn a blind eye to the fact that you're wanted by the FBI for questioning?"

She was magnificent when she was angry. Always had been. Her blue eyes took on an amazing electric hue, and the atmosphere around her crackled with energy. He felt drawn to her, despite himself, and took a helpless step forward. "Livvie—"

"Don't." She held up her hand, a pained look replacing the fire in her eyes. "Please don't call me that."

"I know you have questions. But I've spent the last two hours riding a bicycle in the bitter cold. I'm tired. I'm freezing. I haven't eaten since yesterday. It's snowing out, and I need shelter. Food, if you can spare any. In exchange, I'll tell you everything I've been doing for the past two years, and if you still want to turn me in to the FBI after that, then fine. I'll accept that. Because I'm sick to death of running."

Her forehead creased as she considered what he'd just said. "You'll turn yourself in if I say so?"

He nodded, meaning it. He hadn't realized it until he saw her again, but he really was through running. He'd trusted the wrong person once and lost his freedom for a month—and damned near lost his life in the process.

But he had to trust someone, or what was the point of going on? He couldn't keep living under the radar forever.

And he'd already gone nearly two years without seeing Olivia Sharp. There had been a time when he couldn't have imagined such a thing, couldn't have considered even a week without her, much less a lifetime without her spreading out in front of him as far as the eye could see.

"Were you working with the Blue Ridge Infantry?" she asked, breaking the tense silence between them.

He met her gaze, took a deep breath and answered the question with the truth.

"Yes," he said.

Chapter 2

Hearing Cade Landry admit what she'd spent the past year trying not to believe shouldn't have felt like a kick in the teeth. But somehow, it did. It hit her hard enough that she took an involuntary step backward, her foot catching on the braided rug in the cabin's entry.

As she started to lose her balance, Landry lurched forward and caught her before she could fall, his arms wrapping around her waist. His hands were cold—she could feel the chill through her sweater—but his touch sent fire singing through her blood.

He'd always had that effect on her. Even when he shouldn't.

She pulled free of his grasp, steadying herself by clutching the edge of the desk. "How long?"

He stared at her, a puzzled expression on his face.

"How long did you work for the Blue Ridge Infantry?" When he didn't answer right away, she added, "Are you still working for them? Is that why you came here?"

He took a deep breath and let it out in a soft *whoosh*. "I was never working *for* them."

She shook her head, shock starting to give way to a fury that burned like acid in her gut. "Don't play semantics games with me, Landry."

His dark eyebrows arched, creasing his forehead. "Are you going to listen to what I have to say or should we just cut to the part where you call the cops to come haul my ass out of here?"

"The latter, I think." She went for her shotgun.

He beat her there, jerking it out of her grasp. "Don't," he said sharply as she changed course, going for the P-11 she'd just emptied.

She froze in place, turning slowly to look at him. Something hot and painful throbbed just under her breastbone as she met his hard gaze. "Just get it over with."

"I'm not what you think I am," he said, lowering the Mossberg to his side. "That's what I was trying to tell you."

"You'll forgive me if I have a little trouble believing you."

His lips pressed to a thin line. "I was really hoping you, of all people, would look beyond the obvious."

She pushed down a sudden flutter of guilt. "You don't get to play the victim card. You're the one who disappeared almost a year ago without telling anyone where you were going."

"I did tell someone," he said quietly, lowering the shotgun to the floor, still within his reach. "I told my

SAC at the Johnson City RA that I had information the FBI needed to know about the Blue Ridge Infantry. And the next thing I knew, I was being bludgeoned and hauled to some backwoods hellhole and beaten to within an inch of my life."

For a second she pictured what he was saying, imagined him tied up and pummeled by the vicious hillbillies who comprised the mountain militia known as the Blue Ridge Infantry, and nausea burned in her gut. She knew from her own investigations that the hard-eyed men who ran the so-called militia as a criminal organization were capable of great cruelty. If they'd ever lived by a code of honor, those days were long past.

Money and power drove them. In these hills these days, money and power too often came from drugs, guns and extortion.

"You told your SAC?" She repeated his earlier statement, trying to remember the name of the Johnson City resident agency's Special Agent in Charge. "Pete Chang, right?"

He nodded. "I didn't think he was corrupt. He's a brownnoser, yeah, so maybe he told the wrong person the wrong thing. I don't know."

"You've been a prisoner all this time?" she asked, looking him over with a critical eye. "Take off your coat."

He looked down at the heavy wool coat he was still wearing, a frown carving lines in his cheeks. "I wasn't a prisoner the whole time," he said gruffly as he unbuttoned the coat and shrugged it off. Beneath, he still wore a couple of layers of clothes—a long-sleeved shirt beneath a thick sweater—but while he looked leaner than she remembered, he definitely didn't look as if he'd been starved for nearly a year.

"Then why didn't you go to the FBI once you were free?"

"I just told you that the last time I told anyone with the FBI what I was doing, I ended up a prisoner of the Blue Ridge Infantry." He pushed the sleeves of his shirt and sweater up to his elbows, revealing what they'd hidden until now—white ligature scars around both wrists.

Olivia swallowed a gasp. It was stupid to react so sharply to the scars—in the pantheon of injuries she'd seen inflicted in this ongoing war between the Blue Ridge Infantry and the good guys, the marks on Landry's wrists barely registered.

It was what they represented—the loss of freedom, the indignity of captivity—that made her heart pound with sudden dread.

Or they could be a trick, she reminded herself sternly as she felt her resistance begin to falter. He could have inflicted the marks on himself to fool people into believing his story.

The fact remained, he'd just stood here minutes ago and admitted he'd been working with the Blue Ridge Infantry. And nobody who worked with the Blue Ridge Infantry was ever up to any good.

"What are you thinking?" Landry spoke in a low, silky voice so familiar it seemed to burrow into her head and take up residence, like a traveler finally reaching home after a long absence.

She fought against that sensation and gripped the edge of the desk more tightly. "That's really none of your business."

"You're not curious?" he asked, his eyes narrowing as he took a step closer to her. "You don't want to hear all the details?"

She held his gaze but didn't speak.

"Or maybe you really don't give a damn anymore." He spoke the words casually, but she'd known him long enough to recognize the thread of hurt that underlay his comment.

"You're the one who left," she said.

"Are you sure I was the one?" He took another step toward her, and she tried to back away. But the wall stopped her.

"You packed your things and left."

"You'd already left. Maybe not your body, but the rest of you—the part of you that really mattered—" He stopped his forward advancement, looking down at the rough planks of the cabin floor beneath his damp boots. "Doesn't change the outcome, does it? We both walked away and didn't look back, right?"

"Why did you come here?" she asked again, not because she believed he'd answer her any more truthfully than before, but because it was better than thinking about just how many times over the past two years, with how much regret, she'd looked back on the life she and Landry had once shared.

"Because I thought—" He looked up at her, pinning her to the wall with the intensity of his green-eyed gaze. "It doesn't matter what I thought, does it? You've made up your mind about me. I get it." He turned away, heading for the door.

She hurried forward and picked up the shotgun. "I didn't say you could leave."

He turned to look at her. "You're going to shoot me to stop me?"

"If I have to." She sounded sincere enough, even

to her own skeptical ears. But her heart wasn't nearly as sure.

She'd loved him once, as much as she'd ever loved anyone in her whole life. Hell, maybe she still did.

If he tried to leave, would she really pull the trigger to stop him from fleeing?

"You won't shoot me," he said softly. "At least, that's what I want to keep believing. So I won't put you in that position."

"You'll turn yourself in?"

He frowned. "I'd rather not. At least, not yet. There's a lot I still need to tell you before you'll understand exactly what we're up against and why."

"What *we're* up against?"

He nodded. "I have to assume someone at that bank in Barrowville will remember the name Cade Landry. And why it's so memorable. They'll call the authorities to report my visit to the bank. And like you said, it won't take long for them to connect us. We were partners, Olivia." He moved toward her, walking with slow, sure deliberation. "Lovers."

His voice lowered to a sensual rumble, bringing back a flood of memories she'd spent two years trying to excise from her brain. "Don't."

"It's too late to undo it, Livvie. I took a risk coming here, and maybe I shouldn't have." He came to a stop just a few inches from where she stood, and she made herself remain in place, though the pounding pulse in her ears seemed to plead for her to run as far and as fast as she could.

Losing him once had nearly unraveled her. If she let him back into her heart—into her bed—again…

"I said I was working with the Blue Ridge Infantry,

and that's the truth. But it's only part of it." His hand came up slowly until his fingertips brushed her jawline, sending a shiver of sexual awareness jolting through her. "Did you know they were targeting The Gates?"

She swallowed with difficulty. "Of course. We've been trying to bring them down since Quinn first opened the doors of The Gates."

"I'm not on their side, Olivia. That's not what I meant by working with them—" He stopped midsentence, his head coming up suddenly. It took a moment for Olivia to hear what he'd obviously heard—a car engine moving up the road toward her cabin.

Landry moved away from her and crossed to her front window, sliding the curtains open an inch.

"Could be a neighbor," she said quietly, suddenly afraid he was going to bolt, even though a few minutes earlier, she'd been hoping he'd leave and not look back.

It was just curiosity, she told herself, the need to know what he'd been starting to tell her about his connection to the BRI. It certainly had nothing to do with the way her jaw still tingled where he'd touched her or the quickened pace of her heart whenever she looked his way.

"They're stopping here," he said bluntly, turning back to look at her. She saw fear in his eyes, raw and wild, and realized she had only a few seconds to keep him from doing something reckless.

She pushed past him and looked through the curtains. The truck that had stopped outside her house was a familiar but, under the circumstances, not exactly welcome sight. "It's Alexander Quinn."

Landry groaned. "Your boss."

She looked at him, wondering how much he knew

about Quinn. "You said you're not on the BRI's side. Neither is Quinn. If you know anything about The Gates, you have to know that."

"That doesn't mean he's going to turn a blind eye to the warrants out for my arrest."

"You might be surprised."

He shook his head and picked up his duffel bag. "I'm going out the back. Just give me a head start."

She caught his arm as he started past her, not letting go even when he tried to tug free of her grasp. "Don't run. Not yet. My bedroom is through that doorway. First room on the right. Let me find out what Quinn wants."

Landry stared at her as if he were trying to read all the way through to her soul. Finally, the sound of footsteps on the front porch spurred him into action. He went through the doorway and veered right into her bedroom, closing the door behind him with a soft click.

Olivia took a deep breath just as Quinn knocked.

Showtime.

Her room smelled like Olivia, that half-sweet, half-tart scent he'd never been able to identify as anything other than her own unique essence. For a few seconds all he could do was breathe, fill his lungs with that scent, store it away for another drought like the two years they'd been apart since he'd left Richmond—and Olivia—behind.

The bedroom was small and sparsely furnished—a bed, a chest of drawers and a small trunk at the foot of the bed. The bedding was simple and neat—two pillows in pale blue cotton cases, sheets that matched and a thick quilt that looked handmade.

Despite the tension running through him like currents of electricity, despite the muted sound of the door knock just a room away, Landry couldn't stop himself from smiling. It faded quickly, but the flicker of sentiment remained—she hadn't really changed in the past two years if she was still decorating with handmade quilts.

She made the quilts herself, a secret she'd kept from her fellow FBI agents with the ferocity of a mother bear guarding her den. "If you ever tell anyone about this," she'd sworn when she'd finally let him in on her secret, "I will hunt you down and kill you."

The sound of voices drifted down the hallway. The rumble of a male voice, barely discernible, followed by Olivia's alto drawl.

"New bike?" the male voice asked.

"Picked it up at a yard sale," Olivia answered.

Landry pressed his ear to the door, trying to hear the conversation more clearly.

"It's a man's bike," Quinn said in a tone that was deliberately nonchalant.

"I bought it from a man," she answered, a shrug in her voice. "Women's bikes are usually too small for a woman my height."

Good save, Landry thought.

"I got a call from Daughtry," Quinn said, still sounding like someone making small talk. "He said you got a hit on some bank account you'd asked him to monitor."

"That man doesn't know the meaning of *honeymoon*, does he?" Olivia laughed softly, but Landry heard the faint strain of tension behind her words.

Did Quinn hear it, too?

"One of the reasons I hired him," Quinn answered. "But that doesn't answer my question."

"You didn't ask a question."

Still as smart-mouthed as ever, Landry thought.

"Whose account did you ask him to monitor?"

"Mine," she replied. "I've been noticing some discrepancies in my bank statement, so I thought maybe someone had hacked my password for that account. It's not a lot of money, but still."

"So there's someone tapping into your account? Why didn't you just change the password?"

"That would only stop them from accessing the account. I wanted to catch someone in the act."

"Did you?"

"Maybe. I have some feelers out."

Landry didn't hear anything else for several long seconds, not even an unintelligible murmur that would suggest they'd merely lowered their voices. The silence was unnerving. If he couldn't hear them, he had no way of knowing where they were.

Or how close they were getting to his hiding place.

Come on, he thought. *Start talking again.*

"As much as I relish the screwball comedy potential of being snowed in with you, Quinn, you're not going to be able to get that truck back down the mountain if you don't make tracks in the next few minutes."

"Now you're just tempting me, Olivia." There was a warmth to Quinn's voice that made Landry's gut tighten.

What the hell?

"Funny," Olivia said, but there was no censure in her voice, only a soft amusement that made Landry want to kick down the door.

"Are you sure you're going to be okay here alone? A few of the agents are bunking down at the office for the duration. It's a little college dorm for my tastes, but

I think you can handle the frat-boy atmosphere if you'd rather tough it out in a crowd."

"No, thanks," she said with a laugh that was too friendly for Landry's peace of mind. "I'll be fine here. I have a load of résumés to go through and some housework I've put off for the past couple of months. But thanks for the concern."

"Are you sure everything's okay?" Quinn asked in a tone so quiet and intimate Landry had to strain to make out the words.

"Everything's fine."

"Olivia, I know you're blaming yourself for how close Daughtry and Ginny came to losing their lives, but you're not infallible. Nobody in this business is. We all make mistakes."

Olivia's response was spoken too quietly for Landry to hear. But Quinn's next words gave him a pretty good idea what she'd said.

"There are a lot of ways to pay for mistakes. Sometimes your own conscience is the harshest judge of all. I think you've already given yourself more penance than I'd have ever suggested. That's why I let you come up with your own punishment."

"I would have fired me."

"That's why you're not the boss."

There was another long silence. Landry clenched his fists to keep from reaching for the door handle.

"Call if you need anything. I might know how to get my hands on a snowmobile." Quinn's voice, tinged with amusement, broke the silence, and Landry started breathing again.

He heard the door close and waited until he heard Olivia's footsteps outside the door.

"Still in there?" she asked quietly.

He opened the door to face her. "I was contemplating escape."

"He's gone."

"I heard."

One sandy eyebrow arched over a sky blue eye. "You were eavesdropping?"

"Was there something you didn't want me to hear?"

The other eyebrow joined the first, creasing her forehead. "What's that supposed to mean?"

He meant to change the subject, talk about what a bad idea it was for him to stick around the cabin with her in case her boss decided to come back to check on her in that snowmobile he'd mentioned. But those weren't the words that came out of his mouth.

Instead, to his dismay, he asked, "What the hell is going on between you and your boss?"

Chapter 3

"You were right," Quinn said. "He's there."

Anson Daughtry's voice over the phone picked up a little static as Quinn eased his Ford F-150 pickup around a mountain curve. "What are you going to do about it?"

"Right now? Nothing. She's going to be snowed in with him for a couple of days, and maybe she'll get some information out of him."

"Did you bug the place?" Daughtry's question was delivered bone dry, but Quinn knew his IT director's unfavorable opinion about eavesdropping, especially on employees at The Gates.

"If I did, I wouldn't tell you," Quinn answered just as drily.

"So, you're just leaving her alone with him, without any way of knowing whether or not she might be in trouble?"

"She knows how to call for help if she needs it."

Daughtry made a sound of pure frustration. "Don't you think he's dangerous?"

"I'm *sure* he's dangerous. To someone. The question is, to whom?"

"So you're just letting Sharp find out for you? In a snowbound cabin?"

"If I can't trust my agents to handle themselves in dangerous situations with dangerous people, what the hell am I doing running a security firm?" Quinn had hired Olivia Sharp because everything he'd ever heard about her told him she was perfectly capable of holding her own in a high-risk situation. She'd been a member of an elite FBI SWAT team for six years, and in every dangerous situation he'd put her in since hiring her, she'd proved her mettle. "Sharp is every bit as dangerous as Cade Landry ever thought of being, and she doesn't have any illusions where he's concerned."

"She was involved with him before."

"What makes you think that?" Quinn asked carefully.

"I hear things."

"Then maybe you heard that they're no longer together. And that it ended badly. Which means she's not going to assume his motives for showing up at her cabin in the middle of a snowstorm are entirely pure."

"Love's not that straightforward," Daughtry said bluntly, in the tone of a man on his honeymoon.

"Let me worry about my agents, Daughtry. You worry about your wife. I'm sure she's shooting you glaring looks by now, considering how long we've been on this call." He pressed the end-call button on his phone and stifled a smile. One of his still-single agents had recently groused that the marriage bug was spreading like a contagion at the office, and Quinn couldn't really deny it.

Take a pair of single, physically fit, energetic and bright people, toss them in the middle of a high-risk, high-stakes situation and step back, because sparks were going to fly. A lot of the time, those sparks fizzled out to nothing once the danger was over, but in some cases, his agents had made real connections with each other, the kind that had a chance to last a lifetime.

Quinn was about as far as a man got from being a romantic, but he'd learned a long time ago not to interfere when a man and a woman wanted to be together.

Very bad things could happen.

Olivia stared at Cade Landry, certain she'd misunderstood his question. Because there was no way in the world he'd just stood there and asked her what was going on between her and Alexander Quinn, as if it was any business of his. He wasn't a fool or an idiot, and only one of those would stand here in her bedroom doorway, two years after walking out of her life without even a goodbye, and question anything at all about her personal life. Especially in that particular tone of outrage.

But here he was, gazing at her with green eyes blazing with fury, his jaw muscles tight and his nostrils flaring.

"We're going to pretend you didn't just ask me that question," she said in a deceptively soft voice. But she could tell from the troubled look in Landry's eyes that he heard the undertones of danger.

"I'm sorry. You're right. I'm in no position to question anything about your life." He looked down and started to move around her, heading toward the front room.

"Where are you going?" She caught up with him as he was reaching for the unloaded pistol still lying on her rolltop desk.

"I shouldn't have come here."

She caught his hand, stopping him as he started to pick up the pistol. "Why *did* you come here? Why now?"

He looked down at her hand covering his, and she felt the muscles in his wrist twitch as he slowly turned to look at her. "Because I don't know what to do next. And you were always my go-to."

Her heart squeezed into a painful knot. "Even now?"

"Maybe especially now." He eased his hand from her grasp. She made herself let go as he took a step past her, back toward the center of the room. "Maybe it's better we're more like strangers to each other these days. You can be objective about what I should do next."

She couldn't be objective about him, but she didn't bother saying so. She needed to hear where he'd been and what he'd been doing for the past seven months.

"Look, why don't you sit down in front of the fire? You still look cold." She picked up the knit throw blanket draped over the back of the sofa and handed it to him. "Get warm. I'm going to heat you up a bowl of soup. You want a sandwich, too?"

He took the blanket but shook his head. "I didn't come here for you to take care of me." A look of frustration creased his face.

"Then why did you come here?" she asked softly when he didn't continue.

"I needed to see you." The words seemed to escape his mouth against his will. The look of consternation in his green eyes might have been comical under other circumstances.

But Olivia couldn't laugh. She knew exactly what that raw ache of need felt like. She knew what it was like to wake in the middle of the night and feel compelled to reach out for someone who was no longer there beside her. For almost two years, she and Landry had been a unit. Inseparable.

She should have known it would never last. Forever was the exception in most relationships, not the rule. And with her family history, she should never have allowed herself to think she might be able to beat the odds.

"I wish you'd wanted to see me two years ago when I tried to reach you."

Landry looked down, one hand circling his other wrist as if to soothe the scars that formed a circle there. "I should have listened to you when you tried to explain."

"You were too angry."

"I felt betrayed."

Her heart ached at the pain in his voice, but she didn't let herself fall into that morass again. She'd spent too much time blaming herself for Landry's anger when there had been nothing else she could do but exactly what she'd done. "I'm sorry you felt betrayed. But short of lying about what I remembered, I couldn't help you."

His gaze snapped up. "I know. I expected too much."

"You expected me to lie?"

He shook his head. "I expected you to believe me, without question. I thought you would know I was telling the truth, even if you didn't remember."

She stared back at him, guilt niggling at the back of her mind. "I do believe that you remember hearing an order to go into the warehouse instead of holding our position. But that's not what you were asking me to say."

He let out a gusty sigh. "I don't know that I was really asking anything of you except your trust and belief in me. But you never could really give me that, could you? Not wholeheartedly."

Guilt throbbed even harder, settling in the center of her chest. "You know blind trust is a problem for me. You knew that going in." She looked up at him. "I warned you, Landry. And you said you could deal with it."

"Because I thought *you* could." He looked away from her, his gaze angling toward the window beside the fireplace. After a second she followed his gaze and saw that the snowfall was starting to reach blizzard proportion, whiting out everything around the cabin.

"The power probably won't hold out much longer," she warned him, moving toward the hall. "If you want something hot for dinner, we should heat it up while we still have electricity."

He followed her down the short hallway to the kitchen at the back of the cabin. "I don't want to put you out."

"It's soup from a can. I'll heat it in the microwave. You're not putting me out." She pulled a large can of beef stew from the pantry and showed it to him. "How's this?"

"It's fine. Thank you. Can I help with anything?"

"Again, soup from a can, heated in the microwave." She shot him a look of amusement. "Sit down, Landry. You look as if you rode a bicycle here all the way from Bitterwood."

"Barrowville," he corrected her with a wry grimace. "Which was a breeze compared to hoofing it here on foot from North Carolina."

Olivia set the can on the counter and turned to look at him. "North Carolina?"

"I don't want to talk about it right now, okay?" As he met her gaze, waning daylight cast his face in light and shadows, emphasizing how much older he looked now than the last time she'd seen him. The past two years had been hard on him. Aged him, left fine lines around his eyes and mouth.

"Okay," she said quietly and returned to the task of preparing soup for their dinner.

He ate as if he hadn't eaten in days, though, as she'd noticed before, he didn't appear thin enough to have skipped too many meals over the months he'd been missing. Without being asked, she opened another can of soup and heated it up for him.

"Thank you," he told her after he'd finished the second can of soup. "I haven't had anything but protein bars and water for the past two days."

She wanted to ask him what had happened to him, but there was a warning light in his eyes when she leaned toward him, as if he'd read her mind.

She sat back and finished her own soup slowly as he took his bowl and spoon to the sink and washed them. When he was done, he walked past the table and went to stand by the kitchen window to watch it snow.

"How long is the snow supposed to last?" he asked.

"It should snow all night. We should get about six or seven inches, and the temperature isn't going to get above freezing for a couple of days after that. There's a slight chance for more snow day after tomorrow, but the weather guys aren't as sure about that." So he hadn't been near a television or radio in the past few days, either, she noted silently.

Just where the hell had he been all this time?

Olivia's cabin was large and tastefully rustic, but Landry had a feeling the place had come fully furnished. Outside of her bedroom, there was little in the cabin that reminded him of her apartment back in Richmond, a small loft apartment that she'd decorated in cool colors and clean lines. Even her beloved quilts had been stitched together in straight patterns, using fabrics in blues, greens and whites. Uncluttered and organized— that had been the Olivia Sharp he'd known and loved.

But he could tell she'd changed, just as he had. She'd left the FBI first, left him and his anger behind. He'd been both furious and hurt at first, but after what he'd gone through over the past few months, hanging on to resentment seemed pointless.

"I don't have a spare bed."

He looked up to find her standing in the living room doorway, holding another thick quilt like the one he'd seen on her bed. "You have a sofa. That'll do."

She handed him the quilt. It was another of her creations; he could tell by the geometric precision of the pattern.

"Still quilting?" he asked as she started to leave the room.

She stopped and turned to face him. "When I have time. Which isn't often these days."

He set the quilt on the sofa next to him and waved toward one of the armchairs across from where he sat. "You like working at The Gates?"

She sat and folded her hands in her lap. "I do."

"Your boss seems very interested in your welfare."

The look she sent slicing his way was sharp enough to cut.

"Sorry. Too soon?"

"Quinn takes an interest in all of his employees," she said flatly.

"He's trying to take down the Blue Ridge Infantry."

She didn't answer, her eyes narrowing.

"I'm not a traitor, Olivia."

"You never told me how you got mixed up with the BRI." She crossed her long legs and sat back, pinning him with a challenging stare. "I know you tried to help McKenna Rigsby when she was targeted by the Blue Ridge Infantry. You talked to one of our agents, tried to warn him about Darryl Boyle's involvement with the BRI. But one question never really got answered, once you disappeared—"

"How did I know about Boyle?"

"Exactly."

He tried to relax, as well, even though he suspected that some of Olivia's placid composure was an act. He knew his unexpected arrival on her doorstep that afternoon had been a shock to her system, but as usual, she was trying not to let it show.

"I suspected, when Rigsby supposedly went rogue, that something very bad had driven her there. She struck me as a good agent. She sure as hell hadn't joined the Blue Ridge Infantry—she hated them with a passion, hated everything they were doing and how they were twisting things like honor and patriotism for their own purposes." He couldn't hold back a smile remembering Rigsby's tirades. "She vented to me. A lot. She was undercover, trying to get close to some of the female militia groupies, so she had to pretend she thought they hung the moon when she was with them."

Olivia's lips curved with amusement. "She's so not groupie material."

"So you know her."

"I do." She didn't elaborate.

"Is she okay?"

Her smile faded. "She's fine."

"I didn't get to find out what happened to her after she was taken."

"Because you were grabbed by the BRI guys."

God, he hated the skepticism in her voice, the hint of disbelief, as if he'd have disappeared for a year just for the hell of it. "You don't believe me."

"I never said that."

He pushed to his feet. "You didn't have to."

She stood, as well, and caught his arm. "Don't do this. I'm trying to understand what's happened to you."

"You're looking at me as if I'm crazy. Is that what you think?"

"Of course not." Her grip softened, her fingers sliding slowly down his arm to his wrist, where they settled against his scars. "I just need to know why you stayed away so long. Where have you been?"

"After I got away from the guys who took me, I headed east into North Carolina." He gave a little tug of his arm and she let go of his wrist.

"Why east?" she asked.

"Because when I got out of that hovel where they were keeping me, that's the way I was facing. So I ran and didn't look back." He looked down at his scarred wrists.

"Until now. Why did you come back now?"

He looked at her, saw the curiosity in those summer-sky eyes and blurted the truth. "Because you're a target. And you needed to know."

Chapter 4

"That's why you're here? You thought we didn't know we were on the BRI's hit list?" Olivia shook her head, not buying it. "I told you already. We know—"

"I don't mean The Gates is the target," Landry said in a quiet tone that made her chest ache. "I mean *you*, Olivia. The BRI is trying to get their hands on *you*."

She stared at him, trying to read past the mirrorlike calm of his green eyes. "How would you know this? You said you hadn't had anything to do with the BRI since your escape."

"I didn't say that."

She thought for a moment and realized he hadn't. She'd assumed it, given that the BRI had taken him hostage and, according to what he had told her, beaten him terribly to get information out of him.

"Maybe you should sit down and tell me what you

know." She waved at the sofa and sat facing him on the coffee table, crossing her long legs under her. "How do you know I've been targeted?"

He leaned forward, resting his elbows on his knees. The action brought him close to her, close enough to touch. All she'd have to do is reach her hand toward him and—

"I got away from the BRI. But I still know some people who lurk around the edges of that group. People who aren't on the inside but are close to men who are."

A cold tingle rippled through her. "Women, you mean. The groupies."

"A couple. Also a few guys who sympathize with the stated goals of the group but don't like their methods or trust that they're what they say they are. There are a lot of people in these parts who've seen the mess government interference has made among their kinfolk and neighbors. You have multiple generations who've known nothing but life on welfare."

"The draw," Olivia murmured. At his quizzical look, she added, "That's what people here call it. 'The draw.'"

"They can't live without it, but some of them hate what it's turned them into, too." He stood up and paced toward the fireplace, leaning toward the heat as if he'd felt a chill. "It makes it very tempting to hook up with people like the BRI."

"I know." She'd grown up poor herself. Had struggled to escape the cycle of poverty and bad choices that had haunted her family for a couple of generations. "People don't want to feel victimized. Being part of the BRI gives them a sense of power."

"There's a young man I got to know over the past couple of months. Little more than a kid, really. We worked a few day labor jobs together over near Cherokee. His uncle is part of the Blue Ridge Infantry, but this kid is smarter than that. They keep trying to recruit him, but he resists. He's saving up all his money, planning to go to a technical college over in Asheville."

"He's the one who told you the BRI is targeting me?"

"Not exactly." Landry crossed to the coffee table and sat on the edge, facing her. He leaned closer, his gaze intense.

Once again, the desire to reach across the narrow space between them hit her like a physical ache. She curled her hands into fists and kept them in her lap. "Then what, exactly?"

"He got me into a meeting where they were planning their next move in the war against The Gates."

She stared at him. "You were in a meeting with the BRI and they didn't shoot you on sight?"

"Well, they didn't know I was there," he said with a grin that carved dimples in both cheeks, sending her heart into a flip. "The meeting was at his uncle's place, and there's a big vent in the den where they met. My friend lived with his uncle's family for a while when his mama was in rehab a few years ago, and he found out that if you listen through the vent in his old bedroom, you can hear what they're saying in that den clear as day."

"He let you listen in? Does he know who you are?"

Landry shook his head. "I told him I was thinking of joining the BRI because I was tired of how the federal government was taking over every aspect of our lives. He sympathized, but he told me the BRI wasn't the way to go. They were nothing but trouble and he could prove it."

"By letting you listen in on a meeting."

"Yes."

"And you overheard them making a threat against me?"

"Not by name."

"Then how do you know?"

"They called you Bombshell Barbie."

She arched an eyebrow at him. "And that told you it was me?"

"No. What told me it was you was that one of them said you were dangerous as hell and wouldn't go down without a fight. The combination of the two—the nickname and the statement about your fighting spirit—that's what told me it was you."

She stifled a smile, not sure she should feel quite as complimented as she did. "Bombshell Barbie, huh?"

He held up his hands. "I didn't come up with it."

"I know. I'm pretty sure a guy named Marty Tucker did. He was up to his nasty eyeballs in the BRI until he shot himself trying to escape a colony of bats."

"Bats?"

"Long story. He lived. Now he's in state prison, serving time for kidnapping and other assorted crimes. Sadly, he's chosen to keep all his secrets about the BRI to himself, so we're not any closer to bringing them down than we were before." She frowned. "Matter of fact, they've been really quiet recently. No chatter coming out of there at all that we've heard."

"Until now."

"Until now." She cocked her head. "How long have you known about this target on my back?"

"Two days."

"And you didn't think to call and warn me?"

He slanted a look at her. "You'd have believed it was me on the other line?"

"Probably not," she admitted.

"I knew you'd need proof."

"What kind of proof?"

"An audio recording of the BRI's plans."

An electric pulse of excitement zinged through her. "You have that?"

He shook his head. "Not on me. I didn't want to risk getting caught with it. I put it in a safe place."

"Where?"

"I can't tell you that. Not yet."

Her spine stiffened, and angry heat warmed her face. "You can't tell me? I'm the one in danger and you can't tell me?"

His gaze flicked around the cozy room. "How do you know this place isn't wired for sound?"

"I check it periodically for bugs," she said flatly, trying to control her frustration.

"Using what equipment? Something you got from work?"

"Yes." She met his questioning look without flinching, even though she knew where he was going with the question. "And yes, I realize Quinn probably has a way to get around a bug detector he himself supplied. But I trust him with my life."

Landry's eyes narrowed and he pulled back. "Really? Well, I don't."

She bit back a protest and counted to ten. Landry had no reason to trust Quinn, after all. Or anyone else, she supposed, considering what he claimed he'd been through over the past few months. "Fair enough."

"It's safe for now."

"But the BRI is still after me?"

He nodded, easing forward again. "I don't know the timing of what they have in the works. I know only what they're planning to do. What you need to look for."

Another chill washed through her, raising goose bumps on her arms and legs. "Do you mean to keep that a secret, too?"

A small flicker in the corner of his eye was his only reaction to her blunt question. "No, of course not."

"So what do I look for?"

"First, it's not going to be your standard hit. No sniper shot, nothing like that."

She had an unsettling sense of unreality, listening to Landry speak of her impending death as if it was just another case to be investigated. "Is that good news or bad news?"

His gaze snapped up to meet hers. "None of this is good news."

"Right."

He suddenly reached across the space between them, closing his hand over hers. As if he'd read her earlier thoughts, in an urgent tone he added, "This is not just another case for me, Livvie. No matter what happened between us two years ago, you will never, ever be just another case for me."

As she stared at him, heat spreading through her from the point where his fingers had closed around hers, he let go and sat back, clearly struggling to regain his cool composure.

"I'm sorry," she murmured. "Go on."

"They're going to take you when you're alone. So you need to make sure you're never alone."

"That's impossible."

"Look, I know your boss offered you the chance to stay at the office with some of the other agents. Maybe you should do that."

She looked at the whiteout conditions outside the cabin window. "Too late for that."

He followed her gaze. "I'm sure your boss could come up with some way to get you out of here."

She shook her head quickly. "Landry, I'm safe enough here. For now, anyway. I'm armed and it's not easy to get here in the snow. And you're here, right?"

He nodded toward the rolltop desk. "But I'm unarmed."

She met his warm gaze, trying to be objective, to put everything from their past, good or bad, out of her mind and just assess the situation as an agent.

He'd shown up unannounced, after having disappeared for nearly a year, and told her that he'd been working with the same dangerous militia group he now said had made her a target for assassination. But he'd come alone and warned her of the danger against her. He'd had the opportunity to hurt her earlier, when he'd got the drop on her with her Mossberg shotgun, but he'd done nothing to hurt her.

Was he trying to pull some sort of scam? Was this story about hillbilly assassins part of some bigger plan the BRI had hatched?

Or was he telling her the truth?

"Why?" she asked finally.

His eyebrows twitched upward. "Why did I come? I told you—"

She shook her head. "No—why has BRI targeted me specifically? Do you know?"

"They didn't say. At least, not the part of their discussion I was able to overhear."

"What about your friend? The kid whose uncle is a BRI member. Would he be able to find out why they've targeted me?"

"If I could get in touch with him, yes. But that's very dangerous. Even more so for him than for me. He took a big chance letting me sneak in to eavesdrop on the meeting. If either of us had been caught…"

She quelled a shudder as her mind finished the sentence for him, in vivid, brutal images. She'd seen the lengths to which the BRI would go to carry out a plan. "I get it."

"After the snow thaws, I'll see if I can reach him. But I'll have to be very careful."

She pushed to her feet, nervous energy getting the better of her. "There has to be something I can do while we're waiting. Research or something—"

He stood and crossed to her, closing his hands around her arms and pulling her to face him. His expression was fierce at first, but it softened when she met his gaze.

"I'll tell you everything I can remember from what I overheard," he said in a tone so earnest, so familiar, it made her heart ache. "This all has to be confusing and disturbing—"

"Don't do that," she murmured. "Don't handle me."

Slowly, he dropped his hands away from her arms, but the sensation of his touch lingered, making her feel jittery and unsettled. "Let's sit down, okay? Take a second and breathe."

He was still handling her, but at least he wasn't touching her. She returned to the armchair, and he sat on the coffee table in front of her.

So close. So palpable a temptation.

"They managed to get someone inside The Gates—Marty Tucker, I presume—but he was inside before you got there. They don't assume their limited success with Tucker can be repeated, especially since you're still there, sniffing out any possible traitors in your midst."

"How do they know that?"

"They said Quinn's not trying to hide that information. In fact, he made sure it got out through some of the information channels the BRI already knows are compromised."

Olivia straightened, alarmed. "Quinn put information about me and my role at The Gates out there for the BRI to hear? Deliberately?"

"You didn't know?"

She shook her head.

"See why I'm not sure we can trust your boss?" he asked softly.

She pressed her lips to a thin line, not ready to speak ill of Quinn to anyone, especially Cade Landry. But Quinn should have warned her, damn it! He'd deliberately made her a target by putting the information out there about her role at The Gates.

Was her life a bargaining chip in his plan to take down the BRI?

"He set you up as bait." Landry's voice was a soft growl.

"*If* you're telling me the truth."

"I am."

She wished she could say she didn't believe him. But the truth was, setting her up as bait without warning her was exactly the kind of thing Alexander Quinn would do. He was always, *always* about the bottom line. Get the job done whatever it took.

Even if what it took was putting one of his employees in the line of fire to set a trap.

"So they're targeting me? Do they think he won't find someone else to do what I'm doing?"

"They're not going to kill you."

"But you said I was a target."

"You are. But remember when I said they were going to take you? I really meant take you. They're looking to take you captive."

"Why?"

"They seem to think they can use you to break someone."

She frowned. "Someone? Who?"

Landry dropped his gaze, his expression enigmatic as he silently studied his hands for a long moment. When he finally looked up again, an unspoken question darkened his green eyes. "After listening in to Quinn's conversation with you this afternoon, I think they're planning to use you to get to him."

"Why? Why do they think that would get them anything?"

He held her gaze, the questions in his eyes multiplying. "You tell me. I asked you this before, but you didn't really answer. Is something going on between you and Quinn? Are you lovers?"

"No," she answered bluntly. "I mean—"

His eyebrows quirked. "You mean?"

"We're not lovers. But there have been times—" She swallowed with difficulty, suddenly overcome by the acute awareness that Alexander Quinn might have her cabin wired for sound. She took a bracing breath and continued. "There have been times I thought he wanted to be."

"He's in love with you?"

"I don't think Quinn has ever loved anyone that way," she said with a soft laugh. "But he's a man."

"And you're a beautiful woman. Who seems very alone."

She looked up at him. "I choose to be alone."

"Why?" He shook his head. "You're not a loner, Livvie. You enjoy being around other people. You like companionship."

"That was two years ago. My life is very different now. For one thing, I'm too busy for relationships. My job is dangerous and thankless, and I don't want to inflict that kind of stress on someone else."

"Even one of your fellow agents at The Gates? They're working the same stressful job. They understand the long hours, being on call—"

"Why are you pressing this issue? Do you want me to tell you I've moved on from you? I have. It was two years ago." Her voice rose with emotion. "When I left the FBI, I didn't look back. Are you happy?"

"No." He stared back at her, his nostrils flaring. "No, I'm not happy."

She snapped her mouth shut and looked away.

"I know I drove you away. To this day, I don't know how to trust you again, but I have missed you every single moment. The smell of you haunts my dreams. I can close my eyes and conjure up a vivid memory of the sun glinting off your hair that long weekend we spent on Assateague Island. I can feel the thunder of horse hooves beneath my feet when that wild herd ran past us on the beach. I can remember the way your laugh rang in my ears like music."

He hadn't moved an inch closer, hadn't reached out across the distance between them, but his voice caressed her, seduced her, until she felt a throb of desire pulsing low in her belly.

"I didn't come here to get you back. Or ask for another chance," he said in a deep growl that made her think of long, hot summer nights naked in his arms. "But I don't know if I could keep on living if you weren't."

He moved then, rising to his feet and pacing across the room to the window. Outside, the snowfall continued, barely visible in the deepening dusk. Soon night would fall, silent and deep in the snowbound woods.

And she would be alone with the only man she'd ever let herself love.

She couldn't stop herself from rising to join him at the window. He turned slowly to face her, his face half in shadow.

"They're wrong," she said. "The BRI, I mean."

"About what?"

"Alexander Quinn might very well want to sleep with me. He might even feel some level of affection for me. But he wouldn't hesitate to sacrifice my life if he believed it would serve justice in some way. That's the sort of man he is. So if your friends in the Blue Ridge Infantry believe they can use me to control him in any way, they are sadly mistaken."

"That won't stop them from trying."

She lifted her chin. "Let them try."

His eyes narrowed as he held her gaze, studying her as if he'd never seen her before. "You're different," he murmured finally, reaching up to brush a piece of hair away from her cheek. His fingers lingered a moment, and she felt how work-roughened they'd become since the last time he'd touched her that way.

He dropped his hand to his side. "Do you trust me enough to give me back my weapon?"

Trust might not be the right word, she thought, but she was willing to take the risk. "Yes."

He moved away from her to the rolltop desk and retrieved his pistol, reloading it with both speed and skill. "Any chance you have more 9 mm ammo around?"

"Of course."

His gaze lifted to meet hers, a slow smile spreading over his face, carving dimples into his cheeks and taking a decade off his appearance. "Should've known."

As she started toward the hall closet where she kept her extra weapons and ammunition, the lights went off, plunging the cabin into gloom relieved only by the dying fireplace embers.

"There goes the power," she said with a sigh, detouring toward the hearth to coax the fire back to life.

"Wait," he murmured as she reached for the poker. He was much closer than she'd expected; she hadn't heard his approach.

"What?" she asked, her voice dropping to a near whisper.

"How sure are you that the snow caused the power to go out?"

"It's not unusual during a snowstorm—"

He tugged her away from the window. "Or during a siege."

Chapter 5

Only the soft crackle of the smoldering fire and the quiet hiss of their respirations relieved the sudden blanket of silence that fell over the cabin. Outside, snow continued to fall quietly as Landry listened for any out-of-place noises.

Olivia moved away from the fireplace and picked up the Mossberg shotgun leaning against the wall by the desk. She slanted a quick look at Landry before she started toward the front door and grabbed the thick leather jacket that hung on a hook by the entry.

He caught up with her, closing his hand around her wrist. "What the hell do you think you're doing?"

She shook off his grasp and turned to look at him, her blue eyes glimmering in the low light. "I'm going outside to see if I can tell what knocked the power out."

"Didn't you hear a single word I said about a siege?"

"If there are people out there who want to take me captive, I'd rather get the fight over now than hide like a coward in the cabin."

"Well, you're not going out there alone." He chambered a round in the P-11. "I'll go first."

"Why? Because you're the guy?"

He angled a quick look at her. "Because you're the target, and the target should never be the first person out the door."

She frowned but stepped back. "You need a jacket."

He backtracked and shrugged on the thick fleece coat he'd picked up earlier that day at the thrift store in Barrowville, hurrying in case she changed her mind about allowing him to join her.

But she waited for him at the door, her gaze drawing him all the way in as he closed the distance between them. She was a tall woman, nearly as tall as he was, and if anything, she looked even stronger and fitter than she'd been when they'd worked together in the FBI.

They'd always been a good team, right until the case that had broken them. He hoped the old instincts would kick back in for them now, despite all that had passed between them, because if there really were people out there lying in wait for Olivia, it would take all their skills and a whole lot of luck to make it out of the situation unscathed.

An icy blast of air greeted them as they stepped out onto the cabin porch. Wind had swirled snow beneath the porch roof, depositing about two inches halfway onto the porch's weathered wooden floor.

Landry paused at the top of the porch steps and surveyed the cold white expanse in front of him. If there had been anyone moving around out here in the past little while, they hadn't come close to the porch. The snowfield was pristine and undisturbed.

"The snow probably knocked a branch on a wire somewhere between here and the nearest transformer." Olivia's low voice, only inches from his ear, sent a ripple of pure sexual awareness darting down his spine.

He turned to look at her. "We should check all the way around the house before we let down our guard."

Her eyes narrowed, but she didn't protest as he led her down the steps into the thickening snow. Almost five inches covered the ground, even more gathering at the edges of the porch where the wind had blown the snow into rising drifts. It was a soft, wet snow, flattening under his boots as they slowly circled the cabin, looking for any signs of intruders.

But nothing had disturbed the snow around the cabin, save for a small set of tracks belonging to what he guessed was probably a foraging raccoon, looking for a meal.

"It was just the snow," Olivia murmured, giving him a nudge toward the front of the cabin.

He trudged back through the tracks they'd left in the snow and nodded for her to precede him up the porch steps. She climbed the steps with a soft sigh he recognized as a sign of impatience and turned to face him when he joined her in front of the door.

"Fine," he said. "It was just the snow. This time."

Olivia shook the slush from her boots and opened the cabin door to head inside. He knocked the snow from his own boots before he followed her in.

She closed and locked the door behind him, shrugging out of her damp coat. "Are we going to do this every time you hear a noise you can't identify?"

He tamped down a flood of annoyance. "If I think it's necessary."

She released another sigh as she hung the coat back on its hook. "Okay, fair enough. Let's get the fire cranked up. I'm freezing."

He took off his coat and hung it on the hook beside hers. "How can I help? Need more wood?"

"It's in a bin by the back door. Straight down the hall."

He found the wood bin and grabbed a couple of pieces for the fire then returned to the front room. He found Olivia kneeling in front of the hearth, adding newspaper as kindling to the charred logs still glowing faintly red. He added the wood to the fire and looked around for matches.

Olivia reached into a small steel canister on the mantel and withdrew a narrow fireplace lighter. "Here."

He touched the butane flame to the kindling. It ignited with a soft *whoosh*, and the logs soon caught fire, emitting a delicious wave of heat into the room.

"Nice," Olivia murmured, extending her hands toward the flames.

He pulled the room's two armchairs close to the fire. "Sit."

She did as he said, leaning toward the warmth. "Thanks."

He sat in the chair next to her, holding his icy fingers toward the fire until some of the numbness subsided. "No, thank *you*."

"For what?"

"For extending a little Southern hospitality to a poor, weary traveler?" he suggested with a smile.

Her lips curved in response. "You didn't give me a lot of choice."

"Maybe not. But I am grateful to be here in front of this fire instead of out there in all that cold white stuff."

Olivia fell silent, her gaze directed at the flickering fire. Settling back in the chair, Landry allowed himself to study her profile, take in the lean lines of her body only partially hidden by her sweater and jeans. His earlier observation was correct; she was in excellent shape. She'd always been a curvy woman, and that hadn't changed, but the curves were matched with toned muscles and an overall look of vibrant health.

Leaving the FBI and going to work for The Gates seemed to have been good for her, at least physically.

But what about her spirit? The Olivia Sharp he'd known and loved had been a firecracker, full of explosive energy and a fierce inquisitiveness that had taken her very far very fast in the FBI.

But not this woman in front of him. She was quiet, contemplative and remarkably still.

She stirred as he watched her, turning her gaze to him. "I could heat up some milk over the fire for hot chocolate. Or even water for coffee, if you'd prefer that—"

"You've changed." He hadn't meant to blurt the words aloud, but he couldn't take them back.

Her eyelids flickered and she looked away. "So have you."

Now that he'd started down this conversational path, he decided, he might as well go all in. "Are you happy?"

"I'm…content."

He felt an ache settle in his chest at the hint of melancholy in her tone. "Is contentment enough?"

"For now."

"Do you anticipate finding more than contentment at some point in the future?"

She slanted a look his way. "Why don't you just come out and ask whatever it is you want to know?"

"Do you miss me?" He clamped his mouth shut as soon as the words escaped his lips. He hadn't intended to ask such a blunt, self-serving question.

"Yes." Her answer, equally blunt, caught him by surprise.

They fell quiet, letting the crackle of the fire fill the lingering silence. Landry wasn't sure how much time had passed before she spoke again, but the flames in the hearth had already begun to die down.

"I loved you. Like I'd never loved anyone in my life." Her gaze remained directed forward, toward the fireplace, the flickering light from the flames bathing her face in a warm glow. "When things fell apart, I had to keep going. Keep working the job, not let the loss derail me. But I just couldn't keep going, day in and day out, working alone when I'd gotten so used to you being there."

The ache in his chest intensified. "I'm sorry."

"You'd been transferred by then. It's not like we'd have been working together anyway."

"I was a mess," he admitted. "It was hard to care about anything for a long time. I worked the job, but it just didn't mean anything to me anymore."

"I heard you'd started going through the motions."

Guilt flooded him, hot and sour. "I did. Much to my shame. I don't really have an excuse. I just knew I wasn't ever going to get any further up the ladder than I already was, and any screwup would probably be the end of the line for me."

"Easier to keep your nose clean if you're not rocking the boat."

"Yeah. I guess. I'm not sure I gave it that much thought. It's just—nothing meant anything. Every time I cleared a case, three more would pop up to take their place. Bureaucratic crap kept creeping further and further down the line into the field offices. We were dealing with federal-level politics in the Johnson City RA, for Pete's sake."

"Why didn't you just leave the FBI, then?"

"And do what? I spent over a decade solving crimes and protecting lives. It's all I really know how to do at this point."

"You could have come to work for Quinn at The Gates, for one thing." She picked up the fire poker and gave the logs a nudge.

"I wasn't ready." He stopped short as she snapped her gaze up to meet his.

"You weren't ready to work with me again."

"That's not it, exactly."

She turned back to the fire. "Then what is it?"

"I know Ava Trent probably didn't have anything good to say about me. Or McKenna Rigsby, either. But my job was to watch their backs, and I didn't want to leave them in the lurch."

"So you stayed for your partners?" She arched an eyebrow but still didn't look at him.

"I wanted my job to mean something again. I thought if I stuck around, if I did what it took to get through the day, I'd feel that fire again." He shook his head. "As if that fire came from outside of me."

She remained silent for a long time, her singular focus on the flickering fire beginning to make him squirm inside. The Olivia Sharp who'd been his partner, in his work life and his personal life, had been a vibrant force of nature. Quiet contemplation had never been her style.

Maybe that woman really was gone. Maybe he'd lost her in the aftermath of the Richmond debacle just as surely as he'd lost himself.

"I never understood why you couldn't forgive me for not remembering what happened." Her low murmur seemed loud in the snowbound hush of the cabin, yet he was certain he'd misunderstood her.

"What?"

She slowly turned her gaze to meet his, her blue eyes blazing with a mixture of anger and pain. "I had a head injury. I couldn't remember anything that happened right before or right after the explosion. But you seemed to think I should be able to pull those memories out of nothing to prove you weren't lying. That wasn't fair."

"It wasn't what you couldn't remember that was the problem. It's what you told the investigators."

Her brow furrowed. "I didn't tell them anything. I couldn't. I didn't remember anything."

"Yet you somehow managed to remember me pushing you and the other team members to disobey the hold order." His voice sharpened.

"I did no such thing."

He shook his head. Why was she denying it? Did she think he hadn't learned what she'd said in her official statement?

The agents who'd interrogated him had shown him a transcript of her testimony, signed off by Olivia, that had laid the whole mess on his shoulders.

Surely she remembered what she'd told the investi-

gators. The words were certainly burned in *his* mind—
"Agent Landry believed that waiting would allow the
hostage-takers to escape, so he decided to countermand
the official orders and go into the building."

Her eyes narrowed. "What aren't you telling me?"

"Nothing." He was starting to feel sick, his dinner
roiling in queasy waves in his gut. "It doesn't matter."

Her lips flattened with anger. "You're right—it doesn't.
The real problem is that you never trusted me. Not really."

How could he argue with her? His lack of faith—
in anyone and anything—had long preceded Olivia's
presence in his life.

He closed his eyes. "You, of all people, know why I
didn't trust anyone easily."

Her fingers closed around his jaw, tugging his face
around, forcing him to open his eyes and look into her
pain-filled gaze. "I am not her. I never was. I never
will be."

He didn't know what to say in response. She was
right. Of course she was right. And yet…

She dropped her hand away from his face and turned
back to the fire. "We were doomed from the start."

We were, he thought bleakly.

So why hadn't he done the wise thing and walked
away before it blew up in their faces?

The snow stopped around midnight, but the electricity didn't return. The cabin had been built to keep out
the cold mountain winds, but with only the fire in the
hearth to keep the place warm, it hadn't taken long for
the temperature inside the cabin to drop precipitously.

"This is the last of the quilts," Olivia told Landry
as he sat in silent misery by the fire. Without talking

about it, they'd both settled on the thick rug in front of the hearth, huddled together for warmth.

What they hadn't done was speak any more about the past, about the mistakes they'd both made that had led them from the closest of companions to the awkward strangers now sitting side by side under a mountain of handmade quilts.

She'd made it seem that the end of their relationship was entirely his fault, but that wasn't fair, was it? She had her own demons, had made her own mistakes.

"I should have confronted you when you just left without a word."

He made a low, growling sound deep in his throat. "It doesn't matter, does it?"

"I guess not."

He sighed. "I was always a mess. I never should have inflicted myself on you in the first place."

"It never felt like an affliction."

He slanted a skeptical look at her, making her smile self-consciously.

His own lips curved in response. "You can say it. I may be a mess, but I can be honest about my shortcomings."

"I had my own shortcomings. I never felt good enough for you."

He uttered a profane denial.

"No, it's true," she said. "You came from a rich family, and I was from Hick City, Alabama—"

"My rich family left me so screwed up, I walked away from you."

"And my poor family left me so screwed up, I let you go without a fight. Because I'd always figured you'd go, sooner or later." She looked down at her hands, at the short nails she used to wear long and well manicured, and realized so much of the life she'd once lived had been a disguise, a facade she'd invented to make herself feel good enough for the rest of the world. "Little Sand Mountain rednecks like Olivia Sharp don't get to be with rich Savannah boys like Cade Landry. Not for long."

She felt the anger rising off him, as tangible as the waves of heat flowing from the hearth. "You were always the better person, Olivia. You have to know that. You were smarter, stronger, wiser—"

"I never felt that way. And the first time things between us went sideways—"

"I proved you right by walking away," he finished for her.

A soft buzzing sensation from her hip pocket startled her. She'd figured the power outage would have created cell-phone coverage issues, as well, but when she checked the phone display, the signal was strong. "It's Quinn," she said with a glance at Landry.

He nodded at the phone. "Take it."

She answered. "Sharp."

"Quinn," he responded as bluntly. "Is the new bike still parked outside your cabin?"

He knew. She hadn't really doubted he would. "Actually, it's back in the mudroom by the kitchen. Didn't want the snow to rust it."

Quinn sighed. "Damn."

"What do you have against my new bike?"

"Someone's looking for it. Someone with a wallet full of credentials and the full force of the United States government behind him."

Damn it. "You're not suggesting I put the bike back out in the snow to fend for itself?"

Quinn dropped the games. "Landry's a wanted man. If the FBI tracks him to your place—and given his little trip to the bank in Barrowville, it's really only a matter of time before they do—things could get very uncomfortable for you both."

She looked at Landry, who was watching her with troubled eyes. "Any suggestions?"

"I realize travel at the moment is hardly optimal, and you should have at least another couple of days, because the FBI isn't likely to try to make it up the mountain before the snow thaws. But if I were in your place, I would be planning not to be there by the time the roads are passable again."

"Understood."

Quinn hung up without saying goodbye. She closed her own phone and shoved it back in the pocket of her jeans.

"Something's happened," Landry said.

"The FBI is looking for you here in Tennessee. Quinn doesn't think they've tracked you to the bank in Barrowville yet, but it's only a matter of time."

Landry pushed to his feet. "I'll get out of here."

She scrambled up, catching his arm as he reached for his boots. "They won't come tonight. Or tomorrow, most likely."

"That'll give me time to get far away from here."

"Don't," she said, her heart suddenly pounding wildly.

He looked down at her fingers closed around his forearm. "Don't what?"

She swallowed hard, forcing the words from her tight throat. "Don't leave me behind again."

Chapter 6

"Forget I said that." Olivia took a step back and let go of his forearm, turning away.

Landry didn't let her retreat. Not this time. He closed the distance she'd opened up, until the heat of the fireplace filled what little space remained between them. Its glow bathed her face with gold and added sparkling glints to her blond hair. Desire snaked through him, but he ignored its sibilant seduction. Wanting her wasn't enough. It had never been enough.

Maybe that had been the problem. Wanting was easy. Visceral.

Trusting—that was the hard part.

"I can't forget you said that." He laid his hand on her shoulder, keeping the touch light and undemanding. But her gaze snapped up to meet his, her blue eyes darkening with arousal as if he'd caressed her.

He still had that effect on her, just as the mere sight of her made him long for her touch.

"This is a mess of my own making. You're not part of this. I can go, and you can pretend I never darkened your door."

"I can't pretend that." She looked away quickly, as if she could hide the desperation her eyes had just revealed. But it was too late. He'd seen the fear. It echoed the same desperate emotion burning in the center of his chest.

Need. Pure, unadulterated need.

He needed her. His partner. Set aside everything else—the desire, the complicated history, the perceived betrayals and the two-year separation—and the partnership remained, a connection between them that time and distance hadn't been able to sever after all.

"You were a good agent," he said. "A damn good one, actually. And I need my partner one more time, okay? I won't deny it. But it's still your choice. I'm not a good bet here. I'm in a mess and I can't even offer you ironclad proof that I'm telling you the truth."

She turned slowly to face him. "I believe you."

Her simple declaration jolted through him like an electric shock. "Livvie—"

She held up her hand. "I believe you came here to protect me. That's what I believe. But I'm going into this with my eyes open. And the second you keep secrets from me and tell me a lie, that's it. I'll know it. And you'll be out there on a shaky limb all by yourself, because I'll be going to the FBI and telling them everything I know. Including your last whereabouts."

He couldn't hold back a smile of relief. That was the Olivia Sharp he'd known and loved, the tough-minded, no-nonsense agent who'd watched his back and saved his ass more times than he could count.

"Fair enough," he said, holding his hand out to her.

She looked at his outstretched fingers for a tense moment then clasped his hand in hers and gave it a firm shake. "I think we're safe here until morning. So let's pack up the supplies we're going to need to hike up the mountain in half a foot of snow and then get some sleep so we can head out before daylight."

He should have known she'd have a cabin full of survival gear and supplies. Olivia Sharp had set the standard for preparedness during her years in the FBI field office in Richmond. She already had a prepared "bug out" kit, as she called it, containing camping supplies, tools and a 72-hour supply of Meals Ready to Eat as well as changes of clothing.

She had a second backpack stored in the hall closet. Within a half hour, she'd added another three-day stock of supplies and food to that backpack, as well, filling in the blanks with clothes from his duffel bag.

"The cold will be a pain, but these hills are full of places to find shelter," she said in a tone that was all business. He mimicked her brisk attitude as he carried the two backpacks to the front room and set them near the fire while she retrieved extra weapons for them, adding a compact Glock 19 to her Mossberg and handing over a spare pistol.

He looked at the Kimber Stainless II pistol in his palm and smiled. "You remembered."

"It was two years ago, not two decades," she said in a flat tone. "It's loaded, and I put extra ammo in your kit. Now let's try to get some sleep before morning, okay?"

She settled down on a bed of quilts and pillows that

had been warming by the fire while they'd gathered supplies, her back to Landry.

He tucked the Kimber in the borrowed backpack and sat down beside her on the makeshift bed. "We should sleep back to back," he said, glancing at her quilt-covered form.

"Knock yourself out," she murmured.

He stretched out beside her and covered himself with a quilt, as well, easing back until his body collided with hers. "Sorry."

"Shut up and go to sleep, Landry."

Stifling a smile, he tucked the quilt tightly around him and closed his eyes. There were only a few scant hours before morning, and they both needed as much sleep as they could muster.

But he had a feeling, no matter how few hours remained between him and dawn, this was going to be one of the longest nights of his life.

Daylight was still an hour or two away, nothing more than a faint gray glimmer in the eastern sky, when Olivia woke. The fire had died down to warm embers, allowing a bone-aching chill to settle over the cabin's front room. Only the solid wall of heat pressed against her back kept her from shivering and burying herself more deeply beneath the two quilts covering her from chin to toe.

The hot body behind hers shifted and uttered a familiar groaning sound that made her breath catch in her throat.

Landry.

"You awake?" His voice was like rumbling thunder, muffled by the quilts.

"I am."

He shifted, turning over until he was practically spooning her. "I think my fingers fell off during the night. Can't feel them."

She rolled over to face him. His green eyes met hers with sleepy humor, and she felt something hot and tight release inside her, allowing her to breathe deeply again. "You'd better find them," she said with the hint of a smile. "You're going to need them."

He brought his hands out from beneath the quilt and touched her neck. His fingers were like ice.

She batted them away, laughing despite herself. "Stop!"

"Cold hands, warm heart."

Her smile faded. "We need to hit the road soon."

He sighed. "If we can find the road."

They ate a breakfast of protein bars and left the cabin while it was still mostly dark out. As Olivia had hoped, once they got past the clearing around her cabin and into the woods, the snow was thinner on the ground, thanks to the shelter of the trees overhead.

"Keep an eye on the trees," she warned as Landry fell into step behind her. "Limbs can snap without a lot of warning."

"Duly noted."

She'd tasked him with hauling the crude travois she'd fashioned from a rake handle, a hoe handle and a canvas tarpaulin, which she'd loaded with the supplies she'd packed into a waterproof duffel in case they had to find shelter before they reached their destination.

"What is our destination, exactly?" Landry asked as they headed deeper into the woods.

"Well, for tonight, I want us to reach a place called

Parson's Chair." When he didn't say anything else, she turned to look at him. "No comment?"

His green eyes narrowed as he met her gaze. "I come from Georgia. I have no standing to make fun of strange place names."

She smiled. "It's a tall outcropping that kind of looks like a tall, straight-backed chair, hence the name. But beneath the chair is a large cave that will give us shelter if we can reach it by nightfall."

"And if we can't?"

She turned and started walking faster, tugging her jacket more tightly around her. "Let's just make sure we do."

Parson's Chair was near the top of Fowler Ridge, the southernmost peak of the two mountains that flanked Perdition Gap. On a warmer day, with good weather, Olivia could reach the outcropping within a three-hour hike. She and a couple of the female agents at The Gates had made the hike several times over the summer.

But climbing the winding natural trail in subfreezing temperatures, with a slick carpet of snow underfoot, was turning out to be a grueling test of endurance. She had nearly fallen once already, and as she neared the halfway point of their hike, she heard the sound of a hard thud and a guttural curse behind her, turning in time to see Landry slide almost ten feet back down the mountain on his side, the travois he was pulling tumbling with him.

She reached for the end of the contraption, where she'd strapped the poles together, and caught it before it went over the side of the trail, keeping a sharp eye on Landry as he struggled out from beneath the travois and regained his footing. As he crawled back up the mountain, she held out her gloved hand to him, and he grasped it with a grim smile of gratitude.

"Clearly, I don't have any pack-mule DNA in my ancestry," he muttered as he joined her near a clump of boulders.

She shrugged her backpack off her shoulders and settled on one of the smoother rocks. "Let's rest a minute. Rehydrate and warm up." She pulled out a thermos of warm broth she'd stowed in the backpack before they'd left the cabin that morning.

Landry settled on the boulder beside her, retrieving his own flask. They drank in silence for a few moments before he closed the flask and put it back in his pack. "How much farther?"

She looked at him and saw with alarm that he was wiping blood from the side of his face with the sleeve of his jacket. Rising quickly, she eased his hands away to get a better look at the injury. It was a nasty scrape that started in the middle of his cheek and went into his hairline, disappearing under his black ski cap.

"It's just a scratch," he protested.

"It's bleeding like crazy," she growled, grabbing her backpack to find the compact first-aid kit she'd put inside.

"Seriously, it's a scratch. My head's not even hurting." He winced when she pressed an antiseptic pad against the scrape.

"The travois is obliterating our tracks, for the most part, but if you're leaving a blood trail, I'm not sure the snow we're supposed to get tonight is going to be enough to hide it."

He closed his eyes. "And we're about to spend the night in a cave."

"We're not unprepared."

He opened his eyes, giving her a curious look. "When did you learn all this doomsday prep stuff, anyway?"

"I was born with survival skills," she murmured, mopping up the blood from his face. The scrape continued oozing, but it wasn't as bad as the bleeding had made it look. She tucked the used wipe into a disposal bag and shoved it back in the pack, then made quick work of applying adhesive bandages along the length of the scrape. "All better."

He caught her hand as she was about to let it drop away from his face, pressing her palm against the day's growth of beard scruff on his jaw. Dimples flirted with his cheeks. "But do I still have my boyish good looks?"

He was flirting with her, the beast. And worse, she was falling for it, hard. Damn his charming hide.

She tugged her hand free of his grasp and picked up the first-aid kit. "You're assuming you ever had boyish good looks."

He put his hand over his heart, feigning injury.

She put the first-aid kit in the backpack and swung it up on her shoulders. "We should get moving again if we want to reach Parson's Chair before nightfall."

She didn't wait for him to gather his things before she started hiking up the trail again. Behind her, she heard the sounds of his scrambling to catch up, and she took a little pity on him, slowing her pace until he had.

"You've developed a cold side." His voice drifted to her on the icy wind.

"I've always had a cold side."

As the trail widened, he moved up until he was walking side by side with her. "Not like this. Is it because of me? Because I'm not worth it."

She slanted a look at him and saw he was serious. "Trust me when I say you are only a single line on a lifelong list of reasons not to let myself be vulnerable to other people."

"You never talked much about your past."

"It wasn't important."

"It should have been." He caught her wrist as she continued forward, forcing her to turn and face him. "I should have asked."

"It doesn't matter," she said, tugging free of his grasp once more and continuing up the mountain. What was done was done, and there wasn't a thing either of them could do to change it.

Snow started falling again late in the afternoon, a blizzard of tiny flakes at first, creating a fine mist that looked like the tendrils of mist that gave the Smoky Mountains their name. But within an hour, the flakes grew larger and the snowfall thicker, reducing visibility to almost nothing.

Landry had no idea how they'd be able to find Parson's Chair when they couldn't see ten feet in front of them.

"Stay close," Olivia called, her voice almost whipped away by the wind.

"Wouldn't dream of letting you out of my sight," he muttered.

After what felt like another hour of hiking, though a glance at his watch told him only fifteen minutes had passed, Olivia slowed to a halt. "There it is," she said.

He followed her gaze and saw the faint outline of a rocky outcropping visible through the wall of falling snow. "Parson's Chair?"

"Let's go," she said, hiking forward at a reinvigorated pace.

Tightening his grip on the travois, he followed, ignoring the ache in his calves and thighs. When they finally reached the mouth of the cave beneath Parson's Chair, he eased the front of the travois to the ground and stretched his sore limbs. "Remind me to hit the gym more often when I get back to civilization."

She shrugged off her backpack and shot him a look of amusement. "And here I was thinking you were looking lean and ripped."

"That's from walking everywhere I went, hauling around a backpack and eating only a couple of meals a day." He eyed the dark opening of the cave. "Any chance there's a bear inside?"

"They'd be hibernating at this time of year anyway."

"I heard black bears don't hibernate."

"Why don't you take this, go in there and find out?" She handed him a flashlight from her backpack and waved her hand toward the cave entrance.

"Gee, thanks." He took the flashlight and took a step inside, swinging the light in a slow arc to get his bearings.

The cave was larger than he'd expected, a cavern about twenty feet wide with a high ceiling. The back of the cave disappeared into darkness, suggesting there might be a tunnel that went even farther into the mountainside.

"Any bears?" Olivia's voice was right in his ear, giving him a start. He hadn't even heard her approach.

"If there are, they're hiding." He shone the flashlight in her face, making her squint.

"Give me that." She took the flashlight and headed

back outside to grab her gear. He joined her, unloading the travois and helping her take their supplies deeper into the cave.

He had to give her credit; she'd prepared well for a night in a cave. The well-packed duffel he'd been dragging behind him on the travois contained a portable propane heater, two fleece-lined sleeping bags and extra bottled water. "You forgot the portable toilet." He slanted a sly look her way.

She waved her hand toward the cave entrance. "The toilet came with the accommodations."

"Yeah, I've used it before." He folded one of the sleeping bags into a square and sat cross-legged in front of the duffel bag, looking through the rest of the supplies. "No wonder that bloody thing weighed so much. You packed half your cabin."

She followed his example and folded her own sleeping bag into a makeshift seat cushion. "I wasn't sure how long we'd have to be out in the elements." She opened a bottle of water and took a drink.

He grabbed his own bottle of water. It was icy cold, which might have been good about six months ago when he was living through the hot North Carolina summer, but now served to add chills on top of his existing shivers. "How long does that heater last?"

"Six to twelve hours, depending on the heat level. I figured we'd start as low as we can so we can make it last longer. These sleeping bags will help. And we should probably change into dry clothes now, too."

"You want me to wait outside?"

She met his questioning look with one arched eyebrow. "I don't think either of us grew anything new since the last time we saw each other naked. I know I haven't."

He smiled at that as he stood up. "I'll turn my back anyway."

"Chicken," she murmured.

His grin faded as he heard the zip of her jeans and struggled to keep a memory of her sleek curves and warm golden skin from taking over his brain. After shucking off his own wet clothes, he pulled on the jeans and sweater he'd stashed in his backpack. The dry clothes warmed him immediately.

"All done," Olivia said.

Turning, he shook the melted snow out of his hair and used his discarded sweater to soak up some of the remaining moisture. "You became quite the Girl Scout while we were apart. I used to beg you to go camping, with very little luck, and here you are earning your merit badge in disaster prep."

"There's a difference between knowing how to survive in the wilderness and actually wanting to do it for recreation." She settled on her sleeping bag again and took off her boots and damp socks. Her toenails, he noted, were neatly pedicured and polished a bright sky blue that seemed to reflect the azure tint of her eyes. "Hopefully, we won't be up here more than one night."

He sat next to her on his own sleeping bag and followed her example by taking off his snow-stained boots. His socks were still mostly dry, so he didn't take them off. While she donned dry socks and another pair of boots, he asked, "Why *did* we come up here, anyway?"

"Because it's halfway to where I want to go. And I knew we could find shelter here for the night."

"And where is it you want to go?"

She stopped in the middle of tying her boot and looked up at him, her expression hard to read. "We're heading for The Gates."

Chapter 7

"I thought you didn't trust Quinn."

The words, spoken quietly but urgently, were the first words Landry had uttered since she'd told him of her intentions to hike to The Gates for refuge. She had expected resistance, and when he'd merely turned away from her and started sorting through the rest of the supplies to see what food was available for supper, she hadn't known what to think.

The Cade Landry she'd spent almost two years of her life loving had been quick-tempered and just as quick to get over it. But she wasn't sure this slow-simmering version was an improvement.

"I don't trust him to put my safety above whatever mission he's running at any given time," she admitted, taking the MRE he was holding out to her and reading the packet label. "Spaghetti. Discriminating choice."

He managed a smile, though she could tell he was still disturbed by the thought of putting his own safety—and freedom—in the hands of Quinn and the agents of The Gates. "Eat up. It's going to be another long hike into Purgatory tomorrow, right?"

She sighed. "I know you're not happy about going to The Gates, so you can stop pretending that everything's fine."

"What's the point? You're going to go whether I do or not. And since it's your life in danger, I can't exactly let you head off there alone, can I?"

"Why not?" She dropped the MRE on the cave floor in front of her and angled her chin toward him, her own anger rising in a rush. "You had no trouble leaving me behind two years ago, did you?"

"Maybe we should talk about who left whom."

"Maybe we should."

For a moment tension crackled between them like a live wire. Olivia's chest started to ache from the hurt and anger she'd kept pent up for too long. But was a cave in the middle of a snowstorm really the place to have this argument?

"I'm sorry," she said, picking up the MRE she'd thrown down. "This isn't the time or place—"

"You'll tell me when you find that time and place, right?" he asked in that quiet tone she was beginning to recognize as his slow boil.

"Do you really want to hash this out here and now?"

"No," he admitted. "Not here or now."

"Let's just get some food and some sleep, in that order." She opened the MRE and pulled out the packets inside. The entrée was the first place to start, she decided. The most calories, and she could eat it hot.

She could save the items that didn't require heating for breakfast. "You know how to use one of these things, right?"

"Yeah." He picked up the flameless ration heater. "Been a while, though."

"These come with saltwater packets to activate the heater." She poured the water into the heater, activating the chemicals that produced heat. The packet warmed quickly, and she held it as long as she dared, until the heat began to sting her fingers. She shoved the entrée into the heater packet and set it aside. "What sides came in your packet?"

He went through the small packets that had come in his meal. "Cheese and crackers, fig bar, shortbread cookies, raisins—"

"Trade you my peanut butter for the cheese spread, and this yummy oatmeal cookie for the shortbread." She waggled the packets at him.

"Deal on the cheese spread, but I don't know. These shortbread cookies sound pretty appetizing." He held out the packet toward her, pinning her with his gaze. "But I might be convinced to trade it for something else."

Despite the icy chill of the cave, the air between them heated instantly. The familiar fire in his gaze was pure temptation, and damned if she didn't want to tumble in headfirst.

She looked away. "If you want the shortbread cookies, keep them."

He let out a little huff of air. "Here. You can have them. I'll take the oatmeal cookie." He laid the packet of shortbread cookies on the cave floor in front of her.

She looked up and saw something in his expression she hadn't expected.

Sadness.

"Landry—" She stopped. Started again. "Cade."

His eyes snapped up at her use of his first name. "You never called me Cade when we were together. No need to start now."

"Maybe that was a mistake. I mean, you called me Olivia. Why did I have to put that distance between us?"

"That wasn't what put distance between us." He looked down at the shortbread cookies she hadn't yet picked up. "And it wasn't just you. I need you to know that I know that I was a big part of the problem."

"Maybe we were just too damaged for anything between us to have a chance to work." To her dismay, she felt hot tears stinging her eyes, threatening to fall. She blinked hard, keeping them at bay.

"I wish I wasn't in this situation." He growled the words, his voice deep with frustration. "I wish I'd just come to you before, when there weren't people hunting for us both. I wish I'd told you that I loved you and we could figure out a way to make it work."

"I could have tracked you down and said the same thing." She made herself look at him, to face the choices she'd made. "I wasn't ready to make that move, and I wouldn't have been ready to give you a second chance if you'd shown up at my door, either."

"Then why don't I feel like it's really over?" The words seemed to tumble from his lips, fast and desperate, as if something inside him was determined to get the question out before his better judgment found a way to shut him up.

"I don't know," she answered as truthfully as she could.

"You don't feel that way, do you?"

She could lie, she supposed. Tell him what he clearly believed to be the truth. But she'd never been able to lie to him with any effectiveness.

"I do," she admitted, forcing herself to say it. Get it over with. "I do feel that way. I never felt as if we got any closure, the way it ended. You know?"

He nodded. "I know."

"I need you to know. I really loved you. Like I've never loved anybody in my whole life. And when things fell apart, I felt ripped in two." She couldn't stop the tears, as much as she wanted to. She pushed them away with her fingertips, shooting him a watery smile. "Sorry. I know you hate it when I cry."

He reached across the space between them, the pad of his thumb brushing a tear from her cheek. "I know you loved me." He dropped his hand away. "You just couldn't believe in me."

"You said that before. When you first showed up at my cabin yesterday. You said I just couldn't believe in you enough. But I don't know why you think that. Is it just because I didn't tell the panel that I remembered getting an order?"

"No, of course not." He looked puzzled by the question. "I knew you had a head injury, so I get that you might not have remembered the order."

"Then what did I do that was so unforgivable?"

"It's what you told the panel about my obsession with the BRI."

Now she was the one who was confused. "What?"

"Olivia, it's okay. Maybe you were right. Maybe I

was getting a little too focused on bringing them down. I mean, look at the mess that obsession has gotten me into now."

"But I didn't say—"

"Peterson sneaked me a copy of the transcript of your debriefing. I read your statement."

She shook her head. "There's got to be some mistake. I mean, yeah, I was still suffering from the concussion, but I remember really clearly what I told the investigation team, and I didn't say anything like that about you."

"But your statement—"

"Either you misread it, or you didn't see the real transcript," she said firmly, anger rushing heat into her cheeks. "Because I never said anything like that to the debriefing team. Concussion or no concussion."

"How can you be sure? If you had a head injury, maybe you said things you were thinking that you wouldn't have said aloud if you weren't suffering a concussion—"

"I know I didn't say it, because I never thought it. I never thought you were obsessed with the BRI. You were passionate about bringing them to justice, yes. But so was I. We both wanted that group of terrorists stopped."

A look of dismay crossed his face. "Then if you didn't say it—"

A chill washed over her that had nothing to do with the snowy weather outside the cave. "Someone falsified my deposition."

"But who?"

"Peterson's the one who gave you the sneak peek. Could he have changed it?"

"I guess he could have, but why would he? He'd gain

nothing from it. He wasn't on the SWAT team that day." Landry rubbed his chin, his palm making a soft swishing sound against his beard stubble. "Who was in the debriefing with you?"

She frowned, trying to remember. "Definitely the squad leader, O'Bannon. Agents Thompson and Lopez of Internal Affairs."

"What about Darryl Boyle? Was he there?"

She met his urgent gaze. "Yes. He'd been the unit leader that day."

"I've been thinking a lot about that day in Richmond. I've gone over it and over it in my head, replaying every second."

"I wish I could remember."

"No. You don't. I never thought I'd say this, but I'm glad you don't remember." He looked queasy. "You don't remember two of our friends—our brothers— blown up in front of us."

She reached across the space between them, touching his hand. His gaze snapped up to hers, but instead of pulling away, he covered her hand with his own.

"I'm sorry. I'm sorry I wasn't well enough to attend the funerals for Davis and Darnell. I should have been there with you."

"I missed you," he admitted, giving her hand a light squeeze before he pulled away and rose to his feet. There was a faint glow of lingering daylight coming from the mouth of the cave; he walked toward it slowly until he stood in the opening.

She tugged her jacket more tightly around her and followed, stopping next to him in the cave opening. "Snow's starting to slow down."

He glanced at her. "How much more do you think fell?"

She gazed into the gloom, making out only faint impressions of their trek to the cave in the snow. "At least three or four more inches. Looks like maybe nine inches altogether."

With a little shiver, he turned and walked deeper into the cave. "How long before we can turn on the heater?"

"I'd like to wait until we bunk down. Let's eat. The food should be heated by now, and that should warm us up for a bit."

He lowered himself onto the folded sleeping bag and reached for the box holding his MRE.

"Use your—"

He growled an oath and dropped the now-open box on the cave floor.

"Glove," she finished.

"Thanks for the warning." He slipped on his glove and fished the hot entrée out of the box while she did the same. Steam rose from the packets, filling the air around them with the smell of food.

They ate in silence from the entrée packets and drank a whole bottle of water each before stowing away the trash for disposal when they reached town the next day. Outside, night had descended, snuffing out almost all the light from the world beyond the cave.

"I want to get a predawn start tomorrow," she warned as she handed him the flashlight. "Here, hold this where I can see what I'm doing with this heater."

He pointed the flashlight beam toward the small propane heater. "Is it dangerous to run that thing in an enclosed space like this?"

"It shuts off automatically if the oxygen level gets

too low." She made sure the fuel tank was safely seated in place. She turned on the power, and heat rose from the vents. "Plus, this cave has an opening deeper inside. If you wet your finger and hold it up, you'll feel the breeze."

His lips curved and his dimples made a quick appearance. "I'll take your word for that."

"We should probably try to sleep with our backs to the heater," she suggested as she unfolded her sleeping bag and laid it out by the unit.

He followed her lead, setting up his bag on the other side of the heater. "How much more battery time does that flashlight have?"

"Should be plenty for the trip. But let's not waste it." She switched it off, plunging the cave into inky darkness.

For a few minutes, the sounds of movement, hers and his, filled the silence as they unzipped their sleeping bags and slid inside, then zipped themselves up within the fleece-lined cocoons.

Silence reigned again for a long while, broken only by the soft whisper of their breathing and the hiss of the propane heater warming the air between them.

"I'm sorry." His voice rumbled in the darkness a long time later, just as she was starting to relax.

"For what?" she asked, resisting the temptation to turn over to face him.

"For being reckless. Getting that money out of our joint bank account yesterday, even though I knew it was possible—probable—that the account would have been flagged."

"So why did you?"

"I guess I was just tired of being out there alone," he

said after a long pause. "I missed having someone who gave a damn about my life, and since you were the last person who really did—"

"I'm not sorry," she said quietly.

When he didn't respond, she wondered if he'd heard her.

"I'm not sorry," she said more loudly, turning her head to make sure he could hear her. "I've been so worried about you, for a lot longer than just the time you've been missing. I'm glad you came to my cabin. I'm glad I know you're okay."

"For now."

She sighed, turning her back to him again, suddenly overwhelmed by a heavy sense of danger creeping closer.

"For now," she conceded and closed her eyes, giving in to the bone-aching weariness from a day's hike up the mountain.

She didn't think she'd fall asleep easily, despite her fatigue, but the comforting flow of warmth from the propane heater and the soft, steady cadence of Landry's breathing soothed her into deep, dreamless slumber.

Landry opened his eyes and stared into the black void of the cave, listening to Olivia's slow, steady breathing. It felt a little ridiculous, really, to be forcing himself to stay awake just so he could listen to her sleep nearby.

That was how much he'd missed her. Enough that something as simple as hearing her move oxygen in and out of her lungs was the most comforting sound he'd heard in two long years.

Why had he let her go? His reasons had seemed so right, so overpowering, in the heat of his anger and the burning humiliation of what he'd perceived as betrayal. But he believed her now when she said she'd told only the truth.

He should have believed it all along. He should have told her what he'd read and heard her side of the story. She'd have told him the truth, that she hadn't painted him as an unstable obsessive, and then maybe—

Maybe what? Maybe they'd still be together?

He'd have found a way to screw it up. He'd never had a relationship last longer than a few months before Olivia. Looking back, he wasn't sure how she'd put up with him as long as she had.

Maybe her own emotional baggage had made her more patient than she might have been. She'd come from poverty, from an unstable home with a young and irresponsible mother. Her father had been little more than a stranger, and while she'd sworn nothing terrible had happened to her during her childhood, he'd begun to suspect her father's behavior with her when she reached her teens had made her uncomfortable.

"I was lucky," she'd said firmly the one time he'd brought the subject up. "My mom might have been a major mess as a parent, but she never let anyone hurt me that way. Besides, after I hit my teens, we moved away from Sand Mountain, and I never saw him again."

He hadn't said what he'd been thinking, that maybe her mother had chosen to leave their hometown behind to get her away from her father and his discomfiting behavior.

Whatever the reason, he was glad she'd got out of that situation mostly unscathed.

But she hadn't got away without emotional baggage,

any more than he'd escaped his own troubled youth without deep and lingering trust issues.

An unfamiliar sound drifted toward him through the inky darkness, dragging his mind out of the past and back into the cold, uncertain present.

Not unfamiliar, he realized as the noise came inexorably closer.

Just unexpected.

Footsteps approached the cave at a slow, steady pace, crunching the crusty snow underfoot.

They had a visitor.

Chapter 8

Consciousness returned to Olivia in a nerve-rattling rush, leaving her disoriented. Something had awakened her. But what?

"Don't make a sound." She recognized Cade Landry's voice, quiet but urgent. "Someone is moving around outside the cave." His voice was little more than a whisper of breath against her cheek that time.

She tried to sit up and realized she was cocooned in her sleeping bag.

She heard the faint sound of a zipper, and cold air flooded over her, scattering goose bumps across her skin. Wriggling free, she rose to her feet.

Cold steel pressed against her fingers. Her Glock 19. She didn't bother to check the magazine—she'd loaded it before they left the cabin.

"How do you know someone's out there?"

As if in answer, she heard the crunch of boots in the snow outside. She went very still and silent, her nerves instantly on high alert.

Landry touched her arm briefly then moved toward the mouth of the cave, staying out of the semicircle of faint illumination that lightened the cave floor just in front of the entrance.

She joined him there, just a few feet from the world outside, peering through the darkness for any sign of movement.

"Do you see anyone?" She felt his question more than she heard it, a huff of warm breath tickling her ear.

"No."

Suddenly, shockingly close by, a male voice uttered a low oath.

Next to her, Landry's body reacted with a slight jerk. She put her hand on his arm, recognizing the voice. "It's okay. I know who it is."

"Sharp, if you're in there, I think I just broke my damn ankle." The male voice outside spoke in a whisper.

With a sigh, she started toward the cave door.

Landry caught her arm, jerking her back against the hard heat of his body. "Are you crazy?"

"I told you—I know who it is."

"It could be a trap."

"It's not a trap," came the voice from outside, sounding both pained and annoyed.

She pulled free of Landry's grasp and went outside. Sitting on a low boulder nearby was a lean man with spiky brown hair and a pained look twisting his feral features. He had one leg crossed over the other, massaging his ankle through the hiking boot.

"Hammond, what the hell do you think you're doing up here in a snowstorm?"

Seth Hammond made a face. "I could ask you the same thing."

She shot him a pointed look and he shrugged.

"Rachel and I bought a place just up the gap from where you live. I took the baby out to see her first snow and I spotted two idiots climbing up the mountain in a bloody blizzard. One of 'em was dragging something behind him like a pack mule. So I went and got my binoculars. You can imagine my surprise when I saw one of those idiots was you."

"Funny."

"Anyway, I thought I should see what you were up to. And who was with you."

She sighed, looking at her colleague from The Gates. "What if I didn't want you to know what I was up to and who I was with?"

He eased his foot to the ground. "Well, the good news is, I don't think I can hike down the mountain to tell anybody what I saw. I'll probably just sit here and freeze to death, and nobody will ever find out what you're up to."

"Do you really think it's broken?"

"It's not broken." Landry stepped out of the cave, taking up a protective stance close to her. "You would have screamed when you put your foot down on the ground that way if it was broken."

Seth peered up at Landry through narrowed eyes. "You a doctor?"

"No. I'm a guy who's had a broken ankle."

Seth pushed to his feet, testing the injured limb. He

seemed to be holding his weight easily enough. "What do you know? It's not broken."

"Told you it was a trap," Landry muttered to Olivia.

"It wasn't a trap." Olivia looked pointedly at Seth. "Did Quinn send you?"

"No. I told you—I saw you from my house."

"You're not seriously trying to sell me that story."

The look on Seth Hammond's face was pure innocence. "Would I lie?"

She rolled her eyes. "Uh, yeah, you'd lie. You were a con artist for years. It's kind of what you do."

"Con artist?" Landry asked.

"Reformed," Seth said with a feral grin.

"Or so he says." Olivia glanced at Landry. "Think we should just leave him out here? Since he's not crippled or anything?"

"Oh, come on, Sharp. It's damn cold out here, and I think I hear the sound of a heater running in that cave."

"Should have packed your own," Landry said.

Seth gave him a considering look. "Don't believe I got your name."

"Don't believe you did," Landry agreed.

"Might as well let him get warm or he'll sit out here whining all night and keep us awake." Olivia nodded for Seth to enter the cave ahead of her.

Landry caught her arm as she started into the cave after Seth. He kept his voice low. "I don't like this."

"He's a colleague at The Gates."

"I don't care. I don't trust anyone at The Gates except you."

"But I do. And we're going to need help if everything you've told me is the truth."

"Of course it's the truth."

"Then we don't need to try to go up against a whole army of well-armed, morally bankrupt rednecks by our-selves."

Seth's voice wafted out of the cave. "Got any extra MREs in here?"

"No," Olivia and Landry called in unison. She looked up at him, struggling against a smile.

He didn't fight it, grinning down at her, his dimples making an appearance that even the dark night couldn't quite hide. "I don't know, Sharp. You and I always made a pretty good team. Just the two of us."

She took a step back from him, alarmed by the sharp tug of longing that gripped her by the heart. "There hasn't been just the two of us in a long time."

His grin faded. "You trust your buddies at The Gates, but you don't trust me."

"*You* don't trust *me*," she countered, lowering her voice further. "That was always our problem."

"I guess it was," he conceded. "And it went both ways."

She couldn't argue. "But maybe it's not too late to learn to have a little trust in each other." She glanced toward the cave. "I'm telling you, Seth Hammond is a lot of things, but he's not a traitor. He takes his work at The Gates very seriously, and part of his work is watch-ing the backs of other agents. Including me."

"So you're asking me to trust your judgment about a man who claims he hiked who knows how many hours up this mountain just to see what you were doing?"

She couldn't stop a soft huff of laughter at his dry tone. "Yeah. I guess that's exactly what I'm asking."

He looked toward the cave entrance then back at her. "That's a hell of a lot to ask, Sharp."

"I know."

He sighed. "Okay. Fine. We'll let the huckster join our slumber party."

"Reformed huckster." Seth's voice drifted out from the cave.

"Ears like a bat," Landry murmured. "Kinda looks like one, too."

"I heard that."

"Shut up and grab yourself one of those protein bars," Olivia called to Seth. "But keep your mitts off my MREs."

Landry nodded for her to come with him, a little farther from the cave. She followed, trying to hide her growing amusement at his irritation. When they reached the edge of the rock formation that formed Parson's Chair, he stopped and turned to look at her.

"You don't think he really just spotted us hiking up the mountain and took it upon himself to follow us all the way up here on a whim, do you?"

"I'm not an idiot."

"So what do you think? Quinn had him staked out to watch your place?"

"Maybe. Or more likely, he's tracking us electronically in some way."

"You mean GPS?"

She glanced back toward the cave. "Some of the equipment I brought with us came from The Gates. I guess there could be trackers inside some of them."

"Quinn tracks his agents? He doesn't trust you?"

"We had a problem with leaks. We had a mole in the agency, and Quinn's very touchy about it. So for a while, he was tracking all the agents to see where they went. I guess it's hard for him to let go of his CIA instincts."

"So the hillbilly con man in there might be removing all the trackers while we're out here chatting?"

She shook her head. "No. Quinn doesn't care if I find out about the trackers. He's making a point to me with them anyway."

"And that point would be?"

"I might be one of his agents. I might even be one of the ones he's most likely to confide in. But he's never going to fully trust me. Or anyone else."

"Sounds like a couple of people I know."

She made herself meet his gaze. Now that her eyes had adjusted to the dark, she could make out the details of his familiar face, the lean planes of his cheeks and the curve of his full bottom lip, a hint of softness in his otherwise chiseled features. She couldn't make out colors, but she knew from experience that his green eyes held a touch of hazel, shifting hues with his emotions. Right now, she knew, his eyes would be a deep, smoky green, like a forest pool reflecting the earthy colors around it. A hue of green she'd learned long ago meant he was troubled and tense.

"It's freezing out here. Why don't we go back into the cave?" She lowered her voice to an intimate murmur.

He slanted a look at her. "Right now, hearing you talk to me in that tone, I'm really wishing your good buddy the con man wasn't waiting for us in that cave."

She felt a jolt of pure sexual thrill whip through her body like electricity. She'd forgotten how easily he'd been able to seduce her out of a bad mood or a fit of anger. One soft, oblique hint of desire in that sexy growl of a voice, and she was on fire from the inside out.

"Landry—"

He smiled, sighed and gestured toward the cave.

When he spoke, his voice was soft with understanding. "Come on. Let's get inside before he eats all our food."

Landry hadn't expected to get much sleep with a stranger sharing the cave with him and Olivia, but her sense of ease must have been contagious, for he was asleep nearly as quickly as she was and woke to morning light seeping into the cave and the sound of a whispered conversation taking place close by.

"Of course he sent me." That was Seth Hammond's quiet drawl.

"He doesn't trust me?"

"He doesn't trust sleeping beauty over there."

"Landry's not a danger to me."

"Are you sure about that?"

There was a brief pause before her answer, long enough for Landry's stomach to tighten.

"Positive," she answered, and even in a whisper, conviction rang in her words. "He needs my help. I didn't know how to give it to him before, but I'm not going to stop this time until we figure it out."

Deciding to stop his eavesdropping while he was ahead, Landry rolled over and made a low, sleepy groaning sound as he stretched.

"Good morning," Olivia said.

He turned to look at her and his breath caught. Her face was free of makeup, her hair was a tousled mess, but she was still the most beautiful thing he'd seen in ages, and even the presence of Seth Hammond didn't keep him from wanting to cross to her and take her to bed right there on the icy cave floor.

He managed to control the urge and pushed up to

a sitting position. "No more unwanted visitors while I was asleep?"

"No, just me," Seth said with an unperturbed grin. "Let's just get this out in the open, okay? I know who you are. I know the FBI is looking for you. And I know Olivia here doesn't think you're one of the bad guys. And since my track record with the authorities isn't exactly clean, I'm in no position to judge your decision to run instead of turn yourself in."

"How did a guy like you ever get a job with The Gates in the first place?" Landry grabbed his jacket as an icy draft raced through the cave, making him shiver. Olivia had already turned off the heater, and most of the residual heat had dissipated.

Olivia tossed Landry his half of the leftovers from their meal the night before. "Eat some breakfast. We can talk about Quinn's hiring practices later. We need to get on the trail again."

"At least it's downhill from here," Seth said in a cheerful drawl that made Landry want to throw his breakfast at the man.

Instead, he examined the packets Olivia had tossed to him. Peanut butter and crackers, a toaster pastry, raisins and an oatmeal cookie.

"Yum," he muttered.

"Food is fuel," Olivia said briskly as she started rolling up her sleeping bag. "Eat up. Daylight's burning."

Hiking downhill in the snow wasn't a lot better than hiking uphill, Landry decided a couple of hours later as he hit a slick patch and landed hard on his tailbone. The impact knocked the wind out of him for a moment, and the poles lashed together at the pointed end of the travois cracked hard against his chin.

Olivia and Seth both stopped to help him back up. "You want me to pull the mule cart for a while?" Seth asked, nodding at the travois with a friendly grin.

"Let him do it," Olivia told Landry in a dry tone, already heading back onto the trail. "Serves him right for letting Quinn turn him into his personal bloodhound."

Landry handed over the travois poles and caught up with Olivia on the trail. "Are you sure heading into town is the best idea? Quinn clearly doesn't trust me or he wouldn't have sent your huckster buddy back there to make sure you were okay in my company."

Hammond's voice piped up behind them. "Re-formed—"

"Shut up!" Landry and Olivia snapped in unison.

Olivia slanted a quick look at Landry, her lips curving in a half smile. "I don't know if it's the best idea," she admitted, her smile starting to fade. "But it's the best one I have. You have any better ideas?"

"No," he had to admit.

"At the rate we're going, we should hit town in about two hours. Then the pace should pick up because the streets are relatively flat, and you won't be tripping over hidden stones every few yards."

"What's between here and town?"

"Enemy territory," Hammond said, his voice closer. He'd caught up with them despite his heavier load.

"There's a small enclave of people who claim allegiance to the BRI," Olivia explained. "Their cabins are a little ways off the trail, so if we're lucky, we shouldn't have any trouble with them."

Landry caught her arm and stopped her in her tracks. "If we're lucky?"

"It snowed nearly a foot up here in the mountains. Power up this way is spotty on a good week, so they're probably hunkered down, trying to stay warm. It'll be all right."

"You hope."

"I expect," she said firmly. But he saw her grip her Mossberg shotgun more tightly as she started hiking forward again.

They walked awhile in silence before Olivia broke it with a soft question. "Where is your evidence?"

So much had happened between the time he'd shown up at her cabin and this laborious hike down the mountain, it took Landry a moment to understand what she was asking.

"Evidence?" Hammond prodded when Landry didn't answer immediately. "Evidence of what?"

"Of the BRI putting a hit out on me," Olivia answered in a flat tone that belied the feral alertness behind her blue eyes.

"It's not a hit exactly," Landry corrected her.

"So they interrogate me roughly for a few days before they put me out of my misery. Close enough to a hit for me," she said.

"Wait—what?" Hammond wriggled out from under the travois and trudged forward to join them. "Someone's trying to take you prisoner, and you're out here hiking into town by yourself?"

"She's not by herself," Landry protested.

Hammond shot him a hard look. "Close enough. Why didn't you tell Quinn? He could have put a half dozen agents on your place to stand guard."

"So then I'm Quinn's prisoner instead."

"At least Quinn's not looking to put a bullet in your brain," Hammond snapped, all of the folksy humor gone from his demeanor. "Damn it, Sharp, why do you always play it this way? Why don't you let anybody help you?"

Landry looked from Hammond to Olivia, taking in the bristle of anger in her expression and the frustration in Hammond's voice. Apparently, this wasn't the first time Olivia had clashed with her fellow agents at The Gates about her lone-wolf attitude.

He guessed a few things about Olivia hadn't changed in the past few years after all.

"Let's just get to your office and get warm." Landry nodded at the travois Hammond had dropped. "You can call Quinn and tattle on her when we get there."

The sharp-eyed look Hammond threw Landry's way would have intimidated a different man. But after all that Landry had gone through over the past few months, it would take a hell of a lot scarier man than Hammond to make him flinch.

Hammond released a harsh breath and stalked back to the travois.

"You want me to spell you for a bit?" Landry asked as the other man jerked the lashed poles over his shoulders.

"I'm good," Hammond growled.

"You have such a way with people," Landry murmured to Olivia as he caught up with her.

"I don't want people at the agency thinking I need to be wrapped in cotton and put away somewhere safe."

"Do they do that as a rule?"

She cut her eyes at him. "I haven't tested the theory yet."

"If you're so worried that's what's going to happen, why are we going to The Gates in the first place?"

Her voice rose. "Because I have nowhere else safe to go, okay?"

They walked on in silence for another half hour, battling a rising wind that whipped up the mountain, blowing snow around them and limiting visibility to a few dozen yards. The watery sunlight that had offered a brief reprieve against the icy chill had faded behind a sheet of low-lying clouds that threatened more snow.

"What was the forecast the last time you checked?" Landry asked. He'd lost his cell phone months ago and had never bothered to replace it. Whom did he have to call? But he'd seen Olivia checking her phone that morning before they hit the trail.

"It might snow a little more," she answered. "They weren't sure."

"How much more?"

Coming to a sudden stop, she didn't answer. Landry followed her gaze into the blowing snow and saw what she'd seen. Movement, straight ahead.

There was someone out there in the woods ahead.

"How close are we to the BRI enclave?" Landry asked softly.

"Too close," she answered.

Behind them, Seth Hammond uttered a soft expletive.

"Well, now," came a low drawl, "look who just wandered into our territory, boys."

Landry froze, a flash of images flooding his memory so hard and fast he felt as if he'd been gut-punched.

He knew that voice. He'd heard that voice every day for a month, the deceptively gentle tones that had been a sound track for the brutality of his henchmen.

He'd never seen the face—they'd made sure of it. But he'd know that voice anywhere, even in his nightmares.

Landry turned slowly, bracing himself for his first look at the monster who haunted his dreams.

But before he could move, a crack of rifle fire split the icy air, and he threw himself at Olivia, shoving her to the ground beneath him.

Chapter 9

The idiot was trying to protect her!

But in the process, he'd damn near knocked the Mossberg out of her hand. She shoved him off her and rolled onto her stomach, leveling the barrel toward the last place she'd seen their gun-toting intruders.

But they were gone, running through the snowy woods like wraiths, fading into the whitewashed scenery.

As Olivia turned her head to check the rear, Landry pushed her down again, his weapon hand whipping toward a spot behind her. "Don't move."

"Landry—" Hammond began.

"Shut it," Landry barked. "Put the guns down."

"You're outnumbered." The familiar voice sent a shudder of relief ratcheting through her body. She shoved Landry off again, ignoring his growling order to be still, and looked up to confirm what she'd heard.

Six men in arctic camouflage stood in a semicircle around them, eyes alert and rifles raised. One man was clearly in charge, a dark-haired man with dark hazel eyes and lean, chiseled features. He wore the camo like a second skin, which made sense, she supposed, given his decade in the US Army.

"They're friendlies," she said sharply to Landry, putting her hand over the hand that held his gun.

"Says who?" he growled, shoving her hand away.

"I say," she said firmly, circling to stand between his pistol and her colleagues. The second she got a look at his wild-eyed expression, a quiver of pure terror ripped through her gut. In that moment, she realized, he could just as easily shoot her as not.

Then his gaze focused on her. His expression softened a notch, and he slowly lowered the Kimber to his side.

"Friendly to whom?" he asked, his voice raspy and unsteady.

"To me. And you." She held out her hand to him.

For a moment he looked at her as if she'd lost her mind. But she didn't budge.

After a long, breathless moment, he turned the Kimber grip toward her and handed it over.

She slid the Kimber into the waistband of her jeans and turned to face the men from The Gates. "You should have brought Ava," she said to the leader. "He knows her."

"Yeah, well, she and Solano are down in Alabama. Solano's sister had her baby a week early." Sutton Calhoun shrugged and nodded toward the men flanking him. "Somebody go help Seth out. He's too damn scrawny to be a pack mule."

Hammond made a rude gesture at Calhoun, earning a laugh from Calhoun and the other guys on the squad. But he stepped forward and gave Sutton a downright brotherly hug. "How'd you know to come to our rescue?"

"We didn't. We just knew from your last text that y'all were heading down the mountain in the morning, so we figured you might run into trouble here in the redneck red zone. Quinn asked for volunteers, but when nobody spoke up, he made us draw straws." Calhoun grinned. "We got the short ones."

"Funny."

"This him?" Calhoun nodded toward Landry but looked at Olivia for a response.

"What, you don't have my mug shot hanging on the office wall?" Landry's sarcastic tone almost hid his underlying tension.

Almost.

"I'm Sutton Calhoun." Calhoun extended his hand.

Landry ignored it.

"Manners," Olivia murmured.

He looked at her as if she'd lost her mind. When he answered, his coastal Georgia drawl kicked in. "This ain't a cocktail party, darlin'."

Calhoun shrugged and finished the introductions. "This is Fitzpatrick to my right. That's Dennison on the left. Cooper's the big guy. Jackson's the guy on the end."

"And I believe we've spoken before." Nick Darcy stepped forward.

"You answered the pay phone at the Econo-Tel," Landry said, showing the first hint of relaxing. "The guy with the British accent. You were protecting Rigsby."

Darcy nodded. "You probably saved her life with that call. If we'd been even a few steps behind Darryl Boyle—"

"Olivia says Rigsby's okay."

"She's splendid," Darcy answered in a tone so besotted, Olivia couldn't quell a smile.

"I see," Landry murmured, glancing at Olivia.

"We probably shouldn't stick around here much longer," Calhoun warned. "Those fellows might have gone for reinforcements."

"Don't suppose you brought any skis with you?" Hammond muttered.

"You can't ski worth a lick anyway," Calhoun said, clapping his friend on the back before barking an order in the sharp tone he must have learned during his days in the Army. "Move out."

The little town of Purgatory looked like a Christmas card, covered with snow and sparkling with lights in the deepening twilight. The temptation to stop his weary trudge forward and just enjoy the sight was more than Landry could resist.

He'd been in and out of civilization over the past months, slipping into bigger towns when he needed supplies or information, but most of his time had been spent in the hills, bunking down wherever he could find a kind soul who would take pity on his homeless state and give him a hot meal and a place to stay for the night.

He hadn't stayed overnight in a town since he'd got away from the BRI, and he'd begun to wonder if he ever would again.

"Can't linger." That was Sutton Calhoun's voice, gentle but firm in his ear as he nudged Landry forward. "We're almost home."

"Home," it turned out, was a deceptively shabby-looking mansion on a large, tree-shaded corner lot near the center of town. An engraved plaque near the large iron gates read "Buckley Mansion, est. 1895." A smaller, less ostentatious sign on the gates themselves, however, proclaimed that they'd arrived at The Gates.

"Why The Gates?" Landry asked Olivia as they entered through the iron portal and started up the snowy walk.

"I'm not sure," Olivia admitted.

"The gate of purgatory," Dennison offered as he passed them on the way to the front porch. "Though some of us think it's the gates of hell instead. Occasionally."

It looked like heaven to Landry, welcoming lights glowing warm in the windows, though when they walked inside, the front lobby was empty. But there was light and blessed heat, and an instant sense of safety, however transitory it might prove to be. The temptation to relax his guard was almost more than Landry could resist.

"Who else is here?" Olivia asked.

"Rigsby's here," Dennison drawled. "You know Darcy—never leaves home without her. Brand is up with Quinn at his office."

"Delilah's working the storm shift?" Olivia asked.

"Along with Sara and Ivy."

"Sara's Dennison's wife—Ridge County sheriff's deputy," Olivia told Landry. "Delilah and Ivy are married to Brand and Calhoun, respectively."

"They're both local cops over in Bitterwood."

"Y'all have some sort of law-enforcement dating service going on the side?" Landry asked softly as Olivia led him to the winding stairway leading to the second floor while the other men headed out of sight, shedding their outerwear as they went.

She smiled. "Easier to date someone who gets your crazy hours. You should know that better than anyone."

He did. Of course, he and Olivia had shared most of those crazy work hours, which could have been a problem, he supposed. But somehow it never had been. Work was one part of their shared lives that had never been an issue.

Until Richmond.

He put the dark memories out of his head and followed Olivia down a dimly lit hallway to a room at the eastern corner of the house. She gave a soft knock but didn't wait for a reply before she entered.

A sandy-haired man in his forties sat behind a large oak desk, leaning back in his chair with his hands steepled over his chest. He looked up, unsurprised. "You're an hour later than I expected."

Olivia sighed. "We ran into a couple of BRI boys. Slowed us down."

"Everybody unscathed?"

"I'm sure Sutton or someone on the team has already texted you the details," she drawled, nodding at the other man in the room, a tall, dark-haired man with blue eyes who had turned at the opening of the door. "Brand."

Landry froze. "You're Adam Brand."

Brand's dark eyebrows lifted. "And you're Cade Landry."

"You were on the FBI's naughty list, too."

"I was," Brand said with a nod and a faint whisper of a smile. "Unfairly in my case. What about yours?"

The smile hadn't disappeared, but the room felt instantly colder and less hospitable.

"Definitely unfair in my case," he said firmly. "All the way around, as a matter of fact."

"So we've concluded," Quinn said mildly, waving at the empty chair beside Olivia. "Sit. You must be exhausted."

Landry wished he could make a stand, but his aching legs told him to stop being a stubborn fool. He sank gratefully into the armchair, turning so he could keep both Quinn and Brand in sight.

"We know Darryl Boyle was working with the BRI. We have no reason to think you were, despite your unexplained disappearance. Would you like to explain it?"

Landry glanced at Olivia. "Not at this time."

"Understandable. There's hot food in the kitchen downstairs, and you'd probably like to take advantage of indoor plumbing about now. Sharp can show you where everything is."

"That's it?" Landry asked.

Quinn's sandy eyebrows lifted a notch. "Did you expect something else?"

"You're an ex-spook. I guess I anticipated some sort of enhanced interrogation techniques."

"You've already been through enough of those. Haven't you?" The gentleness of Quinn's tone caught Landry off guard. Apparently, it came as a surprise to Olivia, as well; she stared at her boss with a look of confusion.

"Go get settled. Get warm. Eat some food, drink some water and then get some sleep. We'll all still be here in the morning. Maybe you'll feel more like talking then."

Olivia rose first, heading for the door in stony silence. Landry followed her out, catching up with her halfway to the stairs.

She turned to look at him, her eyes snapping with anger. "That bastard's trying to play you."

Landry nodded. "Yeah, I know. We used to interrogate suspects, too, remember?"

She let out a long, slow breath, visibly trying to relax. "I know. And I know he needs the information. Hell, I still don't know everything that happened to you, either. And I'd like to."

He shook his head. "No, you wouldn't."

She put her hand on his arm, her fingers still icy from the hike in the snow. "I need to know. So when you're ready—"

He covered her hand with his for a moment then gently pulled her hand away, taking a step back from her. "I'm not sure I'll ever be ready, Olivia. Can you deal with that?"

She gazed up at him, her blue eyes troubled. "Can you?"

He nodded toward the stairs. "Quinn said something about food and water?"

She pressed her lips to a thin line. "Yeah. Follow me."

She headed down the hallway toward the staircase, her spine rigid with annoyance. He couldn't hold back a smile at the sight of a pissed-off Olivia Sharp stalking ahead of him like a lioness on the hunt.

He'd missed the hell out of this woman.

Olivia was finally, blessedly warm. A hot meal, a long, steamy shower and the marvel of central heating had managed to drive away the last of her chills and leave her feeling toasty and half-asleep.

In fact, she must have dozed off for a few moments, for when the soft knock at her dormitory door jarred her awake, the shock left her nerves jangling and her head buzzing.

"Olivia?" Landry spoke quietly from the other side of the door.

She pushed herself to a sitting position on the bed. "Come in."

He slipped inside, stopping just inside the room. "I'm sorry. Did I wake you?"

She resisted the urge to rub her gritty eyes. "No. I'm up. For now."

He walked a few steps closer, flashing a lopsided smile. "Same here. I just wanted to check on you. It was a long hike."

"I'm fine." She patted the edge of the bed. "Sit."

He sat, turning to face her. "I know I gave you a hard time, but thank you for making me come down here. I guess over the past year, I forgot I don't always have to be an army of one."

She'd had to learn the same lesson, she realized. Especially since she'd come to The Gates specifically to investigate a few of her fellow agents suspected of being the source of the devastating information leaks that had put people's lives at risk.

"The people who work here are rough around the edges, but they're good agents. And we really do have each other's back. Quinn wouldn't have it any other way."

"I'm still not sure I like him. I know I don't trust him."

She couldn't blame him for that. "I don't trust him

to pick me over the mission. But I trust his passion for protecting this country and its people."

"But you're a security and investigations company. Not a branch of the military."

"And yet, we stand in the breach. There are a lot of people in these hills who just want to live a decent life without fear. And there are a lot of people in these same hills who prey on those good people because they can. Because they're ruthless and better armed."

He flashed her a bemused smile, triggering the dimples that knocked a decade off his age and made her insides twist with desire. "Still protecting and serving, huh? Without all the bureaucratic crap that used to make you nuts."

"It's not all small-scale like trying to take down the BRI. We have some big clients who pay a lot for our training and expertise. It's just—taking down the BRI is Quinn's passion right now."

"Why's that?"

She shrugged, realizing she'd never bothered to ask the question of her wily boss. "I guess maybe it has something to do with his having grown up in these hills. I don't know. Maybe he knows what it's like to be a victim of the predators."

"Or he was a predator himself," Landry murmured. "And maybe he wants to make up for it."

Olivia looked at her former partner through narrowed eyes. She hadn't ever considered the possibility that Quinn had once been one of the human vipers who stalked the Appalachian Mountains. "I don't know. Maybe you're right."

Landry reached across the narrow space between them, taking her hand. "It doesn't matter what inspired him, I guess. We all have mistakes in our pasts we can't correct. At least he's trying to make things better around here instead of worse."

The feel of his rough palm against hers felt right, she realized, dropping her gaze to their joined hands. She'd missed him so intensely over the past two years that having him here, touching him and hearing him speak in that deep Georgia drawl she'd always loved, seemed like a dream she'd wake from any moment.

"Are you really here?" she asked, feeling immediately foolish.

He smiled at her again, making her heart skip a beat. "Feels a little unreal, doesn't it?"

She nodded. "I didn't think I'd ever see you again."

He lifted her hand to his mouth, brushing her knuckles with his lips. "I used to have dreams of you. That you were beside me again. Nothing big. Just beside me, sitting close enough that I could feel the warmth of your body by mine. Hear your breathing. And then I'd wake up." He let go of her hand and dropped his own hands to his knees. "Doesn't matter. Here you are. Warm and breathing."

"Are you never going to tell me what happened to you when you were taken captive?"

"It's not important."

"I can tell it's still important to *you.*"

"I'm okay." He flashed another smile, but even the distracting dimples couldn't make it look anything but forced.

But she didn't want to push him. If he needed to talk about what he'd gone through, he'd do it in his own time.

She hoped.

"I don't want to keep you up if you're tired." He started to get up.

She caught his hand, holding him in place. "Don't go."

He looked down at her hand on his. When he spoke, his voice was a low rasp. "Are you sure you want me to stay?"

She knew what he was asking.

"Yes."

He sat in front of her again, closer this time. He turned his hand until it was palm to palm with hers, their fingers twining. "I like your hair short."

She laughed at the non sequitur. "I like yours longer."

He grinned again, the expression deliciously sincere. "Couldn't find many barbershops out in the wilderness."

"That's where you've been all this time?"

"Most of it." He took her other hand, twined his fingers with hers.

"Where did you stay?"

"Camped out a lot. Stayed at cheap roadside motels now and then, when I could spare a little cash."

"How'd you get any cash?" She leaned closer, letting the warmth of his nearness envelop her. "Did you steal?"

"Define *steal*." He grinned at her frown. "I might have eaten a crab apple off someone's tree now and then. But mostly I used money I'd stashed away in case of emergency."

She rubbed the back of his hand with her thumb. "You were expecting an emergency?"

"*Expecting* might be too strong a word. I just anticipated the possibility. And tried to prepare for the worst-case scenario."

"And was what happened the worst case?" She looked up at him.

"Not the worst."

"But bad enough."

He gave her hands a squeeze. "Let it go for now, Livvie. Okay?"

She would have liked to argue, but she didn't want to risk making him get up and leave. "Okay."

"Thank you."

"For now," she added.

He smiled again. "Yeah, I know you don't give up. You're like a bulldog with a chew toy."

"Flattering."

"A beautiful bulldog. A svelte bulldog."

"I think that's an oxymoron."

"Who're you calling an oxymoron?"

She laughed. "I missed this."

"Talking nonsense?"

She stroked his hand again. "Talking nonsense with you."

"Know what I missed?" His voice deepened. Roughened.

Her heartbeat sped up immediately in response. When she spoke, her own voice sounded breathless. "What?"

"This." He leaned forward, closing the space between them, and touched his mouth to hers.

Chapter 10

When they'd been lovers, there had been passion. Tenderness. Laughter. Even sometimes anger. But never, ever this tentative, questing sensation, like two strangers coming together for a stolen kiss.

Landry drew back and studied her face, trying to read the nuances of each expression flitting across her features as her gaze met his with the same quizzical alertness.

"You're different, aren't you?"

He nodded. "So are you."

"But I still want you." Her raw admission sent a blazing arrow of desire shooting straight to his core. "I just don't know—"

He curled his hand around the back of her neck and gently pulled her into an undemanding embrace, struggling to dial back his body's physical response to her touch. He wanted to reconnect to her, as the friends they'd always been, even if they couldn't be lovers again. Rushing into something they'd regret was a bad idea.

"That feels good," she said as he stroked his hand lightly up and down her spine.

"I don't want to lose you again." He brushed his cheek against her temple, starting to enjoy the exquisite tension of holding her close without any intention of taking things any further. "We were friends first, and I'd like to be friends again."

She lifted her hands, cradling his face between her palms. "I'd like that, too, but—" Her words cut off with a little huff, and she bent toward him, covering his mouth with hers.

There was no hesitation in her kiss. No tentativeness. Just a slow, thorough taking that made his head spin and his heartbeat crank up to hyperspeed. Any thought of differences, of unfamiliarity, were swallowed up by the rising heat between them.

This. He wanted this.

He wanted *her*. Right now, just as she was.

She tugged him down to the bed, parting her thighs to let him settle on top of her. One long leg wrapped around his legs, pinning him to her.

"Don't think," she breathed against his lips.

Threading his fingers through her hair, he deepened the kiss, tasting the minty hint of toothpaste on her tongue. She curled her fingers in his T-shirt and tugged the fabric upward, grumbling when he pulled away from the kiss long enough to whip the shirt over his head.

As he bent to kiss her again, she splayed her fingers against his chest, running them through the coarse hair.

She hadn't forgotten how much he liked her hands on him, tracing, teasing, arousing—

A hard rap on the door sent a ripple of raw shock through his nervous system. Olivia growled a soft profanity against his throat and dropped her head back to the pillows.

"What?" she barked toward the closed door.

"Quinn wants to see Landry." Seth's quiet drawl held a touch of amusement, as if he knew exactly what he was interrupting.

"Tell him I'm not his employee, and I'll talk to him in the morning." Landry glanced at Olivia, who was watching him through slightly narrowed eyes. "What?" he added more quietly.

"It's possible he has information you might need," she said in an equally hushed tone.

"It's possible I need a cold shower before I can appear anywhere outside this room," he growled, rolling up to a sitting position and leaning forward in an attempt to get his body back under control.

"I'll go stall Hammond, see if I can find out more about what Quinn wants." She stood and unhurriedly straightened her clothes. Landry watched her smooth the fabric he'd held bunched in his hands mere moments earlier, his heart still pounding a steady cadence of lust.

"Maybe if we hurry—"

Smiling, she bent and kissed him, a slow, wet, deep kiss that made his blood ignite. "Stay put. I'll be back."

As he retrieved his discarded T-shirt, he tried to make out the muted conversation Olivia was having with Seth Hammond outside, but they'd apparently moved too far away from the door. He gave himself a quick once-over and realized she'd managed to unbutton his jeans and get the zipper halfway down without his realizing it. Talented girl!

He zipped up and finger-combed his hair, wishing the dorm rooms in the basement of The Gates had come equipped with a mirror. He didn't need to show up at his command performance with Alexander Quinn looking as if a tall, blonde bombshell had just tried to have her way with him.

Even if she had.

The door opened suddenly and Olivia slipped inside, her expression serious.

"What is it?" he asked.

"An agent has gone missing. Grant Carver. Quinn thinks the BRI have taken him hostage."

A chill washed over Landry, despite the cozy warmth of the room. "When?"

"Sometime this afternoon. His wife called Quinn when he didn't come back from a quick run."

"Couldn't he have just gotten stranded somewhere?"

"That was the assumption. Until she followed his tracks and came upon a patch of snow that looked as if there'd been a struggle. Carver's hat was in the snow. So was an alarming amount of blood. She called the local cops. One of the cops who took the call was Dennison's wife, Sara. She called Dennison to let him know."

Landry sank to the end of the bed, feeling sick. "Any reason why the BRI would go after this guy Carver? Has he had run-ins with any of them?"

Olivia sat next to him, close enough to touch. But he kept his hands on his knees, too wound up to trust himself to touch her. There was a lot about his time in BRI captivity he hadn't told her. Things that he didn't like to think about, things that showed up in his nightmares all too often recently.

"Quinn asked Carver's wife that question. She said no. Some of her distant relatives are involved with the local BRI cell, and she thought that was probably why they could live where they do without too many troubles with the militia members."

"Live where they do?"

She turned to look at him. "They live on the bottom slope of Fowler Ridge. Near that BRI enclave we hiked through today."

"You said it happened this afternoon?" Landry's tone was neutral, but his expressive eyes gave away the emotions roiling behind his mask of calm—anger, worry and guilt Olivia had expected, given the possibility that the mountain rescue The Gates agents had pulled off earlier that day might well have led to the BRI's retaliatory attack on one of the company's agents.

But the fear that roiled behind his green-eyed gaze caught her by surprise.

Landry was afraid. And in all the time she'd known him, she'd rarely seen him afraid of anything.

"If you're wondering if it's connected to you, we don't know." Quinn spoke in a calm tone that didn't manage to hide the fact that he believed Landry's presence in their midst might have precipitated Carver's abduction.

"You know," Landry growled, "I should get out of here. All I'm doing is making things that much harder for you."

Quinn shook his head. "We don't negotiate with terrorists. We certainly don't hand over innocent people to them to get our agents back. Carver knew what he signed on for."

"Carver has a wife. A family." Landry glanced at Olivia.

She'd told him about Carver's pregnant wife and two kids because he'd asked, and she wasn't going to lie to him, even to protect his feelings.

"Nobody has come to us with any demands," Adam Brand said from his seat next to Quinn at the conference table. Besides Landry and herself, there were nine agents seated at the long oak table—Adam Brand and Sutton Calhoun at the head with Quinn, Mark Fitzpatrick, Cain Dennison, Kyle Jackson, Nick Darcy, McKenna Rigsby and Caleb Cooper. All good men in a nasty fight—Brand and Rigsby were former FBI agents, while Calhoun, Dennison, Jackson and Fitzpatrick had all been in the military. Darcy had been with the Diplomatic Security Service for several years, Caleb Cooper had been a narcotics cop in Birmingham, Alabama, and Quinn had been in more dangerous hot spots around the globe than any of them, and he'd lived to tell.

Landry could do a lot worse for backup. But Olivia had a feeling it wasn't the quality of people willing to watch his back that was fueling his fear.

She'd seen the same look in his eyes up on the mountain just before the guys from The Gates had shown up to run off their assailants. It had started when that man from the BRI had spoken.

Had Landry recognized the voice?

"Let's just sit tight for now. The local law is out looking for Carver. Let's let them do their jobs," Quinn suggested.

"Do you have any idea what kind of things they

might do to him?" Landry's voice came out in a strangled growl. Olivia put her hand on his arm but he shrugged away her touch.

Quinn nodded. "We have some idea, yes."

"If he's not leverage—"

"There's a limited amount of information Carver could share with the BRI," Quinn said calmly. "Because of his familial connection to the group, we've kept him away from cases involving the militia group. I'm sure they know that."

"So he *is* leverage."

"Possibly. But there's nothing we can do about it at the moment, so I'd concentrate on something else." Quinn's gaze settled on Landry. "Calhoun says you reacted strongly this afternoon on the mountain, when one of the men who challenged you spoke. You had your back to him, so you must have recognized the voice?"

Landry looked reluctant to speak, but after a moment he nodded. "I think I did."

"Do you know who he was?" Quinn asked.

Olivia could tell from Quinn's tone that he already knew exactly who had accosted them on the mountain earlier that day. He just wanted to establish whether Landry knew.

"I don't know the man's name," Landry answered, looking down at his hands twisting together in his lap. He pulled them apart and gripped the arms of his chair. "I couldn't tell you what he looked like, either. But I'd know that voice in a noisy crowd."

"He was one of your captors?" Olivia asked quietly.

His gaze snapped up to meet hers, full of anger and no small measure of humiliation. "One of them. The worst of them."

"I realize you probably would prefer not to remember what happened during your time in captivity—" Quinn began.

Landry cut him off. "If you're thinking of hooking me up with a shrink or hypnotist or whatever you spook types like to use to poke around in a person's brain, forget it. I don't remember anything that could help you find your missing man. When I got away, I just ran as far and as fast as I could. I'm sure they've already moved operations somewhere else. They moved me around a lot before I got away, so I don't think they have a permanent base for their snatch-and-grab operations."

"Fair enough. Meeting adjourned." Quinn stood, the look he gave the other men sitting around the table serving as a silent warning—Cade Landry was off-limits, for the time being, anyway.

Olivia could tell most of the other agents weren't happy about their boss playing softball with Landry, but they knew better than to voice their dissent at the conference table. They could take it up with him privately later—and from the displeasure in their expressions, Olivia was pretty sure that at least two or three of them would.

But for now, she and Landry were free to go.

"I need to get out of here," Landry murmured as he caught up with her down the hall. "I should never have tried to play this straight. Those bastards don't know the meaning of playing it straight."

She caught his arm as he started toward the stairs. "You're not leaving."

"I'm not staying."

"You know what the conditions out there are like. It's only going to get colder now that the sun has set."

"How cold do you think Grant Carver is right now?" His voice lowered to a deep growl. "Do you have a clue what they might be doing to him?"

"Yes," she answered tightly. "I do have an idea. Maybe you should go compare notes with one of our agents, Hunter Bragg. The BRI took him hostage last year. He has the scars to prove it."

Landry looked away from her, his expression queasy. "They're relentless. They're not really any good at interrogations. They don't know how to play the game, how to get any real information. They just do it because they're sadistic bastards who get off on the feeling of power it gives them to make a grown man scream." He tugged his arm away from her grasp and started down the stairs.

She ran down the steps after him, tripping in her hurry to keep up. He caught her before she tumbled, pulling her tightly against him. A jolt of pure animal awareness bolted through her from the point where her hips met his, and she dug her fingers into the muscles of his upper arms.

"Don't go," she whispered.

"I can't stay."

"You can. At least tonight. Stay tonight."

He looked away from her, his gaze scanning the room before it returned to lock with hers. "You know we can't pick up where we left off."

"You mean you don't want to."

For a second his expression softened, and he looked like the man she used to know, the man who had loved her and made her as happy as she could ever remember being.

"You know I do."

"Then stay. We don't have to pick up where we left off, but please, don't go away again. Not yet, not while you're in trouble. Let me help you."

He brushed her hair back from her cheek, his touch so impossibly tender it made tears sting her eyes. She blinked them back, not willing to let them fall. "I don't know if you can. I don't know if it's fixable."

"Then you can just get some rest. Most of the guys will be up all night trying to piece together what happened to Carver and how we proceed at daylight. We should get some sleep so we can spell them in the morning."

"We?" He tugged lightly at her hair.

"You used to be a damn good FBI agent. I don't think you've forgotten everything you learned at the academy, have you?"

"Trying to bend me to your will by dangling a mystery in front of me?"

"Is it working?"

"Maybe." He bent toward her until his forehead touched hers. "You win. I'll stay. For now."

She gave his arms a squeeze. "Come on. Let's get some sleep. Tomorrow's going to be a long day."

He didn't resist as she led him back down to the basement dormitory rooms, stopping outside the door of her room. "As tempting as it is to go back in there with you…"

She smiled. "The goal is sleep?"

He nodded toward the room across from hers, where

he'd stashed his own things. "I'll be there in the morning. I promise."

She pressed her hand to the front of his shirt, feeling the reassuring thud of his heartbeat against her palm. "If you aren't, I'm hunting you down."

He sneaked a quick look around, as if reassuring himself they were alone, then bent and gave her a quick kiss. "Get some sleep."

She waited in her doorway until he entered his own room and closed the door behind him, then turned and entered her own dorm room, flicking on the light.

The bed was the way she'd left it, slightly rumpled and full of recent memories of Landry—the way he smelled, the sensation of his hands on her bare skin, the electric thrill of their bodies pressed close and straining for more. She closed her eyes and sank on the edge of the bed, swamped by memories. Of their first meeting, the literal electric shock that passed between them as they shook hands, making them laugh and snatch their hands away.

The more visceral shock of desire the first time they'd taken a step past the slow burn of attraction and kissed at the end of a long day at work.

She lay back on the bed, opening her eyes to stare at the ceiling. They hadn't planned to start a relationship. For weeks, even months, they pretended what was happening between them was just chemical. Two people enjoying each other, no strings attached.

But there had been strings. Probably from the beginning. Despite her tumultuous childhood with a promiscuous and reckless mother, despite his parents' distant, businesslike marriage, somehow, they'd been foolish enough to believe in the possibility of forever.

And then the bombing at the warehouse in Richmond had blown everything apart.

The tears she'd been fighting earlier leaked from her eyes and slid down her cheeks. She brushed them away, angry at the sign of weakness and glad that Landry wasn't here to see it.

She couldn't start thinking about forever again. She just had to focus on getting through one day at a time. She had to figure out a way to get Landry out of the mess he was in. Give him back the life that the BRI had stolen from him when he'd ended up their captive.

Then maybe she'd figure out how to say a proper goodbye this time.

He'd arrived at his apartment after midnight, the metallic taste of fear in his mouth and his mind reeling with questions he didn't know how to answer. He'd tried to help Agent Rigsby, hadn't he? It had been a risk to try to call her and warn her that someone else from the FBI was coming after her.

But before he'd hung up the phone with Darryl Boyle, supervisory special agent with the FBI's Knoxville field office, he'd known McKenna Rigsby was in big trouble.

Boyle was railroading her. The man had said nothing incriminating, but Landry had heard the flicker of eagerness in his voice when he told Landry Rigsby had called him, as well.

He was going after her. And he had no intention of bringing her back alive.

Landry had tried to help her, but he couldn't reach her before Boyle did. He wasn't even sure where she'd be—she'd set a trap, hoping to ensnare the person who had tried to kill her before, and she might not have been in either of the two locations where she'd told him and Boyle she'd be.

He'd just hoped she'd got away. He'd done all he dared. He had his own trouble with the FBI, with a career that was already on life support. He couldn't risk sticking his neck out, in case he was wrong about Boyle.

What a coward he'd been.

When the four men materialized out of the shadows of his living room, he'd been unprepared for a fight. They took him down with ease, binding him with duct tape and hustling him out to a van he hadn't noticed parked outside his unit.

That had been the beginning of his trip to hell.

Chapter 11

Olivia woke to darkness and a gnawing sense of unease she couldn't place. She knew she was in one of the dorm rooms in the basement of the old Buckley Mansion that Alexander Quinn had transformed into The Gates. She hadn't been awakened by a sudden noise or an unexpected touch in the night. She'd just gone from sleep to animal awareness in one fluid motion, without any idea why all of her senses were suddenly tingling.

She listened to the darkness, waiting for some noise, some sensation to remind her what had summoned her from sleep, but there was nothing but the languid silence of a mostly unoccupied space. Down here, in the rooms built out of the mansion's stone foundation, even the creaks and groans of the old house settling rarely penetrated this quiet sanctuary.

Maybe one of the other agents had come down to catch some sleep before morning, she thought, pushing off the covers and swinging her feet down to the cold floor. Shivering, she felt around for the slip-on shoes she'd retrieved from her desk in the agents' bull pen and slid them on her feet.

She padded to the door, stopping to listen before she opened it and stepped outside into the dimly lit main room. The basement dormitory consisted of one long, wide corridor with six small bedrooms branching off on either side, three to the right and three to the left. There was a large bathroom at the end of the hall. That door was open, as were four of the other doors in the dorm.

Only Landry's door remained closed. Apparently, all of the other agents remaining on the premises were still upstairs with Quinn.

She crossed the hallway and pressed her ear to the closed door, wondering if she'd heard noises coming from the room across the hall. But she could hear nothing from inside, except a faint creaking noise that might have been the bedsprings shifting under Landry's weight.

Or was she simply imagining that she could hear sounds of occupation, because the alternative—the possibility that what had jarred her awake had been Landry sneaking out of the dorm—was something she didn't want to believe?

Just open the door, her anxiety whispered in her ear. *Open it and you'll know if he bugged out on you.*

She turned the door handle, half expecting it to be locked. But it moved easily in her grasp, the door swinging quietly inward.

Landry was there, still in the bed. The creaking noise she'd heard repeated twice, louder now.

He was moving in his sleep, jerky twitches rather than thrashing that might hint at a violent nightmare. But the light angling through the open doorway fell on his face, revealing an expression that was nothing short of terror.

Landry jerked up to a sitting position so suddenly, she couldn't hold back a gasp of surprise. Her hand flexed, rattling the doorknob, and his gaze whipped up to meet hers.

"I'm sorry," she breathed. "I didn't mean—"

He pulled his knees up under the twisted sheets and rested his elbows on them, pressing his face into his hands for a long moment. The muscles in his back flexed, revealing pale streaks she hadn't seen before.

She reached for the switch on the wall and flooded the room with light.

Landry squinted up at her. "What the hell?"

"What are those?" she asked, crossing to the bed to get a better look at the pale scars marring his back. "Oh, my God. What happened to you?"

He looked away from her. "The Blue Ridge Infantry happened."

She touched one of the pale scars. He flinched and she pulled her hand back quickly. "They beat you."

"You didn't think it was a trip to the beach, did you?"

"What did they hit you with?" She tried to school her expression, to approach the question without emotion. She'd seen terrible things as an FBI agent and also working at The Gates. She'd seen some of the worst things people could do to their fellow human beings, and she'd always thought herself to be stoic and controlled.

But the thought of someone wielding a whip or a stick or whatever had made these scars—

"They're healed. They don't matter." He reached over and picked up his discarded T-shirt, pulling it over his head. "You should be trying to get some sleep."

"I was. Something woke me."

He frowned. "You think you heard something?"

"I'm not sure." She sank onto the side of his bed. "I guess maybe I'm still on edge."

"I can't imagine why," he murmured in a dry tone.

She managed a smile. "Are you sure you're okay? You were tossing and turning when I came in."

"Unfamiliar bed."

"Yeah." She plucked at the bedsheets. "You haven't really had a chance to talk to anybody about what the BRI put you through, have you?"

"Couldn't exactly go into therapy while I was running for my life."

"You know it's not healthy to try to bury a traumatic experience."

He laughed softly. "I seem to remember a beautiful, hardheaded FBI agent who chafed at the idea of post-operation counseling."

"And that same agent didn't cope very well after Richmond, remember? I lost so much after what happened at the warehouse. I lost myself." She blinked back the rush of hot tears burning her eyes. "I lost you."

He looked up at her, his green eyes glistening with pain. "You really think post-trauma counseling would have saved us?"

"I don't know." She shook her head, feeling suddenly helpless. "I just wish we'd fought harder. I wish we'd valued our relationship more."

"You think I threw it away, don't you?" His lips thinned to a hard line. "You think I pushed you away."

"I used to." She rubbed away a tear that trickled from the corner of her eye. "But I pushed you away, too. I knew you were angry with me. I should have worked harder to be certain I understood why. Maybe if I'd tried, you'd have confronted me after what the debriefing team told you about my statement, and I could have assured you they were lying."

"I'm not sure I'd have believed you," he admitted, looking away.

"I'd have made you believe me."

"You shouldn't have had to make me believe you. I should have believed you because of who you were. What you were to me."

His use of the past tense made her stomach ache. "You never could. Could you?"

The sadness in his eyes hurt her heart. "I wanted to." He shook his head. "I guess I was so used to lies spoken as casually as small talk. There were so many things I wanted desperately as a kid to believe. Promises my parents made that they never kept." He laughed bleakly. "You'd think all those years later, I could have just let it go. They never really wanted kids, and when they had one by accident, they figured out a way to go on with their lives as if I had never happened. It had nothing to do with me. Not really. I didn't matter enough for it to be about me."

Growing up poor with a flighty, promiscuous mother, Olivia had pictured the lives of wealthy people as a utopian promised land, where every child had two parents, all they wanted to eat, all the clothes they wanted to wear and every luxury she could imagine.

She'd never realized there were privations that money couldn't alleviate, until she'd met Cade Landry.

"I guess you haven't spoken with your parents since you went missing?" she asked.

"I don't imagine they care."

She shook her head. His parents had done one hell of a number on him with their casual, thoughtless neglect. "What about Mary? Does she know you're still alive?"

He shook his head. "Mary's safer thinking I'm dead."

"You don't think the BRI's reach goes all the way to Savannah, do you?"

"No point in risking it." He shrugged. "Mary's got a new batch of kids to raise. Did you know that? Last time I talked to her, she was working for a lawyer and his wife. Seem like nice people, from what she said. And the kids are stinking cute. She emailed me photos from Christmas a year ago."

His nanny, Mary Allen, had been the closest thing he'd had to a parent growing up. She'd been only twenty years old when his parents had hired her, shortly after Landry's birth, and she'd given him the attention his parents had withheld.

But even she had kept a certain distance, emotionally. Or tried to, Olivia supposed, thinking of a few things Landry had let slip about his relationship with his nanny. Mary had seemed determined to give Landry's parents every chance to be what he needed them to be. She hadn't wanted him to replace his parents with her.

Olivia had met Mary once, on a weekend trip to Savannah early in her relationship with Landry. She'd been a trim, pretty woman with curly brown hair liberally streaked with gray and kind blue eyes that had made Olivia instantly wish she'd had a Mary Allen in her own life growing up.

"I've had a lot of time to think. To navel-gaze, I think was how you used to put it." Landry slanted a lopsided smile at her. "I do wish you'd come to me and told me the truth. I don't know if I'd have believed you right away, but in time, I think I would have."

An ache of regret throbbed in her chest. "You think so, do you?"

"You probably wouldn't have forgiven me for doubting you, so I'm not sure it would have solved anything," he admitted. "But it would have been comforting anyway. Knowing you didn't think I was lying about the order to go into the warehouse."

She turned to face him, catching his hands in hers. "I never once believed you were lying about that. Not once. No matter what other trust issues I had, I never doubted you were a good FBI agent. You didn't ignore orders on a whim, and you didn't put people's lives in danger for selfish reasons. I know you wanted to stop those guys. I did, too. But I wouldn't have defied orders and blundered into that warehouse just because I was eager to make an arrest. And neither would you."

His eyes narrowed briefly. "You mean that, don't you?"

"I do."

He blinked rapidly, and she didn't miss the hint of moisture in his eyes as he looked down at their clasped hands. "Thank you."

"I know a lot has happened since Richmond. I know we can't go back to what we had then. I don't really want to."

He let go of her hands. "Yeah, a whole lot of water under that bridge."

She took his hands again, giving them a sharp tug to make him look at her. "It wasn't enough then. Not for either one of us. It's not something we should aspire to now."

His eyes narrowed. "Aspire to?"

"I don't want to live this way anymore. I want more than half a relationship. I want to be able to trust someone else. I want someone else to be able to trust me, too."

He nodded. "I get that."

"Maybe that person will never be you. That's something you're going to have to figure out. I just know that as much as I loved you then, it wasn't enough. It would never have been enough, not the way it was. Not with everything we held back."

He released a huff of air. "Yeah. You're right. It wouldn't have been."

She let his hands go and stood up. "I'm going back to my room now. You try to get some sleep. And if you need me, you know where to find me."

It took strength to walk out of his room and not look back, but she made herself do it. Made herself walk across the wide corridor, enter her dorm room and close the door behind her.

And if she cried herself to sleep, it was nobody's business but her own.

"We stocked up for the snowstorm," Mark Fitzpatrick told Landry as he passed him a plate of eggs, bacon and toast, steaming hot from the stove.

"Did you buy up all the milk and bread?" Landry asked with a smile, knowing that a fellow Southerner would get the joke.

"What was left." Fitz grinned. "Don't you wonder why people don't make a run on charcoal and grills instead when snow is forecast? Seems those things would be more useful."

Landry joined the other agents who'd gathered at the conference table for breakfast. Their numbers had expanded, he noted. There was a small, dark-haired woman sitting next to Sutton Calhoun, and across from her, a taller brunette had joined Adam Brand and Alexander Quinn, her head close to theirs in conversation.

"Ivy Calhoun and Delilah Brand," Olivia told him as he settled beside her at the table. "They're both cops in Bitterwood. They worked the overnight shift as part of the department's snow contingency plan or something."

"And there's another guy's wife who's a cop, too, right? You said she was called out on Grant Carver's disappearance?"

"Right. Sara Dennison. Dennison headed out last night to meet up with her and see if she could tell us any more about the investigation. I guess they haven't made it back here yet."

Two more people came into the conference room, still dressed in heavy clothing and red-cheeked from the cold outside. One was a tall, rawboned man in his midthirties with wavy brown hair and dark eyes, while the woman beside him was petite, blonde and sweet-faced. They both gave Landry a curious glance.

Then the man did a double take. "Cade Landry."

Landry sighed. He'd spent the past few months trying to look as different from his FBI photo as he could, but apparently there were some things a man couldn't change about himself.

"Landry, this is Anson Daughtry, our IT director, and his wife, Ginny, one of our accountants." Olivia gave Anson and Ginny a pointed look. "Who're both supposed to be somewhere sunny on their honeymoon."

"And miss the fun? Who do you think we are?" Daughtry set down their plates of food and pulled out a chair for his wife before settling across from Landry and Olivia. "We just walked in—anything new on Carver?"

"Not that we've heard," Olivia answered.

Daughtry gave Landry a curious look. "I heard you'd shown up, but I thought you two were stuck in your cabin."

"You knew I was at her cabin?"

"He was the one I had monitoring that bank account in Barrowville," Olivia murmured.

"I see." He arched an eyebrow at Daughtry. "And from that, you figured out who I was and where I was?"

"Well, we knew you had once had a relationship with Bombshell Barb—" Daughtry's mouth snapped shut, and Landry saw Ginny dig an elbow into her husband's ribs. "We knew you were once involved with Agent Sharp, so when the bank activity showed up—"

Landry lowered his voice. "Your boss likes to stay on top of what's going on in all his agents' lives, doesn't he?"

Daughtry rolled his eyes. "You have no idea, man."

At the head of the table, Quinn's cell phone trilled. He answered it with a brief "Hello" and just listened for a moment. "Okay, thanks."

The room had grown quiet, all eyes turned to their boss.

"That was Dennison. A call came in to Sara's radio while they were checking in on his grandmother. Patrol officers just got a call about a body found in the snow about a mile south of Fowler Ridge."

Brand was the first to ask the obvious question. "Carver?"

"We're not sure. Dennison's heading over there with Sara to take a look." Quinn's gaze landed on Mark Fitzpatrick. "You know Carver's wife pretty well, don't you?"

Fitz nodded. "Lexie and I went to high school with her. You want me to go wait with her in case we get bad news?"

Pressure built inside Landry's chest and swelled upward, making his head pound. He had to get out of this room, out of this building.

He had to get as far away from these people as he could, before anyone else got hurt.

He was on his feet and halfway out the door before anyone else reacted. He heard Quinn call his name, heard the scrape of chair legs on the floor as he swept through the door and down the hall.

Footsteps padded after him, hurrying to catch up as he reached the stairs. Olivia's voice rang out behind him. "This is not your fault."

He turned swiftly to look at her. "You're trying to tell me you honestly think the BRI would have taken your colleague if I hadn't shown up at your cabin two days ago like a stupid fool?" He felt sick, the half a plate of bacon and eggs he'd eaten heavy in his gut. "I knew there was a risk. I knew it. I just thought I would be the only one who would suffer if it all went wrong. I should have known better."

"You don't know this had anything to do with you."

"Of course I do. That man on the mountain—he knew exactly who I was! I could tell from the tone of his voice."

"Just because you recognized his voice doesn't mean he recognized you."

"Then why, after all this time of your friend Carver living safely on that mountain, did he get grabbed the very same day that bastard ran into us on the mountain? Can you answer me that?" Agitation rose like bile in his throat, spurring him into motion again. He started down the stairs at a reckless pace, two steps at a time, and bolted toward the front door.

Olivia raced down after him, grabbing him as he reached for the handle. "Damn it, no! Don't you dare walk out on me again! Not like this."

"It could have been you, Livvie." He turned to look at her, his heart contracting at the concern that darkened her blue eyes. "You could be that body they found in the snow. I never should have come here. I never should have brought this nightmare to your doorstep."

"It's not Carver." Alexander Quinn's voice rang in the foyer, making them both turn to look at him. He walked unhurriedly down the stairs toward them, coming to a stop a few feet away.

"Dennison called back?" Olivia asked, sounding relieved.

"Yes. Halfway to the site, they got a call from the patrolman on the scene. The body had ID on it. Driver's license. Some professional credentials."

Beside Landry, Olivia frowned. "Professional credentials?"

Quinn walked closer, his gaze sliding from Olivia's face to Landry's. "To be specific, FBI credentials. Someone you both know, actually."

Olivia exchanged a glance with Landry before she looked at her boss again. "Are you telling us—"

"After all this time, Darryl Boyle finally turned up," Quinn said.

Chapter 12

"I thought we'd never find Boyle's body. I figured he was somewhere down a hole in the mountains where nobody but the bears would find him." McKenna Rigsby looked up at Nick Darcy, carrying out a whole silent conversation in that one glance.

Olivia had been tangentially involved in the ruse Rigsby and Darcy had set up to trap Darryl Boyle, an FBI agent who'd stupidly tried to co-opt the Blue Ridge Infantry to create a domestic terror act devastating enough to make the government finally start rooting out radicals from within the US borders. But Boyle had turned the tables on Rigsby, and if she and Darcy hadn't been able to convince the head of the Blue Ridge Infantry that Boyle wasn't the ally he made himself out to be, it might have been Rigsby lying dead in the snow rather than Boyle.

"I wonder how long he's been out there," Darcy murmured, looking troubled. Olivia knew he had never fully made peace with trading Boyle's life for Rigsby's, no matter how much he loved her. Like the rest of The Gates agents, he didn't like leaving anyone behind, even someone who'd gone into league with the bad guys.

"Not long." Quinn walked into the conference room, sliding his phone back into his pocket. "Sara said the body was pretty fresh."

"He disappeared months ago," Landry said.

"I know." Quinn glanced at Landry. "There were signs that Boyle had taken more than one beating during the time he's been missing."

Landry's face went pale, and he looked down at his hands clasped tightly together on the table.

Olivia quelled the urge to touch him, knowing he'd just shrug her hand away. But she needed to get him somewhere alone, soon, and see if she could get him to talk about what he'd been through. Whatever the BRI had done to him—and she couldn't imagine they'd been kind in any way—he was still suffering the emotional aftermath.

Repressing that trauma wasn't going to make it go away. And anything he could remember about his time in captivity with the BRI might be important in their quest to take down the vicious militia group.

Quinn crossed until he was standing close to Landry. He waited for Landry to look up before speaking again. "You realize the discovery of Boyle's body after all this time is only going to reenergize the FBI's investigation into what happened last spring."

Landry gave a solemn nod. "I know. I should get

out of here before the FBI comes knocking on your front door."

"I didn't say that." Quinn bent and planted his palms on the table. "But we need to consider what to do with you while the FBI is sniffing around."

"Maybe it's time to turn myself in."

"No." Olivia closed her fingers over his arm. "The last time you tried turning yourself in, the BRI took you captive."

"But I was alone then." He squeezed her hand. "Now I'm not."

Warmth flooded her. "No, you're not."

"I don't think we've reached that point yet," Quinn said. "We're pretty sure there are still people left in the FBI who are sympathetic to the Blue Ridge Infantry."

"Darryl Boyle made that pretty clear. We just don't know who or how many." McKenna Rigsby looked across the table at Landry. "I'm sorry, Landry. I feel as if I'm the reason you went through what you did, because you were trying to help me."

He shook his head quickly. "Don't. You were a target, too. You had every right to try to figure out who in the FBI was trying to kill you. I'm sorry I didn't work all that out before things went so wrong. I should have been paying better attention." His gaze dropped and he tugged his arm away from Olivia's grip. "I should have been a better agent."

"You can flog yourself later," Quinn said in a dust-dry tone. "Right now I need you to concentrate on what you might know about the people who took Carver captive. I don't want to lose an agent. We've been damned lucky so far, and I'd like the record to hold."

Landry nodded but didn't say anything more.

"I think we're safe from the FBI until the roads clear, but once they do, we're going to be racing the clock." Quinn looked at the agents surrounding him. "I'd like to stash Landry somewhere the FBI wouldn't think to look for him, but I'm not sure at this point that our established safe houses are a good option. They're too easy to connect to The Gates. Any other suggestions?"

"Rachel's uncle and aunt live over in Bryson City," Seth Hammond suggested. "They've got a guesthouse out back of their place. Rachel and I have stayed there a few times. Nobody'd think to look for Landry there."

"Rachel's his wife," Olivia murmured to Landry.

"A decent option. Any other suggestions?"

"I have family in Alabama who are damned good in a fight," Caleb Cooper said.

"I've considered that option, but I don't want Landry that many hours away."

"What difference does that make?" Olivia asked, not liking the dark gleam she saw in Quinn's eyes.

Her boss glanced at her briefly before turning his pointed gaze to Landry. "Because sooner or later, I believe Mr. Landry will understand the vital need for him to tell us everything he remembers about his time in BRI captivity. And when he does, I don't want to have to drive six hours to hear him out."

Next to Olivia, Landry looked down at the table, his jaw tight with anger. She put her hand on his leg under the table and felt his muscles twitch. "Why don't we start with Bryson City?" she suggested. "As soon as the roads are cleared for travel, I'll drive him there. We'll play tourists for a few days until the FBI gets tired of sniffing around here."

Quinn's gaze remained on Landry's lowered head.

"Very well. The temperature is supposed to rise above freezing this afternoon, with enough sunshine to give us a decent melt-off. The roads could be clear enough to drive by morning."

Olivia squeezed Landry's leg. "Then we'll head out first thing in the morning."

"The Hunters are nice people." Olivia had spent most of the past hour folding the clothes for their trip to Bryson City. She kept a couple of changes of clothing at the office for emergency situations, she'd explained to Landry when she'd pulled the small overnight bag out of her locker in the agents' bull pen. Added to the clothes they'd brought with them on the hike over the mountain, she had enough to wear for four days. If they could find a laundry in Bryson City, they could stay longer if necessary.

But Landry knew it wouldn't be necessary.

He'd put off facing everything that had happened to him in BRI captivity for long enough.

He caught Olivia's wrist as she placed a pair of socks in one of the suitcases Quinn had provided. "We don't have to go to Bryson City."

She frowned. "You want to go somewhere else?"

"I can tell Quinn everything he needs to know tonight. Get it over with and get out of here so you and everybody else can get on with your lives."

The look on her face nearly unraveled his resolve. "You want to leave? Now? After—" Her lips snapped to a thin line and she turned away.

"It would be better for you, Livvie. Surely you can see that. Even if we can somehow prove I'm not a traitor, there's no way the FBI lets me come back. I'm done there. And I'm not sure what other sort of job I can get that's going to be worth anything. I don't know how to be anything else."

"Quinn would hire you."

"No, he wouldn't. I'm too big a risk. He knows that. So do you."

"Because you worked with the Blue Ridge Infantry? Obviously, you were trying to bring them down." Her brow furrowed. "Right?"

She was trying so hard not to have doubts, but she couldn't quite pull it off. He couldn't really blame her. He hadn't exactly given her a reason to believe in him anymore.

"I was. But I wasn't doing it for the FBI or any other organization that could back me up. I have only my word that I was on the side of the angels, and Quinn can't trust my word." He touched her face, letting his fingers slide lightly over the perfect curve of her cheek. "You can't, either, can you?"

Her jaw tightened, her chin lifting. "I believe you."

"Without any proof?"

Her gaze leveled with his, her eyes a cool, crystalline blue that should have chilled him but warmed him to his core instead. "Your word is the proof. I believe you."

She almost convinced him she did.

She released a soft sigh, as if she could read his own doubts. "Let's just go through with the plan, okay? We'll go to Bryson City to stay for a few days. Once we're there, if you want to tell me everything you can remember about your time in captivity, great. If you feel you need to wait a little longer, that's fine, too. I know you'll do the right thing for Grant Carver."

Landry couldn't stop a soft laugh. "Oh, Livvie. Still twisting the knife with a smile, aren't you?"

She arched an eyebrow at him. "Me?"

"I will do everything I can to help find Carver." God knew, the guilt was starting to eat him up.

"I know you will."

Alexander Quinn stopped by the dorm room a few minutes later. "The roads into North Carolina have been deemed passable by the Tennessee and North Carolina Highway Patrols." He handed over a key to Olivia. "There's a Chevy Tahoe parked out back, gassed up and ready to go. It should be able to handle any icy patches left on the road."

Olivia glanced at Landry. "Is Rachel's uncle expecting us?"

"Yes. He's setting up the guesthouse for you. If anyone asks, you're distant relatives from Georgia, up here to enjoy the winter season in the Smokies."

"I don't want to put anyone else in danger," Landry said. The closer he got to leaving The Gates, the more he feared he was making a mistake. "Maybe I should just wait here for the FBI to show up and take me into custody. I can call a lawyer I know in Richmond, make sure he makes noise with the Richmond field office so they'll know someone's watching."

"Why didn't you do that when you got away from the BRI?" Quinn asked.

He wasn't sure he had a good answer. At the time he got away from his captors, his only thought was to get clear of their reach and find a place to hunker down until he could figure out what to do next.

The problem was, he never really figured out what to do next.

"Go to Bryson City. Do some thinking without the pressure of the FBI breathing down your neck," Quinn suggested. "Maybe you'll figure out how you want to handle things with the FBI from a place of clarity."

Clarity, Landry thought. He wasn't sure he knew what the word meant anymore.

The drive to Bryson City took two hours on slick roads through the Smoky Mountains, but the Chevy handled the conditions as well as Olivia could have hoped, and the scenery was so breathtaking she had to struggle to keep her eyes on the road instead of the snowy landscape.

"I wish this was a pleasure trip," Landry murmured as they rounded a curve and came upon another breathtaking mountain vista.

"So do I."

"Do you know anything about this place where we'll be staying?"

"It's actually an extension of a restaurant and music venue, Song Valley Music Hall."

"A music hall?"

She glanced at him, taking in his confusion. "It belongs to Rafe Hunter, Rachel Hammond's uncle."

"Wife of the con man."

"Former con man."

"Whatever."

"Her aunt and uncle have run this place for years. They're actually quite well-known for what they do. Apparently, Rafe Hunter is known in music circles as a brilliant judge of talent. Seth says playing at the Song Valley Music Hall is a badge of honor for a new artist."

Landry was silent for a moment while Olivia eased

the Tahoe into a slushy curve. Once they'd reached the straightaway, he added, "Does this Rafe Hunter know who we are and why we're there?"

"He knows I work with Seth. He thinks you're my boyfriend and this is a winter getaway for us." She glanced at Landry and saw him frowning. "Is that a problem? It seemed like the easiest cover story."

"No, it's fine."

"We aren't going to see much of Mr. Hunter, so you don't have to pretend anything."

"That's not the problem, believe me."

"Then what?"

"Are we going to share a room?"

She slanted another look at him and found his intense green gaze on her. Heat flitted up her neck and into her cheeks, and she forced her gaze back to the winding road. "It's a guesthouse. There are two bedrooms."

His voice dropped to a soft growl. "That didn't entirely answer my question."

Her breath caught. "I don't know," she admitted.

"Then maybe that's the answer." He leaned back against his seat. "I think we should both be really sure about anything that happens between us this time. We both ignored a lot of doubts the last time and jumped into things recklessly."

"That's how you remember our relationship?" She tried to quell the sense of hurt that rose in her chest, but she didn't have much luck. "As a reckless mistake?"

"I didn't say that."

"I think you did."

He fell silent for the rest of the drive, tension stretching between them until Olivia felt that she'd snap in two. The sight of the Song Valley Music Hall through the front windshield of the Tahoe was a palpable relief.

The place was packed, parking hard to come by, but Olivia found a slot for the Tahoe near the far end of the parking lot and cut the engine. "You stay here. I'll go find Rafe and tell him we're here."

"Where's the guesthouse?" he asked, giving the low-slung saloon-style facade of the music hall a skeptical look.

"I'm not sure," she admitted. She'd assumed there would be some sort of residential structure attached to the building, but there was nothing like that in sight as she crossed the gravel parking lot and entered the music hall.

An early dinner crowd filled the place with talk and laughter that rang in her ears after the long, mostly silent drive through the mountains. The smiling man at the bar at the back answered her query by pointing to a short, jovial man talking to customers at a nearby table.

Olivia waited for him to finish the conversation, stepping into his path as he turned toward the next table. "Mr. Hunter?"

He had to look up to meet her gaze. His smile widened. "Lord, you must be Olivia. Seth described you over the phone." The twinkle in Rafe Hunter's eye made her wonder if the nickname "Bombshell Barbie" had come up. She tried not to take it as anything but a compliment, but she tired of everyone focusing on the fact that she was tall, blonde and on the curvy side. She was also smart, resourceful and dangerous.

Then again, being underestimated could often work in her favor.

"How far is the guesthouse from here?" she asked

as she followed him to a back room in the music hall. The cramped little space was clearly his office; he dug through the lap drawer of the desk and retrieved a key.

"Not far," he said with a smile, nodding for her to follow him back to the main hall, where a four-piece bluegrass band was warming up for their first set. Rafe motioned for her to wait a moment while he crossed to speak with the mandolin player. They exchanged a few words and laughter before Rafe returned to Olivia. "Sorry about that—new act, and there's a record-label scout in the audience tonight. They're as nervous as pigs at a barbecue joint." Rafe laughed at his own joke. "I like to put 'em at ease. They play better if they're laughing."

They stepped out into the chilly twilight air. Overhead, stars and a waxing moon glowed through wisps of clouds visible above the trees. "Y'all get a lot of snow over there in Tennessee?" he asked conversationally as they walked toward the side of the music hall, not far from where she'd parked the Tahoe.

"Enough," she answered, his friendly mountain twang coaxing her own Sand Mountain drawl out to play.

He led her around the building and waved his hand at what the music hall's bright facade had hidden. About twenty yards behind the music hall stood a lovely two-story wood cabin, glowing with warm light from within. "That's where my wife, Janeane, and I live. And right behind that house is the guesthouse. We built it for Janeane's mama, thinking she'd come live with us after Janeane's daddy died. But Donna fell in love with the funeral director and eloped about four weeks later." Rafe laughed, apparently finding the story hilarious.

"That was fast," Olivia commented.

"Well, that's Donna. Fast and brash. It's a big part of her charm." Rafe stopped walking and turned to her, handing her the key he'd brought with them. "Just head on down the flagstone walk past the house and you'll see the place. Janeane knows you're arriving, but be sure to pop your head in the back door and let her know you're here so she won't go for her shotgun." He walked back toward the music hall, laughing.

Olivia started for the Tahoe, but Landry met her halfway, carrying their suitcases in both hands, the shoulder strap of the duffel bag full of their supplies draped across his body.

She relieved him of one of the suitcases. "That was Rafe Hunter."

"I figured." He looked past her at the wood cabin. "Is that it?"

"No, that's Mr. Hunter's place. He said the guesthouse is behind their house, down this flagstone path." Nodding for him to follow, she walked down the dark path, animal awareness prickling the hairs at the back of her neck. How much of her unease could be attributed to the danger lurking around them and how much to the prospect of several days alone with Cade Landry in a scenic mountain cabin, she couldn't say.

The guesthouse came into view as they passed the back corner of the Hunters' cabin, a small, pretty one-story cabin decorated with the slow-melting remains of the earlier snowstorm. Boxwood shrubs flanked the steps up to the porch, giving the log cabin the appearance of a quaint country cottage.

"Cute," Landry commented.

Olivia slanted a look at him.

He met her gaze, smiling. But his smile faded in an instant, and his eyes widened as he looked at something behind her.

She heard the unmistakable clatter of the fore-end of a pump-action shotgun sliding back, ready to fire.

"State your business." The voice behind them was female, mountain-accented and deadly.

Dropping the suitcase to the ground beside her, Olivia lifted her hands and slowly turned to face the small, silver-haired woman pointing a shotgun at her chest.

Swallowing the instant flood of terror that came with facing a shotgun barrel, Olivia forced her voice through her tightened throat. "Janeane Hunter, I presume?"

Chapter 13

"I told her to poke her head in the back door and tell you she'd arrived." What Landry assumed was Rafe Hunter's plaintive voice was audible over the phone Janeane Hunter held to one ear. The shotgun remained in her other hand, though she'd dropped the barrel until it pointed toward their legs instead of their midsections. Landry wondered if they could make a run for it before Janeane Hunter could whip the barrel up and give the fore-end a pump. After another look at her sharp-eyed gaze, he decided it would be folly to try.

Janeane made a face at the phone. "That might've got her shot for sure, you old fool."

"I would have knocked," Olivia offered helpfully.

Janeane flashed her a pointed look, and Olivia pressed her mouth to a thin line. Landry quelled the urge to laugh, despite the jittery adrenaline flooding his system.

"Did she show you any ID?" Janeane asked.

"No, but hell, she looked like what Seth described, and there can't be too many that do," Rafe said. Landry couldn't argue with his logic. Rafe was right. There weren't many women in the Smokies, or anywhere else, like Olivia Sharp.

"Well," Janeane said doubtfully, "if you're sure."

"Let the kids go, hon. I've got to run. A new set is starting."

Janeane hung up the phone and engaged the safety on the shotgun before she set it down in the corner by the fridge. "Sorry about that. Been having some home invasions in these parts recently. Damn meth heads." She extended her hand. "Janeane Hunter."

"Olivia." Olivia shook the woman's hand. "This is my friend Jack." Jackson was Landry's middle name, and Quinn had suggested using that name instead of Cade, since it was a little less uncommon.

"You work with Seth?"

Landry could tell from the woman's smile that she liked her niece's husband. He was a little surprised, given the man's rather colorful history.

"I do," Olivia said with a smile.

"He's an interesting character," Janeane said drily. "But good people, deep down. Loves our Rachel, and he's real good to her. Have you seen pictures of the new baby?"

"Yes, ma'am," Olivia said with a laugh. "Beautiful like her mama."

Janeane beamed. "I think so, too." She caught herself up, her smile turning a little sheepish. "Here I've held you at gunpoint and now I'm talking your ear off about my little grandniece. You folks must be tired.

You hungry? I could have Rafe send something from the music-hall kitchen down to the cabin."

"Actually," Olivia said, "I think we're going to head back to the music hall after we unpack. I've heard good things about the food and the entertainment."

"Well, you know I agree," Janeane said with a bright smile as she walked them to the door. "I've got to get this month's books done tonight or I'd join you." She remained on the back porch, watching while they walked to the guest cabin a few yards away.

Inside, the small cabin was clean and casually furnished with a cozy leather sofa and a pair of matching armchairs filling the front room. They explored the rest of the cabin, finding a small but complete kitchen in the back and two bedrooms, each with its own full bath, on either side of a narrow central hallway.

Unlike Olivia's cabin, which had been originally built as a tourist rental cabin and was outfitted with the sort of luxuries vacationers preferred, the Hunters' guest cabin was simpler, designed for everyday living. The bedrooms were reasonably large, but there was no hot tub on a back porch or roomy claw-foot tub in the bathrooms, just a simple toilet, tub and sink. Landry washed up, unpacked his bags and met Olivia in the front room a half hour later.

"Were you serious about going to the music hall?" he asked, noticing she'd changed out of her travel clothes into a pair of tweed trousers and a slim-fitting sweater the color of the Gulf of Mexico in the summer, a brilliant blue green reflected in her bright eyes.

"I thought it might be nice to get out and eat something besides a protein bar or a can of soup. Seth says the music's really good if you like bluegrass, and I know you do—"

"What if someone spots us?"

"You can wear that farm-supply cap I packed for you. You haven't shaved in a couple of days, and a beard always makes you look a little different. And here." She reached down and picked up a tweed newsboy cap and a pair of steel-rim glasses he hadn't noticed sitting on the coffee table nearby. She set the cap on her head, covering most of her short blond hair, and donned the glasses. "I'll wear these instead of contacts. My own mother wouldn't recognize me."

"If you don't want to be noticed, you probably shouldn't wear that sweater," he said with a wave of his hand.

She grinned so brightly at him as she took a step closer, he felt certain his heart skipped a couple of beats. "You like?"

"I love. But you'll turn every head in the place if you wear that."

She sighed. "I can keep my jacket over it. I don't want to change because it's cashmere and it's so soft."

He reached out and touched her shoulder, letting his fingers trail down her arm. She was right. The cashmere was as soft as a kitten's fur and warm from her body heat. The urge to let his fingers continue exploring the warm, soft curves of her cashmere-clad body was nearly impossible to resist.

He shoved his hands in the pockets of his jeans. "Yeah."

Those azure eyes locked with his for a long, electric moment before she looked away. "I know it's a little bit of a risk, but I'm getting cabin fever already and we just got here." Her lips curved up in the corners. "And I bet it's been a long time since you just went out and had some fun, isn't it?"

"You have no idea."

Her smile faded. "I guess I don't. I'm sorry. I didn't even think—"

He caught her cheeks between his palms, making her look at him. "It's okay. I'm glad you don't dwell on it. It helps me feel more normal, and it's been a really long time since I've felt that way."

"I know what you mean." She covered his hands with hers, holding them in place against her cheeks. "Let's just do this. Let's go, eat some good food, listen to some good music and pretend like we're both normal for a little while. What do you say?"

Impulsively, he gave her a quick, fierce hug and let her go. "Just point me to that cap and we'll get out of here."

Seth had told Olivia the truth. The food at the Song Valley Music Hall wasn't fancy or complex, but it was delicious, fresh and prepared with care by someone who clearly knew his way around a country kitchen. The music didn't disappoint, either; the band Rafe Hunter had booked for the evening was young but wildly talented, doling out an inventive blend of bluegrass, country, rockabilly and blues that kept the patrons clapping.

After a trip to the bathroom a little after nine, Olivia returned to find the waitstaff clearing out a space in the center of the restaurant. Circling around the buzz of activity, she found Landry at their table, chatting with Rafe. Both men stood at her approach, the courtly gesture making her smile.

"What's going on?" she asked, nodding at the hustling waiters hauling tables away from the center of the room.

"Dancing, darlin'," Rafe drawled, winking at Landry as he wandered away to talk to a couple of patrons nearby.

"Dancing, darlin'," Landry repeated, holding out his hand. "Shall we?"

She let him draw her onto the dance floor as the band fired up a brisk two-step.

"If I'd known about this place when we were both in Richmond, I would have suggested a weekend trip to check it out," he murmured in her ear a few minutes later as they swayed to a bluesy arrangement of "The Tennessee Waltz."

"Do you ever wish—" She stopped herself.

"Do I ever wish what?" he prodded when she didn't continue.

"It's stupid. Never mind."

He leaned back to look at her, his green eyes warm and soft in the mellow light of the dance hall. "No, tell me."

She took a deep breath. "Do you ever wish you could go back to the day of the warehouse explosion and do things differently?"

"Of course. All the time."

"What would you have done differently?"

"I would have questioned the order to go in, for one thing. I should have questioned it then, but I thought maybe someone had seen something inside the warehouse, some move by the bombers to take out hostages—"

"I know. I mean, I don't know what that moment was like, because I can't remember it. But I can imagine it. I think my reaction would have been the same as yours. Maybe it was. I wish I remembered."

"I'm glad you don't." His plaintive murmur made her heart hurt. "I'm glad you don't remember any of that moment. I wish I didn't."

"It wasn't your fault." She touched his cheek, enjoying the sensual scrape of his beard stubble against her palm. "You did what you were told."

"How many people's lives have been ended at the hands of someone who was just doing what he was told?" His eyes darkened to a murky forest green, his expression etched with regret. "I should've made a better choice without being told."

She dropped her hands to his shoulders and squeezed, trying to contain a sudden rush of anger for the hell he'd clearly gone through since that horrible day in Richmond. The lives lost, the careers damaged, the nightmares, the second-guessing and the ravening sense of guilt—none of it ever should have happened.

But it had. Neither of them could change a damn thing about that fact.

She kept her voice low, well aware of the crowd around them, but what she was going to say needed to be said. For her sake as well as Landry's. "Look, I know what it's like to have regrets. I get trying to figure out what you could have done differently—God knows I've pored through the notes on that case for two years now, trying to figure out what could have been done to stop any of it from happening. That's natural. But *you* didn't strap a bomb to your body and take innocent people hostage. *I* didn't hit the detonator in a room full of civilians and FBI agents. That's on those BRI bastards, not us."

"Can we get out of here?" he asked, his gaze sliding away from her face to take in the crowded music hall.

"Of course."

They called for the check, paid and tipped the server and headed out into the cold night after saying a quick good-night to Rafe on their way out.

After the doors of the music hall closed on the noise behind them, only the hiss of their frosty breaths in the night air and the thump of their shoes on the flagstones broke the frigid silence until they reached the guest cabin. Olivia unlocked the door, let them in and locked up behind them.

"Thanks," Landry said as he shrugged off his coat.

"I'm sorry. I shouldn't have pushed you to go out."

He turned quickly toward her. "No. I enjoyed it. I did. It's been a long time since I've been able to sit in a crowded restaurant with a beautiful woman, eating good food and listening to good music."

"I shouldn't have brought up Richmond."

He touched her cheek, his fingers cold against her skin. "It won't go away if we don't talk about it. It might be worse if we don't."

Taking his hand, she led him over to the sofa. She pulled him down beside her, turning to face him. "You want to talk about Richmond?"

"No. But I think I need to."

It had been a pretty day, he remembered. Bright blue sky and mild temperatures as fall edged toward winter. The scene was so clear in his head—the sprawling warehouse south of Richmond, gleaming a creamy bone white in the midday sun, the black-clad SWAT team surrounding all the exits while the negotiation team held a tense standoff with the bombers.

"I go over and over that day in my mind. We'd been there less than two hours." He met Olivia's gentle, direct gaze. "That's nowhere near the longest we've waited for a hostage negotiation to produce results. I don't remember being tired or impatient. I just remember worrying that nothing we were doing that day was going to stop someone from dying."

Her expression was so serious, so intense, her brow furrowed as if she was trying to wring a memory from somewhere deep inside her forgetful brain. "Was there any indication that the bombers were about to make a move? I've read the incident-report files, but maybe you've remembered something since then you didn't remember at the time?"

"There was nothing. It was quiet. Eerily so. When we first got there, I could hear hostages talking and crying. But after a while, even that stopped. It was like they were resting. Holding their breaths for something to happen." He managed a faint smile. "You know that feeling."

She nodded. "The incident report said we got the order to move by radio, but the other teams said they heard no such order."

"I know. I'm not sure how it happened. Believe me, I've relived those moments a thousand times, trying to figure out how it could have happened."

"Do you remember changing the frequency at any point?"

He shook his head. "Definitely not."

"Were you in possession of your radio the whole time?"

Frowning, he replayed the moments before the radio order. He and Olivia had been on the east side of the warehouse, along with the other two agents on their team, Len Davis and Kevin Darnell. Both Davis and Darnell had died in the bomb blast. Olivia had suffered a concussion when debris had knocked her backward into a wall.

Landry's injuries had been minor scratches from shrapnel. Even though he'd been in the lead, by some fluke of fortune, he and Olivia had just moved behind a large air-conditioning unit, which took the brunt of the blast, sparing them more serious injury.

Davis and Darnell, who'd gone in the opposite direction as they started to spread out, had been hit with a blast of metal shrapnel that had killed them instantly.

Landry would never be free of those images, watching the split-second, senseless deaths of two good men. But he was damn glad Olivia had been spared that particular memory.

"Any chance someone else could have changed the radio frequency?" Olivia prodded.

He dragged his mind back to the present, meeting her curious gaze. "Yes. There was. I don't know why I didn't consider that possibility."

She licked her lips. "When?"

"Just about fifteen minutes before all hell broke loose, Agent Boyle came by with water. Remember?" He kicked himself when she ruefully shook her head. "I'm sorry. Of course you don't. It was the first time we'd seen him all morning. I guess I must have assumed he was back at the staging area, conferring with the negotiators. He gave us each pep talks."

She frowned. "Boyle gave us pep talks?"

"I know that wasn't his way, but we both know the way he felt about domestic terrorists. He was rabid, and that's kind of what the pep talks were about. He told me, and I guess he told the rest of you, too, that whatever happened, we were patriots for trying to stop the bombers."

She shook her head. "Patriots. Interesting choice of words, now that we know he was working with the BRI to stage a big incident."

"In retrospect, I have to wonder if he didn't stage the incident in Richmond."

"Or maybe it was just a target of opportunity. Maybe he let his zealotry get the better of him and took advantage of the situation to create an incident."

"We weren't supposed to live, were we?"

She met his gaze solemnly. "I don't think we were. When we did, and you told the debriefers about the radio call, it sounded like a lie."

"A bad agent covering his ass." Landry shook his head. "And suddenly the story became about FBI malpractice instead of a domestic terror attack. No wonder Boyle sabotaged me. He must have been so furious."

"You said it was the main negotiator, Williams, you heard on the radio. Are you sure it wasn't Boyle?"

"As sure as you can be about a voice over a radio. I didn't know Williams that well, but he has that distinctive Brooklyn accent. Definitely not a Baltimore accent like Boyle had."

"Their voices are around the same depth, though," Olivia murmured. "A Brooklyn accent is so distinctive, it's easy to mimic, especially over a radio. And none of us on the team were from Brooklyn, so it's not like we'd have been able to distinguish a real accent from a fake one."

He followed her unspoken logic. "Fifteen minutes before the radio call, Boyle came by and took us one by one to talk to us. I remember he put his hands on my shoulders because at one point, he made my shoulder radio squawk with static, and I nearly jumped out of my skin."

"He was changing the radio frequency." Olivia let out a soft curse. "The bastard set us all up to be killed for his obsession."

A shivery sense of relief washed over Landry, spreading goose bumps along his arms and legs. In the rush of excitement, he reached up and cradled Olivia's face between his palms. "That's it. Oh, baby, that's exactly how it happened. You have no idea how much that question has haunted me. How did I not see it before?"

She closed her hands over his. "You just needed your partner to help you talk it out."

Emotion swelled in his chest, choking him. A flurry of thoughts, of images and pent-up feelings, swirled through his brain, but the lump in his throat wouldn't let them come out in words.

But he could see those unspoken thoughts shining in Olivia's eyes.

Two words finally escaped his tight throat. "I forgot."

Her lips trembled in a whisper of a smile. "Forgot what?"

"Us. I forgot us." Swept up in an irresistible whirlwind of emotion, he curled his hand around the back of her neck and pulled her closer, fitting his mouth to hers.

The first time he'd kissed her after so long apart, it had seemed like kissing a beautiful stranger. The desire had been there, but not the familiarity. Not the sense of knowing.

The second kiss, initiated by Olivia, had been an explosion of fiery desire, almost faceless and nameless in its intensity. Two mouths, two bodies, looking for pleasure and completion.

But this kiss, this melding of lips and tangling of tongues, this symphony of touches and breaths and long, deep sighs—

This kiss felt like home.

Chapter 14

Us, she thought. *This is us.*

Landry's hands moved in a slow, sweet exploration of her face before sliding down to her shoulders and sweeping lightly down her arms. His fingers clasped hers. Entwined with them. And it felt so familiar, so perfect, that she wondered how they ever could have let go of this sense of completeness.

She let go of his hands and lifted her fingers to his face, tracing the little nicks and contours she'd once known as intimately as she knew her own face. That scar on his chin was a high school baseball injury, when he'd taken a cleat to the face diving to tag out a runner stealing base. The dimples that creased his cheeks when he laughed had come from his grandfather on his mother's side, he'd once told her, though his mother didn't have dimples.

"At least, I don't think she did," he'd said when she'd

asked about the dimples that still had the power to make her heart skip a beat. "I never saw that much of her, and when I did, she wasn't smiling."

The image of his distant, unsmiling mother made her heart break a little each time she thought of it.

She drew back from the kiss, opening her eyes. Landry stared back at her, his gaze soft but intense. Slowly, he smiled, triggering the dimples, and she couldn't stop a soft laugh.

"What?" he asked.

"Those dimples."

His smile widened, the dimples deepening. "Missed 'em, did you?"

"I did."

"I missed *you*. Every single inch of you."

"All seventy of them?"

He laughed. "Yeah. And even more when you're wearing heels."

She pressed her forehead against his. "How did we let it fall apart? One day we were fine, and the next—"

"I don't think we were fine." He leaned back, putting a little distance between them. Cool air seeped in between them, giving her a chill.

She rubbed her arms. "You're right. We weren't."

"This is such a bad time to be considering this." He rubbed his jaw, his palm rasping against his beard stubble. "I have no idea what's going to happen next. I'm wanted by the FBI, and you've been targeted by the BRI, and in case it's not clear, those bastards aren't going to just let me go unscathed if I run into one of them in the woods one day and they figure out who I am."

"All the more reason we should stick together." She lifted her chin and pinned him with her more determined gaze. "Maybe it'll all go wrong again. Hell, maybe it's inevitable. But right now we need each other, as partners if nothing else. We just work better together than apart, and you know it. Tell me I'm wrong."

"You're not wrong." He bent toward her and pressed his lips against her forehead. She snuggled closer and he wrapped his arms around her, holding her close. "I just don't think we need to get ourselves all tangled up in plans and promises when we're not sure what tomorrow's going to hold."

She sighed, wishing she could argue with his logic. But he was right. Rushing into things never worked out well, in her experience. "Okay. We'll slow it down and just concentrate on the work for now. Agents Landry and Sharp, back on the job."

"That sounds good." He gave her a quick kiss on the temple then let her go. "In the morning, that is. It's late and we've had a few long, stressful days. Let's get some sleep and we'll get started first thing in the morning. Deal?"

"Deal." She extended her hand toward him.

He shook her hand, his grip lasting a little longer than necessary. In his green eyes she saw a sweet, intense longing that echoed in her own chest. Finally, he let go and smiled. "I really did miss the hell out of you."

"Back at ya." She made herself turn around and head for the bedroom she'd staked out earlier in the evening, closing the door behind her. By the time she'd snuggled under the warm blankets, she heard Landry's footsteps enter the hall outside her room.

His footsteps faltered as he neared her door. Olivia waited, breathless, for him to make another move.

When his footsteps moved on, and the door to his

bedroom opened and closed, she let out a pent-up breath, well aware he'd made the smart decision.

But she didn't have to like it.

Her cell phone hummed on the bedside table where she'd left it. It wasn't her normal phone; she'd left that back at The Gates locked in her desk. Instead, Quinn had provided both her and Landry with untraceable burner phones for their trip to Bryson City. Her late-night caller could be only one person.

"It's nearly midnight, Quinn," she said into the phone.

"You didn't check in when you arrived."

He was right. She hadn't. "Sorry."

"Everything okay?"

"Everything's fine," she assured him, tucking her knees up to her chest. "No problems on the road, got here in time to have some good food and listen to some good music and now we're safely tucked in our beds for the night."

Quinn was silent for a long moment.

"Is something wrong?" she asked when he didn't speak.

"Are you alone in that bed?"

Her spine straightened. "Is that any business of yours?"

"No. Not the way you mean."

"Then in what way *is* it your business?"

"I remember the Olivia Sharp who walked into my office looking for a job. She was— I'm not sure I even know the right word for it. Broken, I guess. Not in a way that was obvious. But there were pieces missing, and I could see it."

"Thank you for the analysis, Dr. Phil."

"I'm not trying to psychoanalyze you, Olivia. I'm not sticking my nose where it doesn't belong. If you're going to continue to be a vital member of my team, you have to be smart and focused and emotionally centered."

"I am all of those things."

"Good. Keep it that way." Quinn's voice lowered. "I take it from your answers that you really are alone in your room?"

"Quinn—"

He laughed softly. "That time, I was sticking my nose where it doesn't belong."

"I'm fine," she said, realizing he'd thrown in the last question just to break the tension. "And I know what I'm doing. I promise."

"I hope whatever happens with Landry is a good thing for you. I really do. But I need you to put your own safety first. Carver's missing, and for all we know, he's already dead. I don't want to have to call up your mother and tell her that you're gone, too."

She tamped down a flush of guilt. She hadn't talked to her mother in over a week, she realized. Carla Sharp hadn't exactly been a great role model, but Olivia had never once doubted her mother loved her. And she loved her mother, too, even when Carla exasperated her beyond words. Maybe especially then.

"I don't want you to have to do that, either," she said. "I'll be careful."

"You do that," Quinn said. "Call if you need anything."

"Will do." She hung up, set the phone on the bedside table and stared up at the darkened ceiling, wondering if she was going to be able to keep her word. Carver was missing; she and Landry were both hunted. She'd chosen the work she did willingly, knowing the dangers, but she was nearly thirty-five now. Her window of opportunity for having a child of her own was closing quickly, if having a child was even what she wanted.

Was it? She and Landry had been partners and lovers, but one thing they'd never seriously talked about was getting married and starting a family. In fact, in retrospect, she could see that they'd gone out of their way to avoid talking about marriage and kids.

Why? What had they been afraid of? That they wanted different things out of life? In some ways, she knew Landry as well as she knew anyone in the world, but in others, she didn't think she knew him at all.

Because he'd wanted it that way? Because she had?

Maybe they were crazy to think they could make their relationship work this time.

Maybe they were crazy to try.

Olivia was already up the next morning, scrambling eggs, when he wandered into the kitchen. She turned around to flash him a quick smile. "Good morning."

Her face was freshly scrubbed and free of makeup, and her hair was damp and tousled from the shower, but she was still the most beautiful thing he'd ever seen, especially in that Alabama T-shirt and houndstooth-patterned running shorts, her long, tanned legs stretching for miles beneath the hem.

"Good morning," he replied, looking over her shoulder. "Need any help?"

"The toaster is over there on the counter. There's bread in the pantry—the Hunters stocked the place with some essentials for us, it seems. Janeane left a note so we'd know everything's fresh."

The kind gesture touched him more than it probably should have. "That was nice of her."

Olivia must have heard something odd in his tone, for she turned away from the stove to look at him. "It was."

He smiled. "I guess it's been a while since I've experienced much human kindness."

Olivia reached out and touched his arm briefly. "Give yourself a little time to get used to it again." She turned back to the eggs.

He hoped he'd have reason to get used to it. The thought of returning to a life of running and hiding was deeply disheartening. He'd grown accustomed to living a mostly solitary life, his only relationships shallow and transient.

But he'd never grown to like it.

The toaster took four slices at once. He put bread in the slots and pushed down the lever. "If we can't figure out a way to prove someone in the FBI set me up, I'll have to go back under the radar."

"We'll figure it out," she said, her voice firm.

"You can't know that."

She moved the skillet from the stove eye and turned to look at him. "I will not rest until we figure it out."

God, he loved her when she stuck out her chin and made declarations of intent. She was fierce and formidable and as sexy as hell.

He lifted his own chin in response. "Then neither will I."

She flashed him a big, toothy grin. "There's the Cade Landry I remember."

He hoped she was right. He hoped he was the man he used to be, because the man he'd become didn't seem to be a damned bit of good to anyone.

As they were cleaning up after breakfast, Olivia outlined her plan for the morning. "I brought files with me that I want you to go through. They're dossiers we've gathered on the bigger players in the Blue Ridge Infantry, and I was hoping maybe you could tell us if any of them were involved in your abduction."

"I didn't see faces. They wore masks."

"Maybe there will be something else that you'll be able to identify about them. Or maybe something in their files will spark a memory." She put the last cup in the dishwasher and straightened. "I set up everything for us in the front room."

He followed her into the living area and saw that she'd stacked fifteen manila folders in a neat line on the long coffee table in front of the sofa. "How long have you been awake?"

"A couple of hours." She slanted a sheepish smile at him as she took a seat on one end of the sofa. "Early riser, remember?"

"I remember." He sat beside her and picked up the first dossier. "Calvin Hopkins."

"Head of the Tennessee branch of the Blue Ridge Infantry. Anything familiar about him?" Olivia asked as he flipped open the folder.

The photos in the dossier appeared to be candid shots taken with a telephoto lens. "Who took these shots?"

"Grant Carver, among others," she answered soberly. "One of the benefits of his living near the Fowler Ridge enclave."

"If you know where they're living, why hasn't someone gone in and staged a raid?"

"Because they learned a little something from the meth cookers with whom they've aligned themselves. They don't bring their drug business home. We think they've set up meth labs in other places in the hills.

Abandoned cabins up high in the hills, maybe. Or even some of the old, abandoned marble quarries north of here. A few of those places are still private property, with absentee owners. All kinds of activity could be going on there without anybody but a few locals knowing it."

Landry rubbed his jaw, realizing he was already falling back into the habit of not shaving. Reentering civilization after nearly a year of living on the fringes was proving to be more difficult than he'd expected.

"Take a close look at some of the people with Hopkins," Olivia suggested as he flipped to a photo of Hopkins talking to a clean-shaven man wearing khakis and a light blue golf shirt. "That guy isn't in the BRI, we're pretty sure."

"Maybe he's just some tourist asking for directions."

"Maybe. Or maybe he's one of those other FBI agents Darryl Boyle spoke about before he disappeared."

He looked up at her, frowning. "What other FBI agents?"

"You said you thought there was someone in the FBI who had contacted the BRI when you tried to report Boyle's treachery to your superiors. I just figured you knew that Boyle wasn't the only one."

"I did but I didn't realize Boyle had actually admitted it." Landry looked at the photo of the man in the khakis. "I don't recognize him. Do you?"

She shook her head. "But I left the FBI before you did. I was hoping maybe he was someone in one of the local field offices. Probably not an agent, but maybe one of the support staff?"

"He might be with the Knoxville office, I guess," Landry said doubtfully. "Though you'd think Rigsby would have recognized him."

"She didn't."

"If he was with the Johnson City RA, he was either there before I came aboard or after I left."

Olivia sighed. "I guess it was too much to hope for."

"Sorry."

She shook her head. "Don't be. We have a lot more files to go."

They continued working their way through the files, concentrating on photographs first. Then when none of those pictures triggered any memories, they started to go through the written reports The Gates had gathered from their agents as well as civilians who lived or worked in areas influenced by the Blue Ridge Infantry.

"Your files are amazingly thorough," Landry commented a couple of hours later when they stopped for a break. She had coaxed him into his jacket and boots for a walk in the woods behind the guesthouse, where the evergreens had sheltered much of the remaining snow from the melting rays of the sun.

"Unfortunately, we've had a lot of run-ins with members of the Blue Ridge Infantry. And a few of their drug-dealer and anarchist buddies."

"I'm not sure the FBI's files on these groups are as detailed."

"The BRI has become really savvy about covering their tracks. We can outline how we think they're committing crimes, but producing evidence of their involvement is another thing altogether."

"I know. I was part of a task force trying to round some of them up, remember?"

"Right." She gave him a sidelong look. "You never told me how you were working with the BRI. I know you weren't sanctioned to get involved with the BRI undercover while you were on that task force. When Quinn got us involved in trying to keep McKenna Rigsby safe, we did a lot of digging with our FBI sources and we found out that much. But you ended up working with them anyway. How did it happen?"

"The contact fell into my lap. A guy who lived in the apartment next door was doing some jobs for them. Transporting contraband, that kind of thing. They made a mistake with him—he wasn't a meth head, but he was a drinker, and when he got drunk, he liked to talk. I figured out that I could pick his brains easily enough if I made sure to be his designated driver. So I ended up spending my nights at his favorite bars, looking for a chance to scrape him up off his bar stool and take him home."

"What kind of information did he give you?"

"Upcoming runs for the BRI. When they'd be moving drugs from one place to another. I went to Chang and told him what was up. I figured we could interdict the next run, if that's the way they wanted to go, but they didn't think there was sufficient evidence to warrant a raid." He frowned at the memory.

"That's ridiculous," she said, sounding confused. "What was their reasoning?"

"They didn't say. And I wasn't in any position to push them on it, given my shaky status with the Bureau." He shook his head, angry with himself. "I should have pushed anyway. I knew there was something hinky going on. But I just—I just didn't much care at the time."

"You must have started caring at some point, if you ended up working with the BRI anyway."

He nodded. "I did."

"What happened?"

"Rigsby disappeared."

The curious look she sent his way was tinged with suspicion. "I knew you were part of the team running her undercover op, but I wasn't aware you'd become close."

He almost laughed at the thought. "We weren't close. But I knew she was a good agent. She certainly didn't go rogue for the hell of it, so I knew something had gone really wrong. And I might not have been running on all cylinders as an agent, but my gut told me that whatever had gone wrong had gone wrong on the FBI end of the operation."

"What did you do?"

"I tried to get Chang to let me go undercover and see what had gone wrong. I had a ready way in, through my neighbor, and I was still pretty new to Tennessee, so it wasn't like anyone in the BRI would know my face. At least, that's what I figured. I didn't know about Boyle at that time."

"Chang said no?"

"He ran it up the Bureau chain of command and came back with a no," Landry corrected her. "I think he might have contacted the Knoxville field office and got the no-go from Boyle. He was the Knoxville liaison person."

"So he would have known you were trying to go undercover. He must have tipped off the BRI."

"That's the thing. I don't think he told them anything. At least, not at first." Snow crunched beneath their boots as they hiked through the woods, stretching their limbs. Landry's legs were still a little sore from their long hike over the mountain, but the exercise helped loosen the aching muscles and tendons.

"It must have suited his purposes for you to go undercover," Olivia mused. "Do you know why?"

Landry shook his head. "When Rigsby called me to

meet her at the Econo-Tel, I had a gut feeling I shouldn't follow protocol. But I just didn't trust my instincts. Instead, I went through proper FBI channels. I called our task-force liaison to report the contact."

"Darryl Boyle."

"I knew when he told me not to contact anyone else, something was wrong. I even tried reaching Chang, but I never got through."

"So you called the number Rigsby had used to contact you, trying to warn her about Boyle."

He nodded. "I got Nick Darcy instead. By then, Boyle was already on his way to the other meet site Rigsby set up, along with some of his BRI buddies."

"So you knew then that whatever contacts you'd made in the BRI were compromised."

"I knew I couldn't trust Boyle. So I went home to pack some things. I knew I couldn't stay there anymore. I went to the bank and got a few thousand dollars out. Stashed it somewhere safe where I could access it if I needed to. I contacted my landlord and broke my lease. Told him to keep the deposit for his trouble."

"That made you look like you were on the run."

"I was." He looked at her. "I had no idea who to trust. Or if there was anybody left at all who could help me."

"You could have contacted *me*." The look she gave him was half fury, half dismay, as if she wasn't sure whether she wanted to give him a whack upside the head or burst into tears.

"I wanted to. I knew you were working for The Gates, so I knew where to find you. But I made a mistake."

"What mistake?"

"I gave the FBI another chance."

Chapter 15

"Who did you contact?" Olivia asked, dread settling in the pit of her belly. Since leaving the FBI, she'd taken her share of emotional blows where the people she'd worked with were concerned. First Boyle. Then for a while, she'd come to fear that Landry was a traitor, too.

"I went over Chang's head," Landry answered. "Called someone at FBI headquarters instead. Dallas Cole."

Her eyebrows lifted a notch at the name. Dallas Cole? "The visual-information specialist at headquarters?"

Landry smiled at her surprise. "Yeah. Exactly. I figured, who would bother to corrupt a guy who designs brochures?"

She tried to picture upright Dallas Cole taking a bribe. "You're not telling me someone did."

"Honestly, I don't know. I haven't tried to contact him again to see what happened, for obvious reasons.

He was always a pretty straight arrow—maybe he didn't listen when I told him to skip the chain of command and go straight to Assistant Director Crandall to tell him where to contact me."

"Actually, the Dallas Cole I remember wouldn't break chain-of-command protocol for anyone," Olivia said. "And if Boyle had thought ahead and made a few calls…"

Landry sighed. "Cole would have reported my contact and they'd know where to find me. Which must be exactly what he did. Because it wasn't twenty minutes later, while I was waiting for a call back from Crandall, that a bunch of big, bearded guys ambushed me and hauled me off for interrogation."

Olivia touched his arm, horrified by the pictures his words painted in her mind. "No wonder you didn't think there was anyone in the FBI you could trust."

"Now you know why I didn't turn myself in to the authorities when I got away from my captors."

"I'm sorry. I'm so sorry you felt so alone. That you didn't feel there was anyone you could trust."

He touched her hand then gently removed it from his arm and took a few steps away. "We should probably get back."

"Wait." She tugged him around to face her, not ready to let him leave. Not before she told him what she'd spent most of the night before thinking about. "You know what we said last night, about the wisdom of trying to recapture what we had together?"

He met her gaze with wary eyes. "Yeah?"

She took a deep breath. "I don't think we should try."

His eyes flickered, as if she'd caught him flat-footed. "Oh."

She realized he didn't get what she was saying. "I'm

sorry. I didn't say that well. What I mean is, we aren't the same people. I know I'm not, and I think you'd agree that you're not, either. Right?"

His expression shuttered. "Right."

He started to turn away from her, but she was still holding his hand.

"So let's not try to recapture our relationship." She caught his other hand in hers and stepped closer until her heat enveloped him. "Let's make something new."

She let go of his hands and rose to kiss him, her arms wrapping around his shoulders to pull him closer. As Landry tightened his arms around her waist and pulled her flush to his body, the cold dissipated. The rustle of wind in the trees disappeared, swallowed by the thunderous pounding of Olivia's pulse in her ears.

It was so easy to let herself be swept up in the memories of their time together, the whirlwind of crazy hours, high-octane SWAT missions and stolen moments of pleasure in a world sometimes gone insane. They'd lived on passion and adrenaline, glossing over the missing pieces of their relationship as if they didn't matter. Things like trust and commitment, the building blocks of a relationship that had lasting power.

No wonder it had all fallen apart.

As if he sensed her sudden doubts, Landry's grip on her loosened, and he drew back to meet her gaze, his green eyes troubled. "What's wrong?"

"We made so many mistakes before."

His lips pressed flat as he nodded. "I know."

"I don't want to make those mistakes again."

He let her go, turning so that his profile was to her. "Okay. I get that. We should probably go back to the cabin and get back to work anyway."

"That's not what I mean." She moved closer to him, missing the heat of his body. "I want it to work this time. Don't you?"

He turned slowly to look at her. "Of course."

"We never thought past the next day." She shook her head. "Hell, most of the time we never thought past the next hour. We lived in the here and now, and we thought it was enough. But it wasn't. Was it?"

"No." He shook his head. "It wasn't nearly enough."

"If we do this, I don't want to settle for less than everything."

"You mean marriage and kids and mortgages?" His expression shuttered, and she felt the first hard flush of dismay.

But before she could answer him, she felt a quiet buzz against her hip. "Damn it." She pulled her vibrating phone from her pocket. It was Alexander Quinn, of course.

"What, does he have you wired for sound?" Landry muttered as she pushed the answer button.

"Hello?"

"Carver showed up at home, a little scuffed but okay."

Relief swamped her. "That's amazing news! Did he escape?"

"Carver?" Landry asked softly. She nodded.

"Yes, but I'm not a hundred percent sure they didn't let him go."

"Why do you say that?"

"Because he came back with a message. And I think maybe it was one they wanted him to deliver."

"What kind of message?"

Quinn's voice lowered. "You're not on speaker, are you?"

Olivia glanced at Landry. "No."

"Carver said the men who took him told him there's a reason Cade Landry came out of hiding and sought you out. That the story he told you about being a target is true. But it's not the Blue Ridge Infantry who's after you."

"Then who?"

"It's Landry."

Something was wrong. Very, very wrong. From the sudden shift in Olivia's posture to the blank expression on her face, Landry knew that whatever Quinn was telling her had hit her like a brick bat.

Was it something about Carver? Had something bad happened back in Purgatory?

"That's not possible." She spoke in a careful tone, still looking at Landry even as her expression remained frozen in neutral.

Whatever Quinn said to her didn't do anything to improve her demeanor. She finally looked away, her gaze going south toward the guest cabin barely visible through the trees.

"I understand. You don't have to worry." She hung up the phone and took a deep breath before she slowly turned to look at him.

"Carver's okay?"

"He escaped. He was a little beat up, but Quinn says he's going to be fine." Something in her voice suggested she wasn't telling him the whole story, but she turned and started walking toward the cabin before he could ask anything else.

He hurried to catch up. "Wait a minute—what else was Quinn telling you? What's he worried about?"

"I'll tell you when we get to the cabin," she answered, picking up her pace until they were almost jogging through the trees.

The hair on the back of his neck rose as she beat him inside and disappeared almost immediately into her bedroom and closed the door. Adrenaline pumped into his system, feeding his rising alarm.

Get the Kimber, his instincts screamed. *Get it now.*

He pushed down the rising fear, held it in check. This was Olivia. Whatever had gone down between them, she wouldn't hurt him. Not without reason. He had to believe that, or he had nothing at all to believe in anymore.

Remaining where he stood in the middle of the front room of the guest cabin, he waited, his ragged breathing slowly subsiding and his pounding heart easing to a slow, steady beat.

When the door of her bedroom opened, the click of the latch sent a little jolt through his nervous system, but he fought against the fight-or-flight instinct and made himself remain still while she slowly emerged from the hallway and walked back into the front room.

She was holding her Glock in her right hand, the barrel facing the floor. Moisture glistened in her eyes but she wasn't crying. He could see the effort it was taking not to let the tears fall.

She didn't look at him as she spoke. "Quinn thinks the BRI let Carver escape on purpose. He said that Carver overheard something his captors said, and Quinn thinks they planned it that way. They wanted to give us a message without delivering it directly."

Landry swallowed with difficulty. "What message?" he asked, though he had a sick feeling he already knew.

"He heard them say they're not the ones who are after me."

The cold certainty deepened, rippled like an icy

breeze down his limbs, scattering goose bumps. "Then who is?"

Olivia's gaze lifted and locked with his. "You. They said it's you."

He saw pain in her eyes, and his heart contracted. Did she believe Quinn? Was that why she was carrying the Glock?

For her protection against him?

She lifted the Glock and he braced for whatever came next, knowing he couldn't do anything that might hurt her, no matter what she did next. When she set the Glock on the top of the glass-front cabinet that stood against the wall and dropped her empty hands to her sides, he released his pent-up breath.

"Landry, the one thing I know, the one thing I believe with absolute certainty, is that you didn't come in from the cold in order to hurt me."

Relief rolled through him, threatening to make his knees buckle.

She took a step closer, her gaze holding steady with his. "I'm not sure what the BRI is up to by sending a message through Carver the way they did. Maybe it's an attempt to turn us all against each other. Or maybe whatever operation you overheard them planning that day through the bedroom vent wasn't a sanctioned BRI operation, and this is their way of letting us know. I honestly don't know. But I know you. No matter what went wrong, no matter how many problems we overlooked instead of fixed, no matter how much time we've spent apart, I know you. You won't hurt me, because it would kill you. Just like I won't hurt you."

He glanced at the Glock she'd laid on the cabinet and forced a smile. "I have to admit, I wasn't so sure you weren't going to hurt me the other day when you pulled your shotgun on me."

She smiled back, the tears welling in her eyes trickling down her cheeks. "I had the safety on. You didn't notice?"

"I couldn't see past the barrel stuck in my face." He took another deep breath and let it out. "So the BRI is spreading the word that I'm the big bad, huh? I guess Quinn was pretty quick to buy into it?"

"Quinn's not exactly the trusting sort."

"You don't say." He walked back to the front door of the cabin and looked outside, scanning the yard. The sun was already high in the sky, hot enough despite the chilly temperatures to melt away half the snow that had been in the yard that morning when he woke. "Does the BRI have any idea where we are?"

"I don't know. Sometimes I think they have every inch of the Appalachians under surveillance."

"How much do you trust Quinn?"

"Enough," she said after a moment's thought. "You asked if he believes this story about you. I think by calling me, he gave us the answer."

"He believes it."

"Actually, no. I don't think he does. He gave me the choice of what to do by calling me. If he truly believed you were the bad guy in this scenario, he and a dozen other agents from The Gates would have shown up without warning and gotten me out of here before calling the FBI to come get you."

"So that call was about giving you the facts at hand and trusting you to make the right decision?"

"That's how Quinn works. He says he has to be able to trust his agents to make the right decision in the field."

"So what's your decision in the field?"

"I think we're about as safe here, for the moment, as

we'd be anywhere." She looked around the cabin, her eyes narrowed as if she were assessing the cabin's utility as a fortress. "I wouldn't mind shoring up our defenses a bit, though."

"What do you have in mind?"

"Short of building a moat?" She flashed him a grin that made his heart flip-flop, and for a second, he felt as if he'd been transported to three years earlier, when they had still been together, still partners. Still lovers.

He forced himself back to the present. She had been right earlier, when she'd said it was folly to try to recapture the past. The past, for all its delights, had also been riddled with mistakes and lost opportunities.

They had a chance to start fresh. And that was what he planned to do.

"How much do you think we can trust Rafe and Janeane?" he asked.

"Seth Hammond trusts them. And he's a pretty good judge of character. He made his living off being able to read people, you know."

"Interesting choice of hires for The Gates," he murmured.

"Quinn's a pretty good judge of character, too." She crossed to him and took his hand. "We're going to figure all of this out. You're not going to spend the rest of your life running. Do you hear me?"

When she said it, he could almost believe it. "I hear you."

"We've just got to figure out a plan. Something more proactive than hunkering down and hoping nobody finds us. Making this place or any other place a fortress is the same as making it a prison. I have no desire to live the rest of my life in a prison."

She never had been the wait-and-see type, he thought. It didn't seem that the time they'd spent apart had quelled her propensity to take action.

Waiting had never been one of his strong suits, either. Which was why he'd spent the previous night working out potential plans of action in his head when sleep proved elusive.

Putting his life in the hands of the FBI wasn't something he was willing to try again, even if it was unfair to the thousands of honest, trustworthy agents and staffers in the Bureau's employ. He didn't know who could be trusted, so he had to work on the premise that he could trust none of them.

But Olivia was right. He may have escaped BRI captivity months ago, but that didn't mean he wasn't still trapped behind the invisible bars of life on the run.

It was time to come out of hiding.

"You have something in mind, don't you?" Her eyes narrowed a twitch, a faint smile playing with her lips. "Come on, Landry. Spill."

"I do have something in mind," he admitted as he crossed to the fireplace and added logs and kindling to the cold hearth. Despite the rising temperatures that continued to melt the blanket of snow outside, the cabin was chilly, sending shivers down his spine.

Or maybe it was the plan he'd been formulating that was giving him the shakes. Because he'd figured out last night, lying in a strange bed in the dark, listening to the moans of the wind in the eaves and the thud of his own pulse in his ears, that there would be no easy solution to his problem.

He was a wanted man, and he had no proof of his contentions about what had happened almost a year ago when he'd tried to do the right thing and had ended up bound and beaten for his efforts.

The only way out was to get the proof.

And the only way to get proof was to bait a trap.

"Are you going to tell me or not?" Olivia's voice was close behind him, her breath warm against his neck.

"I can't prove I'm not a traitor. Because I can't prove I was set up. Especially not while I'm hunkered down and hiding."

Suddenly, she was standing in front of him, her eyes wide and scared. "What exactly are you suggesting?"

He took her hands in his. "It was my fault that McKenna Rigsby's plan to trap Darryl Boyle went sideways."

"Because you followed protocol and contacted Boyle in his capacity as the task-force liaison?" Olivia's grip on his hands tightened. "How were you supposed to know he was one of the bad guys?"

"I think I did know, deep down," he said bleakly. "But that's not what I'm trying to get at." He tugged her hands up, pressing her knuckles against his chest. "I'm saying that if I hadn't screwed up and called Boyle, her plan might have worked. Boyle wouldn't have been forewarned, and he might have walked right into Rigsby's trap. It was a good plan. It just might be a great plan."

"You want to set a trap."

"Yes."

Her voice rasped. "With you as bait."

Chapter 16

"This is a crazy idea."

Stopping in the middle of making notes on the files he was studying, Landry slanted a look Olivia's way. "Just an hour ago, you agreed it would work."

She put her hands over his, tugging the pen from his fingers. "I said it *could* work. Could is not would."

He closed his eyes. "Livvie."

"Don't Livvie me, Cade Landry. You're already working out the logistics of a plan when we haven't even considered other options."

"What other options?" He pushed aside the notepad and turned to face her, his expression tight with exasperation. "There are no other options. I've known since I got away that one day, sooner or later, I was going to have to put myself out there as a lure to get the BRI and their friends in the FBI to show their hands. It's time to stop avoiding the inevitable."

"I think you're being reckless."

"And I think you don't want to face the fact that there's no safe way out of this mess. Not for me, anyway." He took the pen from her grip. "I still think it might be a good idea for you to call Quinn to come get you. Take you back to The Gates until whatever happens to me happens."

Anger burned lava-hot in the center of her chest. "Who do you think I am? Do I look like the kind of person who would hide behind the walls of The Gates to save myself while you're out there with your neck on the line? Do you think I could do that to the man I—" She bit off the word, not quite ready to say it aloud, even though the emotion swelled in her chest, threatening to burst forth no matter how hard she tried to keep it bottled up.

He cradled her cheeks between his palms, gentle understanding in his gaze. "No. I know you couldn't. But I'm not the man who could let you risk your life without trying to talk you out of it."

She pressed her forehead to his. "We should call Quinn, at least. Get some backup for this operation."

"Livvie, you've told me yourself that you've had leaks at the agency."

"But we stopped the leaker."

"You stopped *a* leaker. Are you sure there aren't other traitors in your midst?"

As much as she wished she could say she was sure, she wasn't. Not really. There hadn't been any sign of information leaks since the police had taken Marty Tucker into custody after he'd tried to kill Anson and Ginny Daughtry when they'd figured out his secret. But that didn't mean there wasn't another mole in the agency biding his time before he could make a move.

"No," she admitted. "I don't think there is. I really don't. But I can't be a hundred percent sure."

"Then we do it my way."

"How exactly are we going to document what happens when the bad guys spring the trap? We're not exactly rolling in cash or audiovisual equipment." She gave him a pointed look.

"There's a music hall not a hundred yards from here that has its own recording equipment."

Her brow furrowed with suspicion. "And you know this how?"

"When you went to the ladies' room last night, I chatted a bit with Rafe. You remember that balcony that goes around the whole music hall, kind of like those old-timey Western saloons?"

"Yeah?"

"I noticed there was a guy up there recording the music sets. I was curious, so I asked Rafe about it. He said he invested in some audio and video equipment a couple of years ago when he started working with talent agents to get their clients' work in front of prospective record labels. They pay him to record the sets live, and those sets go on public video-sharing sites. They can only upload the ones where the artists still retain the rights to the music, but Rafe said it's gotten several of the bands who debut here a closer look from the record labels looking for fresh talent."

"And you think Rafe will just hand over his expensive equipment to you for your sting?"

"I hope so."

"And if he doesn't?"

"I still have some money left over from the funds I took out of our joint bank account the other day. I'd just rather not tap into it if I don't have to." He flashed a smile. "Might need it for bail money."

"If this plan doesn't work," she muttered, "you're not likely to be granted bail."

He put down the pen, pushed his notes away and pulled her into his lap. She snuggled closer as he wrapped his arms around her waist and buried his face in her neck. "We have to try something, Livvie. This waiting for something to happen is going to kill me."

She kissed the top of his head, wishing she could argue. But he was right. He'd already spent nearly a year in hiding, and the longer it went on, the more dangerous it would become. He needed his life back.

She needed *him* back.

"I think you may be right about backup, though." He leaned his head back to look at her. "We have no idea how many people might be involved in the FBI branch of the Blue Ridge Infantry. If it's more than two, we'll be outnumbered."

"I don't want to be outnumbered. We don't have to be."

"I know you trust the people you work with."

"I want to trust the people I work with," she corrected him bleakly. "But after this past year and the leaks—"

"You said you thought you'd caught the only leaker."

"And you asked me if I was sure, and I said no."

"I've been thinking about that, too." He rubbed his chin against her collarbone, his beard prickling her skin, sending lovely little shivers of sexual awareness skittering down her spine. "Everybody who was in that conference room yesterday knows where we are. You trusted them enough not to change our plans."

She thought about the men and women who'd helped them figure out the logistics of their trip to Bryson City. She would trust her life to any of them. Perhaps more to the point, she'd trust Landry's life to any of them. "I did. I do."

"So they're the ones we contact. But I don't want to go through the phone system at The Gates or their cell phones. If there is a leaker at your agency, they might have access to anything that could be connected directly to the company. Do you have other ways to contact them?"

She had home phone numbers for most of them in the address-book app in her phone, coded in case someone ever managed to sneak a peek at the saved information. "I do."

"Good. We can call them when we get our plans finalized. Tell them how they can help." He gave her hip a little slap. "As tempting as it is to cuddle here with you on the sofa, we have to work out a lot of logistics."

She sighed and slid out of his grasp, settling on the sofa next to him. "Starting with figuring out if Dallas Cole is still with the FBI."

Ice crusted on the banks of the Potomac, an incongruous contrast with the cloud-streaked brilliance of the January sunset, reflected in all its fiery glory in the glassy surface of the river. The Jefferson Memorial was little more than a murky silhouette in the distance, a reminder that for all the beauty of its natural surroundings, Washington, DC, was a city built on power. Powerful men, powerful institutions, powerful ambition and powerful greed.

He had seen it all during his time in the capital. Idealism had died a million deaths on the altar of compromise. Good intentions soon became swallowed by desperation to score an elusive win at any cost.

Governing a free country could be a very nasty business, indeed.

He sighed and spoke into the phone. "When did you get the call?"

"Ten minutes ago." The voice on the other line was deep and well modulated, though even if he hadn't known the speaker already, he'd have been able to detect the hint of eastern Kentucky in the man's inflections.

Dallas Cole had tried to leave coal country behind him, but there were things a man couldn't escape no matter how hard he tried.

"Why you?"

"He said he was giving me a second chance to get it right." Cole's voice betrayed a touch of guilt, a hint of uncertainty.

"Get it right?"

"He said the last time he called, he had trusted me to do as he asked, and I failed."

"And what did he ask?"

"For me to take the message directly to you instead of going through channels."

Assistant Director Philip Crandall didn't speak right away as he watched an egret rise from the water and take flight, its wings flapping slowly as it glided across the flaming sky.

"Did I do the wrong thing?" Cole asked as the silence extended.

"Of course not," Crandall said. "You made the right call, Mr. Cole. I'll take care of it. Please don't discuss this call with anyone else."

He hung up the phone and took a couple of deep breaths. In and out, cleansing the tension from his neck and shoulders.

Finally. *Finally.*

He'd begun to think he'd never find a way to end the nightmare.

Son of a bitch.

Son of a *bitch*!

"What have I done?" Dallas Cole met his own gaze in the reflective glass of his office window. His office in the J. Edgar Hoover Building was little more than a closet with a single window he thanked his stars for every day, considering he'd started out in an even smaller closet without a window in sight. Support staff might be a vital cog in the FBI machine, but cogs didn't get corner offices and great views of— Well, okay, not many people at that ugly behemoth of a building had great views, period, despite FBI headquarters taking up prime property a hop, skip and a jump from the White House and other DC landmarks.

"Did you say something, Cole?"

The lilting female voice drew his mind out of self-imposed chaos and his gaze to the door. Michelle Matsumara, his supervisor, stood in the open doorway, neat and pretty in her trim blue suit.

"Talking to myself again, boss." He flashed a sheepish smile, feeling sick. Matsumara just gave a delicate shrug and continued down the hall.

He pressed his face into his hands. To say he'd been

shocked by the phone call from a man claiming to be Cade Landry was an understatement of epic proportions. He'd spent the past year utterly certain Landry was dead and buried in some deep, dark hollow in the southern Appalachians.

Cole was from Harlan County, Kentucky. He knew all about deep, dark hollows.

Landry hadn't answered any of his questions, just told him to get it right this time. "Tell AD Crandall where he can meet me. And tell him I want him to come alone."

This time Cole had done as Landry asked. Bypassed Matsumara and her superior, Kilpatrick, and gone directly to Crandall, even though he knew, gut-deep, that both Matsumara and Kilpatrick were honest, trustworthy public servants—as good as they came, especially in a place like the capital.

After his phone call with the assistant director, Cole didn't think he could say the same of Crandall.

It hadn't been anything Crandall had said. His response had been everything anyone could have expected—an expression of concern about the contact from Cade Landry, reassurance that he'd done the right thing by calling him directly and, of course, an admonition to keep the call to himself.

But there'd been something else in Crandall's voice. Something as deep and dark as any hollows a man could find in the hills of Kentucky.

Cole looked at his office phone, his mind reeling. The phone Landry had used to make the call had apparently been equipped with number blocking, for the phone display had been blank. It wasn't likely redial would work, he thought, but he picked up the phone and tried it anyway.

Nothing happened.

Damn it, Landry. How could he warn the man about Crandall?

Would Landry even believe him? Nothing Crandall had said would strike anyone as suspicious. Hell, if Cole hadn't heard the man himself, he wouldn't have given a second thought to Crandall's responses.

Never ignore your instincts, boy. His grandmother's voice rang in his mind. Leona Halloran was a big believer in hunches and listening to the still, small voice in a person's head. "It's the warnin' voice of angels, Dallas. They're tellin' you, watch out! There's trouble ahead."

He pulled out his cell phone and stared at the screen, thinking about his options. Who might know how to reach Landry after all this time?

The answer hit him like a gut punch. *Of course.*

He pulled up a search application on his phone and found the number he was looking for. As he started to dial it, the hair on the back of his neck rose, prickling the skin as if a cool finger had traced a path across the flesh.

Warning voices of angels, he thought, and shoved the phone back in his pocket. It was almost six o'clock on a Friday. Like most of the employees who worked in the J. Edgar Hoover Building, he didn't exactly watch the clock. But he'd worry about trying to impress management another day. He had a phone call to make.

And not from a phone that could be connected to him.

"Do you think he went straight to Crandall this time?"

Landry looked up at the sound of Olivia's voice. She

stood in the open doorway of his bedroom, dressed for bed in a sleeveless T-shirt—the Atlanta Braves this time instead of Alabama. Her shorts might have hit midthigh on a shorter woman, but Olivia was a statuesque Amazon goddess, and there was enough skin visible to inspire some of his favorite fantasies.

"I have no idea," he admitted, dragging his mind back to business. "I guess we'll find out tomorrow. Are Quinn and the others set for tomorrow?"

She nodded. "All set."

He patted the edge of the bed, well aware that he was wearing nothing beneath the sheet covering his lower half. He could tell by the flicker of awareness in her blue eyes that she was aware, as well.

But she crossed slowly to the bed and sat down beside him, facing him. Slowly, she reached out and pressed her palm against the center of his bare chest. "I guess this could be it. Freedom or—" Her throat bobbed as she swallowed the rest of the thought.

"I have to believe it's going to be a win. I think we've both earned one, don't you?"

Her fingers brushed over his chest muscles, lightly tracing the contours and sending delicious shudders down his spine. "I'm not sure wins can be earned. Not in a world this ruthless."

He curved his palm around her hip and saw, with visceral pleasure, the way her eyelids flickered at his touch. He could still affect her. Still elicit a physical response, deliver on the unspoken promise of pleasure.

"So it's all luck?" he asked in a growl, pressing his thumb against a point just below her hip bone that he knew could make her squirm.

Her soft gasp sent a jolt of raw desire racing straight to his core.

"Landry—" Her response ended on a soft groan as he flicked his thumb across the sensitive point again.

When he reached for her, she came willingly, her long limbs tangling with his. Her hips settled flush with his, and he was the one who groaned as his arousal amplified a thousandfold.

"I want you," he whispered against her throat.

She arched her neck as he flicked his tongue against the tendon just below her jaw. "You don't say."

Cupping her bottom, he positioned her more snugly over his sex. "Need proof?"

Her laugh was like cello music, deep and fluid. She stretched out, her body sleek against his, and he felt his heart begin to pound. "I was willing to take it on faith," she said, "but if you insist."

Suddenly, her hips began to vibrate against his, sending shock waves through his whole nervous system. In the middle of lowering her mouth to his, Olivia stopped short and growled an impressively profane word.

Pulling back until she straddled his thighs, she pulled her cell phone from the pocket of her shorts and glared at the display.

"Really, Quinn?" she snarled at the offending device.

"His sense of timing is really something to behold," Landry murmured, trying to get his breathing back under control.

She answered the phone in a low, hostile voice. "What?"

Landry watched her expression shift from frustration to puzzlement. "Really. He called the agency?"

"What is it?" Landry asked.

"Hold on. I'm putting this on speaker so Landry can hear." She pulled the phone away from her ear and tapped the screen.

A moment later Quinn's voice came over the phone. "Cole called around six thirty, asking for you. We told him you were gone for the day and he flat out asked if you were with Landry."

Olivia arched her eyebrows at Landry. "And you responded how?"

"We told him we'd make sure you got his message."

"And did he leave one?"

"No. But we were able to get a trace on the number he was calling from. It's a gym not far from the National Mall. We haven't dug any deeper, but we'd probably find out that Cole is a member there."

"No, you wouldn't," Landry disagreed. "If he bothered to use a phone that doesn't belong to him, he'd use a number that isn't easily traced back to him. What we need to do is call him back on his cell phone."

"You think he'd answer?" Quinn asked.

"I think he'd have to chance it," Olivia said. "He called me for a reason. I don't think it's to catch up on my life these days."

"He thinks you know how to reach me," Landry said.

"He called for a reason. We need to find out what it is." She shifted until she was sitting on the bed instead of his thighs. Missing her warmth immediately, he stifled a sigh.

"Well, give it a try and call me back." Quinn hung up the phone.

Olivia edged closer to him on the bed until her hip was warm against his, as if she needed to be close to him as much as he needed to be close to her. "You have his number handy?"

Landry had it memorized. It had been the last phone number he'd dialed before the BRI had ambushed him, and he'd spent a good bit of his captivity repeating the number to himself to keep from thinking about his predicament.

He rattled it off to Olivia, who arched her eyebrows at his quick reply. But she didn't say anything as she dialed the number and put the phone on speaker so he could hear the call.

The phone rang four times before Dallas Cole's voice answered with a cautious "Hello?"

"You called," Olivia said bluntly.

"Right. I can't believe you actually called me back."

"Why did you call?" she asked, not bothering to hide her impatience. Olivia could be a sweet, considerate woman, but there were times when she could intimidate a bull moose. This was one of those times.

"Cade Landry called me."

"I know."

"He's with you, isn't he? I knew he would be."

"Why did you call back?"

"I did what he asked this time. I bypassed Matsumara and Kilpatrick and went straight to AD Crandall."

Olivia darted a look at Landry, clearly surprised. "What did he say?"

"He thanked me for telling him and said he'd handle everything as you asked."

"Well, that's good, then." Olivia frowned at Landry, clearly disappointed that Cole hadn't reacted as they'd thought he would. He wasn't happy himself. Now they'd have to figure out another plan—

"No, it's not." Cole's blunt tone interrupted Landry's thoughts. His accent, which usually was carefully neutral, held a strong hint of the Appalachian backwoods. "You and Landry thought I'd go through channels again, didn't you? That's why he called me again, even though the last time he came to me for help, he ended up in a hell of a tangle."

"Yes," Landry said.

"I'm sorry about that, man. You told me what to do, but I did it my way and you ended up paying for it. So this time, I did it your way. But Crandall's not what you think. He's not what I thought, either."

"But you said he agreed to handle it."

"He did. But I don't think he's going to—" Cole's words cut off on a soft expletive.

"What?" Olivia prodded.

"I've picked up a tail. At least I hope it's just a tail." His voice rose a notch, tight with tension. "Two sets of headlights, coming up fast."

"Where are you?"

"Driving south on 231, north of Ruckersville. Thought I should get out of town for the weekend— Son of a bitch!" His words were almost drowned out by the squeal of tires audible over the phone line.

Then the call cut off.

Olivia stared at Landry. "What just happened?"

Feeling sick, he reached for his phone. "I think Cole just got run off the road."

Chapter 17

Mulberry Creek Diner wasn't nearly as picturesque as its name, but it offered Alexander Quinn the three things he was looking for in a staging point—lots of strong, hot coffee, free Wi-Fi and a large private room where eight men and four women could meet in relative privacy to discuss their plans to set a trap for a traitor.

"Still nothing from the Virginia State Police," Sutton Calhoun informed them after getting off the phone with his wife. "Ivy has a friend there who's promised to keep her informed if they get any accident reports from the Ruckersville area, but nobody's reported anything so far."

Almost twenty-four hours had passed since Dallas Cole's phone call had come to an abrupt end, and still no word about his whereabouts. Quinn didn't have a good feeling about Cole's chances for survival, but he was the FBI's problem. Quinn had his own agents to worry about.

"Maybe they weren't intending to kill him," Landry muttered. He was sitting near the end of the table, his chair pulled close to Olivia's, as if he didn't want to get too far away from her.

"Landry thinks someone might have taken him captive to question him," Olivia explained.

"Because that's what happened to you?" Nick Darcy asked. He sat to Quinn's left, McKenna Rigsby on his other side.

"Cole told me he didn't trust Crandall. He said something about their conversation made him feel really uneasy." Landry turned his coffee cup in circles in front of him. "I figure if a graphic designer's warning bells were going off during that conversation, an assistant director of the FBI might have had some suspicions, too."

"I wish there was a way to track Crandall. See if he's really on his way or if this is another wild-goose chase," Rigsby said.

"I'm working on that," Quinn said vaguely. Nobody asked him to elaborate. He wouldn't have done so if they had. He might not be in the spy business anymore, but he still knew what "need to know" meant. "I'm not sure it matters right now if Crandall shows up himself. To be honest, it's not that likely. You don't get to be an assistant director of the FBI if you do your own dirty work."

"Then what are we doing here?" Darcy asked, his dark eyes snapping up to meet Quinn's. "What do we think is going to happen?"

"We're setting a trap," Rigsby said.

"A trap Crandall's probably already seen through if he's sent people after Dallas Cole," Olivia muttered.

Adam Brand took a sip of coffee and grimaced. "We still run with our plan, in case that's where Crandall wants to make his stand."

"He won't," Olivia insisted.

Quinn didn't think he would, either. "He's put Dallas Cole on ice for a reason. What reason?"

"Setting up a new scapegoat?" That suggestion came from Seth Hammond, who sat across the table from Quinn. Covert Ops weren't his area of expertise, but he'd been in on this case from almost the beginning, tracking Landry and Olivia up the mountain and keeping an eye on them for Quinn. He'd wanted in on the finale, so Quinn had added him to the team.

"You mean, he wants to pin everything on Dallas Cole?" Rigsby asked. "But what about Landry? I thought he was already the designated patsy."

"Thanks, Rigsby." Landry made a face at her.

"You know what I mean. Crandall must know you suspect him by now. Or does he think you still believe he's one of the good guys?"

"I don't know. Maybe he sent people to grab Cole in order to keep him from communicating anything more to Olivia or me." Landry looked at Quinn. "Cole went to the trouble of not using a phone that could be connected to him. So Crandall may not know he's been in touch with us already."

"Wonder if Cole had reason to think he was under surveillance?" Hammond suggested.

"I think most people in the government assume their communications can be accessed easily. Especially someone in the FBI," Olivia said.

"And Crandall knows that." Quinn pushed away the half-drunk cup of coffee in front of him. "I think Olivia's right. Phil Crandall won't show his face here. That's not how this game is played."

"It's not a game," Landry muttered.

Quinn sighed. "You're right. Bad choice of words."

"You think nobody will show up at all?" Olivia asked.

"I didn't say that. Landry's a wild card, and if I were Crandall, I'd take one more shot at eliminating him. I'd be thinking, maybe Landry can't connect me to any of this mess, but what if he can? And I hate to say it, Olivia, but Landry is probably right about your being a target. Crandall must know by now that Landry's made contact with you."

"But if they know we're setting up a trap, why would anybody show up at all?" Hammond looked confused.

"They're not going to show up at the meeting point," Brand agreed. "We know that much already."

"But they'll do their own surveillance and go after Olivia and Landry once we close down the operation," Quinn explained. "This is a trap on top of a trap on top of a trap."

"Like running a long con," Hammond murmured.

"Sort of."

"I don't think we'll be able to prove Crandall was behind any of this just because someone tries to take out Landry and Sharp," Brand warned.

"No, but we may be able to finally bring some provable charges against some members of the Blue Ridge Infantry. Then the police can get search warrants, warrants to pull phone records, and maybe that will lead to even more warrants and searches—"

"*If* we can pull this off," Landry finished. "It's a big if."

"That could very well depend on the two of you," Quinn warned him. "We're going to have to fall back and leave you two exposed for a little while. I'm not going to lie and tell you it won't be dangerous. It will."

Landry's gaze shifted toward Olivia. "I don't think Olivia has to be part of the bait this time. She can fall back with you, and I can go it alone."

"No." Olivia shook her head. "Not happening."

"She's right." Quinn didn't like the idea of Olivia in the crosshairs, either. She was a good agent, a very good asset to his company, and he'd come to like and trust her during her time as one of his agents, as much as he ever allowed himself to trust anyone. "They almost certainly know you're together. They'll be very suspicious if you part company now."

"It's a chance I'm willing to take."

"I'm not," Olivia said. "This could be your best chance to clear your name and get your life back."

"If you're talking about the FBI, there's no way they'll take me back, even if I get out of this without criminal charges."

"There's more to life than working for the FBI." Olivia put her hand over Landry's, just a brief, firm touch, but in the gesture Quinn saw all he needed to know about where Olivia's loyalties ultimately lay.

Good thing they were chronically understaffed at The Gates these days. If everything worked out this afternoon, it looked as if he'd be adding a new investigator.

"We don't have time to fight this out," he warned. "We're an hour from meeting time, and the roads are still messy. We need to get rolling."

"I'm not leaving you, Landry. So deal with it." Olivia's low, fervent tone left no room for argument. Landry met her gaze and sighed.

"Okay. Fine." He looked at the rest of the men and women at the table. "Let's get this party started."

Quinn pulled Olivia aside as they lined up to pay their dinner checks. "I meant what I said—our best chance to make this plan work is if you stick with Landry. But it's your choice. If you have any doubts…"

"I don't." Her chin lifted and her gaze met his without wavering.

"Good luck." He touched her arm and walked past her to the checkout counter, hoping this was one of those rare operations that went off without a hitch.

Olivia supposed that sometime in history, somewhere in the world, an operation had gone exactly as planned.

She'd just never been part of such a thing herself.

The meeting time had come and gone about an hour ago, and as they'd expected, Crandall had been a no-show. So had Dallas Cole or anyone from the Blue Ridge Infantry. But Seth Hammond had sent her a text message a few minutes ago to inform them the covert backup team had spotted about a half dozen men observing the meeting place from a distance.

Quinn and half the crew from The Gates were now headed back to the agency, while Landry and Olivia were on the road to Bryson City. The trip would take them through any number of potential ambush points, with only their stealthy backup team to help them out until more reinforcements could arrive.

By midnight, they'd passed almost all the potential ambush points the operation team had mapped out for them. They were five minutes from the Song Valley Music Hall and the Hunters' guest cabin.

"Do you think they figured out our plan?" Olivia asked as she forced herself to stay relaxed and focused.

"Check with the backup team."

Before she typed a letter, a text from Seth Hammond came in. "The men they've been following have just peeled off and seem to be heading back to Tennessee."

"I don't like this," Landry muttered.

Olivia didn't, either.

The Song Valley Music Hall was dark when they pulled into the driveway that wound past the restaurant toward the houses behind it. A couple of lights were still shining in upstairs rooms of the main house, but the guest cabin was dark and quiet.

Prickles of unease crept down Olivia's spine. "Do you think the Hunters are still awake? There are lights on."

"What are you thinking?"

"I don't know," she admitted. "My danger radar is still going off like crazy, but I don't know if it's because I'm still on high alert from playing out this plan."

"I can't shake the feeling that it's not over," Landry admitted. "I don't trust that they've backed off tonight. Patience isn't something I've ever associated with the Blue Ridge Infantry."

Olivia felt sick. "And we've just put the Hunters in danger."

Without warning, Landry pulled the Tahoe to a stop in front of the Hunters' cabin and cut the engine. "We'd better tell them what's going on."

The sense of unease strengthened exponentially once they left the relative safety of the Tahoe and headed up the flagstone walk to the Hunters' cabin. The weight of the Glock tucked in the holster under her jacket was a partial comfort, but every instinct Olivia had was screaming warnings to stay on guard.

"Wait," she said as Landry started to reach for the screen door.

He glanced at her. "What?"

She reached in her pocket and pulled out the flashlight she'd carried with her on the operation. She flicked on the light and ran the narrow beam up and down the front of the screen door. She was about to shut off the light when something glinted in the beam, catching her attention.

"Do not move," she said with quiet urgency.

Landry went still. "What did you see?"

"There's a wire sticking out between the door frame and the screen door. It might be a loose wire from the screen, but—"

"But it might be a trip wire."

"Right." She took a step backward. The floorboard beneath her boot gave a loud creak, and her heart skipped a beat.

A moment later she heard a muffled shout coming from inside. "Get away! The house is rigged!"

"That was Rafe," Landry growled, stopping his retreat. Olivia saw him eyeing the windows, looking for another mode of entry, but she had a feeling the windows might be rigged with explosives, as well.

She put her hand on his arm and pulled out her phone, punching in a message to Hammond. "We're not bomb-disposal experts. We can't get them out of there by ourselves."

"This is all my fault."

"No, it's not." Her phone vibrated and she checked the screen. Hammond's text in reply was blunt and profane. "He's informing Quinn. Quinn has contacts in the local law-enforcement agencies. He'll make sure the best bomb squad available shows up to take care of this situation. But we have to get away from this house." She turned toward the door and shouted, "Rafe! We're getting help. Hang in there!"

"The guest cabin's probably rigged, as well, in case we went there first," Landry growled.

"The music hall may be, too. We need to get the experts here before we make things worse."

Cade resisted for a moment when she gave his arm a sharp tug, but finally he turned and hurried her down the steps and back to the Tahoe.

As she reached for the door handle, something thudded hard against the front panel of the SUV just as she heard the crack of rifle fire echoing through the trees nearby.

"Get in the car!" Landry shouted, already opening the driver's door.

Olivia heard the click of the passenger door unlocking and jerked it open as another bullet shattered the side mirror in an explosion of flying glass. One small shard nicked her cheek with a sharp sting.

"Go, go, go!" She flung herself onto the passenger seat and jerked the door shut behind her.

Landry jerked the Tahoe in Reverse and whipped it around in a semicircle until they were facing the road.

Where three dusty pickup trucks blocked the driveway, each one manned guerrilla-style by men in camouflage standing in the truck beds, rifles aimed directly at them.

Chapter 18

"Get down, get down!" Landry jerked the Tahoe in Reverse and swung into a sharp J-turn even as rifle fire split the night air. He heard more than saw Olivia hit the floorboard, putting three rows of seats between her and the shooters. She started speaking and he realized she'd called 911.

"We're taking rifle fire and we're hemmed in. I'm not sure there's any way to evade them." Olivia's voice was breathless and pitched a little higher than usual, but there was no sign of rising panic, no hint of fear taking over.

He wished he could say the same for himself. The mere thought of bringing in the authorities had his heart pounding and his mind reeling. He'd been stuck in fight or flight so long, the idea of turning over his fate to the authorities was almost more than he could fathom.

But they were out of options. Even as he swung the truck across the uneven yard behind the music hall, twisting the steering wheel back and forth to avoid the obstacle course between him and the other end of the music hall, he knew there was little chance of mistake. In the cracked glass of the rear window, he saw that only two of the trucks had taken up the pursuit, which meant the third vehicle was probably circling around to cut them off.

There was a small gap between the two trucks behind him, but if he timed it right—

He jammed on the brakes and the Tahoe's wheels slid on the lingering patches of melting snow as he jerked the wheel around to reverse course again and aimed for the narrowing gap between the two pickup trucks now barreling across the slippery ground straight at him in a terrifying game of chicken. Finally, as the grille of the Tahoe came a few short feet from the front of the trucks, the drivers swerved out to avoid a head-on collision.

The men in the truck beds were too busy clinging to the truck to get off any shots, and with a scrape of metal on metal as the SUV slid against the side of one of the trucks, the Tahoe shot the gap and raced up the driveway toward the road.

The trucks behind him had to avoid each other, slowing down their attempts to reverse course, and the third truck that had gone around the music hall to cut them off had no idea what had happened.

His heart pounding, Landry gunned the Tahoe down the driveway, increasing his lead as he swung onto the road in front of the music hall and tore away from the pursuit.

Olivia had pulled herself up into the seat and was

giving the 911 operator a play-by-play of what had just happened, peering through the gloom ahead to make out the sign on the next crossroad they passed. "We're still heading north on Valley Road, just past Soldier Junction." She listened a moment, turning around to look out the back. "They're still behind us but falling back. No, we didn't get any license numbers."

Suddenly, headlights came on, bright and blinding, from two vehicles parked on either side of the highway. Landry's heart jumped into his throat. "Son of a—"

Olivia's hand closed over his arm, and he darted a quick look at her.

"The Gates," she said, and he realized what she was telling him.

He drove past the two trucks parked on the shoulder and kept going. With a glance in his rearview mirror, he saw that the parked vehicles had pulled out behind him, blocking both lanes of Valley Road.

"They'll have vehicles trailing the trucks," Olivia said softly, the phone pressed against her chest. "They're going to hem them in."

"There'll be a firefight."

"Maybe. But those vehicles have bullet-resistant windows and armor. Just like this one."

Landry looked at the bullet holes in the rear window and realized they hadn't penetrated the glass. He released a harsh breath. "You could have told me."

"When?" She put the phone to her ear and told the 911 operator they'd evaded their pursuers and arranged for a meeting point with the sheriff's-department deputies responding to the call.

Landry eased the Tahoe to the shoulder where she indicated they should stop and put it in Park, though instinct told him not to cut the engine. Those jerks in the trucks weren't the only dangerous people in these hills.

"Are you okay?" He turned to look at Olivia, taking in her disheveled appearance and searching for any signs of injury. He saw a dark rivulet of blood running down the right side of her face. "You're bleeding!"

She reached up and touched her cheek, looking at the blood that came away on her fingers. "I got nicked by flying glass from the side mirror. Barely even stings. I'm fine. How about you?"

If he'd been injured, he couldn't feel it. He reached for her, tangling his fingers in the hair at the back of her neck, and pulled her across the gear console and into his embrace. Electricity seemed to flow through his veins like blood, sparking everywhere it traveled, until his whole body felt like a live wire, utterly on edge.

But slowly, as she lifted her hands to draw soothing circles across his back, the frantic energy ebbed, until he finally felt his pulse return to some semblance of normal.

Even the wail of sirens in the distance, moving inexorably closer, wasn't enough to jar his nervous system into another flight of panic. One way or another, his ordeal was over. The authorities would believe him or they wouldn't. But there would be no more running.

He might well be doomed to spend the next few years of his life behind bars, but he thought he could handle it now.

Now that Olivia was on his side.

"How much longer are they going to interrogate him?" Olivia couldn't stop her restless pacing beside Alexander Quinn. He sat with annoying calm in one of the two chairs that faced the empty desk of Ridge County Sheriff Max Clanton, who had insisted on observing the interview.

"You know the FBI. They like to swagger around and play the big dogs." The look Quinn shot her way was full of amusement, making her want to kick him in the shin with her hiking boots.

Instead, she stopped pacing, slumping in the chair next to him and stretching out her long legs, which had begun to ache. Dropping her chin to her chest, she glared at the empty desk chair and tried not to think about what Landry was going through in the interview room down the hall.

The Bryson City Police had picked up the men who'd been chasing Olivia and Landry, but so far, they hadn't been able to get much out of them. Quinn had told her it was possible they wouldn't be able to connect them to the Blue Ridge Infantry at all.

At least the Hunters had been safely rescued from their booby-trapped house. The bombs had been small pipe bombs, two hidden in the decorative urns on either side of the porch set to blow if anyone had opened a door or a window on the first floor. Fortunately, one of the officers on the Bryson City force had been an explosive-ordnance expert in the Marine Corps and had managed to disarm the simple explosives without incident.

But they still hadn't figured out how the men who'd accosted them had known to look for them in Bryson City at the Hunters' place.

"I get the feeling something's up with this interrogation," Quinn said a few minutes later, breaking the tense silence and drawing her thoughts back to the present.

"Good or bad?" She wasn't sure she wanted to hear

the answer, but she couldn't go through life avoiding things that frightened her.

"I don't know. I just can't shake the sense something's changed."

She looked at him, trying to read his expression. A fool's game—Quinn never gave anything away he didn't want to. And sometimes when he wanted to, what he gave away was a lie he wanted you to believe.

Before she could ask another pointless question, the door to the office opened and Max Clanton entered, his sandy eyebrows lifting in surprise as he spotted them waiting in front of his desk. "Y'all know it's nearly five a.m., right? Figured you'd have moseyed on home for the night."

Olivia rose to face him. Max Clanton was a tall man, fit and trim, looking young for a man in his midforties, and from the handful of things she'd heard about his time on the Knoxville Police Force before he ran for Ridge County Sheriff, he was tough as a bull. But he must have seen something fierce in her expression when she turned to look at him, because his forward progress faltered and his expression shifted from affability to wariness.

"Where is Cade Landry?"

"I'm not sure." Avoiding her gaze, Clanton continued to his desk and sat in his chair, making a show of straightening the files on the corner of his desk.

"You're not sure?" she pressed, starting to grow alarmed. "An hour ago he was in your interview room down the hall, talking to the FBI. I thought that's where you were, too."

"I was called away on a different case," Clanton said

apologetically. "When I checked in again, the interview room was empty."

"Empty?" Olivia took a step toward the sheriff's desk.

Quinn rose and put his hand on her elbow, holding her in place. "Thank you for allowing us to wait in your office. If you have any further questions for Ms. Sharp or any of my employees, we'll be happy to oblige." He guided Olivia out the door and into the narrow corridor outside, shutting the door behind them.

"Where the hell is Landry?" she asked, keeping her voice down.

"My guess is, he's been taken into custody by the FBI, at least temporarily."

"And the Ridge County Sheriff's Department just let them take him?"

"Technically, he's committed no crimes in Ridge County that would give the sheriff primary jurisdiction." Quinn nudged her down the hall and out into the main foyer. "I'll make some calls, see if I can track down where he's been taken."

"That won't be necessary." A tall, dark-haired man with clear blue eyes and a Southern drawl stepped in front of them as they started toward the door. He handed Olivia a card.

It read "Will Cooper. Federal Bureau of Investigation." She looked up at him, her eyes narrowing.

"Where's Landry?"

"My guess is, he's currently on the way to The Gates. The FBI has released him under his own recognizance while the details of his situation continue to be sorted out." Cooper nodded at Quinn. "Nice to finally meet you, Mr. Quinn. I've heard a lot about you. I'm Will Cooper."

"One of the Alabama Coopers, I assume?"

Will smiled. "My brother Caleb gave me a call because I'm on a multistate task force investigating and interdicting domestic terror incidents. I've just been assigned temporary duty in the Knoxville field office to review some recent undercover operations run out of that office as well as the Johnson City resident agency."

"You got Landry released."

"He's got some details to work out, but unless different evidence arises, there aren't likely to be any charges pending against him." Will nodded toward the door. "I'd like to talk to you, Mr. Quinn, about your investigation into the Blue Ridge Infantry, if you'd be willing to discuss it with me."

Quinn looked at Olivia. She nodded. "Go ahead. I'll meet you there." She peeled off toward her car in the visitor's parking lot and pulled out her phone as she settled behind the steering wheel.

It was a long shot to think Landry would still have possession of the burner phone Quinn had given him. The cops had probably confiscated it as evidence. She'd just have to hope he was waiting for her.

When she arrived at The Gates, the agents' bull pen was buzzing with activity, agents making up for lost time after the snow days. Olivia caught Ava Solano's arm as the other woman edged past her in the doorway. Ava had worked with Landry briefly when they'd both been in the FBI's Johnson City RA. "Ava, have you seen Cade Landry?"

Ava's dark eyebrows lifted. "I thought he was at

the sheriff's office, being questioned still. Did they let him go?"

"Seems to be the case, at least for now. Have you been here for the past hour or so?"

Ava nodded. "I have tons of paperwork I'm catching up on. If I see him, I'll tell him you're looking for him."

Olivia made herself slow down as she left the bull pen and headed for Quinn's office to see if he and Will Cooper had arrived. Maybe Cooper had misunderstood and the FBI agents who'd come from Knoxville to interrogate Landry had simply taken him to Knoxville for more questioning.

As disheartening an idea as it was to think he was still in deep trouble with the Bureau, it was a better option than the panicky fear starting to take up room in the back of her mind.

Face it, Olivia. There's always the chance he's run again.

But how would he run? He no longer had the Tahoe to drive. When he'd shown up in her front yard a few days ago, his only means of transportation was a thrift-store bicycle.

Which brought up another question. If he'd left the sheriff's department the way Will Cooper said, how had he managed it? On foot? Called a cab? Hopped on a bus?

She settled down in the chair in front of Quinn's desk and tried to think. Could he have caught a ride with another agent from The Gates? As far as she knew, she and Quinn had been the only ones there at the sheriff's office this afternoon, but Dennison's wife worked there as a deputy. She supposed Landry could have run into Dennison at the station and asked for a lift.

As she was dialing Dennison's number, Quinn and

Will Cooper entered the office, their pace faltering a little when she stood and took a step toward them.

"Cooper, you said Landry had left and you thought he was headed here, but he's not here. Can you tell me how he left the sheriff's department?"

Cooper looked momentarily nonplussed by the question, then apparently caught on to what she was asking. "One of the deputies going off duty offered him a ride."

"Male? Female?"

"Female. Dark hair, dark eyes, midthirties—"

That could fit Sara Dennison. "Thanks." She headed past them into the corridor and pulled out her phone. Sara's number was saved somewhere in her call list, wasn't it?

She found it as she was heading down the winding staircase to the first floor and made the call.

Sara answered on the second ring. "Dennison."

"Sara, it's Olivia. Did you give Cade Landry a ride this afternoon?"

"I did—he said he needed a lift to your place because he'd left a lot of his stuff there when y'all had to bug out. Frankly, he could do with a shower after sweating out an FBI interrogation, so I dropped him off at your cabin. I hope that was okay. I talked to Cain and he said you and Landry were friends."

"It's fine," Olivia assured her, already out the back door to the employee parking lot.

The bicycle was still where Olivia had put it, in the small storage shed behind her cabin. The metal was icy cold but dry, protected from the snow by the sturdy shed's tin roof.

Landry ran his hand over the cold steel handlebars

and remembered the ride up the mountain to this place, the snowfall increasing with every mile. He'd been terrified he was making the worst decision of his life.

He should have known better. Being with Olivia was always the right choice. How could he have ever thought anything different?

For a moment the sound of a car engine approaching up the mountain road sent a little ripple of alarm darting through him. But he made himself remain calm, though he didn't entirely relax his guard. He might not be stuck in fight-or-flight mode anymore, but there were still dangerous people out there who might be willing to take another shot at bringing him down.

The FBI hadn't given him back the Kimber or the Kel-Tec P-11 he'd had on him when they'd taken him in. He supposed they wanted to hold them as evidence until they fully settled his case.

That was fine. He had nothing to hide now.

Fortunately, he'd stashed his extra weapon in the locked cabinet in the shed, along with some ammo. He located the key in the hidden spot Olivia had shown him and unlocked the cabinet to retrieve the compact Ruger and its holster. He clipped the holster to his belt and loaded the magazine into the grip as the approaching vehicle came to a stop nearby. The engine cut, and he heard a door open, then close with a slam.

Olivia's voice rang out in the cold afternoon air. "Landry!"

He shoved the Ruger into the holster and edged through the shed door.

"Landry, are you here? Please say you're here!" The anxiety in Olivia's voice caught him by surprise, making him hurry as he rounded the side of the house toward her voice.

She was halfway up the porch steps when he reached the front yard.

"I'm here," he said.

She whirled around to look at him, her blue eyes wide. "Landry."

As he started to cross the yard, she came back down the porch steps and met him at the bottom. "Livvie."

She reached out and touched the front of his jacket, her gaze settling somewhere around the middle of his throat. "I thought you'd gone."

He put his hand over hers. Her fingers were cold and trembled a little beneath his touch. "You think I'd go without saying goodbye?"

She tugged her hand away and stepped back, her expression shuttering. "Is that why you're here? To say goodbye?"

"Let's go inside. Get a fire started and get warm." He put his hand under her elbow and nudged her toward the steps. She seemed to resist for a second, then gave in and went upstairs and unlocked her front door.

She went straight to the wood bin by the fireplace and went about the job of building a fire in the hearth, her movements quick and efficient, like everything she did.

She was radically competent, brilliantly resourceful and marvelously self-sufficient. She was, in short, a magnificent woman, and he could spend the rest of his life trying to be worthy of her without getting anywhere near his goal.

But he had to try. Because the alternative was walking away from her again. And he knew now, with utter certainty, that he didn't have it in him to do that again.

"I'm not sure my trouble with the FBI is over," he said, breaking the tense silence that had risen between them.

She gave the fire one last poke and turned around to look at him. "I really didn't expect them to let you go on your own recognizance, given that you've been a fugitive for so many months."

"I've offered to testify in front of a Senate subcommittee on domestic terrorism, which seemed to mollify my interrogators a bit." He moved closer, holding out his hands to warm them in front of the fire. "There was a new guy, Cooper—seemed to think I won't be charged with anything given the circumstances of my disappearance."

"That's good."

She still hadn't looked at him since they'd entered the cabin. Her shoulders were tense, her chin set and a little on the belligerent side.

"Livvie, I'm not leaving."

Slowly, she looked up at him. "You say that now…"

"I will never leave you again. Not if I have a choice. As long as you want me to hang around, I'm in. No doubts."

She raised one of her eyebrows a notch. "You? With no doubts?"

He caught her hands, tugged her around to look at him. In the firelight, she was a golden goddess, as beautiful and luminous a creature as he'd ever seen. His heart seemed to swell near bursting, so full of gratitude and love that he didn't know what to do with all the emotion.

"I lost you because I was a stupid idiot. But somehow, when everything seemed hopeless, I closed my eyes and looked for an answer, and there you were. Like a light in my darkness. So I found you. Because you were my hope. You're my home."

Her eyes glowed like jewels as she met and held his gaze. "Landry."

"I love you. I have loved you since almost the first day we met. There was never a point in time after that when I didn't love you, and there never will be." He touched her face, his thumb brushing against a sparkling tear that slid from one of her eyes. "So you tell me what you want."

"You." She slid her hand around his neck and pulled him to her. "I want you."

He kissed her then, a long, slow, intimate exploration that left them both breathless. Olivia finally broke away just enough to whisper against his mouth, "Say it again."

He didn't have to ask what she meant. "I love you."

Her answering smile was bright enough to light up the Eastern Seaboard. "Do you realize in all the time we were together, we never said those words to each other?"

He brushed her hair away from her cheek. "Technically, one of us still hasn't said them."

"I love you, idiot. If I didn't love you, I'd have probably shot you that first day you showed up in my front yard with that stupid bike."

"So let's do it, then."

She shot him a wicked look. "Do it? Here? Now?"

He laughed. "Well, yes, but I was actually thinking about getting hitched."

She took a step back, looking surprised. "Hitched?"

"Yeah. You know, married. Blissfully wed. Fitted with the old ball and chain."

"You were doing so well there for a minute."

He laughed again. "Marry me, Livvie." His smile faded as he realized she might not have experienced the same epiphany he had about trust and devotion. "Unless you're still not sure you can trust me."

"No, that's not it." She brushed her thumb against his lip. "I just never thought I'd marry. I thought I'd be like my mom, always looking but never finding."

"Is that what you still think?"

She looked up at him, her gaze frank and open. "No, it's not. I know what I've found. I know it's worth keeping."

"So is that a yes?"

Her slow, sexy smile warmed him to his core. "Yes," she said and kissed him again.

Epilogue

The thin gold band on her left ring finger felt right, she decided after sneaking a peek for the sixth time in the past hour. It fit perfectly, neither loose nor constricting, as if it had been forged specifically for her alone.

"It's just a wedding ring," Landry murmured from his desk across from hers in the agents' bull pen on the second floor of The Gates. "It's not going to come alive and bite you."

She looked up at him, flashing him a quick, sheepish smile. "I like the way it looks. And the way it fits."

"I like the way it looks on you." The grin he shot back at her came with a full display of dimples and a softness in his green eyes that was endearingly shy.

She looked pointedly at the thicker band on his own ring finger. "Right back at ya."

"Oh, my God. Why didn't y'all just go on a real honeymoon instead of inflicting all this newlywed bliss on the rest of us?" Seth Hammond perched on the edge of Olivia's desk, shaking his head. "Have a little mercy on us, will ya?"

Sutton Calhoun thumped Hammond on the back of his head and dropped a file folder on Olivia's desk blotter. "I seem to remember a couple of months of you on the phone babbling disgusting endearments to your own bride, Hammond. Leave the newlyweds alone."

Calhoun waited for Hammond to wander back to his desk before he motioned Landry over. "Here's everything we could find on Dallas Cole. Any chance he's not a victim? Darryl Boyle hinted to Rigsby that he wasn't the only one in the FBI who was a true believer, and so far, we're just not finding any dirt on Philip Crandall."

"We just don't know," Landry admitted. "Given my own recent history, I'm in no position to assume a man's disappearance is evidence of his complicity in a crime. But Dallas Cole could have been trying to set us up so we wouldn't go to Crandall for help. It might have been a ploy to slow us down until the BRI could get their assets in place."

"Well, it's a place to look," Olivia pointed out. "If he *is* one of the bad guys, we need to find him."

Calhoun's slate blue eyes darkened. "And if he's not one of the bad guys?"

"Then he's in trouble and could use our help," Landry answered. "If he'll take it."

Olivia reached out, putting her hand over her husband's, her wedding band clinking quietly against his. His gaze flicked up to meet hers, and his dimples made a quick appearance.

A hint of amusement tinted Calhoun's voice. "Either way, Quinn wants us to find Cole and bring him in before the BRI gets their hands on him. He wants you two in charge of the investigation, since you know the most about him."

"We don't really know that much," Landry warned. "We could pick him out of a lineup, maybe, but—"

"We're investigators," Olivia reminded him. "It's our job to find out all we can about him now."

She picked up the folder Calhoun had placed on her desk blotter and opened it to the first page, a grainy photo of a dark-haired man with brown eyes and a guarded expression on his lean face. He was thirty-four, according to the notes clipped to the photos. Six foot one, approximately one hundred and eighty pounds, no distinguishing features.

"How does a graphic designer get mixed up with a backwoods terror group?" she asked in a murmur.

"That's what we have to find out," Landry answered.

Olivia looked at the photo again, trying to see beyond the flat, expressionless surface of the image.

Who was Dallas Cole?

And which side was he really on?

* * * * *

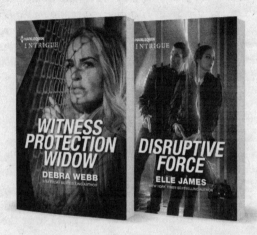

He was challenging her already and they hadn't even really
started working together, but if they were going to survive
several weeks of training, honesty was going to be the best
policy.

"My husband was a marine," Piper said, but didn't make
eye contact with him. Instead, she whirled and started
walking back in the direction of the outdoor training ring.

He turned and kept pace beside her, his gaze trained on
her face. "Was?"

Challenging again. Pushing, but regardless of that, she
said, "He was killed in action in Iraq. Four years ago and
yet…"

Her throat choked up and tears welled in her eyes as she
rushed forward, almost as if she could outrun the discussion
and the pain it brought.

The gentle touch of his big, calloused hand on her forearm stopped her escape.

She glanced down at that hand and then followed his arm up to meet his gaze, so full of concern and something else. Pain?

"I'm sorry. It can't be easy," he said, the simple words filled with so much more. Pain for sure. Understanding. Compassion. Not pity, thankfully. The last nearly undid her, but she sucked in a breath, held it for the briefest second before blurting out, "We should get going. If you're going to do search and rescue with Decoy, we'll have to improve his obedience skills."

Rushing away from him, she slipped through the gaps in the split-rail fence and walked to the center of the training ring.

Shane hesitated, obviously uneasy, but then he bent to go across the fence railing and met her in the middle of the ring, Decoy at his side.

"I'm ready if you are," he said, his big body several feet away, only he still felt too close. Too big. Too masculine with that kind of posture and strength that screamed military.

She took a step back and said, "I'm ready."

She wasn't and didn't know if she ever could be with this man. He was testing her on too many levels.

Only she'd never failed a training assignment and she didn't intend to start with Shane and Decoy.

"Let's get going," she said.

Don't miss
Decoy Training *by Caridad Piñeiro,*
available April 2022 wherever
Harlequin Intrigue books and ebooks are sold.

Harlequin.com

Love Harlequin romance?

DISCOVER.

Be the first to find out about promotions, news and exclusive content!

Facebook.com/HarlequinBooks

Twitter.com/HarlequinBooks

Instagram.com/HarlequinBooks

Pinterest.com/HarlequinBooks

YouTube.com/HarlequinBooks

ReaderService.com

EXPLORE.

Sign up for the Harlequin e-newsletter and download a free book from any series at **TryHarlequin.com**

CONNECT.

Join our Harlequin community to share your thoughts and connect with other romance readers!
Facebook.com/groups/HarlequinConnection

HARLEQUIN

Heartfelt or thrilling, passionate or uplifting—Harlequin is more than just happily-ever-after.

With twelve different series to choose from and new books available every month, you are sure to find stories that will move you, uplift you, inspire and delight you.

Get 4 FREE REWARDS!

We'll send you 2 FREE Books plus 2 FREE Mystery Gifts.

KENTUCKY CRIME RING
JULIE ANNE LINDSEY

TEXAS STALKER
BARB HAN

FREE Value Over **$20**

UNDER THE RANCHER'S PROTECTION
ARDEN FOX

OPERATION WHISTLEBLOWER
JUSTINE DAVIS

Both the **Harlequin Intrigue®** and **Harlequin® Romantic Suspense** series feature compelling novels filled with heart-racing action-packed romance that will keep you on the edge of your seat.

YES! Please send me 2 FREE novels from the Harlequin Intrigue or Harlequin Romantic Suspense series and my 2 FREE gifts (gifts are worth about $10 retail). After receiving them, if I don't wish to receive any more books, I can return the shipping statement marked "cancel." If I don't cancel, I will receive 6 brand-new Harlequin Intrigue Larger-Print books every month and be billed just $5.99 each in the U.S. or $6.49 each in Canada, a savings of at least 14% off the cover price or 4 brand-new Harlequin Romantic Suspense books every month and be billed just $4.99 each in the U.S. or $5.74 each in Canada, a savings of at least 13% off the cover price. It's quite a bargain! Shipping and handling is just 50¢ per book in the U.S. and $1.25 per book in Canada.* I understand that accepting the 2 free books and gifts places me under no obligation to buy anything. I can always return a shipment and cancel at any time. The free books and gifts are mine to keep no matter what I decide.

Choose one: ☐ **Harlequin Intrigue Larger-Print** (199/399 HDN GNXC) ☐ **Harlequin Romantic Suspense** (240/340 HDN GNMZ)

Name (please print)

Address   Apt. #

City   State/Province   Zip/Postal Code

Email: Please check this box ☐ if you would like to receive newsletters and promotional emails from Harlequin Enterprises ULC and its affiliates. You can unsubscribe anytime.

Mail to the **Harlequin Reader Service:**
IN U.S.A.: P.O. Box 1341, Buffalo, NY 14240-8531
IN CANADA: P.O. Box 603, Fort Erie, Ontario L2A 5X3

Want to try 2 free books from another series! Call 1-800-873-8635 or visit www.ReaderService.com.

*Terms and prices subject to change without notice. Prices do not include sales taxes, which will be charged (if applicable) based on your state or country of residence. Canadian residents will be charged applicable taxes. Offer not valid in Quebec. This offer is limited to one order per household. Books received may not be as shown. Not valid for current subscribers to the Harlequin Intrigue or Harlequin Romantic Suspense series. All orders subject to approval. Credit or debit balances in a customer's account(s) may be offset by any other outstanding balance owed by or to the customer. Please allow 4 to 6 weeks for delivery. Offer available while quantities last.

Your Privacy—Your information is being collected by Harlequin Enterprises ULC, operating as Harlequin Reader Service. For a complete summary of the information we collect, how we use this information and to whom it is disclosed, please visit our privacy notice located at corporate.harlequin.com/privacy-notice. From time to time we may also exchange your personal information with reputable third parties. If you wish to opt out of this sharing of your personal information, please visit readerservice.com/consumerschoice or call 1-800-873-8635. **Notice to California Residents**—Under California law, you have specific rights to control and access your data. For more information on these rights and how to exercise them, visit corporate.harlequin.com/california-privacy.

HIHRS22